THE STAG AT HAND

THE CHALAM FÆRYTALES, BOOK VI

MORGAN G FARRIS

MINoR 5
PUBLISHING

CONTENTS

PRAISE FOR MORGAN G FARRIS

Fantasy the way they used to write it — full of mystery and magic and wonder.

— WYATT, READER

Her writing is pure poetry. Her stories are pure magic.

— EMILY, READER

Epic. Poetic. Breathtaking. And so many twists!

— JIM, READER

A hardcover edition of this book was published in 2022 by Minor 5 Publishing.

ISBN 978-1-7331668-9-8

For those of us who've walked through darkness.
There is magic in hope; we get to take it with us.

MAP

KERACH SEA
BORRAS
BORRAS PROVINCE
CHERETH PROVINCE
EDEN OCEAN
SHEFA SEA
Port Challon
TSULAH PROVINCE
HASAMAYIM PROVINCE
HINNOM PROVINCE
MAJESTIC MOUNTAINS
HARAVELLE
Massahd Castle
Lake Yerah
Shalem
NEHAR PROVINCE
Chesedelle Castle
KINNERETH PROVINCE
MEDINAH
Chesedelle City
Melamed Estate
Har Omer
Northern Pass
Dupree Estate
Ramleh
TSAFONE PROVINCE
Adina's House
Goleath Palace
MIDVAR
BENALLE PROVINCE
GAV PROVINCE
Eh'tsem Valley
Gaevasi
NAVAH
QADIM PROVINCE
Benalle Palace
Benalle City
WILD WOOD
N'VEH SEA
the Secret Place
TEMAN PROVINCE
Teman City
Fount Barakah
THE GREAT SEA

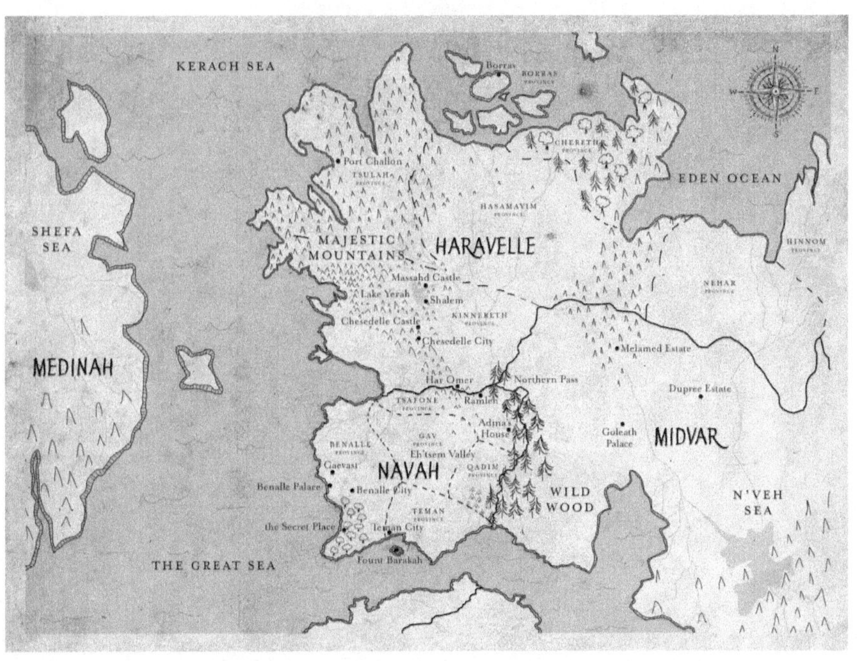

PROLOGUE

Bound by the sea
For all eternity
Leviathan awaits her destiny.
By fire and flame
She sets the world ablaze
For the coming of the new age.

"Get your nose out of that book, Miri. It is not proper for a young lady to read."

The words set her teeth on edge, but young Miriam Sasson sighed in resignation and silently slid her gaze to her cousin beside her, who only raised his eyebrows, his gaze remaining on the book between them. But it was no use—she could see the smile he was attempting to purse. She swallowed a giggle and turned her attention back to their book, squaring her shoulders like a proper lady for good measure.

They had been devouring the dusty pages for the better part of the afternoon. A Fæ adventure. A story of men who could shift to wolves and waylay enemies on the battlefield. It had been an excellent story. And though it had been chosen as an alternative to a glorious, sunny day after a rather heated conversation with her mother about *obligations* and *being a lady* and *blah, blah, blah,* Miri could not complain. Then again, she rarely had a reason to complain when the day's prospects included time with her cousin, Ari.

Why her mother had insisted she and Ari stay in the drawing room while her father had some *boring* conversation with some *boring* priest about something that had to do with *boring* politics —her father's favorite subject—Miriam couldn't say. But apparently their excursion into Fæ for the afternoon was not to be either, for even without looking up from the daily paper she feigned to read, her mother's warning had hit its mark.

Miriam laughed weakly and reached for her cousin's hand. "Let's go, Ari. Surely we're only a bother here."

Ari nodded his agreement, tapping a small, golden bookmark in his hand. It whirred to life and crawled like a spider across the pages before settling like a cat might curl up in the sun, marking exactly where they had stopped reading with one long, spindly, tail-like extension. Satisfied, Ari grinned at the clever little contraption and folded the book closed, setting it aside. He stood, taking Miri's outstretched hand.

But before they could so much as take a step, her mother went on, repeating her earlier words, "You will stay in here. You must stop all this nonsense and learn to act like a civilized young lady."

From behind her mother's back, Miri rolled her eyes for Ari's benefit. He breathed a laugh and shook his head. Reaching into the pocket of his trousers, he retrieved two amber candies, handing one to Miri as he mouthed, *You must learn to act like a civilized young lady,* his pale brows furrowed as he waggled his finger.

Miriam eyed the candy with a hint of disdain, picking lint from the treat and snickering a little too loudly at Ari's uncanny resemblance to his aunt.

This time, it was not her mother's warning that gave her pause.

"Miriam," her father growled, cutting off his conversation on the other side of the room with the lanky young priest. The tone of his deep voice sent shivers down her spine. Ari straightened, too, knowing too well exactly what would happen if they crossed her father. The bruise on his cheek was almost gone, but hints of it lingered in fading shades of green and brown. Ari had never told her how he got it. But Miri knew anyway—at least she knew enough that when her father barked a warning, they both listened.

Ari pressed his finger to his lips, shaking his head again. "We'll read more later," he whispered. He popped the small piece of barley sugar into his mouth and winked, the emerald in his eyes sparkling in the filtered afternoon light.

Her father's conversation caught her ear, and she turned her head slightly to listen.

"She has just as much claim to the throne as those imposters that sit on it now," her father said to the priest, his greasy words dripping over her. Miriam shot her gaze to Ari, but his attention was also fixed on her father—the Lord of Teman City.

"Careful, my lord. You speak treason with such claims," said the priest. But there was no true warning in his words and a smile threatened his narrow mouth.

Her father chuckled, handing the priest a glass of whiskey.

"It will be an uphill battle," her father went on, turning to face the great windows of the sitting room that overlooked perfectly-manicured lawns. Above them, the sky was bright and blue, and an airship floated through the clouds, no doubt taking passengers from the city to the coast. Its black sails resembled the wings of a great bat, a dark, menacing contrast to the bright summer skies. Miri had been in awe the first time she had seen the new invention—a product of the magic man had learned to master in recent years.

A revolution—that's what her father had called the modern era. A revolution of industry and magic and power.

But it seemed a silly waste to harness magic for things like ships that flew and lamps that needed no flame and ink that never ran dry.

Conveniences, yes. But not the stuff of revolution.

The airship floated lazily in the fat, white clouds, a faint glow of light and shimmer trailing from its stern. She wondered if she would ever have reason to ride in such a vessel. Or if she'd ever muster the courage.

"The royal family is well loved," her father went on, and Miri tore her eyes from the airship and back to the slender, severe-looking man who watched her father with a hint of a smirk on his narrow mouth. "And with the alliances they are making with Medinah, their legacy on the throne could be impenetrable."

"The wrong family has sat on the throne for thirteen generations, Lord Sasson," said the priest. "Regardless of the bullshit progress they've made in magic and the peace treaties, it is time the true line was restored."

Miri was surprised to hear the priest use such language. It did not seem fitting for a man of his station. But even more surprising was the subject of their conversation.

Treason. Her father and the young, slithering priest spoke treason. Though they were not technically wrong—the original royal family, descended from King Ferryl and Queen Adelaide, no longer sat on the throne of Har-Navah. King Daegan's family, the

Ramagis, had overthrown the royal family some three hundred years ago in a great uprising and claimed the throne for their own. And since the Ramagi family had spent the better part of the last few centuries honing and perfecting the craft of magicked weaponry, no one had dared challenge them—not then and not since.

But it was illegal to speak of that uprising. King Daegan's grandfather, King Decimus had declared it a treasonous act, punishable by death. So to be plotting against the Ramagis? To speak of restoring the throne to the Adelaidian line? The priest was brazen to even hint at it.

She did not like the way he looked; though thin and reed-like, the priest seemed anything but weak beneath those mantis limbs. Where her father was a double-edged sword—all strength and might and bellowing intimidation—the priest was a stiletto, slender and wicked and hidden to strike at the most opportune moment. Miriam absently watched him take a long pull on his glass, his spindly, narrow fingers wrapped around the crystal. There was very little of the amber liquid left when he was done.

"There are some who would say it is her cousin who is the true heir." The singsong warning came from Miriam's mother. Dressed in a gown much too formal for the afternoon, the Lady of Teman City sat demurely on the settee with perfect posture as she feigned reading the gossip section of the morning paper. Just as she pretended to read it every day—a perfect way to act as if she wasn't eavesdropping on everything going on around her. Beside her, a tea kettle buzzed with magic, keeping the liquid inside warm without the aid of flame.

"It's a shame that your sister bore a bastard then, isn't it?" said Lord Sasson.

Miriam clenched her teeth, taking in a breath to protest the nasty things they were saying about her beloved cousin. But Ari just squeezed her hand and kept his attention on the conversation in silence. Three years her senior, Ari had always quietly accepted the way people spoke of him, the things they said. *Bastard born. Disgrace to the family.* It sickened Miriam any time she heard it, for Ari had been nothing short of her very best friend for all of her life and the kindest soul she had ever known. It was not his fault that his father had left him.

"Besides, if the royal family can put a woman on the throne, so can we," Lord Sasson went on.

"So they have signed the decree," the priest said.

"Indeed, Tomas," said her father. "Princess Rachæl is the first female heir since Queen Adelaide. For *now*," he added with an emphasis Miriam didn't like.

"My lord?" asked Tomas, cocking his narrow chin to one side.

Lord Sasson smirked, raising his glass to his mouth. But her father did not take a drink. "My family lineage can be traced back more than a hundred generations. Our family predates Har-Navah itself. My daughter is as close as anyone can claim to true heirship, and her blood can be traced in many lines back to King Ferryl himself."

Her father took to pacing, slowly swirling the contents of his glass as he walked the length of the room. He hadn't spoken a lie —the Sasson family could be traced back to King Ferryl. The problem was, so could most of the noble families in Har-Navah. A thousand years after the fabled king's reign, most could find some way to trace their lineage to him. Or to Adelaide. A cousin of a cousin of a cousin, once removed. A marriage seven generations back. It did not matter, in the end. Most never bothered to check the accuracy of such claims.

But they *would* check those claims—if Miriam were to name herself the true heir in some public fashion, those claims would most certainly be checked. And likely found paltry, at best.

She wondered why her father was naïve enough to think such a thing could work.

"She shall need a profitable marriage if she is to reclaim the throne. Someone who can offer her power. Influence. I can get her the support of the council. But she will need someone who can help her achieve the support of the Sanhedrin."

Tomas's brow raised. "My lord?" he asked, cocking his narrow head to one side, all prowling jackal and anything but holy.

"It is all but done," said her father. "We need only a few more signatures and your title is official."

"My title, my lord?"

"It's a tragedy, really. That our beloved high priest found himself on the wrong side of history. Rumor has it the king is brokenhearted over his betrayal. He was found floating face-first in Lake Yerah only days ago. Suicide, they say. His shame could not be overcome."

Her father turned, facing Tomas once again. The priest looked positively giddy. At her side, Ari had gone deathly still.

"We will need someone to rule as high priest immediately. To keep peace. And to restore faith in the holy council. We need someone who can reunite the royal court and the holy faith. And you are the man to do it."

Tomas beamed like a child offered a shiny new toy. "I don't know what to say."

"Stick with me, *Phinehas,*" said her father, clasping the priest's shoulder. "And we'll both get what we want."

"Phinehas?" Tomas asked.

"The first high priest of Har-Navah. Appointed by King Ferryl himself when he began construction of the temple in Benalle City nearly a thousand years ago. It is only fitting that the most powerful high priest in the kingdom's history should bear the same name as the very *first* high priest, is it not?" The grin on her father's face was positively vulpine.

So was Tomas's.

"I WILL NOT MARRY HIM!" Miriam barked, pacing across the plush carpets of the library.

Ari took hold of her arm when she passed by him. In the dim light of the vast space, his fair hair looked like spun moonlight.

"Breathe, Mir. Nothing is set in stone."

"I don't want the throne. I don't want to be queen. Why must Father use me like a pawn in such ridiculous games? Can you believe it, Ari? He wants to marry me off to that...that snake. And for what? More power? For a throne that's not mine!"

"You're only thirteen. Marriage is a long way off. A lot can happen between now and then," Ari tried. But it was no use. He always underestimated her father, what he was capable of, what he would do if it meant more money, more power, more influence.

"Everyone knows *you're* the true heir to the throne," she said wildly. "Why do they act like you don't exist?"

It was true. Though he was bastard born, both Ari's and Miri's mothers were supposedly direct descendants of King Ferryl himself. As Ari was male, that would have given him priority to the throne. But Ari's father had died when he was very young. Most knew the truth of his story, though—the man who everyone knew as his father had only married Ari's mother to save her from the scorn of giving birth to a bastard. Ari never knew his true father. No one save for his mother knew who had truly sired him. The man who had taken him in, had raised him, had been a good man. Kind enough. But when he had passed, he had taken his protection with him. And by the time Ari had reached his teenage years, most knew he was a bastard-born nobody. No one in their right mind would consider him for the throne of Har-Navah.

Ari's emerald eyes flickered. "It is hard for people to accept what they cannot understand," he said, and Miri blinked, unsure what he meant. In his hand, he fiddled with what looked like a small, gold coin. Covered in glass, the inside whirred with cogs and wheels that turned of their own accord. "They say this thing can tell you the weather," he said, half amused as he watched it in his palm.

Ari had always harbored a curiosity for all manner of oddities, particularly of the magical sort. And in this modern world, there was certainly no lack of clever contraptions and gadgets of convenience to inspect.

Miri, conversely, had never had an affinity for such things, finding them more a nuisance than anything. Why in the world would anyone need a small coin to tell the weather when a window would suffice quite nicely? She crossed her arms and huffed with annoyance.

Ari smiled, pocketing the whirring coin. "I wouldn't worry about it, Miri. And I certainly wouldn't let it bother you."

"How can Father agree to marry me off to that snake?" she asked, resuming her pacing. Ari folded his arms across his chest. It was positively unacceptable that he should be walking around a noble Har-Navarian home without an afternoon jacket, his white shirt nearly threadbare and about a size too small for him, tucked haphazardly into his brown breeches. But he had never cared much for fashion. Or aristocratic protocol. So he had never really minded that Miriam's parents—his aunt and uncle—hadn't bothered to provide him proper attire. As if by doing so, they emphasized to any observer that Ari was bastard born. And certainly not a part of their picture-perfect world.

Bastard nephew. But nephew all the same. Come to live with them some years ago after his mother had passed suddenly of the pox.

"You will not marry him, Mir. Trust me." Ari's words brought her back to the present—to the prospect of marrying that reed-thin priest with eyes that spoke of too many secrets.

"How can you know that?"

Ari took her hand when she passed him again, squeezing it gently. She could have sworn she saw a tiny flash of light pass from his palm to hers. "My father will protect you."

"Your father?" she asked, furrowing her brow. "What do you mean? Your father is dead." Just as the man who had reared him was gone, in all likelihood, the man who had sired Ari was gone too. For no one had ever learned who he was, much less what had become of him. Ari was an orphan in every sense of the word.

Her cousin breathed a laugh, pressing a gentle kiss to her brow. "He is not dead. You will see. In due time, you will understand."

"Understand what? What do you—"

Ari squeezed her hand a little harder, and this time, she was certain she saw a light, soft and blue, warming her hand and fingers, sinking into her skin.

"There is only one true magic, Miriam. Never forget that. Let it guide you. Wherever you go, whatever happens, never forget it."

"What do you mean, whatever happens?" She looked up from their joined hands. "Ari, what is going to happen?"

Ari did not answer, instead lifting a necklace over his head with his free hand.

"What is this?" she asked, perplexed. Another trinket in his collection of oddities, no doubt. But she had never noticed Ari wear a rough stone around his neck. Not once. Ever.

The light in his palm flared, a burst of stars and galaxies before it dissipated into the air as if it had never been. Her hand tingled, and a warmth unlike any she could explain settled into her very bones as she looked again at their clasped hands. Before she knew what he was doing, Ari placed the necklace around her neck.

Pulsing. She could feel the stone pulsing at her breast.

"What just happened?" she asked, her eyes still fixed on her faintly glowing hand.

But before her cousin could answer, the dinner bell rang. "C'mon," he said, folding her hand into the crook of his arm. "Your father will not want us to be late."

THE PRIEST STAYED FOR DINNER. And dinner the next night. And the night after that. Plotting, planning, scheming with her father. She hadn't been wrong—the things they spoke of, they were treason. If the wrong person heard so much as one word of what they spoke...

Miriam needed a break. All this talk of thrones and advantageous marriage and priests and Medinah, the western kingdom, and *blah blah blah*... It was enough. She didn't want to be queen. She figured she had enough to worry about as the daughter of a powerful lord. But to be queen? To deal with the burdens of an entire kingdom? No, thank you. Not to mention being queen meant being married to Tomas...Phinehas...whatever name he would go by.

Please. He was an old man. Or at least much older than she. The thought of calling him husband...of holding his hand...of letting him—*kiss* her...

She kicked a stone, blowing a strand of her fiery red curls from her eyes in a huff. The spring breeze picked up, carrying with it scents of salt and sea and fresh flora. She eyed the grounds of her father's estate—the thick grasses, waving lazily in the breezes, the fat trees, ripe with blooms, the dandelions...

She bent and picked one, another, then another. She picked dandelions until she had a fistful.

Standing again, Miri's eyes caught something bright and white through the trees ahead. Moving to get a better view, she could just make out the form of the creature through the thick forest.

A stag.

As white as summer clouds and as bright as the summer sun. He stood tall, with proud antlers that climbed so high it was hard to tell where they ended and the branches of the trees began.

The stag seemed to hold her gaze, and even from such a distance, she could see that his eyes were a familiar shade of emerald.

"Do you have a fondness for weeds?"

Startled, she whirled to find Tomas the priest walking behind her, his lanky arms clasped behind his back. She practically growled at the stick-like man.

"They're not weeds, they're dandelions. I'm gathering them for the færies."

"Aren't you a little old for that?" he asked, tilting his pointed chin to one side.

"I would have thought that as such an *important* holy man, you of all people would not think anyone was too old for the things of Providence," she sneered, turning her back to him, a chill running down her back. If he retaliated…if he was anything like her father…

She glanced again into the forest, peering around trees and brambles. The white stag was nowhere to be found.

So Miri walked further down the path that led away from her father's manor, into a thicket of gnarly oaks—a place she knew the færies frequented. "I always gather dandelions for the færies in the Spring. They use them to make things. Like a textile. But this time of year, the wind carries off the fluff so quickly that I like to help them."

"I thought only children played with færies," Tomas said, his unhurried steps crunching on the gravel and grass behind her.

"I *am* a child," she said, looking around the thicket of trees for a particular nook—there. She found the nook, but inside… Gone. It was gone.

"You are thirteen. I would say you are a young woman."

"Is that why you agreed to marry me?" she scoffed over her shoulder. "Because you consider thirteen to be a woman?"

Miri looked back at the nook in the tree, disappointment bubbling in her throat. He had found it, taken it down. Again.

Every time she built a færy house, no matter how well she hid it among the nooks and crannies of the trees, her father found it. And destroyed it. Miri ground her teeth to keep from huffing a word against her father in front of his new ally.

She only remembered Tomas was behind her when she heard him breathing a throaty chuckle. "Your father told me you were— spirited." He caught up to where she stood on the path, stopping only a foot away from her. She could feel his eyes on her, knew they were traveling down her body and back up again, the hair on the back of her neck standing on end at his appraisal. "Nothing that cannot be broken, I'm sure."

"How old are you?" she blurted, whirling to face him.

His eyes raked back to hers. "I am twenty-nine."

"And was this your ambition, then? To marry a child?"

A serpentine smile quirked the corner of his narrow lips. "My goals have little to do with marriage, girl."

"What then?" she asked, flinging her fists to her hips.

"My goals are the same as Providence, of course," he said piously, lifting his chin.

"And what would you say is Providence's plan?"

"He no longer bothers with such trivialities as færies, Miriam."

"What does he bother with, pray tell?"

"Power. Magic is power, Miriam. Never forget it. He has ruined men and waylaid kingdoms with that power."

"Is that your plan?" she asked. "To ruin men and waylay kingdoms?"

That smile quirked a little more. "I am at Providence's bidding. Just as you are at mine."

"I am not your wife."

"Not yet," he said with that same serpentine grin. She huffed and rolled her eyes.

"Do you not wish to be queen?"

"Why should I? I do not have royal blood!"

Tomas stepped close. Dangerously close. His foul breath assaulted her mouth as he spoke dangerously low. "I would be careful of what you say, Miriam."

She did not back down, squaring her shoulders and refusing to wince. "Why should I be careful to say the truth?"

"The truth can damn you. It can damn us all."

"I thought truth was the way of Providence," she said.

A breathy laugh. "You have much to learn, Miriam."

She allowed herself to back up only a fraction, his nearness too unsettling. "I don't want to learn. I don't want to play these stupid games of yours. Or my father's."

"You will soon learn that it does not matter what you want."

Miri looked over her shoulder, eyeing the nook where her carefully crafted færy house had been only yesterday. "I've already learned that. A long time ago." She turned from him then, placing the delicate dandelions at the base of the branch and turning away, marching back towards her home.

"Where is Ari?" Miriam asked as her father, mother, and the priest sat down to dinner. "I haven't seen him all day."

"He is away," said her father matter-of-factly as he began slicing his cut of meat.

"Away where?" Miriam pushed.

"It is none of your concern," her father answered, never bothering to lift his eyes.

She slammed her fist on the table, the crystal glasses jumping at her outburst. "What have you done to him?" she demanded.

Her mother looked up, her beady eyes near boredom. Tomas looked up too, but it was not boredom in his gaze. It was something else. Something much worse.

Her father slowly slid his eyes to her, his face flat, emotionless. "He will no longer be living here."

"Where will he live?" she blurted, panicked. Ari would be homeless without them.

"He is not our concern, Miriam," her father said calmly.

"Of course he is!" she yelled. "He is family!"

"He is a distant cousin," said her father dismissively before returning to slicing his meat. "We are hardly obligated to clothe and shelter him all of his life. Besides, he is a man now and—"

"We are the only family he has left!" she protested, her breath coming up short.

Her father appraised her for a moment, and despite his mask of indifference, she could see the irritation rising, pounding in the vein at his temple. "He is an obstacle that will no longer block our path."

Miriam erupted, grabbing her glass of wine and throwing it across the table, aiming straight for her father. It missed him, unfortunately. But the wine did not, showering him with a blanket of crimson liquid.

Calmly still, too calmly, her father picked up his napkin, wiping his face and cravat. The wine staining the fine white cloth...it looked like blood dripping down his neck. But behind her father's calm she could see his rage simmering to a boil. A tremble settled along her bones.

That's when she noticed it—a heat, a warmth coming from

the palm of her hand. She looked down to see a faint glow growing along her skin. She fisted her hand and hid it in the folds of her skirts. From the corner of her eye, she could feel Tomas appraising her with unblinking vigilance.

Her father finished wiping his face and stood. Slowly. As if the world itself had slowed to a snail's pace. He crossed the room, her heart pounding in her throat with every menacing step he took. The rage burned brighter the closer he got, until he was face to face with her, nose to nose, breath to breath.

"You will regret that," her father breathed.

"You will regret sending Ari away," she sneered, despite the fear pounding in her veins.

Her father lunged, grabbing her throat, shoving her to the ground. Her mother screamed as her father landed above her, one knee painfully lodged on her belly as he dealt one bone-splintering blow after another. The world slowed a little more, until all she could see, all she could comprehend was the blood as it splattered on the ornate carpet beside her, the drops glistening in the gaslight, peppering the floor with more and more and more, until it was no longer spatters, but pools of crimson liquid, absorbing into the fibers of the bright colors around her.

Somewhere in the distance, she could hear screams, cries, shrieks. A woman calling for help, for someone to stop. But for Miriam, all she knew was the strange sensation as fist after fist landed across her face, her nose, her cheeks, her chin.

The blows slowed, and she sputtered, spitting blood on the carpet beside her. From somewhere above her, she saw a man— the priest—pulling, clawing at her father. To remove him? To stop him? No one could stop him. He was a great man. A brute of a man. Nothing short of a miracle could stop him.

A light flared. Blue and hot. Preternatural, impossible light.

Magic.

There is only one true magic, Miriam. Never forget that.

Her beloved cousin's words rang in her ears as the light flared brighter. She reached for her father, taking his face in her hands, shocked at the scream that tore from his throat at her touch.

But the scream was short-lived, and the rage that had previously boiled in her father's eyes—it erupted. An inferno. A storm. He lunged for her again, a lethal blow coming for her face inch by crawling inch in this world where time had slowed, crawling at a sickeningly slow pace.

But the blow did not land. Her father flew suddenly back like a sack of flour tossed across a table.

Tomas. The gangly priest had bested her father somehow. He lunged for Miriam, scooping her into his arms, fleeing the room with shocking speed.

"Come with me," he breathed as he ran. "He won't hurt you again."

And she believed him. Providence help her, she believed him, and clung to her rescuer as he escaped in the night.

PART ONE

CHAPTER ONE

Present Day: One Thousand Eight Years After the Great War

"Well, blessed be. Look what the cat dragged in," Galina purred, sipping from her cup. Her pointed chin mimicked the perfect point to her brow, that constant devil-may-care look on her face. Kohl lined her almond-shaped eyes, and her darkened lashes rested like raven feathers on her cheeks every time she blinked. If Miri could choose a phrase to describe her, it would be sin made flesh.

Miriam ignored the insufferably beautiful acolyte as she finished tying her ginger curls into a knot on the top of her head and sat down at the table in the kitchens beneath the temple in Teman City. She poured hot water over a little bauble of leaves and spices, watching absently as a silver spoon stirred the tea for her, gradually turning the water a lovely shade of amber. The whole temple buzzed with servants, packing and preparing, chattering and fussing.

The festivities from last night still swirled in her mind.

Phinehas had gathered all the lesser priests of the Sanhedrin, all the sages, and all the acolytes to the temple sanctuary. He had lit a thousand candles and stood amongst the cloying, amber smoke of the censer, a god of his own making, and announced to them all that he had done it. He had gotten the final signature from the king's council. The last one required to make it official.

Phinehas was now the high priest of Har-Navah. The youngest in the kingdom's history.

It had taken seven years. Seven years to finish what Phinehas and her father had started. To achieve the impossible. All the work and scheming; all the meetings and parties and dinners and banquets; all the obsequious conversations and relentless flattery and *promises, promises, promises* had led to this moment.

They had all celebrated into the wee hours of the morning.

It was not only the announcement of his appointment that had surprised Miri last night. It was his announcement that he would relocate—that Phinehas and a few of the priests and sages of the Sanhedrin would move to the north. To the mountains of Old Haravelle. To be at the *seat of power,* as he had put it.

A lord—a Medinian ambassador from the continent across the sea—would be coming to Har-Navah soon. Specifically, to the northern provinces. To stay at Chesedelle Castle with the royal family, deep in the heart of the mountainous region of the king-dom, and far, far away from the sunny, warm life on the southern coast. Phinehas had practically drooled announcing it. And the sages and priests had not stopped talking about it since. Appar-ently, the Medinian ambassador had a taste for unmitigated cruelty.

But while the rest of the priests couldn't stop gossiping about the ambassador, Phinehas couldn't gush enough about the *glorious* grand duke who lived near Chesedelle.

He's the second most powerful man in the kingdom. Next to the king, the people of the north have answered to the Kelach family for generations. It's high time the Sanhedrin had more influence, Phinehas had said. *And he will help us get it.*

The king of Har-Navah, the ambassador from Medinah, and a young, impressionable grand duke—easily influenced, Phinehas had pointed out—all in one place. The high priest could not resist such a melting pot of power.

And in light of all that, Phinehas had announced that they were moving.

Today, she and Phinehas would leave their lives in Teman City behind. Today she would leave these insufferable acolytes behind too.

Hopefully forever.

She swallowed the satisfied smirk threatening to curl her lips and looked out the windows of the temple kitchen to the sprawling city just beyond. Winged airships traversed the skies, their tattered sails and bat-like wings bloated by the winds, likely bringing goods and minerals from the north. Steam carriages whizzed along the city street, splattering passersby with whatever questionable liquids littered the road. And people. People everywhere, moving to and fro like ants on a mound.

In the distance, towering rails crisscrossed the bright blue skies; the railcars would be completed soon, their tracks built on stilts high above the bustling city below. Great steam engines, pulling countless cars behind them, speeding along skyward tracks towards glorious and faraway places. Teman City—a beacon of modern industry. Progress. Magic.

She swallowed back disappointment that she would not see the rails completed before they left. She had very much been looking forward to seeing that miracle of modern magic for herself. Perhaps even experiencing a ride on them sometime.

But leaving behind all of this progress and industry was a small trade to make if it meant also leaving behind the acolytes with whom she currently shared a table.

They would not be taking those steam cars to the northern mountains. No, wherever they were going did not boast any rail-cars. It probably did not boast much of anything—except political advantage.

"Wipe that longing look off of your face, Miri. It does not suit you," chimed Galina, fiddling with one of her perfect curls.

"I do not have a longing look," Miri countered, turning her attention back to her tea.

"If you're so worried about leaving, perhaps you should stay behind," Galina offered icily. She flicked her nails across her thumb as if she were counting off her victims, a smirk threatening the corner of her voluptuous lips.

"It's much too early for your antagonizing, Galina," Kata said, rolling her eyes as she helped herself to her second serving of eggs and toast.

"I'd be careful with that if I were you," Galina purred to Kata. "Phinehas likes a woman with curves, not rolls."

"How would you know what Phinehas likes?" asked Nerissa, another of the acolytes, her long curls spilling over her shoulder much too perfectly this early in the morning. Her breasts were on generous display beneath her gauzy white dress this morning—a promise of worshipful pleasure to any priest or sage who glanced her direction. "He wouldn't even know where your chambers are."

"Perhaps he doesn't have to." Galina did not bother to look at any of them as she spoke.

And at the implication, Miriam rolled her eyes. Yes, leaving all of this progress behind would not be so bad after all. She was sick of having to stomach breakfasts that consisted of cold eggs and catfights.

The acolytes were a necessary evil in the temple, as Miri had discovered when Phinehas first brought her here. Young women, no older than twenty-two, who served the priests and sages, not to mention wealthy and powerful patrons. They lit candles and sang chants, offering blessings to visitors and patrons alike. But that was only their public face.

Under the cover of darkness, the acolytes' true mission came to life. With whispered promises and quiet, knowing glances, the acolytes served the priests and sages of the temple. In whatever manner they desired.

Phinehas and the rest of the priests kept up the pretense of piety, presenting the girls as vestal, holy virgins. Miri—and the rest of the world, it seemed—knew better.

In the dark of the night, the acolytes were nothing more than holy lightskirts.

Miri hated every one of them. And had ever since she'd arrived seven years ago.

She had only tolerated them all this time for the sole reason that she knew Phinehas did not entertain any of them. He didn't need to, after all.

But that didn't keep them from fighting over him as if he were a prize to be won. A god to be worshipped.

Kata rolled her eyes, casting a sidelong glare to Miriam. Kata's mousy brown hair hung limp, and she pushed the weak braid off her shoulder. "Galina's particularly feisty this morning, isn't she?" she asked, taking another bite of toast. "Perhaps she's upset that Phinehas hasn't invited her to come to Kinnereth with him as his personal companion."

"Better that than his castoff," Galina replied, sipping indignantly from her tea. Kata burned with disdain, but said nothing when Miriam squeezed her friend's arm.

Ignore her, she said with her eyes. *She's not worth it.*

It was true; Galina was not worth the argument most days. Her auburn curls, which Miriam knew full well she spent hours preparing each day, were pinned artfully around her face—the perfect balance of youthful innocence and mysterious allure. Her gauzy white dress was not as sheer as most of the girls'. What Miri had once thought was modesty on Galina's part turned out to have the opposite effect on most men. Whereas the other girls preferred having their assets on display at all times, Galina preferred a much more clandestine form of seduction. As if her body were a present to be unwrapped, a secret to be discovered. Miri and all of the acolytes watched night after night as Galina's innocent glances and bashful blushes worked wonders on any man who came within a mile of the woman. Galina was a master among the acolytes.

So of course it drove her mad that Phinehas had nothing to do with her. The other priests? They visited her chambers regularly. But it was Phinehas she was after—his power, his pull at the temple, even in the city. Galina would not be satisfied until she had the high priest in her clutches. In her *bed*. But Phinehas refused to have anything to do with her. And nothing irritated Galina more.

Just then, Jordie bounded into the kitchen, her blonde locks tied in a mess of a knot on the top of her head. The youngest of the acolytes, she hadn't quite figured out that delicate balance of allure to mix with her wide-eyed youth. Even so, the lesser priests and sages indulged her all the same. And at only fourteen years old, Miriam often wondered what happened to Jordie to land her in the company of temple prostitutes.

Then again, Miriam herself had been barely thirteen when Phinehas had brought her here. And it was within a matter of weeks that he had first taken her to his bed. In her innocence she had not understood what he had wanted from her, had not understood what he asked.

But she had trusted him. He had saved her from her father's wrath. Nursed her back from the brink of death by his careful ministrations. And all of the hate, all of the loathing she had experienced upon first meeting him at her father's estate had melted away the first time he had run delicate fingers under her chin, the first time he had called her his *innocent dove,* the first time he had held her in his arms.

She had given herself over to him—wholly, completely, without question.

Her brutal savior.

But that did not make her an acolyte.

Even though she had spent her days among them for the last seven years, even though most assumed that's all she was, Miriam had always been special to Phinehas. He always told her so. He certainly made her feel so every time he took her to his bed. It had always driven the other girls mad with envy—and breakfast had become the battlefield on which they let out their aggressions.

Above them, the gaslight lamps flickered, whirring and buzzing as the gears that kept the fixtures turning sputtered.

"Useless things," Galina chided, glaring above her. "Someone needs to fix them, for Providence's sake."

"Whatever happened to just plain old candles?" Kata asked, taking another tart. "Why does everything have to run on magic these days?"

"Because magic is better." Jordie smiled, stuffing three tarts into her mouth before plopping down into a chair next to Kata.

"Magic is *power,*" Galina corrected.

"Blessed be," said Nerissa, although Miri couldn't help but think the declaration sarcastic.

Indeed, it seemed that magic these days had been reduced from the splendor of the days of King Ferryl and Queen Adelaide, to nothing more than minor conveniences and quicker modes of transportation. She wondered what her cousin Ari would have thought of such things—if he was even alive.

"Why are you so chipper?" another acolyte asked—Raisa. Twenty-four and far past her prime, she mostly hovered quiet and unnoticed around the temple, knowing that there would be little mercy for her in the world should she be kicked out. Miri remembered the day the other girl had turned twenty-three—how quiet Raisa had been. How reserved. From that moment forward, Raisa had kept her head low, her words few, as if by going unnoticed, she might not have to leave the temple as so many before her had been forced to.

In Miri's seven years here, she had watched Phinehas remove no less than thirteen acolytes once they had grown too old. Every time it happened, he'd told her the same thing. *The role of an acolyte is youth and innocence, worship and servitude. It is no place for a woman.*

And one after another over the years, the aging acolytes had been left to fend for themselves on the streets of Teman City. The world took even less kindly to them than to the temple girls. Miri had been nauseous for three days when she learned that every single one of the former acolytes had become nothing more than street whores.

"Phinehas said I could go with him to Kinnereth." Jordie beamed, popping another tart into her mouth.

"What?" Miriam asked, frozen. She glanced at Kata, who only shrugged. Jordie had to be mistaken. Phinehas had made it clear in last night's revelry that only a few from the temple would move north. The rest would stay here in Teman City. Miriam had been certain he would not take any of the acolytes with him. He had no need of them.

But Kata looked down, not meeting her eyes, and that's when Miriam realized Kata's cheeks burned red.

"Don't look so surprised, *your high-and-mightiness,*" Galina said, sipping her tea. "Or did you think you were the only one worthy of His Holiness's new mission?"

Miri's heart struggled to find a regular pattern.

"We're all going, aren't we?" Jordie asked with her wide, inno-cent eyes.

Galina grinned triumphantly. "Well, the ones that *matter* anyway."

Raisa slammed her fork on the table and pushed her chair so hard it scraped with a great shriek across the floor. She huffed as she marched out of the room without a backward glance.

"What's gotten into her?" Nerissa asked, looking up from her breakfast.

"She's just upset that she wasn't asked to come to Kinnereth." Galina tossed her curls.

"Who *was?*" Nerissa asked carefully, looking around the table. Miri was privately thankful the acolyte had asked the question she hadn't had the nerve to ask.

Galina's eyes narrowed to slits. "Well, I suppose if you don't know, then you're not on the list, are you?"

"You can be such a bitch, Galina," Kata snapped.

"Now, now. Is that the talk of a holy servant?" Galina chided icily, nibbling on a single grape, her perfect figure evident even under the fur-lined robe she insisted on wearing every morning. As if she were the queen of Har-Navah herself.

A lesser priest ambled by the door just then, tall and somewhat handsome, and even from the corner of her eye, Miriam could see the way he slowed his pace just enough to leer at the girls. No, to leer at Galina. His whole demeanor shifted when Galina flicked her eyes to him for the briefest second. And Miriam knew that flicker—the promises it entailed.

Galina would visit the priest later. *To pray,* as she would declare.

"Who *is* going to Kinnereth?" Miriam asked quietly, unable to stop herself.

Galina shifted triumphant eyes to Miriam. "Were you not invited?" the auburn-haired acolyte hummed, tilting her head to one side.

"Of course she was," Kata snapped. "Do you really think he would leave her behind?"

Galina snorted, returning to her tea.

"It eats you alive, doesn't it?" Kata said to Galina. "Knowing he visits her every night. And not you."

Every night. Miri wondered what Kata would think—what *any* of the girls would think if they knew that Phinehas hadn't visited her that frequently in a long, long time—a fact that Miri hadn't let herself linger on. He was a busy man. An important man. She had not allowed herself to worry about why his visits had slowly begun to wane. She had especially not let herself think on it when she had turned twenty last month.

Still...at least he didn't visit the other girls. And every time she tried to worry about Phinehas's waning attention, she reminded herself of that comforting fact. She'd figure out the rest later.

"All those nightly visits... It does make you wonder," Galina responded, tracing her delicate finger through a puddle of berry juice on her plate. "If Phinehas can only stomach Miri when the lights are out."

Kata erupted. Standing from her chair so fast, it tumbled behind her, she launched herself across the table, plates and bowls and the remnants of breakfast scattering as she flung her arms out, ready to strangle Galina.

"Girls," came a voice from behind.

Kata froze, her breaths shallow, her eyes red with rage. Miriam did not miss the fear that glazed Galina's eyes, watching Kata like a hawk even as the sage spoke.

"His Holiness is preparing for prayer. You are to meet in the sanctuary in ten minutes," said the sage.

"*Praise be to Providence,*" said the girls in unison.

The sage shot a quick glance to Jordie, whose cheeks heated at his attention. Another invitation. Another man in this temple looking for pleasure before most of the girls here departed forever.

Miri had been wrong. So very wrong.

"Do not be late," said the sage. He glanced once more at Jordie before disappearing from the dank kitchen, and Jordie made no effort to hide her gaze as she watched him leave.

"Well, *I* for one have had enough of your pettiness. It is unholy. I'll see you in the sanctuary," Galina said, standing to her feet with casual elegance, as if Kata had not just threatened to choke her to death. She brushed rogue lint from her robe. "We'll be off to the north today. And, Jordie—perhaps you should freshen up. That sage's standards may be low enough to take interest in you, but you will not represent His Holiness with your unkemptness. It's sinful."

Jordie was indifferent to the comment, twirling an errant curl around her finger as she absently watched where the sage had disappeared.

But as Galina turned to leave, the rest of the girls eyed each other around the table, all asking the same question with their worried looks—who was going to Kinnereth? And who was staying?

Miriam ignored the apologetic look on Kata's face as she turned to head to her chambers. It was supposed to be a new chance. A new life. And now her hope of starting over was gone before it had fairly taken hold. Miriam would not be the only one to move north with Phinehas.

She swallowed back the lump in her throat and walked in silence.

THE DOOR near her bed creaked, and Miri whirled to see Phinehas slip through. Made to look just like the wall—with picture frame paneling and rich tapestry that blended in—Miriam had always thought it was less like a door and more like a secret passageway.

She had been only thirteen when she was given this room in the temple, and her young imagination had danced around the idea that the door led somewhere magical.

The truth was, it just led to Phinehas's chambers. And over the years, only *he* had used it. Frequently.

Despite the summer day, a cool draft spilled into the room with him and Miri wrapped her arms around her torso to warm herself.

"You were not at prayers," the priest said flatly without preamble.

Miri looked down, fiddling with her fingers, watching from the corner of her eye as the priest made his way into her chambers, clad in a thick, brocade bib and a gold tunic beneath. Phinehas always wore the finery afforded to the devout—richly embroidered bibs; tall, pointed hats adorned with the eight-pointed star of Providence; golden slippers; brocade robes. He was a walking picture of wealth, piety, and power.

He moved to a table nearby, sampling one of the small tarts perched upon it. "I expect you at prayers, Miri darling," he went on, looking pointedly in her direction.

Miriam sighed. "Are we really moving away?"

"Don't you start, too," Phinehas grumbled, plopping down in the chair next to him, which granted him better access to the tray of tea and cakes. No doubt one of the girls had set it out for him.

Miri held back a huff. Nothing rubbed her the wrong way more than coming into *her* room to find little gifts waiting for Phinehas. Gifts *she* hadn't given him. Phinehas would always brush her off, telling her she mustn't let her own selfishness stand in the way of the girls' desire to serve Providence. Miri had never quite figured out how leaving treats and gifts and baubles for the priest all over the temple was serving Providence.

"But what's it like?" she went on, pointedly ignoring the priest as he indulged in the pastry. "Kinnereth? I've never been to the mountains."

"Mountainous, I would hazard," Phinehas said. The sunlight spilled across his golden tunic, casting it in a glow Miri knew was meant to make him look holy, ethereal even. Today, it was working. He looked positively godlike.

At thirty-six, Phinehas was by no means old. But neither was he young. Not really. It seemed he had lived several lifetimes in those three and a half decades. And he was now officially the youngest high priest in the history of Har-Navah. A feat he had achieved without the help of her father, after all. It turned out Phinehas was more than capable of securing his place as a powerful high priest on his own.

Miri was privately relieved. For now that he was high priest, he would not need her to continue with the rest of her father's ridiculous plan to put her on the throne of Har-Navah. It was a subject they did not often speak of—her father's plan to make her queen of Har-Navah with High Priest Phinehas at her side. As her king. She shivered when she thought of such a couple. Of such power.

Power she did not want. Power she would never be strong enough to handle.

So when that last signature had finally come, Miri had been glad. Phinehas was high priest of Har-Navah. A task seven years in the making. It was done. The politics—the endless dinners and parties and balls, the countless lords of this and dukes of that lining up to cling to the tails of Phinehas's robe, the incessant games and flirting and promises and secrets—it could all finally end. And Miri could go back to something normal. Simple.

She would no longer have to play a role in the games of kings and priests. No longer have to be a pawn to be used and toyed with by grasping aristocrats and slithering noblemen.

"I am glad, anyway," she said, taking a seat on the carpet at his feet—a place she knew he liked her to be. When she was young, sitting at Phinehas's feet had made her feel like a child under the protection of a loving father. Over the years, she had begun to feel more like a servant at the feet of a ruthless god.

She was no longer sure which she preferred.

"I am tired of the scheming and plotting. It will be nice to start fresh. To end these silly games of the aristocrats of Teman City."

Phinehas chortled, a laugh deep from his throat. "Oh my little dove, you are not as young as you used to be, but you are still quite innocent, aren't you?"

Her brows knitted in a silent question as he went on. "Nothing has ended now that I am high priest. In fact, it has only just begun. I will need you more than ever."

"No, Phinehas," she said, standing so that she might walk away, put distance between them. "I won't be your pawn anymore. I'm tired of it. They all want the same thing."

The flirting, the playing, the scheming. Nobleman after nobleman had been sent her direction, offering promises of support for Phinehas in exchange for one thing: her.

She had played along. For far longer than she was comfortable, for the sole reason that she knew Phinehas would allow nothing less. If she had done anything to get in the way of his becoming high priest, the price would have been much higher than simply giving her body to strangers.

But it was over now.

Phinehas was high priest.

She would not be party to those games again.

"And what exactly would you do then, my darling?" Phinehas's question was laced with humored pity. "Go back to your father's estate? The one he plundered away? I did you a favor that day, taking you from that miserable man."

She drew a breath. "I know. I—"

A chortle sounded in his throat. "You have nothing, my dove. There is no place in this world for you now. Not without me."

She hated it that she did not have an answer. Hated that he was right. That somehow, in saving her from her father's prison of hate and scheming, he had imprisoned her in a world of shimmering censers and holy chants. A farce of lies and games no different than the one she had escaped.

"My little dove," he said, standing, the hem of his bib falling heavily to his ankles as he made his way to her. The pity on his face was enough that she turned her face away. "You are my secret weapon. My siren." He slithered towards her so smoothly, so slowly, that he reminded her of a snake. "Those wild, wanton curls," he said, reaching her, taking one and twirling it along his spindly finger. "Those wide, innocent eyes. I will need you more than ever."

She shook her head, hating the lump forming in her throat.

"Use Galina," she said. "She will be glad to take my place."

"Galina has other uses," Phinehas said, but before Miri could ask what he meant, he was moving her, one slithering step at a time, his body against hers, ushering her back, back, back until the back of her knees hit the bed. A chill spread along her skin as he began unfastening the delicate buttons that ran down the front of her shirtwaist. She had never worn the gauzy, barely-there excuses for a dress that the acolytes wore. She had opted for simple clothing—shirtwaists and bottoms of her own design, billowy enough to look like a dress, but fashioned in a way that they were more like trousers. She had always felt comfortable in her pants-that-were-not-a-skirt. Protected. Safe, even.

But as Phinehas revealed her body to him, one button and hook at a time, she felt exposed. Vulnerable.

A lamb at the slaughter.

His eyes glazed as he raked them over her skin, and with one flick of his long fingers, her skirt-like pants fell to the ground in a billow of linen.

He ran a knuckle along the skin of her shoulder, her chest, and down farther as he said, "I have been unable to resist your wiles, my dove." He pressed a single kiss to the soft skin at the swell of her breast before he went on. "I doubt he will either."

"*He* who?" she tried. But Phinehas was lowering her down onto the bed.

The high priest of Har-Navah doffed his bib with economical movements, loosening his trousers and lifting his tunic before settling himself upon her. He did not meet her eyes as he moved, swift and rough. Powerfully. He held a power over her that she could not describe. From the very beginning, she had been at his bidding.

Maybe that powerful feeling was love. She hadn't been sure. But she had read the holy texts enough to know what transpired between a man and a woman was supposed to be a holy act, meant for those in the covenant of marriage. She had often wondered why it had never felt holy with Phinehas. Never felt as tender or loving as she imagined it should.

But it had always felt powerful. And perhaps that was enough —that this love was more powerful than any simpering ideas of tenderness she might have had as a young girl.

Phinehas groaned, his movements becoming swifter, harder. Miri shut her eyes against the pain, wincing as the priest unleashed his brutal affection. "Phinehas," she tried, but the high priest did not answer, his eyes shut, the tendons in his neck straining as his body grew as taut as a bowstring.

With a mighty groan, Phinehas found the satisfaction he sought and soon stilled, catching his breath with his head buried in the crook of her neck.

She willed her breath to calm, willed her mind to stop reeling, willed herself to find comfort in his affection. "Phinehas, my darling," she said, mustering as much affection she could into her quavering voice. "I love you."

Phinehas shifted, lifting away from her in one fluid movement. With his back to her, he refastened his trousers, straightened his tunic, and reached for his bib. She slithered to the edge of the bed, taking the blanket with her, wrapping it tightly around herself.

When he finished the work of straightening his clothes, he turned to face her, taking her chin with his thumb and forefinger. She resisted the urge to wince at his grip. "Never forget, my dove. You are mine and mine alone. You would be nothing without me."

Miri could not speak, could not think of anything to say. So she opted to merely nod.

Satisfied, Phinehas relinquished her chin and made his way to her hidden door. "Dress, my dove. The work of Providence awaits."

CHAPTER TWO

"Why is it so small?" Galina sneered, finger-combing her auburn hair.

Five weeks, four days, six hours, and what felt like ten thousand minutes later, the traveling party now stood before a temple in the heart of a quiet mountain village somewhere in old Haravelle. More than a month of enduring Phinehas's daily ancient text readings in the bumpy carriage; of the girls' quiet bickering; of the sights and smells and monotonous *riding, riding, riding* deeper and deeper into the heart of old Haravelle. Across barren plains and the dusty heart of old Navah. Through the rolling hills of Tsafone Province and the vast vistas of the foothills in the Majestic Mountains. And finally the winding, climbing roads through the labyrinthine mountains and towering aspen and pine trees.

Only to arrive at an ancient, quaint stone temple nestled at the base of a towering mountain.

Thanks to the iron horses that pulled their carriage, they had not exactly had an uneventful journey. Magic, while convenient for most things, required a lot of maintenance to keep going. And a carriage pulled by iron horses made of more gears and parts than Miriam could ever imagine was not exactly a problem-free way to travel, the intricate mechanics and delicate magic that powered the rusty beasts a questionable wonder of modern invention

It was for these reasons and a dozen more that Miriam practically leapt from carriage when it finally came to a stop in the rustic village. The crisp air had captivated her from the moment they had crossed into the mountains more than a week ago. But here...higher, deeper into the purple, jagged peaks, the air was brighter. Invigorating. The mountains were not quite the rugged wilderness she had expected. Galina hadn't been wrong in her observation; the temple was small. Rustic, even. Nothing like the sprawling city temples in Teman City. In fact the whole village of Shalem where they would now live was *different*. A step back in time, if such a thing were possible. Quiet. Small. Unhurried. A nod to the past, before the hustle and bustle of modern magic changed everything about Har-Navah.

And the temple itself was like looking at a painting—all lithe columns and brightly-colored frescoes, it was nothing if not a portrait of bygone times.

In fact, the temple seemed to be at direct odds with the larger-than-life man who would rule from its seat. Tall, lanky Phinehas seemed to gobble up the tiny place with one foot through the door. They started down the long aisle that cut through the center of the sanctuary, the acolytes and sages following the high priest.

Jareth, a sage with arms as long as a mantis, carried several bags under and along his arms and said, "The temple was built in the year 327, during the Adelaidian Era. The paintings are a tribute to the ancient queen and—"

"We didn't ask for a history lesson, Jareth," Galina said, cutting him off. Her eyes were fixed on a young priest who had entered the temple sanctuary from the other end. He had not taken his eyes from Galina the moment he had spotted her.

Jareth ignored her and kept walking down the smooth stone aisle with his burden of bags, most of which were Kata's, Miriam didn't fail to notice. He had always quietly taken care of her needs. And Kata had always brushed it off.

He's a sage. That's his job.

But it wasn't. He was a historian. A keeper of legends and knowledge. Not a servant to an acolyte. Miriam had stopped bothering to point that out to her friend after about the millionth time. But Jareth hadn't once missed an opportunity to do something for Kata. Though he always made a point of keeping a healthy distance from her. And he very rarely looked her in the eye.

Miriam turned her attention to the paintings he had mentioned before he was so rudely cut off. Evergreens and mountains. A scarred and fractured fresco of Chesedelle Castle. And there, in the midst of the forest, a mated pair of winged horses—one black, one white.

"King Ferryl and Queen Adelaide's mounts. It is said that all remaining winged horses today can be traced back to them," said Jareth.

Miriam smiled softly, appreciating Jareth's love for the rich history of their kingdom. Having spent countless hours with Ari in her father's library, devouring book after book, it was inevitable that in all that reading, they had learned a thing or two about the story of Har-Navah. About its mysterious inception after the wars of sons, Hasse and Neshaun—the heirs who would become the first kings of Haravelle and Navah. And Midian—the son of a temptress who became the first king of Midvar. The winding, twisting tale of Har-Navah had all come to its culmination with the marriage of Prince Ferryl and Princess Adelaide, the reunification of two mighty kingdoms, and the defeat of the evil of Midvar.

And this was supposed to be the Golden Era — in the aftermath of the ancient king and queen's reign, the people were supposedly basking in the golden age of the fruits of those endeavors.

The age of the Mashiach.

Except the Mashiach—the supposed Promised One—had never come.

In the early years, many had assumed King Ferryl's own son, Prince Derwin was the fulfillment of those ancient prophecies. When he had built the great temple at Benalle only a few years into his reign, many believed him to be so.

But he had died like every other king. Simply died an old man —nothing particularly remarkable about him.

The same was true for his son, and his son after that, and every descendant of King Ferryl for generations. Just men. Kings. But nothing more. Some of them legendary, some of them about as useful as a felt pot, some unholy and selfish.

But none of them had been the fulfillment of the ancient prophecy. At least not as far as anybody could tell. If any of the sons of Ferryl had truly been the Promised One, the famed legend had been an underwhelming prospect to be sure.

Over time and over generations, the fervor for such a thing waned and faded like the moon until nothing was left but legend and lore, ancient religions and fringe zealots. More people idolized King Ferryl and Queen Adelaide than any legend of a promised savior.

Now, a thousand years after the reign of the storied king and queen, people had simply stopped caring. Stopped hoping. And certainly stopped waiting for the fated one who was supposed to save them all.

Save them from what exactly? That was something else the old prophecy wasn't clear on.

"It is certainly a change," said Phinehas. "May change be the blessing of Providence." Coming up behind Miri, he folded his long fingers before his stomach. Dressed in a fine tunic of rich embroidery, the delicate threads wove an intricate pattern of color on his breast: crimson and emerald, sapphire and ochre, violet and golden. The billowing white fabric of his robes trailed behind him as he moved like a cloud down the aisle. Behind him, another sage carried a censer, hanging from heavy golden chains and adorned richly with gems of all colors. Smoke billowed thickly, casting a cloying purple haze in the room that shimmered faintly in the candlelight.

Magic. It looked like magic.

Never mind it was nothing more than a mixture of herbs and dried fruits, burning slowly inside the censer. "We are humbled and honored to serve," Phinehas went on, his words delivered with a godlike timbre. "Whatever the appointment to which Providence has assigned us." With that, the priest lit several candles at the altar without the aid of a match and knelt before it, muttering prayers. The act was meant to strike awe in the hearts of any who saw it—a priest who could light a candle with his own hand. Miri herself had been amazed by it for years before she discovered that Phinehas carried a small, magicked contraption in the hem of his sleeve—one he'd had fashioned by a tinker to light candles with a discreet flick of his wrist. When Miri questioned him about it and the deception, he had struck her so hard across the cheek that she tasted blood. She hadn't dared ask again.

As Phinehas breathed his chants, speaking in the ancient tongue, the sage behind him continued to wave his censer, the ethereal cloud surrounding Phinehas, encircling him as if he were Providence himself.

"Praise be to Providence," said the three acolytes who had been invited to join them—Galina, Jordie, and Kata—trailing behind him in a perfect line, gowned in their traditional, gauzy white dresses with gold bands on their upper arms, their kohl-lined eyes

glazed with adoration for the man before them. In his presence, they often spoke in unison as if of one mind. Miri hated it.

A few more sages and lesser priests followed behind the girls, carrying the bulk of the luggage and trunks they had brought.

"A humble abode for a humble, holy man."

Miri whirled, her attention flying to the unfamiliar voice. A man—a *massive* man—stood at a door off of the side of the temple sanctuary, the candles behind him casting him in muted, flickering gold light. Miriam thought perhaps he looked like an angel, fallen from the skies. Except in the ancient legends, it wasn't angels who had fallen from the heavens, but demons doomed to wander the earth and infest it with their darkness. Some of those demons had even been cursed to take the form of wolves.

She wondered if the man before her weren't a demon wolf himself.

She swallowed as a pious, vulpine smile spread across his mouth. Under his fine clothing, it was apparent that he had been gifted with brute strength, his thick arms straining the fabric of his plum damask jacket, adorned with silver buttons down both lapels. He wore black leather pants that perfectly matched his black leather boots. And peeking out from the neck of his ruffled collar was a tattoo. It was hard to tell, but it looked like it could be the top of a skull.

"Allow me to introduce myself," said the man. "I am Gian of Borras. I am come to welcome Your Holiness to Kinnereth." Gian bowed low, that smile never leaving his face.

Miriam didn't fail to notice the wealth of weapons on him—a rapier hanging from his belt, a bandolier of knives glinting from within his jacket, exposed when he bowed.

He straightened again, his gaze slowly coming to rest on Miriam, though he still spoke to Phinehas. "You are most welcome here."

Miri couldn't help the greasy feeling of dread that washed over her as his keen, ice-blue eyes lingered...and lingered.

"It has been a long journey," Phinehas said. "But one worthy of its cause, praise be."

"Praise be to Providence," parroted Gian, that vulpine grin spreading his mouth thin. The massive man bowed again, this time dropping to one knee. "I offer my services to you, Your Holiness. It would be an honor to serve and protect a man of Providence."

Phinehas looked on the man with a hint of skepticism. But he nodded for Gian to stand again and simply said, "I do not make it a practice to refuse the devout to the service of Providence."

Gian rose, nodding his approval before sliding his eyes over the rest of Phinehas's party, at last landing on Miri again, his leer setting Miri's teeth on edge.

"We are humbled and honored to take up our residence in such an *historical* village," said Phinehas regally with a slight bow of his head. "Providence's goodness knows no bounds."

"*Praise Providence,*" said the acolytes, all bowing their heads in unison.

Historical. Right. Miriam knew full well the reason Phinehas had chosen such a place had everything to do with political advantage and nothing to do with an appreciation for history. The duke—the glorious grand duke of Kinnereth Phinehas couldn't seem to quit prattling about—resided here somewhere. *He rules half the kingdom, Miriam,* Phinehas had told her last night at the inn in the mountains south of here. *Anyone with that kind of power, no matter how disinterested he may be, needs to be steered towards the proper interests.*

What interests are those? Miriam had asked.

The interests of Providence, of course.

Standing before this dark enigma named Gian, surrounded by her priest's masquerade of piety here in this forgotten temple in the middle of nowhere, Miriam wondered exactly what were the interests of Providence these days.

"HE'S OFFERED himself as personal guard to Phinehas," said Jordie, plopping down on the small chair nearest the fire. A common room connected the many sleeping chambers below the temple. Outfitted with a number of rugs and a warm fireplace, it was at least cozy, though humble in size and furnishings.

No private access to her chambers anymore. That had been the first thing Miri noticed when she moved her things in. If Phinehas wanted to visit her, he'd have to cross the common space, the anteroom outside everyone's chambers.

For everyone to see.

Galina stood near the high windows, peeking out at the mountains beyond, fiddling with her curls. Miriam didn't like that she'd have to crane her neck so high just to get a glimpse of the outside world. But considering their rooms were mostly underground, she supposed it was better than having no windows at all. At least she'd have an idea of the time of day and the weather.

"They say he was a pirate," said Galina. "And now he lives at court. He is said to strut about Chesedelle Castle, fighting and fucking as he pleases."

"Where did you hear that?" Kata asked.

Galina did not answer immediately, curling her mouth into a smirk instead. "Men talk."

"Barely here for a few hours and Galina is already taking to her *prayers,*" Kata sneered.

Galina merely fussed with her nails, unbothered by the snide remark. "Devotion beckons at all hours."

"The young priest?" Jordie asked jealously.

Galina said nothing. It did not surprise Miri. Not really. Men threw themselves at the voluptuous acolyte most of the time. If they had something that might benefit her, she usually accepted their advances. And since Phinehas provided for the girls' every need in exchange for their devotion, it meant that sleeping with men often involved payment that had little to do with coin. Gossip was, for all intents and purposes, Galina's favorite currency.

"Phinehas will be officially named high priest at a state dinner tomorrow night," said Galina. "It's only fitting that such a man should have proper security."

Perhaps that was true. But a pirate? It seemed...odd.

"Who would hurt a priest?" Kata asked, munching on a berry tart she had found in the kitchen.

Galina turned a feline smile to the acolyte. "A man must protect his interests."

"I don't like him," young Jordie said. "He scares me."

Miriam couldn't help but agree. "Jareth told me there are rumors that he is a secret mercenary for the king."

"He certainly has a reputation," said Galina, obviously enjoying every word. "He is ruthless and brutal. They say he protects the interests of the king at any cost."

"I thought you said he would protect *Phinehas's* interests," Miri pointed out.

"Phinehas *is* the king's interest," Galina said, and turned her attention back to her curls.

Outside, the day was bright and golden, the sunlight streaming down from the high windows in skinny shafts. It would be several more hours until sunset. And Miri found she didn't much feel like sitting in this nearly-windowless room with the girls arguing politics or the fact that they were apparently living with one of the king's spies. She had been cooped up in a carriage for a month and a half. She certainly didn't feel like staying here in an underground room that mostly resembled a dungeon cell, thank you very much.

"I'm going out," she said, turning on her heel.

"Where?" Kata asked. "We have prayers in an hour." And it was clear from her tone that she wished Miri would invite her to come. Though she knew it was selfish of her, Miri did no such thing. She just needed to be alone.

"Out," was all she repeated, before she disappeared behind the door.

The hall outside her chambers was dim and silent, the stone walls marred with decades—if not centuries—of wear and grime. The few lamps that hung from the low ceiling were not outfitted with modern gaslighting, but rather burned with real flame, as if any of the previous priests who had governed these sacred halls hadn't deemed an upgrade important. Not for the first time, Miri found herself surprised that Phinehas had deigned to reside in such a primitive place.

She had lost herself in those thoughts when the subject of them found her near the end of the long hallway.

"What has you in such a hurry, my darling?" Phinehas asked with saccharine curiosity.

Her thick ginger curls whipped around her neck as she spun to face him. "I thought I'd explore the village. It looked interesting when we came through earlier." Haberdashers. Apothecaries. Mercantiles. Cozy restaurants and tempting little bakeries. All surrounding a lake in the heart of the tall mountains. She wanted to explore as much as she wanted to escape from the acolytes.

Phinehas didn't seem keen to argue, thank Providence. He took three steps to stand before her, surprising her when he placed a small handful of shekels in her palm. "See what trouble you can get into, darling."

"You could join me," she offered.

"You'll have much more success on your own, I'm sure," he

said before he turned on his heel and disappeared back into the dank darkness.

BREATHTAKING.

That was the only way to describe the village of Shalem. Jareth said in the old language, the name meant *perfect peace*. She believed it. Surrounded by towering granite mountains, kissed with pockets of snow, the village curled around a glassy lake at the base of those imposing peaks. Homes and buildings of all colors and sizes climbed the lush mountainsides, interspersed between thick green trees and brilliant wildflowers. At the base of the mountains, the village sprawled along the lakeshore.

Magic was not completely absent in the town, for Miri passed a shop full of whirring gadgets made of brass, magicked to offer small conveniences—a contraption that kept your bath warm. A writing pen that cleverly siphoned ink from the well every time it rested. A candle that lit itself every time you walked by it. And those were only the ones she could see from the window.

People bustled about the village around her, greeting one another, going in and out of the colorful buildings around the lake's edge. A town tinker called merrily as he pushed his clanking cart down the cobblestone, offering wares of the mostly non-magic variety. Soaps and perfumes, spices and fats, goose grease and pigs' feet. On the end, he offered baubles of polished amber and rough-cut crystals. Some of the passersby stopped to shop, purchasing some of his small wares.

She couldn't help her smile as she passed the villagers, some arm in arm talking and whispering to one another.

"Acolytes."

The word snagged her attention, and she looked across the

way to a pair of ladies talking over a small table set with tea and cakes outside a quaint eatery.

"What is an acolyte?" the other woman asked.

The first woman donned a look that told Miri she was both mortified and thrilled to share such titillating news with her friend. "Lightskirts. Who live at the *temple!*" It took her friend a minute to catch the meaning of the word, but when she finally did, the woman added, "The high priest brought with him an entire harem. I saw them getting off of their iron carriage just today."

Miri turned away, unable to listen to another second of the conversation, a knot forming in her throat at how quickly such news had already traveled through the village. She walked as quickly as she could without drawing attention to herself, putting more and more distance between her and the disdainful gossipers.

Farther into the village, a boardwalk hugged the edge of the blue water, and most of the shops were accessible from both the lakeside and the mountainside by a wooden promenade, edged in some places with intricately-painted, turned wooden railings.

At the heart of the village, the temple stood out against the rest of the buildings, the ancient gray stone stark next to the cheery paints of the other structures. A steeple climbed to the skies from the highest gable, an eight-pointed star atop its peak, pointing straight to Providence. The Star of Ferryl—a symbol of the Mashiach to come, glistened in the sunlight.

But just down the cobblestone road that cut through the steep mountain village she could see another structure—one unlike any she had ever seen before. Great white marble columns sculpted with winged creatures embracing their tops held a white marble balcony with equally ornate embellishments. Windows lined the front of the building—tall and formidable, with golden light twinkling inside. Chandeliers. She could see them even with the setting sunlight competing for attention.

A theatre.

Her heart thundered as she watched the villagers pour into the giant doors, opened as if greeting old friends. There was a show tonight.

The shekels in her pocket seemed to burn.

She had never been to a theatre, despite how often she had begged her parents growing up. They never seemed to have the time to take her to one. And Teman City, as bustling as it was, did not boast a single theatre or opera house.

That a quant village hidden among remote mountains should have such a proud theatre was a marvel.

Somehow, she found herself standing in the ticket line behind a throng of eager attendees.

When at last she reached the ticket clerk, he gave her an uncomfortable once-over before asking flatly, "How many?"

"Just one, please," she said, reaching into her pocket for the money Phinehas had given her earlier, hoping it would be enough.

With his nose crinkled and his eyes narrow with disdain, he said, "We only have the mezzanine left." She tried not to let his disgust get to her. Surely he could not know who she was. Then again, this was a small village. If the gossiping ladies were any indication, perhaps everyone knew of the new high priest...and the acolytes he brought with him.

But she was not an acolyte. Despite the fact that nearly everyone in Teman City had decided she was. Here, in this place far from anyone who knew her, she would start over. She would finally just be Miri. Nothing more.

"Oh, that's fine," she said, ignoring her pounding heart. She didn't even know what the mezzanine was. But any seat would be divine. She just wanted to see the show.

"Eight shekels," the clerk said flatly.

"Only eight?" she asked, surprised that the show should be so affordable. For such a place, she had half expected him to ask for ten gold talents. Not that she had ten gold talents. She had no money of her own. Nothing but the pittance Phinehas would occasionally give her.

"I could charge you more, if you're so eager to part with your *—hard-earned* money," said the clerk. And the implication...

"Have I offended you, sir?" she asked, unable to stop herself.

"I know who you are," he said, not bothering to temper the disdain in his voice. "His Holiness is most welcome here. Though I cannot say the same for the rest of you."

"I am...his wife," she said wildly, wondering how even a ticket clerk in this tiny town far from the rest of the world had already gotten word of what she was.

Disappointment unfurled in her gut.

"And I'm the king of Har-Navah," he said.

She furrowed her brow and handed him the money through the little hole in the window that separated them. He handed her a single red ticket and said wryly, "Enjoy the show."

WITH THE HELP of the usher, she found her seat on the mezzanine. It was a glorious view, despite what the ticket clerk had implied. She was on the front row, even if it was far to one side. From here, she could see the whole stage, the wings, and she could even peek just a little behind the side curtains to the actors bustling backstage.

As she looked around the great, golden room, she understood just how severely underdressed she was. Ladies were dressed in exquisite gowns decorated with jewels and pearls and feathers. Lords with top hats, crisp cravats and tails. She had opted to wear loose-fitting pants and a shirtwaist today—her favorite. The pants, as usual, were billowy enough to pass as a skirt if no one paid much attention. But the fabrics were plain and nowhere near the finery of the women around her. She had at least bothered to pull her hair into a neater bun on the top of her head, if you could ever call her hair neat. Her messy, fiery red curls were about as cooperative as a dandelion in a wind storm. But if she pulled tightly enough, she could coax them into a bun for a few hours. So far, only a few tendrils had spilled loose around her temple and ears.

But she didn't care. Not one little bit. For when the gaslights dimmed and the lone note of the orchestra began, her heart found a new rhythm, and the hairs on her arms stood on end. The show had begun.

Magic. Music was nothing short of its own kind of magic, and the anticipation—

Miri froze, keeping her eyes locked on the orchestra, she dared not move. She scarcely breathed. For reasons she couldn't explain, she had the distinct feeling of being watched. And in fact when she turned her attention to the box perpendicular to her, she realized she *was* being watched. By a man.

A man far too beautiful for words.

His hair, as black as quill ink, was neatly combed, but here and there, strands seemed to stick up and away from the rest, rebels against his otherwise polished presentation. But that was about the only thing unkempt about him. He was clad head to toe in black, the light of the gaslights dancing along shimmering threads, painting a pattern of glossy damask on his broad chest and thick arms. His eyes—Providence above, his eyes were a shade of golden so fierce, it rivaled the chandeliers. And he watched her without remorse, without blinking. If she were any closer, she might have snapped at him, hissed for daring to stare so brazenly. Most men would have at least pretended to play a game—to dance a dance of half smirks and come-hither glances. But not this man. No, this man watched her unapologetically. He did not seem as if he would be bothered if she crawled across the chairs and clawed his eyes out, for his appraisal was as unrelenting as it was branding.

It was a moment before she realized that a woman sat next to him in the private box—surely his wife. She too had hair as black as a raven's feathers. Dressed in a fine gown of peacock-blue and gold, the swell of her belly rested on her lap. Pregnant.

Miri did not miss the fact that he showed no affection towards his wife. No arm around her. No holding her hand. No paying her any heed, really, his attention fixated solely, brazenly on Miriam.

She decided to cock her head to one side, raising her brows. At this, the man's mouth turned up into a smirk, and she saw his chest puff with a laugh.

Ass.

Something you'd like to say, sir?

It was hard to tell in the wan light, but she could have sworn that smirk turned into full-fledged smile. But then the man bowed his head once and returned his attention to the stage.

Heart pounding, Miri also turned her attention away from the mysterious man with midnight hair. But for the rest of the play, she could feel his eyes drift to her now and again. She willed herself not to look back.

"Where did you go?" Kata asked, barraging Miri with questions the moment she returned to the temple.

"Exploring," Miri said, marching past her friend. Tired and still unnerved by the lingering attention from the mysterious stranger, Miri wanted nothing more than a bath and bed. Especially this late at night.

"Why didn't you wait until after prayers so I could go with you?" Kata asked, hot on her trail as they marched down the steps to the underground living quarters.

"I'm sorry," she said when she saw the hurt in Kata's eyes. "I just needed some air."

"We had only been here an hour," Kata said.

"That's an hour more of Galina and the girls than I can take." They never discussed it—the fact that Kata was an acolyte, too. She never really acted like one. But Miri and Kata both knew that Kata offered herself to the lesser priests and sages in exchange for a place to live. Miri had never bothered to ask her friend why, always keeping Kata in a category all her own. Acolyte. *And* friend. And that had always been enough.

"You think I like being around them?" Kata demanded. "Galina is positively insufferable since we left Teman. Like she knows something we don't."

"I know. It's ridiculous," Miri agreed.

"And that new guard scares me," Kata added, lowering her voice. They made their way down the dark hall to the door at the end. "He wanted to know all of our names and what our business is here. He was particularly interested in you."

"Gian—interested in me?" Miri asked, freezing in her tracks. Kata looked solemnly at her.

"He said you were Phinehas's most prized possession and so he'd have to keep his eyes on you the most."

"Possession! I am no possession!" Miri growled.

"The point is, he's watching us, Miri," said Kata. "He's watching all of us. You most of all."

"I have nothing to hide."

Kata raised her brows, as if she thought it a brazen lie. "You have a way of finding trouble, Miri. And Phinehas has never kept you on quite as short of a leash as the rest of us."

"That's because I'm not the *rest of you,*" she said before she thought better of it.

Hurt flashed in Kata's eyes. Hurt that Phinehas had never shown interest in her. And while Kata swore she didn't want it anyway, Miri knew it bothered her friend. But not nearly as much as it would have bothered Miri if Phinehas *had* been interested in her. And that was yet another subject the girls had never discussed.

Miri couldn't help but wonder when the delicate balancing act they all kept up would finally come crashing down around them.

CHAPTER THREE

"I hate these things," said Kata, standing beside Miri. Sparkling wine in hand, she appraised the tittering crowd gathered in the banquet room at the back of the modest temple. Built behind the sanctuary itself, the room was by no means sprawling. Jareth had told her that its original purpose was for the priest to host a gathering or meeting, and occasionally for private prayers. Miri couldn't help but wonder if the ancients who had built this place ever imagined it would be teeming with nobility waiting in line to adulate a fledgling high priest.

"Rather tedious, aren't they?" Miri said in agreement.

Kata chuckled and Miri breathed a laugh as she watched the crowd of noblemen and women. She had put on her finest gown tonight, an amethyst ensemble of velvet and feathers. A bit scandalous, it offered a generous view of her assets as it hugged every curve of her body before spilling onto the floor in a pool of heavy velvet. Great plumes of delicate purple feathers sprawled from her shoulders, dancing at her slightest movements, while a deluge jewels sparkled along the plunging neckline. Phinehas's favorite.

The crowd had surprised her. For such a quaint, isolated

village in the heart of the mountains, there were a lot of people here tonight. Lords and ladies from all around coming to pay homage to the newly minted high priest of Har-Navah. His ceremony had been unbearable—incense and a loquacious speech on the merits of Providential Law and unflinching piety and *blah blah blah* until they had finally adjourned to the banquet room for dinner and loquacious flattery.

Lamenting the fact that her unruly bun was particularly tight on the top of her head in the vain hope that it would stay in place tonight, Miri tucked an errant curl behind her ear and took a drink of her wine.

Kata stood beside her, watching the crowd silently as she sipped from her glass. One of the lesser priests spotted them from across the room and began ambling closer. Miri didn't know his name—she had never really bothered to learn any of the lesser priests' or sages' names except Jareth. And she had only learned his name because of the attention he paid to her friend. But judging by the look on Kata's face, *she* knew this priest's name. Knew him well.

"Sheol," Kata spat under her breath as the lanky priest made his way closer.

Miri knew why Kata was disappointed. She didn't know what to say, either. It was awkward to be standing right here, to watch the silent conversation unfold. The priest said nothing as he approached, merely raking his lust-glazed eyes over Kata before nodding his head to one side. He turned and walked towards the edge of the room and the corridor that led to stairs and then down to the private quarters.

Tonight, Kata would earn her keep.

She eyed Miri for a second, a look of wry disgust in her eyes, then handed Miri her glass of sparkling wine and threaded her way through the crowd in the direction of the priest.

Miri swallowed once, thanking Providence that her days of

entertaining whatever aristocrat who glanced her way were over. Things would be different here. They would start over. Something new. Something better.

In the early years, Phinehas had convinced Miri of the merits of entertaining noblemen. Giving them what they wanted in exchange for their loyalty to Phinehas and his cause. In the beginning, Miri had been naïve enough to trust that giving her body to one man after another would please Phinehas—help his cause.

And maybe it had. He had certainly gotten the necessary votes for his surprise appointment to the prestigious title despite his lack of experience with the Sanhedrin. But now that he was appointed, now that it was done, so, too was Miri. She would not go back to that life—to those kinds of games. Here, in Kinnereth, she would start anew.

It was then that she spotted a man across the room, eyeing her with hungry greed. She looked away, sipping from her wine and hoping her lack of interest would dissuade him.

It did not.

Apparently her reputation had followed her, despite her hopes to the contrary. She swallowed back bitter bile and did her best to ignore the man.

The nobleman slithered through the room towards her, brazenly eyeing her up and down. This time, she did not back down from his gaze, but held his eyes with a contemptuous glare. By the time he made it to her, his swagger hadn't diminished in the least.

"My lady," he said, taking her hand and lifting it to his mouth. He did not kiss it, but hovered over her skin for a moment too long.

"Is there a reason you are here?" she asked with all the petulance she could muster.

He did not seem terribly bothered. "I have heard of you," he said. "I wanted to meet you for myself."

"I'm afraid I'm going to have to disappoint you," she said.

The nobleman put on a distasteful grin. He let his eyes wander over her body as if she were a mare at auction. When his eyes reached her breasts, on full display in her gown, he practically drooled. "I am afraid the rumors were wrong," he said, the soft lilt of his northern accent slanting his words like stalks of wheat in the wind. "The famed acolytes are even more alluring than the lore would imply."

Miri did not resist the urge to roll her eyes. "Well unfortunately for you, I am no acolyte."

He huffed a laugh as if she had made a joke. "You humor me, my lady."

"Funny. You disgust me."

At this, his swagger diminished a bit. "I beg your pardon? Are you implying you are not the priest's most prized whore?"

Well then. At least he was done with implications. "I'm afraid you'll have to play your own fiddle tonight, my lord. His Holiness does not take kindly to bawdy implications about his temple dwellers."

At this, the nobleman was at last taken aback. He eyed her skeptically for a moment, his mouth opening and closing a few times, as if he could not think of how to respond. Finally, he decided to merely huff before turning to march away. She smirked and sipped again from her sparkling wine, content with her impudent victory.

"He's harmless, my pet," came a whispered voice in her ear. "Though I do not blame you for turning him away. There are much more important men here tonight." She turned her head to find Phinehas standing just behind her, a smirk on his narrow mouth.

"I'm done playing those games, Phinehas," she said.

Phinehas donned a piteous frown. "Can you blame him for trying?"

"I just—" she started but instead looked down, fiddling with the stem of her wine goblet.

Phinehas ran a featherlight finger along the top of her hand. "You *are* a rather delicious prize, my darling."

Miri looked up, unable to hide her frown. "I thought moving here—I thought it would be different."

"You look positively sinful," he pointed out. "Did you really think men wouldn't notice?"

"*You* picked out my gown!" she spat.

Phinehas tilted his chin to one side, a look of pious reproach on his narrow face. "Remember, darling, you are foremost a servant of Providence."

Miri huffed, turning away from him. But his hand found her upper arm, gripping her with a strength that did not match his mantis-like limbs. He yanked her around to face him again.

"You are not so very young anymore, are you?" His words were light. Too light. The warning behind them sent a shiver down her spine.

"I'm barely twenty," she said, mimicking his lightness.

"You've become quite the woman," Phinehas said. But it wasn't pride in his voice. It was something else—something she couldn't quite place. He ran a finger along her collarbone, down... Such brazen attention. Here. In a room full of people here to meet the new high priest. She could think of only one reason he would display it...

"Do me a favor and use that to our advantage."

She narrowed her brows. "Phinehas."

The high priest of Har-Navah breathed a throaty chuckle. "My darling," he said. He pressed a soft kiss to her brow that did not match the harsh tone of his quiet words. "We did not move to this shit-hole village for nothing. All I want is for you to make friends." He eyed her breasts on display in the gown and then said, "The *right* friends."

"I don't want t—"

"The grand duke is here tonight. You'll make fast company, I'm sure," he said. And then without another word, he disappeared into the crowd.

She almost followed him—almost insisted he understand. She did not want to play games. He was high priest now. What else was there to accomplish? But she found herself gaping after him instead.

Quite the woman.

Miri huffed a sardonic laugh. She had never felt more like a child.

Reeling, she took another sip of her wine and watched the guests mill about. From one corner of the room, the nobleman who had tried to win her tonight was deep in conversation with Jordie, who smiled coyly as she sipped from her glass. Not far from there, Jareth stood a head taller than the rest of the crowd. He watched a corner of the room as if he had seen a ghost. Miri understood his silent vigil when she followed his line of sight to the place where Kata had disappeared on the arm of the lesser priest. Not even a year ago, that could very well have been Miri, disappearing into a dark corner with a stranger at the behest of Phinehas. Nausea roiled in Miri's gut, and she turned away from the sight.

But Miri soon forgot about the games of acolytes, her breath frozen in her lungs...

The man from the theatre. The man with raven black hair. He was here. And he was watching her.

He was dressed in all black again. But tonight, silver toggles and trim and shiny buttons adorned his fine jacket. His shirt and cravat were black too. And she did not fail to notice how tan was his skin—as if he spent a lot of time in the sun. The man watched her from across the room as brazenly has he had last night at the theatre. No apology. No explanation. Just bald appraisal—as if he might devour her with his eyes.

She wanted to sneer, to lift her chin and spin away from his unflinching gaze, but she did not have the chance before a crowd of people cut between them and she lost sight of her mysterious observer. She sipped her wine instead, wondering what she would do about him. What she would say to him if given the chance.

A moment later, the crowd parted again and she could see him once more. Engaged in a conversation, he no longer watched her. But she could see the eagerness of the aristocrat speaking to him...and the near disinterest in his eyes. The nobleman was prattling on and on—no doubt patronizing, since the man in black seemed quite important, if the subservient posture and mannerisms of the man speaking to him were any indication.

Their conversation ended, and Miri quickly found something else to occupy her gaze before the man in black spotted her ogling. But she couldn't help cutting her eyes to him again—to watch him from a distance just as he had watched her at the theatre. Yet another nobleman was speaking to him, fawning over him. And once again, the man seemed positively disinterested.

She wondered exactly who this man was. Why so many of the noblemen here seemed eager to get a word with him. She turned away. Another glass of sparkling wine was in order.

"I do not believe we have met," said a voice from behind.

She whirled, only to find herself face to face with the man in black. As if he had flown across the room—one second a world away, the next second disconcertingly close...

"I believe you were at the theatre last night," he said.

She allowed herself to look at him. This close, she could see the smoothness of his skin, the spattering of faint freckles on his cheeks, the dimple on the right side of his mouth. He was even more beautiful up close. She quickly reminded herself that he was a married man with a child on the way.

"What is your name?"

"Would your *wife* approve of you knowing my name?" she quipped, not bothering to temper her disgust.

"My *wife?*" he said, nearly choking on the wine he sipped from an ostentatious golden goblet set with rubies and emeralds. "I would have bet money that everyone had heard the news by now. Interesting."

She did not know what meant. Nor did she care.

"The woman with you last night. She was certainly quite pregnant with your child," said Miri. "So if she's not your wife—"

The man burst into laughter. "Providence help me if I ever had to marry her." He sipped his wine casually, his shoulders still bobbing from his silent laugh. Easy. Effortless. As if he were carrying on a conversation with an old friend.

"Mistress, then? Yes, it would be quite an inconvenience for you to have to make an honest woman of your *paramour*," Miriam sneered. His arrogance irritated her. The brazen way he just...*talked* to her. Like he had a right.

"Good Providence, woman," he said, appalled. But there was something else there. Something that sounded a lot like amusement. "Are you always so impudent?"

"I'm usually worse," she said, turning away from him.

The man did not leave, however. "That was my sister," he said, a hint of a laugh remaining in his rich voice.

"Your *sister,*" said Miri flatly. Right. She did not buy his line for a minute. She had met too many men like him before—cocksure, arrogant, letting their wealth give them a sense of superiority. As if the world bowed to them for the sole reason that they existed.

"Her name is Esther. And she will be as horrified as I am that you thought us married. I do look forward to telling her," he said, chuckling. Genuine humor colored his dark, chiseled features.

"Right. Well, don't let me get in the way of you and your *sister.*" Miri fixed her attention on the tittering crowd.

"She is nearly halfway through now. I do look forward to another niece or nephew."

The way he said it...the delight in his voice... Miri could not help but turn and face him again.

"Another?" she asked.

"This will be my second. The first—John Junior—well, he's positively perfect, if I do say so myself." The man's eyes lit up like a thousand stars on a summer night as he spoke of his alleged nephew.

He let a moment pass between them, humor dancing in his liquid gold eyes. "I am Ezra, by the way. Ezra Kelach." He extended his hand to her, but she did not take it. He kept it extended anyway, undaunted by her snub.

"I better go," she said, turning away.

"You forgot to tell me your name."

She turned, facing him again. "I do not recall offering it."

A smile ghosted his mouth. "No, I suppose you didn't. But I'll ask for it all the same."

She turned away from again, keenly aware of his eyes on her as she walked away. "Would you ask my name so brazenly if you knew you were speaking to the high priest's wife?"

She didn't know why she lied—why she said such a thing. But his speechless, gaping mouth was satisfying enough that she relished saying it all the same.

"You told him you're his wife?" Jareth said, standing beside her. Apparently, in this crowd of tittering nobility, Miri seemed a safe refuge to the sage tonight—at least without Kata here.

The guests had begun gathering around the banquet table.

Dinner would soon commence. Miri waited patiently along the wall for Phinehas to motion where he'd like her to sit.

"You heard that?" she asked, momentarily horrified by the thought of who else might have heard the lie.

"What are you going to do when he finds out you're not married to Phinehas?" he asked.

"Why should he find out? And even if he did," Miri said flippantly, "why should I care?"

The guests had almost all found their places, though Miri did not fail to notice only a few seats remained. Jareth raised an eyebrow, but said nothing more before he made his way to the other end of the table, far away from the guests of honor. She watched him walk away, watched him glance about only once— no doubt looking for Kata—before he finally took his seat. By the time everyone found their seats, there was only one left beside Phinehas—near the head of the table.

Miri hesitated before she took the seat beside him. And he, engaged in a conversation on his other side, didn't even acknowledge her.

It wasn't until she sat down that she realized the man in black —Ezra. Whatever—had found a seat opposite her. Of course. He caught her eye immediately, a gleam of mischief shining, and tipped his head once. Miri ignored him, forcing herself not to react to his breathy chuckle.

At the head of the table, a nobleman tapped his fork on his glass.

"My lords," he said. "If I may." The quiet conversations around the table hushed at last, and the lord went on. "We are humbled tonight to honor such a great man of Providence and the youngest high priest in Har-Navarian history." He raised his glass. "Your Holiness," he said, looking to Phinehas. "It is an honor that you have chosen the village of Shalem of Kinnereth Province to call your new home. Here's to a bright future and to a new era of cooperation between the monarchy and the Sanhedrin."

The nobles around the table raised their classes, all agreeing in unison. *To a bright future.*

Phinehas raised his glass too, a smile curling his mouth before he took a sip of his wine. Miri dared to steal a glance at the man in black. He did not join the toast, but he raised his glass and drank of his wine nonetheless, his eyes never once leaving Miri.

She tried to engage in conversations around her. She really did. But Phinehas would only pat her hand when she tapped his shoulder, never once turning to face her. And she knew no one else around her, the acolytes all either on the edge of the room or tangled with a nobleman somewhere else, no doubt.

So she had no choice...

"Is something on my face?" she barked when the the dark stranger wouldn't take his eyes from her.

"On your face?" he asked, tilting his head to one side.

"Surely I must have sprouted a mustache. Or perhaps I've grown toadstools for my brows. There can be no other explanation for your insistent appraisal, sir."

"That would be a sight," he said, humored. He sliced a piece of meat with his fork and knife, not quite finished chewing his bite before he continued, "Does that happen to you often?"

"Funny," she said flatly, beginning her own dinner.

At her side, Phinehas laughed, and she turned her body at an angle that made it clear she was done conversing with the man in black and keen to get in on whatever Phinehas was talking about. But the priest did not so much as acknowledge she breathed, his body angled in such a way that she wouldn't be able to join in his conversation. Frustrated, she started slicing another piece of meat.

"Careful. You're about to cut right through the table," said the man across from her.

"Is there a reason you're so keen to torture me, sir?" She bit the piece of meat so hard her teeth sang with the impact of the fork. Around them, conversations continued, oblivious to their exchange.

"I hadn't realized you'd consider lighthearted conversation a form of torture," he said, a twinkle of humor in his eyes. "Then again, you won't give me your name. So perhaps you're terrified of making new acquaintances."

She met his eyes, holding his gaze, her face expressionless. But a wicked grin slowly curled her mouth when she finally said, "If it's the acquaintance of an acolyte you're seeking, I'm sure I can introduce you to several who will suit your needs."

"You consider conversation an invitation to my bed?"

Her eyes flared and she blinked once. The man was utterly unfazed by her. "You, sir, are too forward."

He breathed another laugh. "Well. For reasons I have yet to understand, I have gotten off to the worst possible start with you, Lady Without a Name. For this, I sincerely apologize."

She slammed her fork down and grabbed her goblet of sparkling wine, guzzling down the fizzing liquid without an ounce of forbearance. A servant passed by, and she shoved her glass in his direction, silently demanding he refill her drink.

"That's not enough," she said curtly when the servant only filled her glass a respectable amount. Reluctantly, the servant poured some more. When he stopped again, she snarled, "I'll tell you when to stop."

The servant shot his eyes to Ezra across the table, who wasn't bothering to hide his chuckle. Miri bit down on her retort and watched the servant fill the glass. The golden liquid poured much more freely now, and she did not stop him until the glass was filled to the brim. Enough to intoxicate three men.

"Have a nice trip," Ezra said as Miri took her first drink. She eyed him with disdain over the rim, but he seemed undaunted so Miri guzzled the beverage without a hint of contrition.

"It would be a pity for you to lose your inhibitions," he added.

"And why is that?" she asked, despite herself. At least the pause offered her a chance to take a breath.

"In vino veritas," he said, grinning.

She did not know the phrase, but she recognized the cadence of the words. He had uttered something in Medinian.

Before she could say anything, he went on, "Careful, now. You might make a new friend."

THE ROOM SPUN, and Miriam steadied herself behind a chair as the nobility slowly ebbed from the room. Just a little longer and she could take off this stupid gown and go to bed—and put this pointless night behind her.

Dinner had continued without any more conversation with the man from the theatre. Ezra. Whatever his name was. Which had been just fine with her. He had slipped from the table before dessert was over, and she hadn't seen him since. She hadn't been looking for him either. Not at all.

She wondered if he left early or had simply vanished into thin air.

But she didn't care. No, she didn't care one tiny little bit.

Miri pinched the bridge of her nose, willing away the headache that was blooming from the copious amounts of sparkling wine she had consumed at dinner.

"She wasn't here again," Miri heard. Two noblewomen huddled nearby, gossiping over their nearly empty glasses of sparkling wine.

"She hardly shows her face anymore," said the other woman. She made a point to hold her glass just so, displaying a rather ostentatious pearl-and-sapphire ring on her right hand. The thing looked like a burden, it was so large and ornate. Miri wondered why she wore it like a trinket instead of the costly piece it was.

"She uses her pregnancy as an excuse," said the first woman. "But if I had such a dolt for a husband, I wouldn't want to be seen with him either."

"They say he's not even the father," said the other.

The first woman chuckled. "It *is* a bit odd—to finally give your husband an heir after *such* a long time."

The other woman smirked. "Why, it's positively *miraculous.*"

"And what about our dear downfallen Mrs. Rennius? I noticed she is absent tonight too."

"Her husband decided to show up, though. Did you see him? I'm sure he's wearing one of the duke's hand-me-downs just to fit in."

The two women snickered, and Miri rolled her eyes, turning away from their meaningless, hateful banter.

Kata emerged into the room just then, looking mussed and flustered. The lanky priest who had claimed her was nowhere to be found. Miri was about to wave her friend down when she overheard another conversation somewhere behind her. One with a familiar voice.

She turned, the room spinning a bit too slowly after her, to find Ezra engaged with one of the other noblemen just on the other side of a column. Close enough that she could hear but far enough away that she might not be spotted eavesdropping.

"Do you find it odd?" the man asked.

"Odd? Perhaps," said Ezra. "But if he's the man of Providence people seem to believe, then I am glad of his presence. Perhaps he can talk some sense into His Majesty."

The other man breathed a laugh. "You're talking treason, brother."

Ezra's lighthearted smile did not meet his eyes. "You and I both know the king needs as much sense as he can get, John."

John clasped Ezra on the shoulder. "What made you come tonight, anyway? You never show up to these things. Especially not lately."

Ezra seemed to brush off that last observation quickly. "It's not every day a high priest moves to your village."

"A priest with a harem of acolytes," added John. Miri cringed, hating that they knew. That everyone in this village seemed to have already found out what she was. And why any of them were here.

Ezra gave him a wry look. "I'd like to learn everything I can about the man who is to rule so closely with our king."

"Growing political? Not you, Ezra!" John mocked, a hand to his chest.

"Never," said Ezra with false piety. He patted John on the shoulder and said, "Go home and take care of my sister."

"She's rather cranky," lamented John.

"She's always cranky when she's with child," Ezra said, as if offering a casual reminder.

John sighed. "Yes. Yes, she is."

Ezra breathed a laugh. "And you're madly in love with her."

"Yes. Yes, I am." John set down the goblet he had been nursing. "Goodnight, Ez. We'll come by later this week."

"Night, John," said Ezra, clasping John on the shoulder before he walked away.

Miri watched him for a moment with quiet appraisal. But when he turned toward the crowd—toward her again—she whirled quickly, putting her back to him as she leaned on the column to steady herself.

But then—

"He loves Esther very much," came a voice from behind. "He's a good husband to her. Otherwise I would never have let him marry her."

"I wasn't eavesdropping," she protested as Ezra moved to stand beside her. Why was her tongue so thick?

Ezra merely gave her a knowing smirk and sipped from his goblet.

"I wasn't," she said again.

Ezra didn't argue, turning to watch the crowd fizzle out, offering their well-wishes and blessings to Phinehas as they departed. "Your priest is quite the phenomenon around here," he said.

"Surely you've had a priest here before. It's not as if this temple is new."

"Yes," he said. "But not a high priest. That's quite a different thing entirely."

She wondered what he meant by the distinction. A high priest was nothing more than a glorified political figure, wasn't he?

"And so you're not very political?" she asked.

He faced her. "I thought you said you weren't listening."

Heat found her cheeks, and she turned away from Ezra once more. But he didn't seem bothered, and instead breathed a laugh as he said, "Not usually, no. I find politics to be a bit exhausting, as a rule. But sometimes, politics find you."

The way he said it...it was like he lamented his birth. His obligation to this world of games and whispers and maneuvering.

"My name is Miri," she said, wondering much too late why she had offered it. "Miriam Sasson."

"Sasson," he said. "You are the daughter of Lord Sasson of Teman?"

"You knew him?" she asked, surprised.

"I knew *of* him. I was sorry to hear of his passing."

She bit down on her retorts, her lack of sorrow for her own father's untimely passing. Or the way he had died. Some angry nobleman had come to collect the exorbitant amounts of money her father had apparently been frittering away right under their noses—Miri had no idea on what. And the man had taken his debts with both her father and her mother's lives. Miri hadn't felt the slightest bit of remorse when Phinehas had broken the news to her not a month after he had taken her from her home. Good riddance. Even if it had left her with nothing.

Miri sighed and continued to watch the crowd thinning from the room.

"It's an honor to meet you, Lady Miriam," Ezra said.

"It's just Miri," she said, not bothering to look at him.

"Just Miri, then," he said. "Perhaps I will see you again soon. Perhaps at the theatre."

She looked at him, furrowing her brows. But before she could think of what to say, Ezra smiled, exaggerating that dimple in his right cheek and said, "Goodnight, Lady Miri."

"It's just Miri," she repeated, stumbling on her words. But Ezra merely tipped his head and made his way to the door. He didn't offer his blessings to Phinehas. He didn't even bother saying goodbye to him. He just found his top hat and coat and slipped out the door.

CHAPTER FOUR

T he very next morning, a bit groggy from the sparkling wine, Miri wasted no time in escaping the temple. Not bothering to eat breakfast in the stuffy kitchen and certainly not interested in engaging in petty arguments with the girls over who got more attention from whom last night, Miri dressed in her favorite billowy, mint-colored pair of loose pants and twisted her curls into a reckless bun on the top of her head.

One gust of breeze outside in the mountain air and that bun was hanging on for dear life, her curls tickling her face and getting in her eyes. But Miri didn't care. She was outside. And could really get used to this mountain air, the smell of pine and aspen thick and inviting.

Passersby walked through the streets—some with hurried purpose, others with lazy strolls. Lovers hand in hand, sharing coy glances as they made their way down the cobblestone. Businessmen with coats and top hats marching to their destinations. Women eyeing pretty dresses in a clothier window. But it was not business or dresses that captured her today.

Bread. Cinnamon. Vanilla. Chocolate. The scent of baked

goods wafted through the village, and she followed her nose into a bakeshop near the middle of the street, suddenly ravenous for something solid to eat. A bell clinked above her head when she pushed through the brightly-painted door, and a man busy wiping the counter lifted his gaze at the sound, greeting her with a smile.

"Good morning, my lady," he said, the lilt of his Haravellian accent curling his words gently. The bakery was adorned floor to ceiling with all manner of trinkets, brightly colored paint on every wall and trim: rich ceruleans, warm greens, bright yellows, and cheery crimsons. Pictures and signs and anything that could be hung from a nail covered every inch of the walls: keys, locks, bits of chain, toggles, carriage wheels, medallions.

"They each have a story," came the voice from behind the counter. She spun to face the baker again. He was an older man—perhaps in his fifth decade or so. He wore a crisp white apron that brought out the silver that peppered his chin and temples. He was not portly by any means, nor was he slim and svelte. If his body was any indication, he happily dined on the pastries and breads and cakes and muffins that surrounded him.

A woman Miri assumed was his wife came to his side, her cheeks rosy and her belly just as round. The man wiped the counter between them with a bright white rag while the woman set out more cakes on a pedestal plate and said with an even heavier accent, "What can I get for you?"

"What's your favorite?" Miri asked, approaching the scarred counter that separated her from the bakers. Their aprons were spotted with what looked like cinnamon or cloves. As she watched the woman set out more and more delectable goodies, she was glad she had a few bekas left from the money Phinehas had given her.

"Definitely get the chocolate challah," came a familiar, amused voice from her side.

She whirled to find Ezra smiling back at her, those golden eyes of his so intense it was as if he had pinned her feet to the floor. "Good morning Joshua, Winona," he said, tipping his head to the man and woman. He was wearing all black again today, this time with a fine thread of gold embroidered throughout his jacket. A band of the same fabric was fashioned around his top hat, which rested under his arm.

"Ezra, darling," said Winona. "What a pleasant way to start the day." Winona bustled around the counter, motherly concern all over her face. "We've been worried about you," she said, putting her hands on either of Ezra's cheeks.

Ezra's smile looked genuine, if a bit dismissive. "You needn't worry."

Winona kissed his brow, which was a feat considering how Ezra towered over her. But he happily bent to allow her such liberties. "Well, you know I will. I was so sorry to hear the news."

Miri watched the exchange in mute curiosity. He kept his gaze on Winona as he said, "It was my decision."

Winona was clearly taken aback, for she let go of his face, furrowed her brows, and jutted her chin backward at the declaration.

Whatever *that* meant.

"I thought..." she started, but Joshua cut her off.

"I told you not to listen to idle gossip, dearest," he said plainly. "I'm sure Ezra has a story he'd love to regale you with another time."

Ezra breathed a good-humored huff, took hold of Winona's hand, kissing the top of it chivalrously and with what looked like genuine affection. "There's not much of a tale to tell. But what's done is done and all is well, I assure you. Now, how about that challah?"

Winona puffed a flattered sound. "Ol' Wy'll fix you right up, love." With that, she moved to bustle back behind the counter.

Ezra turned his attention back to Miri, winking once before he said, "Let's make it two challahs. And two coffees."

Breakfast. He wanted her to join him for breakfast.

"I don't drink coffee," she said quickly. She wasn't sure why she was flustered.

"Have you ever had it?" asked Joshua from behind the counter as he poured the steaming beverage into two cups.

"No," she admitted. "How would you even know to ask that question?"

"It's obvious you're from the south, my dear," said Winona with a smile. "You're tea drinkers down there, are you not?"

Miri raised an eyebrow and stubbornly repeated, "I don't like coffee."

"How do you know you don't like it?" Ezra asked with a snicker. He took the two steaming mugs the older man offered him. "Thank you, Joshua."

"Of course, milord. I'll bring the challah to you right away."

Ezra nodded and looked at Miri, mugs in hand. The steam climbed slowly up to his face, like two wispy fingers stealing a touch of his smooth cheek. "Shall we?"

"Shall we what?"

"The roof is my favorite, although the veranda is quite nice, too," Ezra said, ignoring her confusion.

"I've kept it open for you, milord," said Joshua with a smile.

"You're too kind." Ezra nodded to the baker over his shoulder. Joshua stooped to retrieve a heavy sack of flour before turning back toward his kitchen.

"It's this way," Ezra said, nodding toward an open doorway just on the other side of the small dining space. The door was cracked open enough that she could see stairs behind it.

He didn't wait for her to follow him but turned and began walking. When his foot hit the first step, he glanced back at her. "You coming or not?"

For reasons she would consider later, she followed him.

The narrow, windowless stairway was a bit dark, but there was enough light to see that it was painted in rich sapphire and a patina that had chipped away over the years to reveal scarred plaster beneath. The rail along the wall was made of slender wrought iron twisted into delicate patterns. She ran her fingers along the artful metal as she followed Ezra up, up, up until he pushed open a door into the blistering morning sunlight that spilled onto the roof of the bakeshop.

She tried not to gasp at what met her eyes.

The mountains towered around them, the lake spreading out from the edge of the village, vast and glassy in impossible shades of cerulean and emerald, a perfect mirror of the village above. The wildflowers that bloomed on the mountainsides burst in riotous colors on the lake's surface. And here and there, pockets of mist floated above the water with haunting beauty. A kaleidoscope of color and splendor.

Further out, something sparkled on the surface of the lake, moving gracefully over the waters.

"Careful, Miri. The mountains will get into your soul."

"What is that?" Miri asked, pointing to the thing glistening across the lake.

Ezra followed her gaze and smiled, a bit conspiratorially, she thought. "A glass gondola. Terribly romantic. They say no woman can resist falling into a man's arms when she's in one of those."

Miri gave him an incredulous look, and Ezra chuckled, turning towards the tables nearby.

"Have you always lived here?" she asked, mechanically following him as he selected a table on the edge of the roof. As if they were friends. As if she trusted him. She wondered at the feeling.

As Joshua had promised, the roof was empty of patrons,

despite the many inviting tables scattered around its small expanse. Ezra pulled a chair out and turned to face her.

"Yes, I've always lived here. And I've never had a desire to live anywhere else, unlike so many."

"Who would ever want to leave such a place?"

"Those who want to see the modern world," Ezra said. "It's alluring, all that magic," he said wistfully, looking out across the lake as if he could see the bustling cities somewhere behind all those mountains.

"I don't know," she said, following his gaze, taking in the mountains. It was... "Breathtaking," she heard herself say as she took the seat he offered, distracted by the glorious view. There was something about this place. Something she couldn't quite name. Its peace, its tranquility, its simplicity...

What she thought would be a sentence to a life of missing out felt much more like a promise of better days on the horizon.

The breeze picked up her unruly, fiery curls, tossing one across her mouth. She pulled it away absently as Ezra pushed the mug of steaming coffee toward her. She took a moment to tighten her bun again, afraid it might fall in this breeze.

It's a mop of hair, isn't it? Phinehas would have said—or rather, mocked. He hated her hair as much as her mother had. Then again, so did she.

"Yes, it is," said Ezra, sipping from his mug.

"What?" she asked, whipping her head toward him.

"This place. It's breathtaking."

"Oh," she said. "Yes."

He watched her for a moment, his eyes colored with that signature humor of his before he said, "Are you going to try it?" When she didn't answer, he eyed her mug.

"Oh. I'm not sure I'll like it," she said.

He furrowed his brows, a smile threatening his mouth. "How do you know?"

"I've never understood the appeal of *boiled bean water*."

He breathed a laugh. "Yes, you southerners and your tea. I suppose we northerners don't understand the appeal of boiled *leaf* water, as it were."

She raised a brow, a counterargument failing her. She had never understood why the kingdom had held onto that invisible dividing line between the north and the south—what had once been the kingdoms of Haravelle and Navah. The people of the south still held on to distinctly Navarian traditions, just as the Haravellians had held on to theirs, choices of warm beverages included. So she stopped objecting, picked up the mug, and pressed it to her lips.

"Wait!" he said. She narrowed her eyes.

"Not like that!" Ezra took her mug and added some cream from a porcelain creamer on the table. Next, he drizzled honey from a comb into her cup. "I think this is how Providence himself drinks it."

She raised a single brow. "Oh, you think Providence drinks coffee, then?"

"Of course he would! It is a superior beverage, to be sure." He finished drizzling the honey and pushed the cup a little closer to her.

"If it needs so much help, why bother?"

Ezra smiled. "Some things are just better with a little extra love." He did not choose the magicked spoon that would stir for him, but instead opted for a plain, silver spoon with which he finished stirring her coffee.

Skeptically, she picked up the mug again, pressing it to her lips. The steam wafted to her nose, the smell inviting despite her misgivings. Timidly, she took a sip.

Bitter. Creamy. Warm. And somehow sweet.

"Well?" Ezra asked.

"It's..." She eyed the milky brown contents. "Fine."

"Liar," Ezra quipped. She lifted her eyes to his as he went on. "It's an acquired taste."

"Apparently," she said, sipping again and crinkling her nose. Ezra chuckled.

The baker appeared from the steps, two mismatched hand-painted plates in hand. And the smell coming from those plates...

"Now this is most definitely *not* an acquired taste," said Ezra. "Thank you, Joshua. You are an artist."

Joshua bowed, pride squaring his shoulders at the compliment.

Indeed, Miri had to agree. The bread was expertly braided in layers and layers of glossy dough and rich, velvety chocolate, sprinkled with white, powdery sugar that looked a bit like the first dusting of winter snow.

"You are too kind, milord," said Joshua. "Do you need anything else?"

Ezra looked to Miri, and Miri, taken aback by the fact that he cared at all for whether or not she had what she needed, found herself unable to come up with an answer.

"I think we're fine," said Ezra at last.

Joshua bowed. "You know where I'll be," he said, and then turned to leave.

"You didn't have to get my breakfast," Miri said. "I can pay for my own."

"I wasn't trying to imply that you couldn't," said Ezra. "I did not mean to offend."

Miri eyed him skeptically. "What did Winona mean earlier?" she asked before she had a chance to stop herself.

Ezra merely tilted his head and waited for her to explain.

"She said she was sorry to hear the news. What news was she talking about?"

Ezra looked down, slowly swirling the coffee in his cup.

Too far. She had gone too far. "I'm sorry. I didn't mean to pry."

Ezra looked up. "No, it's just... Well, I'm surprised you didn't know. I did not figure a soul would be in the dark on the news by now. New to the village or not."

"Good news travels fast and all that?" she said, an image dancing in her mind of the way the ticket clerk had looked at her at the theatre.

"Exactly," Ezra said with a soft laugh.

"You did have a lot of people groveling at your feet last night. Was it because of your *good news?*"

At this, Ezra nearly choked on his coffee. "No, it was most certainly *not* because of my good news."

"I see. I suppose when you're a *terribly important* aristocratic male, everyone is getting in line to lay it on thick."

Ezra didn't stop the laugh that shook his shoulders as he said, "Yes, Miriam Sasson. I'm a terribly important aristocratic male."

She eyed him with a skeptical smirk and took a bite of her bread.

Good Providence.

She nearly moaned at the pillowy dough and the most decadent chocolate she had ever tasted. When she had at last recovered from her momentary respite into chocolate paradise, she said, "Don't expect me to fawn over you like the rest of your admirers."

"I wouldn't dream of it." He smiled at her. And his smile...

She stopped herself from looking at it for too long and said instead, "You seemed a bit hesitant of Phinehas's appointment as high priest." She took another bite of the ridiculously good bread. Somewhere nearby, a bird chirped merrily.

"Hesitant, no," he said. "But I confess I'm not a fan of the political world into which I've been born."

"Poor nobleman must deal with nasty men and all those terrible impositions like obligations in order to keep his title," she mocked.

"Exactly." He laughed again as he sipped his coffee and looked out over the lake, its placid waters rippling softly in the breeze. "The world is changing, Miri," he said. "I'm not sure I'm ready for those changes."

"What do you mean?"

He met her eyes across the small table. "The king has many plans for this kingdom. Plans that will change everything. I'm afraid your husband is now an integral part of it."

Husband. She nearly choked on the word, forgetting that she had lied to Ezra about the nature of her relationship with Phinehas.

"And you don't like them?" she asked.

"Not particularly. But I'm not so naïve to believe I can do anything about them."

"Isn't that your role? As nobility? To influence politics?"

He breathed a sardonic chuckle. "Something like that. I'm coming to realize at the ripe old age of twenty-six that politics are like those steam cars they're building in Chesedelle City. On rails of their own, high above the rest of us, they're moving whether we're on board or not."

She knew that the larger cities in nearly all twelve provinces of Har-Navah were implementing the steam cars just like the ones they were building in Teman City. Great tracks that towered above the buildings, built on long, spindly legs that curled and climbed and trailed through the city skies, carrying car after car of passengers, eager to get somewhere faster. Faster. Always faster.

She thought Ezra's analogy might be a perfect description of the games Phinehas liked to play. Always striving. Always grasping. Always wanting more, more, more. Always climbing higher, higher, higher.

She looked up to find Ezra watching her again.

"You are lost in thought, Miriam Sasson."

"It's nothing," she said. "Breakfast is delicious. Thank you."

"It is good, isn't it? Joshua is a regular genius in the kitchen. I don't patronize him enough."

"You come here often?" she asked, tilting her head to one side.

"As often as I can," he said with a smile.

"As often as you go to the theatre?" she asked.

"I don't go anywhere as often as I go to the theatre."

"You like it that much?"

"Didn't you?"

"It was perfect. But I didn't think it would appeal to that many people. I was surprised at how full it was, for such a small village." She fussed with her bun again, which was threatening to fall, her heavy curls battling the lake breezes.

"If anyone doesn't like the theatre, they just haven't given it a fair chance," said Ezra. He watched her fingers working to coax the curls back into submission before he said with a chuckle, "Giving you trouble?"

"Always," she said, rolling her eyes.

Ezra watched her fuss with it a bit more before he asked, "If it's such a bother, why do you put it up?"

"Because otherwise it's a force to be reckoned with."

"Like a wildfire."

"A horrific, destructive force of nature?" she quipped, at last satisfied with her bun. She returned her attention to the last bits of the glorious challah on her plate and wondered if it would be rude to ask for a second piece.

Ezra chuckled. "Is it really so bad?"

"It's a nuisance."

Ezra gave her hair a once-over before he went on. "Well, I am merely a casual observer, mind you, but perhaps its wildness is a masterpiece of its own kind."

"Are you always so full of bullshit?" she asked. "Or do you fancy yourself a philosopher?"

Ezra tilted his head back and barked a laugh. "A little of both, I suppose."

She couldn't help laughing too. This man... He did not balk at her attempts to offend him; in fact he seemed downright amused.

"I think I should very much like to be your friend, Miri," he said, still recovering from his laugh.

"Is that so?" she asked, feigning indifference.

"Yes, you see, in addition to being a philosopher and a curator of bullshit, I also happen to be an excellent judge of character. And I had a feeling when we met that we would become fast friends."

"So *that's* why you wouldn't quit staring at me at the theatre."

A grin and a nod was his response. "No, I wouldn't quit staring at you because with one glimpse of your hair, I was convinced my beloved theatre was on fire."

It was her turn to laugh. "Well, that settles it. You're definitely full of bullshit, Ezra Kelach."

He laughed with her. "Indeed."

She fiddled with the crumbs on her plate, thinking that Ezra was right—she could effortlessly become friends with him, thanks to his easy smiles and good-humored personality. She hadn't met someone with whom she had such a connection in... well, she could not remember meeting anyone like Ezra before. Ever.

Fast company, indeed.

"Can I get you anything else, milord?" Winona asked, giving Miri a bit of a start as she made her way across the bakery roof, a pot of coffee in hand. She refilled both cups without asking.

"Would you like anything else?" Ezra asked Miri.

"No," she said swiftly, clearing her throat.

Winona bowed her head and ambled away. Ezra watched her in silence, waiting until she disappeared behind the stair door before he returned his attention to Miri.

"I'm sorry I pried earlier," Miri said, knowing she needed to apologize for her nosiness. "It was none of my business."

"I suppose I should get used to the questions. I know everyone is asking them, if not to my face."

When Ezra toyed with a crumb on his own plate, Miri couldn't help asking, "Is everything all right?"

"Yes, I'm quite all right. That's the trouble of it, I'm sure. Everyone is waiting for some harrowing tale. I'm afraid the truth is rather mundane."

When she didn't retort, he went on. "I've been betrothed since I was eleven years old. Two weeks ago, I called it off." He shared the matter with surprising nonchalance, as if he were prattling about the weather.

"Oh," she said. It was not the story she had expected to hear. "Oh. I'm sorry."

"It was a long time coming. A decision I should have made years ago."

"I take it not everyone agrees with your sentiment," she said.

"Not at all," he said, and a smile warmed his eyes.

That smile gave her the gumption to go on prying. "May I ask what happened?"

"Sufficient to say, we were two very different people. And it would never have worked."

"How do you know it would never have worked?"

Ezra held her gaze for a moment, as if considering his answer. Then, "Would you find it rather melodramatic if I told you that it was my gut and nothing more?"

She snorted a laugh, looking down, running her fingernail along the detail carved into the table. "No," she said. "Idealistic, perhaps. But not melodramatic."

"I take it you are not an idealist," he offered.

"Ha! I'm about three opinions away from being permanently branded a curmudgeon."

Ezra laughed. "Well, you're in luck. I'm rather well versed in curmudgeonry. My sister is about as opinionated as they come."

While the words were a bit harsh, the way he said them didn't feel like annoyance or even frustration. More like good-humored observation.

"You are close to your sister?"

"She married my best friend. I suppose that makes her doubly important to me. She's all the family I have left."

She wanted to ask what he meant, but decided she had pried enough for one breakfast. So instead, she asked with a smirk, "Is that why you're so desperate for friends?"

Ezra barked another laugh. "Oh, absolutely. I'm desperate for company. So desperate that I was hoping you'd join me at the theatre," Ezra said to her surprise. "And Phinehas too, of course," he added quickly, scratching his jaw.

"I will ask him," she said, searching Ezra's face. But there was no game in his eyes. No ulterior motive she could detect.

A smile threatened his mouth, deepening the dimple on the right side of his face. "And perhaps I might even run into you at breakfast again."

"Perhaps," she said.

CHAPTER FIVE

"Oh," said Miri, nearly stumbling when she realized Phinehas was standing on the other side of her bedchamber, staring out the high windows. Outside, dusk had begun her march across the skies. "I didn't realize you were in here."

"Is my presence unwelcome?" the lanky priest asked, turning slowly to face her.

"Of course not," she said, coming to him. "We missed you at dinner, my darling."

She slipped her arms around his slender waist, but his arms did not come around her. "Where were you?" she added.

"Busy," was all he said. "Where were you today?"

She leaned back so that she might see his face, unable to read his temper from the tone of his question. "Out," she said. "Exploring."

"All day?" he drawled, a brow raised.

"Yes," she said, though she hated that she could feel her cheeks heating. After she and Ezra had parted ways at breakfast, she had spent the rest of the day exploring the marvelous little village. With only a few copper coins in her pockets, she hadn't found anything she could afford to buy, so after hours of mindless wandering, she finally came back to the temple around dinnertime. Phinehas had not been there—*in a meeting,* according to Galina. Miri was surprised to find him in her room when she finally retired from dinner.

"I hope you were doing something useful," he said.

"Phinehas, what's wrong?" she asked, removing her arms from around him. She took a step back when he moved to begin walking.

"It was a shitty day." He rubbed the patchy stubble on his narrow chin.

It worried her, the unseemly word on his tongue. Phinehas only uttered colorful language in private, and only in times when he was particularly frustrated. Miri watched him carefully as he made his way to the small chair on the other side of the small, sparse room. No lush tapestries like her chambers in the temple at Teman. No plush carpets and soft furniture. No shelves of books to occupy her. Just a bed, a worn chair, and a table beside it with a tiny window near the ceiling.

But the paltry view from that tiny window more than made up for the lackluster interior. The sunset had begun to stain the sky in wild swaths of color, the majestic mountain peaks glowing as if they had caught fire—a beacon to signal the last vestiges of day. They seemed to tower over the whole world here, as if the mountains themselves were standing guard, watching. Biding time.

"I can tell you're terribly worried," he added sardonically.

"I'm sorry," she said, whirling away from the view that had stolen her attention. She made her way to him and knelt before his chair, resting her hands on his knees. "Tell me all about it, my darling."

Phinehas rolled his eyes. "You are the worst liar, Miri. You can't even pretend to care anymore."

"I do care," she said, his words stinging more than she expected. "I do."

Phinehas fussed with a loose thread on the arm of the chair.

"I think last night was a success," she tried. "Everyone seemed thrilled by your presence here."

He met her eyes. "Were they?"

"I think so," she said eagerly. "Everyone I spoke to seemed to be." Lie. But one he apparently needed. She hoped he wouldn't see through this one so easily.

He raised a brow. "From what I saw, your time was occupied most of the night by only one person."

"Ezra?" she asked, hating how quickly the name had slipped from her lips.

"A first-name basis? I'm not sure whether I should be thrilled or appalled."

"You told me to make friends."

He ran his finger under her chin, tilting her head up. That finger found its way to her mouth, running along her lips. "I did, didn't I?" he asked, his tone shifting. He practically purred when he said, "I suppose you don't need as much of my help as I thought."

"Help with what, my darling?" she asked.

He pressed a dry kiss to the corner of her mouth in lieu of answering. Then he stood, taking her hand and lifting her to stand with him. He began working the buttons of her shirtwaist until her corset was exposed, his eyes glazing the more he revealed.

There was something predatory in his touch. Possessive.

Jealous.

It was jealousy in Phinehas's touch. Miri could not understand it.

He kissed her décolletage, working his way up her neck as he worked the laces of her corset loose, pushing her shirtwaist away. Bare before him, he breathed a guttural "My little spider" before he ran his finger along her face, wrapping a ginger curl around his knobby finger. "Go and lie down."

Miri did as she was bade, vexed by his quiet brooding. By the words he wasn't saying. She made her way to the bed and propped her pillows so she could watch him from across the room. He took a decanter of whiskey from a small table near her fireplace, pouring himself two fingers, which he downed in a single swallow. And in that moment, Miri wondered if she had been wrong to avoid the temple all day. Maybe he needed her.

Maybe he even *wanted* her.

He breathed a deep sigh, staring into the empty fireplace before at last turning to face her.

"Something is bothering you," she said softly.

"A damned prophet," he said, the words almost inarticulate, his eyes fixed in a blank stare.

"A what?" she asked, propping herself up on her elbows.

"A godsdamned prophet, Miri. He's going to ruin everything if I don't do something."

"Ruin what, my darling?"

"He's a vagabond, that's what. A rutting drifter." Phinehas took to pacing the room as he spoke. Miri wasn't sure she had ever seen him so vexed. Or so open. "I have no doubt he smells of shit and piss. And these stupid mountain simpletons listen to him. They *listen* to him, Miri! If I had known... If I had realized he was here, I would have done something about him long before we arrived."

"What does he say?" she asked, unsure what in the world Phinehas was talking about. But he was talking to her. Sharing. He never shared anything with her. So she listened. She watched him pace and she listened to the youngest high priest in Har-Navarian history lament this apparent obstacle to his goals.

And something within her deflated with a realization.

The games—they were not over. They would never be over.

"He says that we will fall. That the Sanhedrin will fall. The *monarchy* will fall."

"That will never happen," she said, sitting up more.

Phinehas at last faced her, a quiet, simmering rage in his tight shoulders, his narrowed eyes. "I say let him come here. I say let him learn who he is dealing with." Phinehas began marching across the room towards her. "I want you to find out where the grand duke's loyalties lie."

Heart pounding, she wondered how in the world she would do that. "I don't—"

"You will ensure he chooses wisely. Do whatever it takes, Miri. Do you understand? Whatever it takes."

She did not understand Phinehas's fear of a no-name beggar. Why a stranger should upset him so. But she felt his fury, his rage as he crawled onto the bed towards her. As he grabbed her thighs and yanked her down the length of the bed to meet him halfway. She understood the full measure of his wrath as he practically ripped the billowy split pants away, the cold night air kissing her legs and thighs as she laid exposed to him. She understood as he worked the buttons of his trousers, not bothering to remove them all the way before he unleashed his temper upon her.

"So grown up," he groaned. "You're no longer my innocent little angel, are you?"

"Phinehas," she tried, tears falling involuntarily down her cheeks. He gripped her arms so tightly she wondered if she would bruise. But he did not look at her, did not meet her gaze. He simply took and took and took—her decency, her dignity. He took until he could take no more.

Soon, he collapsed beside her, resting the crook of his arm

over his eyes. Miri watched him for a long moment, wiping the tears from her cheeks, wondering what it was that haunted him so. Wondering what she could do to help. Wishing she knew how.

She sat up, pulling her shirtwaist back down before she fetched the blanket at the foot of the bed and lovingly covered Phinehas. He did not move, did not show that he even noticed her care. So she curled herself up next to him, draping an arm over his hard, slender chest, pressing a kiss to his temple.

"Stay with me tonight, my darling," she tried.

A taut silence stretched between them before he finally removed the arm from over his eyes and looked at her. With his face blank, he at last uttered, "For a while."

She could smell the whiskey on his breath as it caressed her face, his narrow chest rising and falling under her hand. She ran a finger along his torso, to soothe. To remind him why he had chosen her. Why he wanted her. But Phinehas did not allow her such liberties, grabbing that finger to stop her ministrations before they began.

A change in subject. That's what he needed. Something else to think about. Not this apparent prophet, whoever he was.

"I've been thinking," she said. Phinehas's eyes fixated on nothing above them, and he made no notion that he was listening. She spoke anyway. "Perhaps it's time we make it official."

His hand slackened on hers as he turned to face her. "What?"

"We're here now. Starting our new life. So let's start that new life fully. Let's finish what we started."

"And what exactly did we start?" he asked.

"You remember what my father wanted," she said sweetly.

He cocked his head to one side. "What? For you to get off your ass and do something about your inheritance?"

"Phinehas," she tried, surprised by his sudden shift in tone. "You and I both know that's a farce. My claim to the throne is as great as anyone's. But together we could—"

Phinehas scoffed as he shoved her off of him, getting off the bed. "You don't want anything that matters. You just want to sit in here like a pampered princess while I do everything."

"Phinehas."

Roughly, he began buttoning his trousers. She slid her way across the bed, taking the blanket and wrapping it around her bare shoulders as she stood.

"My love," she tried.

"You may have become a woman, but you're still a spoiled little brat, Miri. It's time to grow up."

"I want to give you what you want. I want to help you, but you won't tell me."

"What I *want?*" he barked. When she winced, he calmed himself. But only just. He placed his hands on her arms. "What I want, Miri..." He stopped, taking in a breath. "Do you understand the pressure I'm under now that I'm high priest? And you want to marry now?"

"Wasn't that the plan? To be together?"

"And here I was thinking you had forgotten it. We were to marry when I was high priest and you were queen. We were to rule this kingdom by the laws of Providence.

"I've done my part, Miri. It's about damn time you did yours."

Without another word, Phinehas disappeared through her door.

FOR A LONG WHILE, Miri sat in silence. For the last seven years, she had been so focused on Phinehas's appointment as high priest, so determined to help him in that endeavor that she had thought the subject of the throne was moot. She had thought it was over. A needless distraction.

Tonight, she understood: it was not.

But it was a preposterous, futile plan, to put her on a throne that was not hers. She had never wanted all the power her father and Phinehas had lusted after. She had never cared about it the way they did. She was not cut out for these political games, and she was certainly not smart or cunning or clever enough to be someone of import.

She was no one. She was nothing.

It was her cousin, Ari, who was the true heir to the throne. The last direct descendant of King Ferryl himself. Everyone had known it. Perhaps it was the reason her father had hated him so. Had sent him away. Because he was an obstacle to the plan.

She did not know if Ari was even alive. Or if he was alive, she did not know where he was. If he was all right. And sometimes, when she was alone at night, she would pray quietly to herself— not because Phinehas had instructed her to, but because she was desperate. Desperate to see Ari once more. To know that he was alive. That he was well. She would beg Providence in the darkest hours of the night that one day she would know if Ari was okay.

And then in the daytime, she had done the priest's bidding, doing her best to obey Phinehas as a thank you for saving her life, for giving her a second chance. Every day she had bowed her head low, thrown aside her dignity, and done as Phinehas bade.

She had thought it would be enough.

It was clear it was not. *She* was not enough.

A tear fell down her cheek. She swiftly wiped it away and turned towards the window again, the first hints of moonlight spilling from the high windows and bathing the tattered carpets in rippling silver patterns as it slanted through the leaves of a nearby tree.

She wished she could see the mountains right now. Wished they were not cloaked in night. Or that they were not so difficult to see from such a small, high window. She would let them sink into her soul. She would let them take her away—their foreboding power. Their breadth that reminded her with one glance how small she was. How little was this world of hers. How much bigger were the things of Providence.

Careful, Miri. The mountains will get into your soul.

Ezra's words clamored through her mind as she wiped the tear from her cheek. She wrapped the blanket more tightly around herself and pulled a nearby chair under the window. Climbing up, she used the added height to push open the window and let the mountain breeze sweep in, cooling her cheeks. She shut her eyes and took a deep breath, the smells of conifers and aspens now a familiar balm. When she opened them again, she wasn't sure if it was a trick of the wan light, but she could have sworn two small creatures flew in.

Glowing. The tiny creatures were *glowing*—one silver, one blue.

"Færies," she breathed, extending her hand. Those færies landed on her palm, their wings, tattered into shreds, fluttering in the wind behind them. Simultaneously, they bowed.

"Do not let your heart be troubled, Miri," said one of them. A female. "I am Malkah Neharah, Queen of the Light."

"And I am Melekfa," said the other. "Færy King."

The female, whose hair glittered sapphire and amber and gold and amethyst, grinned, her black-and-white wings hanging limply from her back. She was beautiful. Not glamorous or ethereal. Just a simple kind of beauty that radiated from her bright eyes and kind face.

"It's time," the tiny færy said.

"Time for what?" Miri asked.

"Prepare the way, Miri," said the male. His silver hair shone like moonstone in the evening light, with a great streak of obsidian coming up from the center of his brow. He, too, was beautiful, even if he was scarred and battered. She wondered how old he was. How many battles he had seen.

"Too many," he said, smiling. The female came to his side, taking his hand and lacing her fingers through his.

Miri ignored the fact that the færy had just read her mind and instead said, "You're married."

"Fa is my Mate," said the female, smiling proudly. "I've put up with him for the better part of a millennium."

A millennium? "A thousand years? You're a *thousand* years old?"

"Older than that," laughed Fa.

They didn't look it. Færies or not, they didn't look any older than she.

"The time has come, Miri," said the king.

"Time for what?"

Without explanation, the female kneeled on Miri's hand, placing her tiny palm flat against Miri's.

Splendid, cobalt light erupted from the færy's palm.

Light that reminded her so much of another time, another place. A lifetime ago, when her cousin had taken her hand. He had given her light in a flash, there and gone again so fast that she had hardly understood it.

"You took care of us. Our kind. When you were a girl. We have not forgotten it," said the female. "Nor has Providence forgotten you. Or your cousin."

"My cousin?" she asked, her heart suddenly a pounding drum in her chest. "He is alive?"

"Prepare the way, Miri." The female smiled. Malkah. "My friends call me Meren," the færy queen said, as if she were reading her thoughts. "And it's time for the world to know the True Magic."

Miri paused for a moment, taking it in. Taking it all in. She looked back to her palm, watching the light as it danced in patterns along her skin—like spring vines growing along a cliff. Slowly, it faded into her hand, disappearing as if it had never been there. But she could feel it. Beneath her skin, she could still feel the warmth of the light.

Like warm embraces and quiet laughs and bright, green fields and sunny afternoons. Magic. The light was *magic.*

The magic of Providence.

"The Mashiach," Miri finally managed, finding it difficult to speak around the lump in her throat. "The Promised One."

"*The stag is at hand,* Miri. Prepare the way."

Without another word, Fa and Meren leapt from her hand and onto the high windowsill. She stood, watching them leave, their useless wings floating behind them. She wondered if they would fall to their death, but then, in the span of a breath, a great eagle swooped down, catching them on its back and flying away.

CHAPTER SIX

"Rachæl! To what do I owe the pleasure?"

"Don't start," the blonde barked, pushing past Ezra into the foyer. Her curls spilled down her back with glossy perfection, as usual. Rachæl never had a single hair out of place. Ever.

"Please do come in," he said sardonically as she marched past him, closing the great door behind her. From across the vast foyer, he caught the eye of his housekeeper, who lifted her brow and nothing more. He winked at her, and she perched her arms on her wide-set hips to let him know she disapproved of the princess's gumption. Ezra stifled a grin and shook his head. His house-keeper, Helena, nodded once and disappeared down the adjacent hall.

The crown princess of Har-Navah whirled to face him, her billowing skirts still twirling about her legs after she stopped. "We need to talk," she said.

"I gathered that from your rather adamant entrance," he said.

"You can leave your silver tongue here. This is serious."

Ezra bit down on his grin. "Well then, by all means." He

gestured with one hand to the sitting room across the marbled foyer. The princess turned and marched towards it without a word—as if she owned the place. Ezra followed, wondering why he had agreed to come to the door when Helena had told him who had come to call. This was going to be fun.

The princess handed her shawl and parasol to Thaddeus, the stiff-backed butler, without acknowledging him and abruptly sat on the nearest settee without invitation. Thaddeus eyed her belongings with a hint of disdain before disappearing with them.

Chin high and all harsh angles, Rachæl did not wait for Ezra to find his own seat before she began speaking. No preamble. All business. Typical of her.

"I have reason to believe that my father is in league with Medinah."

"Medinah?" Ezra asked, taking the steaming cup of coffee a maid offered him as he sat down in his favorite armchair.

"The western continent." With an annoyed wave of her hand, Rachæl huffed, refusing the coffee she was subsequently offered by the maid. The maid curtseyed to the princess nonetheless, and Ezra offered her a placating smile as she turned to leave the sitting room.

"I believe we were tutored in geography by the same governess, Rachæl. Thank you for the reminder. I fail to see the alarm, however. His Majesty is in league, as you put it, with many kingdoms. Trade deals. Tariffs. Peace treaties. It's rather commonplace for—"

"This is no trade deal," the Crown Princess interrupted. "I have reason to believe this is more."

"More? Like what?" he asked, sipping his coffee, just barely sweetened. Perfection. Exactly as his servants knew he liked it. He needed to give them all a raise for the way they doted on him.

The princess did not sit back, despite the plushness of the settee. Her back stayed ramrod straight, her shoulders tight and her chin high. Ezra could not help but wonder what would happen were he to balance a few books and a kettle on the top of her head.

She went on, ignorant of the rather entertaining picture in his mind. "I have reason to believe that my father is working on a treaty with Medinah that would change the state of our kingdom. Permanently."

"What kind of treaty?" Ezra sat up straight, no longer imagining the array of objects he'd like to attempt to balance on the princess's head.

"I am unfamiliar with the details."

"But you are concerned about them?" he asked, tilting his head to one side.

The princess fussed with one of the delicate lace gloves on her hand, not meeting his eyes.

Ah.

Ezra sat back again, sipping from his coffee once more. "Rachæl," he said, his tone shifting. "What's this really about?"

"The kingdom," she answered testily, meeting his eyes.

He dipped his chin, raising an eyebrow and schooling a knowing smirk.

"Stop that," she spat, sitting even more stiffly, if that were possible. A perfect blonde curl fell across her shoulder, and the jewels that cascaded from her ears glittered in the afternoon sun.

"Why are you really here, Rachæl?"

She looked away, her attention suddenly consumed by the servants working in the manicured garden outside the window.

"Your roses are blooming quite nicely," she said.

"Grandmother would be thrilled that I haven't killed them yet."

The princess huffed a small laugh, her eyes still fixed on the garden.

The gesture was so unlike her that Ezra leaned forward again, taking her hand across the gap between them. "What's going on?" he asked gently.

Rachæl did not speak for such a long moment that Ezra thought she might not. But then, "I need you to help me."

"You've never needed help a day in your life," he said, and it wasn't an insult. The princess was as formidable as any man. He had always admired that about her—that tenacity. That unapologetic ferocity. Had always hoped it would be enough.

It hadn't been.

At least not to think of her as anything more than a friend.

When he caught the silver in the corner of her eye, he took hold of both her hands. "Hey. Look at me," he whispered softly.

She obeyed, her stoic face in stark contrast to the tear that held strong as if it, too, had no desire to show its hand. For a brief moment, he was back there in Chesedelle Castle, in a quiet antechamber, just the two of them, sharing a private conversation about a council meeting or state dinner. She with that frank stare of hers, regaling her opinions on her father's reign. He with his dismissive grins and useless advice. He had never been good at politics. And she had never minded.

They had always worked well together. Had always had an easy camaraderie between them. Friends. They were genuine friends.

He supposed it was why it had taken him so long to end the betrothal. And why now, she looked at him as if she thought him the world's biggest fool.

She might not have been wrong in that regard.

"Tell me why you are here," he said gently.

"You made a mistake. I am here to make you fix it," she said.

"I see," he said, her plan becoming clearer to him, whether she realized it or not. She'd found something she thought he might take interest in. Something to give him a sense of importance. As if boredom had been the reason he had ended things.

"You were to be my partner. We've always had each other's best interests at heart. You left me to face all of this alone." That she would admit that much aloud told Ezra much more than she realized. But before he could interject, she added, "You know that being prince consort is not nearly the insult you think it is, Ezra. You were my partner. In every sense of the word."

Ezra smiled, but it wasn't in jest or mockery. He lifted her hands, brushing a chivalrous kiss across the delicate lace gloves. "I'm still your friend, Rachæl. That you think my becoming consort was an issue tells me how little you know me."

For that's what he would have been. Had he married the crown princess, he would have one day been prince consort to the queen of Har-Navah. Not a king, but a sanctioned lover and bestower of land, dowry, and well-bred heirs. A brood-stallion, for lack of a better term.

But that had never bothered him.

"We've known each other our whole lives, Ezra," she said. Providence help him, it was the first time in his life he'd ever seen the princess give any indication that she might have lost.

"Yes, we have," he said gently. "Which is why I am sorry that this did not happen sooner."

"Must you be so cruel?" she asked.

"It is not my intention to be cruel," he said. And he meant it. "Quite the opposite. Rachæl, you deserve so much more. You are bold and fierce and formidable, and you deserve someone who will love you boldly and fiercely and formidably."

"Just not you," she said sardonically.

Ezra moved to sit beside her on the settee, pulling a handkerchief from his jacket. Though he offered it, she did not take it.

"I swear to you that I tried," he said. The truth. That's what he would give her. She deserved nothing less.

"But I am not enough," she said, squaring her shoulders again, looking straight ahead of her, that stoic face returning.

He took hold of her hand on her lap once more. "It is me who is not enough for you."

She scoffed. "That is such a pathetic thing to say. I thought you were better than to reduce yourself to rehearsed lines, Ezra."

Ezra breathed a sigh, unsure what to say. How to make her understand. He couldn't marry her. He respected her. He even liked her most of the time.

But he was not in love with her. It took walking away to understand that he never had been. And as childish as it made him look, when it came to it, he realized it mattered. It mattered a great deal. And he knew it would someday matter to her, too.

"You want to marry for love. Like your grandparents," she said, as if she could read his thoughts.

"Don't you?"

"Love will come, Ezra," she said. "You just didn't give it a chance."

"How much of a chance was it supposed to take?" he asked. "We've been betrothed for fifteen years."

"I wouldn't have minded, you know," she said, fiddling with her fingers and still not looking him in the eye. "You could have taken any lover you wanted. I wouldn't have stopped you."

"Listen to yourself, Rachæl. Is that really what you want? To be married to a man who warmed any bed he pleased? To never know whose arms he was in, just that they were not yours?"

Rachæl did not say anything. Ezra placed a warm hand on her back. "You are better than that. And I'll be damned if I let anyone break your heart. Myself included."

When she did not speak, did not retort, he laid a gentle hand on her arm. "One day," he started, gathering his thoughts. Making sure he knew what he wanted to say before he spoke. "One day you're going to fall in love. One day you're going to find someone who loves you the way you deserve. And one day you're going to thank me for not tethering you to a loveless marriage."

"There is no place for such idealistic sentiment in our world, Ezra. It doesn't work that way."

Ezra huffed a small laugh, a vision of his grandparents dancing in his mind. Smiling, a soundless laugh shining on his grandmother's mouth as his grandfather whispered something for only her ears.

"I know for a fact that's not true."

She whipped her head to face him suddenly. "Is there someone else? Is that why you ended it?"

He wasn't sure why he hesitated. Wasn't sure why it took him a moment to find words. There was no one else, of course. There had not been when he ended the betrothal weeks ago.

"There is no one else," he said at last.

She must have believed him, for she merely nodded, ripping the handkerchief from his fingers and fixing her eyes ahead once more.

"Is there really a treaty with Medinah?" he asked. If she had made it up...

"Yes."

"What is it for? We already have trade agreements."

"As I said, I do not know the nuances of the treaty."

"Then are you truly concerned about it?"

She lowered her eyebrows in disdain, but saved her reprimand. "Yes, Ezra," she said flatly. "I know my father. Or, at least, I thought I did. He's...he's not himself anymore. He's...dazzled. By all the Empress of Medinah has to offer. He speaks of her like...like she's...a goddess or something. Her met her once. Only one time. And he brushes Mother aside like she doesn't exist. It bothers me."

Ezra thought for a moment, letting Rachæl's words sink in.

"Say something," she demanded after a long moment of silence.

"I will help you. Of course I will help, Rachæl. I will look into the treaty. John will help. We'll find out all we can."

"And the priest," she added.

"The priest?"

"The high priest. He is everywhere. All at once. He has eyes and ears everywhere. He knows too much too soon. I do not trust him."

Neither did Ezra, but that had been because of a gut reaction to the weasel and less because of any concrete evidence. He would have been lying to himself if he said he didn't like the fact that someone else had noticed the perfect, perfect priest was a farce.

"What do we do?" Princess Rachæl asked.

"I'll keep my ears open here in Shalem. You find out what you can at the castle."

"And the council?"

"I was planning on coming back anyways," he said.

A raised eyebrow was her response. "Devoted at last?"

"I have a duty to the Crown, do I not?"

She folded narrow arms across her chest. "That's never motivated you before."

Ezra breathed a small laugh. "Let's just say that my quiet little village is not as immune to politics as I would like."

"Nothing in the entire world is immune to politics, Ezra. The sooner you realize that, the better."

Ezra found he had no retort. "Speaking of which... Tonight—"

"You're going to tell me that we should keep our distance," Rachæl said, looking down and rubbing her fingers over her delicate gloves once more.

"It will be our first appearance since the announcement," he said softly.

"I know that you are right," she said, still unable to meet his eyes. "But it will not change how strange it will feel to be at a function like this without you on my arm."

Ezra placed a warm hand on her arm, taking in a breath to speak. But Rachæl cut him off, abruptly standing.

"But I know you are right. And besides, if I'm to find a new suitor, I cannot have you following me around like sad puppy."

Ezra's smile was genuine as he, too, stood. "Indeed, Your Highness."

Her neck stiff and her chin high, Rachæl did not bother to look at Ezra as she said, "I must be off. I have much to do before tonight."

"Of course," he said with a nod.

The princess of Har-Navah turned to leave, but Ezra took hold of her elbow, stopping her. "Rachæl," he said.

She stopped, but she did not turn to face him.

"I'm sorry."

"No you're not," she said. "And that's part of your grating charm."

She walked out with her back to him.

CHAPTER SEVEN

"Is it strange?"

Ezra met John's eyes. "What? To be here without her?" He tilted his chin toward the subject in question.

John did not answer, merely tilting his head downward while lifting an eyebrow.

Ezra returned his gaze to the princess mingling merrily with a gaggle of people across the room—most of whom were men, he did not fail to notice. But that twinge of jealousy he had expected to feel did not come.

"I told her it would be better this way," Ezra said.

"Is it?" John asked, sipping casually from his goblet of wine.

"Oddly, somehow I feel it would be easier if I *were* jealous," he admitted. He sipped his own wine, observing the banquet room full of aristocrats before he continued. "Then perhaps I wouldn't be riddled with guilt."

"You did the right thing," John offered.

"Yes, well, enough about me. What about you?" Ezra asked, his voice brightening. "Second official dinner in a row? You're turning out to be quite the politician yourself, aren't you?"

John rolled his eyes. The lawyer-turned-brother-in-law had not exactly been welcomed with open arms to formal or royal functions since marrying Esther. Mostly out of snobbish disdain, the nobility of Har-Navah had not accepted John into their inner sanctum of gossip and lies. John hadn't minded most of the time. But to be here tonight—to show up simply because he knew he could. Even if marrying Esther hadn't elevated his formal status among the aristocracy, he had had Ezra's blessing from the beginning. And an invitation to any party from the grand duke of Kinnereth himself was as coveted as gold. Still, for him to be here, knowing how the nobility looked down on him... It was bold. Ezra liked bold.

"I'm tired of the way they treat my wife. By the time she has the baby, I want her back at these functions where she belongs."

"You didn't ruin her life, John," Ezra pointed out. "She would choose you over all of this a thousand times again."

"All the same, they can all go straight to Sheol. I'm tired of playing their games."

"Good for you." Ezra grinned.

"Good evening, Your Grace," came a soft, sensuous voice. Ezra turned his attention to find a young woman standing beside him. Not the one he might have hoped to find standing beside him. He had not seen her here tonight. Not that he had been looking every chance he got.

This was not a woman of fiery red curls, but a girl of no more than fourteen or fifteen. She was beautiful—a stunning sort of beauty that was accentuated by the fall of her golden locks down her flimsy, linen gown. Her lips, parted into the faintest pout, were colored in a violent shade of red, and her eyes were smeared with kohl, giving her an odd mixture of maturity with innocence.

An acolyte.

Acolytes were nothing new, of course. From the earliest centuries of the temple, women had given themselves to the cause of Providence, foregoing carnal pleasures out of devotion. But somewhere along the way, that devotion turned to something darker, for too many figured out just what kind of power they could wield with that innocence. Virginity turned out to be a rather irresistible lure to the most powerful men. Foregoing the carnal pleasures of life became fiction. And over the centuries, the devoted virgins serving the cause of Providence under the careful watch of the priests had devolved into nothing more than harlots, the priests their eager, furtive panderers.

Ezra had heard all his life of their legendary allure and the promises of pleasure that came with it, but he had never witnessed it himself until Phinehas had shown up in his village.

"I've heard much about you, my lord," she went on, her light, young voice at odds with the maturity of her presence.

Ezra was immediately uncomfortable.

"I wondered if you'd be willing to introduce me to some of the noblemen here. I'm such a fool with names," she added with a bubble of a laugh. It was painfully clear from her question that she had no intention of learning about any man here tonight... except the one she was talking to.

"You seem like a nice man," she went on. "Perhaps you can help me." At this, she placed a pale, delicate hand on his arm.

She was a perfect package of wide-eyed virginity and cunning cleverness—all wrapped in soft curves and rich decadence. Providence help any man she turned her attention to, Ezra being no exception.

His eyes fell on the hand she rubbed softly on his arm and lingered there, wondering what tragedy had thrown her into a life of luring strangers into her bed.

"My lady," he finally managed, placing his hand over hers, effectively stopping her from continuing the ministrations that were working much, much too well. "I thank you for the invitation, but I'm afraid I am terrible with names as well. I will not be much help to you."

The acolyte's laugh was as soft as it was sensuous. "My lord, how you tease," she said.

"What is your name?" Ezra asked to distract himself from her long, thick lashes.

"Jordie, Your Grace," she said, dipping into a faint curtsey.

"How old are you, Jordie?"

A blush rose to her smooth cheeks—and Ezra could not tell if it was a question she enjoyed answering...or hated.

"I'm fourteen, my lord," she said under her breath, her words coming from behind an embarrassed smile.

"Jordie," Ezra said, taking her hand in his. The move snagged the young acolyte's attention, a look of surprise washing over her. But whether or not it was a practiced reaction, Ezra could not be sure. "Surely there are more exciting things for a young girl to do than look for the attention of noblemen."

The question in his mind was answered when her face melted into perfect, practiced allure as she placed a hand on his chest and said, "Perhaps you would prefer to join me for prayers."

He did not have to see John on his other side to know that his brother-in-law was observing this exchange with mild shock. Ezra stifled a nervous chuckle.

"Thank you for the offer, Jordie," he said. "But I think I will have to decline."

Jordie nodded once before lifting onto the tips of her toes to press a soft, lingering kiss to his cheek. "If you change your mind..."

That kiss alone would garner a thousand rumors after tonight. So it was a good thing Ezra didn't give a damn what anyone thought.

Jordie winked once before turning away and disappearing back into the crowd.

"Well that was…interesting," John said finally. Ezra turned to face his brother-in-law, an unexpected sense of worry blooming in his gut. What was the priest *doing* with all his acolytes? And why were they so young?

"I don't think I've ever seen you propositioned before," John went on, half-amused, half-horrified.

"I don't think I ever have been, come to think of it," Ezra admitted, taking a much-needed drink from his goblet.

"Providence above, she was…something else. I'm not sure how many men refuse her."

"I don't think she's used to refusal," Ezra agreed.

"Though I do wonder," John added. "When she uses the word pray, do you suppose she spells it with an A or an E?"

Ezra looked to his brother-in-law, who kept his eyes forward even as his mouth slowly curled into a grin.

"Clever," said Ezra, chuckling softly. He scanned the crowd for the young acolyte, but did not find her again.

Instead, he found a room buzzing with nobles, all here for yet another formal dinner as the world welcomed the new high priest. There would be a series of dinners to welcome him, all for different purposes. Tonight had been for King Dægan to bestow his blessings on the man who would govern the religious council of Har-Navah: the Sanhedrin. While the king governed the kingdom, it was the high priest who dictated morality—even for the king. In some ways, that made the man the most powerful in the world.

The previous high priest had been the quiet type, keeping his head low and his opinions to himself—just how King Dægan liked it. When the old priest died a few years ago, Ezra wondered what sort of personality would follow him.

But even with all the politics, even with all the pandering that had ensued—the bloody battle for the coveted title—Ezra still hadn't expected someone quite as slippery as Phinehas.

He couldn't quite put his finger on it, but something about the priest bothered Ezra. Grated on him, actually. Like running a rusty nail down a slate. The fact that he encouraged acolytes much too young for such a life did not help.

Ezra was expected to show up to these ridiculous dinners, whether he liked it or not. So he would be a face in the crowd, a silent observer of this parade of nobility, all vying for a seat at the most powerful table. And he would thank Providence every day that Lord Gray Ornstein had spared him the burden of hosting these pissing contests himself. Lord Ornstein summered in Shalem for the very reason that he could open his estate to the king and so gain his favors.

But it had been just fine with Ezra, for if Lord Ornstein hadn't always opened his home, Ezra would surely be expected to. And having a room full of nobleman in his estate sounded about as pleasant as having his teeth pulled one by one with a pair of rusty forceps.

"She is moving on rather quickly," John said, bringing Ezra's thoughts back to the present. Ezra wondered if John was referring to the young acolyte before he realized his brother-in-law meant the princess across the room. He watched her laughing and blushing.

"Yes, quite," he admitted. It was strange to watch Rachæl flirt with someone who wasn't him. Ezra knew the nobleman she had selected for her attentions this evening; knew him to be a decent man, if a bit grasping. That he was the subject of her focus accounted for the wide-eyed wonderment permanently branded on his face. Ezra stifled a piteous chuckle for the young lord, wondering if he knew exactly what he was getting into.

"Was she angry with you today?" John asked.

"No. She tried to guilt me into changing my mind."

John faced Ezra, raising a single eyebrow. "Did it work?"

"Well, she is over there and I am over here. What do you think?"

"No one can ever accuse her of being weak," John said, a smirk threatening his mouth as he observed the king's daughter—and only heir.

Ezra breathed a sardonic laugh. "I should have done this a long time ago. Perhaps I would have hurt her less if I had."

He knew that brazen flirtation was as much a show for him as it was for everyone here. That she was stronger. That she would not be daunted.

That her show here tonight was as much to convince him as it was to convince herself of such things.

"You were not prepared to admit the truth to yourself a long time ago, brother," John said. "But you are too much of a damned romantic to marry for politics."

"This coming from you," he said, and John snorted.

After all, John had married far above his station when he had wedded Ezra's sister, Esther. But it had been a wild love that far outweighed societal protocol for them. And while Ezra had been privately amused by the debacle that was his sister's so-called scandalous marriage to the working-class lawyer, he had also been partly proud and partly jealous of both his sister and his best friend for standing their ground, despite the fallout.

"Anyway, it's not that I'm a romantic, John. It's simply that I have no desire to marry because it's *what's expected of me.*"

"And for that, I cannot fault you," John said. "I just hope you're prepared for the shit you'll get for it."

Ezra raised a brow, breathing a laugh. "Naïve idealism wins again," he said, raising his goblet.

"Idealism never hurt anyone," John tried.

"Except the crown princess," Ezra retorted, taking a long drag from his goblet. Across the banquet hall, the princess laughed a little too loudly, placing a slender hand on the arm of the gentleman who had humored her. At the sight of that hand—all possessive and flirtatious—the jealousy still did not come. Ezra turned his attention away, knowing the more his gaze lingered on his former betrothed, the more likely it was that people would notice. And speculate.

There was enough gossip going on about him for the time being, thank you.

Ezra realized John was quietly inching away from his side. It was only when he heard the commanding voice on his other side that he understood why.

"I confess, when I looked up at dinner to find you sitting at the table tonight, I was surprised you had the stones to show up," came a familiar, deep voice. A heavy hand clasped his shoulder, and Ezra turned to find the king of Har-Navah staring at him.

"Your Majesty," he said with a bow. "A delight as always."

"Cut the shit, Ezra," said the king, not bothering to look at him as he spoke. The king was about as warm and welcoming as a stone battlement. His broad shoulders and thick arms were clad in rich emerald brocade and medals for all manner of honors. His thick salt-and-pepper beard and wiry brows only added to the intimidation wrought by his booming voice and consuming presence. His attention lay fixed on his daughter across the room, and Ezra's heart beat a little faster. He hadn't spoken to the king since he had called off the betrothal weeks ago.

"I thought you'd stay home and keep hiding," the king went on. "I didn't realize you'd be brazen enough to show your face in my presence so soon."

So it was to be *that* kind of conversation. King Dægan would not sit idly by and let his daughter be scorned. Not that fatherly affection drove him—more like kingly pride. Either way, Ezra wasn't looking forward to the conversation at hand.

"I mean no disrespect, Majesty," said Ezra. "I thought that by

showing my face, the world would see that there is no ill will between Her Highness and me."

"It's not *her* will you should be concerned about, my boy." The term was perhaps supposed to be one of endearment, but there was nothing endearing about the king's tone. "You will regret your careless disregard for your future."

"I promise you that the decision was for the sake of your daughter and her happiness."

The king huffed a scoffing laugh. "You've always been full of shit, you know. Too damn charming for your own good. Rest assured, my boy. Your decision is final. And when you change your mind and realize the mistake you made, it will be too late for you."

"I understand," Ezra said, resisting the urge to clarify to the king that he wouldn't change his mind.

The king huffed a laugh, at last turning his attention away from Princess Rachæl. He gave Ezra an uncomfortably long look, appraising him without remorse before he was interrupted by the sound of someone clearing their throat.

"Your Majesty," drawled a voice rich with bravado, and Ezra turned to find Phinehas standing before them, bowing low and looking ridiculous in a long set of white robes adorned with an embroidered bib of brightly-colored flowers and evergreens. Behind him, two sages dressed in plain white robes carried heavy golden censers, filling the space around Phinehas with a cloying, sickening sort of smoke. Ezra choked on a cough, the smell filling his lungs with a saccharine heaviness that threatened to rob him of his senses. As if that weren't enough, the smoke itself was full of some sort of shimmering dust, giving it the illusion of what he supposed was meant to look like magic.

It looked more like carney tricks.

If the previous high priest had been a humble man of Providence, opting for simple homespun robes tied with homemade ropes and lighting simple wax candles for his prayers, Phinehas was nothing short of the picture of holy piety in his embellished and rather ostentatious get-up and his shimmering, purple smoke parade.

"Your Grace," Phinehas went on, bowing his head to Ezra as well.

Ezra cringed. Most of his closest friends and family had learned by now to just call him by name. The few remaining who still used his title were either kissing his ass or not close enough to him to know how much he hated the superiority of the honorific.

"I am honored by your presence here tonight," Phinehas went on, acknowledging both Ezra and the king. "I trust our new alliance will prove fruitful to the cause of Providence and the endeavors of his holy council."

Ezra swallowed his laugh, wondering how Phinehas would react if he knew just how much his reputation preceded him. Questionable acolytes aside, there wasn't a nobleman in the kingdom who hadn't been bullied into supporting Phinehas's appointment as high priest, save for Ezra. For while it was the Sanhedrin—the holy council—that voted the appointment of the high priest, it was the nobility that financed the cause, offering favors and alliances to the priests of the council who voted one way or another. Ezra had mourned the reek of corruption that had plagued his quiet village as he watched the members of the religious council become bought and paid for by the wealthiest nobles, most of whom were on the king's council. Someone had bought off nearly every one of those nobleman in order to secure Phinehas's vote as high priest, though from where the money had come, Ezra couldn't say. He had commissioned John to investigate the matter the moment Phinehas had announced his intentions to move to Shalem.

So far, that investigation had come up lacking. Phinehas was squeaky clean, which was precisely why Ezra suspected the man was anything but.

"We are grateful for the appointment of such a humble man to be our new high priest," said the king, his words saturated with firm warning. "As we equally trust that you will seek the wisdom of Providence in all things, just as your predecessor before you."

His predecessor. Right. The previous high priest had learned the hard way not to cross the king of Har-Navah. Rumor had it that when the high priest had first been appointed, eager to rid the government of corruption, he had the stones to question the king on a matter of morality and infidelity. Not long after, his family had mysteriously disappeared, only to be discovered floating prone and bloated on the opposite end of Lake Yerah a month later. From then on, the high priest had kept his head down and his mouth shut.

Ezra wondered if Phinehas knew just what kind of king to whom he was pledging his loyalty. But like Phinehas, the king's record was clean, and none of the mysterious punishments and disappearances could be traced back to him.

No, every single one of those, thanks to John's investigations, could be traced back to one man: Gian of Borras. A pilfering pirate turned into the king's prized mercenary.

And it had only been because of Ezra's constant presence in Chesedelle Castle and closeness to the royal family, thanks to his betrothal, that John had figured out the connection. Gian showed up at the castle rarely, and when he did, it was usually to make lewd comments to the princess and kiss some royal ass at banquets before disappearing again. Only after several years of such behavior did Ezra realize Gian was up to more than simply vying for favors from the royal family like most at court. Most of the court knew of Gian's connection to the king. Few knew he was no longer a pirate, but was now the king's favorite lapdog. And his personal assassin.

"Your Grace," said Phinehas, bringing Ezra back to the present. "The reputation of your devotion to the throne precedes you," the priest said. "As I, too, am devoted to His Majesty, I am certain you and I will become fast friends."

Ezra smoothed on a smile he knew did not meet his eyes, wondering what the king thought of that little declaration of devotion—especially considering he had ended his betrothal only a few weeks ago.

Devoted to the king, indeed.

"It would be my honor to be fast friends with such a *holy* man of Providence," Ezra said diplomatically. Though he was certain his definition of holiness was a bit different than Phinehas's.

It didn't seem to bother anyone else here that the newly-appointed high priest had brought with him a whole harem of temple lightskirts. It took everything within Ezra not to cut his eyes to the many young acolytes who bordered the room in their flimsy white dresses and come-hither stares. There were many more where Jordie came from. Phinehas was anything if not devoted to his cause. And considering how the king presently ogled those acolytes, the priest clearly knew exactly what game he was playing, who the players were, and what were their weaknesses. Phinehas had brought his most alluring pawns with him when he arrived in Shalem, that was clear. A vision flashed in Ezra's mind—a picture of a room riddled with webs, black widows lurking in every corner.

Phinehas's eyes rested on the king again, and something like salivating eagerness colored his words when he said, "If it is devotion you seek, Majesty, I am sure that my flock is eager to accommodate."

The king did not take his eyes from one acolyte in particular. Not Jordie, but an older one—perhaps closer to eighteen or nineteen, with glossy auburn curls that spilled down her generous figure. But despite her curves, she was somehow all hard angles, like a swath of luxurious silk draped over a wicked dagger. Ezra was privately thankful that it was young Jordie who had found him tonight and not this one. For her eyes met the king's across the room and did not falter, an expert in this game Phinehas had laid out for both of them.

A black widow luring her prey.

The king said nothing, merely huffing a small laugh before absently handing off his goblet to a nearby servant and making his way across the room to the acolyte, never once breaking eye contact with her. The closer he got, the more she lowered her lashes. By the time King Dægan reached her, she was the picture of submission.

Ezra resisted the urge to roll his eyes.

Across the room, Ezra spotted Queen Gelleia, dressed in a gown of fine brocade, immersed in a merry conversation with a small bundle of lords and ladies. Her eyes were decidedly *not* on the king or his brazen escapades. She had always been excellent at turning a blind eye to King Dægan's many dalliances. But now, with a high priest in tow eager to accommodate the king's entanglements, Ezra wondered just how long that eye of the queen's could remain artfully blind.

Just as he wondered why any priest bothered to keep up even the pretense of purity and holiness when surrounded by such temptation. It was not that priests were expected to remain chaste their whole lives. Many priests married and built families of their own. But indulging in acolytes? That was another thing altogether, and certainly not the behavior of a devoted man of Providence.

"She will be here soon," said Phinehas, and Ezra whipped his attention back to the high priest. "You know how women fuss."

"What?" Ezra asked stupidly, though he knew exactly to whom the priest was referring.

He hadn't seen her here tonight. Hadn't caught sight of those ruby-and-wine curls in the crowd of noblemen and noblewomen.

Not that he had been looking for them.

"She always wants to make sure everything is perfect," Phinehas went on, with a laugh. "You need only say the word, Your Grace," he added, "and she will be at your disposal."

When Ezra met Phinehas's eyes again, there was a grin there that set Ezra's teeth on edge.

Miri.

She was bait.

For Ezra.

A pawn in Phinehas's games.

No different than the auburn-haired acolyte who had been a trap for the king.

Perhaps Jordie had merely been curious tonight. But Miri… Miri was a web woven specifically for him. Disgust roiled in Ezra's gut that he hadn't realized it before now. Hadn't seen the game she had been playing.

A game she had played so well.

Too damn well.

She had waltzed into his world like a wildfire—all smiles and bewitching perfection under those wild curls. The moment he had seen her in the theatre that night, he hadn't been able to take his eyes from her. That impossible beauty. That quiet strength hidden behind wide, innocent eyes and perfect, ruby lips. And like a moth to a flame, he had been drawn to her.

Perhaps it was her beauty that had captured his attention, but it was her smile, the depth of it, that had kept it. That had him coming back for more like a beggar.

Like a fool.

Ezra cursed himself for not seeing it before. For letting her perfection distract him from the politics he so carefully avoided.

He was in the midst of gathering his words, finding an excuse to walk away from this conversation, when the subject of his thoughts walked up.

Clad head to toe not in flimsy linen but in a cobalt gown that hugged her wondrous figure in all the right—*wrong*—places, her unruly tresses piled atop her head in her signature nest of curls, Miri's smile was so damned enchanting that Ezra froze in his tracks and held her gaze for what must have been a thousand years before anyone said something.

Phinehas placed a possessive hand at the small of her back, and Ezra chalked it up to nothing more than the indomitable spell she had cast on him when he restrained the urge to rip that hand off of her and replace it with his own.

"Miri, darling," said Phinehas. "You remember His Grace."

Miri's smile remained, but she did not play the coy acolyte, as Jordie had for him earlier. She did not dip her head in subservience, nor did she look at him through lowered lashes. She was good. Too good at her game. With her eyes bright and her smile wide, Miri simply said, "Hello, Ezra."

And at the use of his given name...

Ezra took her hand and kissed it. No gloves separated his lips from her skin and... Providence save him, her hand was so warm, so soft...

He dropped her hand immediately, muttering an excuse and smiling perfunctorily before whirling around to march off.

A FEW MINUTES later he realized John was on his heels. That John must have witnessed the entire debacle from not far away.

"Are you breathing, brother?" John asked, a laugh hovering under his question.

"I need a whiskey," said Ezra, marching through the room

without bothering to offer his excuses as he pushed aside one aristocrat after another.

"What happened?"

Ezra took the crystal snifter offered to him by a servant on the edge of the room and pushed through a set of glass double-doors onto a veranda outside the banquet room. The cool evening breeze was a welcome reprieve, soothing his pounding heart.

There was little that could rile him. Little that could upset him. So why it bothered him so...

"What's gotten in to you?" John asked.

Ezra rested his forearms on the balustrade of the veranda overlooking the green lawns that spread before him, the lake lapping lazily just down the way. The moonlight glinted off the small waves, the mountains towering around the expanse.

"I need some air," Ezra said at last.

"You act like you've been skewered by a boar." John laughed, resting his arms along the railing as well.

"It's sobering," he said at last. "Realizing how blindly I've stepped into a spider's lair."

"Yes," John agreed. "You of all people should keep your wits about you."

Ezra privately agreed, taking a long drink from his glass, the irony not lost on him as the amber liquid burned a welcome trail of fire down his throat.

Fire. Like her thick, lustrous curls...

Shit.

"What I'm not sure I understand is why it's upset you so," John added unhelpfully.

"What's that supposed to mean?" Ezra asked. "Should I not be outraged that the priest would try to play me?"

"Of course," John said. "But you're not outraged about that. You're outraged about the fact that it was working."

"Is everything all right?"

Both Ezra and John whirled from their perch on the quiet veranda to find the subject of their conversation standing at the doorway, looking too damned beautiful for her own good in that vibrant gown. The light from the banquet hall spilled past her, washing her curls, her slender shoulders, her narrow waist in gold. Her cobalt skirts stood absurdly far from where her feet were hidden beneath, a product of what had to be a rather cumbersome petticoat.

And before he could let himself keep thinking about her petticoat, Ezra tore his gaze from her and took the final gulp from his glass, lamenting how quickly it was gone.

"Of course, my lady," said John, pushing himself from the rails. "If you will excuse me, I must be getting home. My wife will be waiting up for me."

Liar. Esther would be sound asleep. Or at least trying to sleep with her belly swollen with his child. But before Ezra could protest the lie, John disappeared, not bothering to even nod at Ezra as he left the two of them alone on the quiet veranda.

"Did something upset you earlier?" Miri asked after bidding farewell to John. Ezra merely turned his back to her and leaned once more on the balustrade.

"No, my lady. Pardon me. I simply needed some air."

"The room *is* full of hot air tonight, isn't it?" she asked with a hint of disdain, leaning on the stone beside him. He stole a glance at her, but when he caught sight of the way the moonlight spilled across her décolletage, he quickly looked away again.

"What's bothering you?" she tried again.

"There is nothing bothering me, my lady," he said, unable to meet her eyes despite the fact that she had turned to face him.

"Why are you calling me *my lady?*"

"Is that not a proper honorific for you?"

"What happened to our names?" she asked, crossing her arms. He dared not steal a glance at how that movement might accentuate the soft swell of her breasts peeking out of the top of that godsdamned gown.

"Is it proper for me to be on a first-name basis with you, considering you are married to His Holiness?"

He wasn't sure why she wasn't fighting back—why she wasn't defending her character and reputation. Why she wasn't keeping up the pretense of innocent, wide-eyed acolyte.

"Pardon me, but I thought you said you would like to be friends," she said, looking away, her gaze falling across the manicured lawn before them. From inside, laughter spilled through the glass door that John had left open a crack.

Silence yawned between them for a good moment before she said, "Everyone is talking about you in there."

Not surprising, considering he had recently ended his betrothal to the crown princess and then spent an evening accosted by not one but *two* acolytes...

Providence help him tomorrow when he'd have to hear the whispers for himself.

He turned to look at her, but her gaze remained firmly before her. "You didn't tell me you were engaged to the *crown princess*."

"It was a betrothal, not an engagement," he heard himself correct rather quickly.

"Same difference."

"There is a great deal of difference." Why was he talking? He needed to shut his damned mouth.

"Why did you end it?" she asked, facing him again.

This time, he let himself meet her eyes. "Why does anyone call off a betrothal?"

"I did not take you for a simpering romantic," she said.

"What did you take me for, then? A fool?" He asked the question before he thought the better of it. But she was a statue of marble—as smooth as glass and as solid as stone.

And he was an ass with an empty snifter in his hand.

"No. I just took you for you," she said softly.

There it was. That quiet strength he had seen in her, even from the balcony of the theatre the first time he ever laid eyes on her. A strength he had verified the first time they spoke. It wasn't obstinance or stubbornness, but something else. Something much more honest. Resolve.

And in that moment, Ezra realized that either she was damned, *damned* good at this game she was playing...

...or she meant what she said.

He was not sure which bothered him more.

He was equally unsure which *should* bother him more.

Her gaze remained solemn as the candlelight from within the banquet hall spilled across her curls like they were a living flame.

Wildfire.

That's what she reminded him of.

A raging, terrible, beautiful wildfire.

He had taken her at face value. Running into her, sharing breakfast with her at the bakery, she hadn't seemed like she was playing any sort of game with him. But tonight, realizing the impossibility of her *not* being a pawn in Phinehas's games...it set him on edge, the idea that her laugh hadn't been genuine, her smile probably faked.

"Well I've done something to terribly upset you, obviously," she said, turning away and moving to leave.

"No," he said, taking hold of her arm. "I'm sorry. I'm just... distracted. Please. Stay."

She looked down to where he still held her arm, and he quickly dropped it. When she met his eyes again, he found a quiet sadness there. One he hadn't seen before. And he wondered what it meant.

She did not leave, nor did she move to return to the balustrade of the veranda. Instead, she crossed her arms again, taking hold of her upper arms with her small hands.

"Are you cold?" he asked when he noticed the gooseflesh along her skin. The summer evening wasn't exactly hot, but it was by no means cold.

"No," she said quietly, but she did not meet his gaze. "I just hate this gown. Phinehas insisted I wear it."

"He tells you what to wear?" he asked, knitting his brows together.

It was hard to tell for sure in the moonlight, but he could have sworn color kissed her cheeks and neck. "Never mind," she said. "It doesn't matter." She turned, taking the few steps to cross the veranda and rest her arms once more on the ornate stone. "Am I the only one here who thinks this whole spectacle is a farce?"

The non sequitur nearly made Ezra bark a laugh. Instead, he said, "Most of the world is a farce."

"That seems rather incongruous of you," she said.

"Why is that?"

"I thought you said you were an idealist."

"I am. About most things," he said, privately wondering at her ability to draw confessions from him so easily. "But when it comes to the political world, I'm afraid my mind is hopelessly made up."

"I cannot say I blame you. Knowing half the men in there, there's no reason for optimism."

"What do you know about them?" he asked, his curiosity getting the better of him.

"Enough that I wouldn't trust them with my worst enemy," she said. "But what would I know? I'm just a whore."

He resisted the urge to growl at the word and instead settled on saying, "I thought you were a wife."

She breathed a scoffing laugh. "A wife who is dolled up and put on display like a prize to be won."

"You are married to perhaps the most political man in the room, my lady. You expect to be immune to the effects of politics?"

"Immune? No. But I suppose you're going to say I'm a fool to hope there's more to life than politics."

"I suppose you are not the only fool in the room, Miri."

"All I mean is that when you have kohl on your lashes and your breasts on display, the world assumes you're as stupid as you are wanton. You can learn a lot when no one thinks you are listening."

Providence above. This woman.

"Most people here are not what they seem," she went on. "Until tonight, I thought you might be the exception to that rule."

It bothered him. It shouldn't have. But it bothered him that she thought him to be as two-faced as the majority of the fools here tonight. It bothered him that she thought he was playing a game with her. But he could not tell her the reason for his behavior. He could not reveal to her that he knew *she* was the one playing the game. That she was the two-faced liar in this conversation.

Miri sighed, resting her elbows on the balustrade while she rested her chin in her delicate hands. A rogue curl fell from the pile atop her head, but Miri didn't bother to put it back in its place. Instead, it spilled long and glossy down the side of her arm, dancing on the breeze. "In times like these, I miss my cousin most keenly."

"Your cousin?"

"He always knew how to navigate these politics. Never let anyone get the best of him. I never quite learned that art."

Ezra watched her for a moment, contemplating the sentiment with which she spoke of this cousin. Earlier this evening, he had noted the fact that he had felt no jealousy as he watched his former betrothed flirt with a room full of men. He wondered why he should feel it now at the thought of this woman missing another man.

"Were you in love with him?" Ezra asked, surprising himself when the question just came out.

Miri shot her gaze to him, confusion quickly melting into a disbelieving grin. "No!" she laughed. "Heavens no. He was more like a brother than anything." She chuckled, shaking her head. "Providence help me, I can only imagine the Sheol he would give me if he heard you thought I was in love with him."

He smiled. "Well, I suppose it's only fair considering you assumed I was married to my sister."

Miri laughed again, and the sound of it—bright and merry—rattled him to his very bones.

"Where is your cousin?" Ezra asked, realizing she spoke of him in past tense.

The smile fell from her face, replaced with a quiet worry that settled on her shoulders. "I don't know. Dead probably. My father never told me where he sent him."

"Your father sent him away?"

"He was an obstacle to the *plan*. And Providence forbid we do anything that might obstruct the *plan*." She spoke the last sentence with sardonic disdain.

"What plan?" he asked gently, understanding he was prying into a sensitive subject just from the way she spoke the words. But for reasons he was not about to unpack, he asked anyway.

"Phinehas becoming high priest was part of it."

"And the other part?"

"Wishful thinking," was her only answer. And when her hands began to tremble, Ezra decided not to pry any further.

"Sufficient to say, I have always been and remain a disappointment."

"Well, you're in good company. I make a terrible grand duke."

"Grand duke?" she asked, looking up at him. Something washed over her soft features. It looked a lot like fear. *"You're* the grand duke?"

He huffed a disbelieving laugh. "Of course." She, of all people, surely knew that, what with the games she and Phinehas were playing.

"It's you?" she asked again. "*You're* the grand duke?"

"Of course, Miri. You knew that."

She didn't answer, shaking her head in horror. She backed away from him as if he were the plague.

"Did I say something wrong?"

Miri didn't answer, just kept shaking her head as she backed away, step by step.

"Miri?" he tried, moving towards her.

"I have to go." And before he could stop her, she whirled and disappeared through the doors.

CHAPTER EIGHT

He was the grand duke.

Ezra was grand duke of Kinnereth. The second most powerful man in the entire kingdom. And until a few weeks ago, he had been engaged to the crown princess.

Royalty.

And he had been the one Phinehas wanted her to bait.

To find out where his loyalties lay.

To ensnare him into Phinehas's ever-growing tangle of indentured disciples.

Ezra was one of the main reasons they had moved to this remote mountain village to begin with. To ensure his loyalties were the correct ones.

She was going to be sick.

"Whatever you did to him, keep doing it," Phinehas said by way of greeting as he barged into her chamber.

"What are you talking about?" she demanded, unable to hide her frustration. The darkness of the room hid most of his features from her. And since she hadn't bothered to light a fire, she had nothing but candlelight to go by. It was hard to tell if he was pleased or annoyed.

"He was in a state after you left. Asking if you were all right. If you needed anything." Phinehas sat down in the small chair on the edge of the room, taking a tart off a plate Miri hadn't even noticed yet. "He is yours, darling. Yours to command."

"I don't want him," she said.

Phinehas's chuckle was dark and anything but humorous. "Oh my darling, if only I believed you."

She tore across the room in three steps, throwing herself to her knees before him. She took hold of his shins as she spoke. "I don't, my darling. I only want you."

He patted her head with an affection that felt...fatherly.

Priestly.

"My little dove, you *are* mine. And you are doing well."

"I don't want to do well!" she blurted. "I don't want to play games. I want—"

"Yes?" Phinehas asked, the word dark. Dangerous.

"I want..." she tried again, calming herself. "I want to be taken seriously."

The high priest of Har-Navah said nothing, tilting his head to one side.

"Perhaps if you stopped taking the herb—"

"The what?" he asked, jutting his chin back.

"The herb," she said, meeting his eyes. "Perhaps if we conceived, people would—"

"Miriam," he said. His tone shifted entirely. It was almost... piteous. "Oh Miri, my darling." He pulled her up from the ground, onto his lap, running his hand along her hair, now a mess of curls down her back. He eyed those curls with distaste as he said, "Miri, my darling, I'm not taking the herb."

"What?" She sat up to meet his eyes. "Of course you are."

Of course he was! She had long-since concluded that Phinehas took a regular regimen of the herb that prevented unwanted children.

"My darling. Why would a chaste priest need to take the herb?" His words were soft. Piteous. But they were laced with a hint of warning.

"But you're not chaste," she said. Confused. She was so confused. Of course he had been taking the herb. Of course he had. How else could she explain the fact that she had not conceived his child after seven years in his bed?

"Of course I am chaste, my darling. I am high priest of Har-Navah. I am untouched. Just as you are. Just as all the girls are. I have no need for the herb."

"Phinehas," she tried, but he gripped a heavy hand over her mouth. And that warning in his tone and eyes was no longer a hint. His grip became a vice, his eyes raging.

"Do you know the consequences, my darling? Do you know what would happen if the world were to see me as anything but holy and blameless?"

But everyone *already* knew. Surely everyone knew they were together. That Phinehas had chosen her. She wondered what he would think if he knew she had told Ezra they were married.

"Is having a family with me so unholy?" she asked, shoving his hand off of her mouth. Shoving her thoughts aside just as violently.

Phinehas's quiet warning turned to something sharper.

Something like the edge of a blade.

"A priest," he said, taking her chin roughly, "cannot possibly consort with a whore."

She did not sleep. Not for a single minute. She hadn't cried either.

She had just reeled.

She had thought back to every dinner. Every dance. Every party with Phinehas. Every time he had dolled her up in a gown of his choice and paraded her on his arm. Whether back in Teman or here in Kinnereth.

She had thought it was because she was special. Because he had chosen her. Because he loved her.

But not once had he ever presented her as anything more than an acolyte.

Oh, she *was* special.

A prized mare. A shiny plaything on display for men to see but not touch.

Not without a price.

And men had paid that price. Phinehas had offered her time and time again. Just as he offered her to Ezra.

And tonight, she understood. Tonight, the light shone like a rising dawn. And shame and humiliation washed over her as the truth became clear.

She was the trap. *She* was the game.

And the prize this time was the loyalty of one grand duke of Kinnereth—the most powerful man in Har-Navah besides the king.

Miri vomited, the motion so violent she doubled over in her bed and nearly fell off the side. She knelt on the floor, clambering for a rag, a towel, anything to clean up the mess she had made. She found a robe—Phinehas's robe, actually. She spat the remnants of bile onto it, using the clothing to clean up the mess of sick beside her bed. When she was done, she tossed the robe into the empty hearth across the room and made her way into her bathing chamber.

She managed to clean herself up enough that she returned to her sleeping chamber and passed out atop her bed, still in her dress.

THE NEXT MORNING, Miri did not feel rested. Nor did she feel any less rage. Any less pain. She needed to leave. Get out. Think.

To figure out what in Sheol she had done to her life. And what in Sheol she could do about it now.

She slung a shawl around her bare shoulders and marched her way out of the temple. The sun had risen, and the day had blossomed in the sleepy mountain village, washing the mountains in rich, golden light. Aspens shimmered in the morning breeze like a coven of færies gathered to bestow blessings. Pines and spruces towered into the rich blue skies. She wished the beauty would do something to assuage her guilt, her anger, her rage.

But it did not help. She pushed a rogue curl behind her ear and decided breakfast was in order.

What she didn't expect was the person she ran into just outside the bakery, her face planted in his chest with such force it should have knocked him over. It would have knocked a smaller man over. But Ezra was anything but small. And this close, he might as well have been a mountain himself.

"Miri," he said, grabbing hold of her to keep her from toppling over. "I didn't see you there!"

"Sorry," she said, straightening his jacket and lapels from the disarray caused by her rather ungraceful collision. "I'm so sorry."

"There is no need to apologize," he said, righting his top hat on his head.

She fussed with his shirt, his jacket, and his cravat, her harried emotions still coursing through her veins like an army on the march.

"Miri," he said, taking a moment to replace the shawl that had fallen down her shoulders. And at the softness of his words, at the gentleness of his touch, she finally slowed enough to meet his eyes.

"I was worried about you last night," he said. "You left in such a hurry."

"It was nothing," she said, shaking her head. She looked away, at anything but him, swallowing back the frustration that threatened to fall down her face in the form of tears. Embarrassment burned in her cheeks as she realized she was still in that ridiculous gown from last night.

"I was rude to you, and I want to apologize. I don't know what got into me, I just—" Ezra paused, taking hold of her chin. But where Phinehas had held her face with a firm, unforgiving hand last night, Ezra's fingers were...

At the realization that Miri's hands were still resting on his chest, she abruptly dropped them to her side.

"Miri," Ezra said gently, not letting her chin go. "I'm sorry for how I treated you."

"It's fine," she said, trying to brush him off. "It's nothing." She could feel tears threatening to fall. She hated them. She looked down, trying to avoid Ezra's gaze.

"Is something wrong?" he asked gently.

Miri could not look at him, couldn't find an answer, couldn't even order her mind enough to know where to start.

"Come here," he said, wrapping a solid arm around her back. "I have an idea."

He began walking, ushering her along with him. His arm was gentle as he guided her.

"Ezra!" came a merry voice from within the bakery as they entered.

"Good morning, Winona," said Ezra warmly. "I was wondering—do you think you could fix us up something to take with us?"

"I think we could manage that." Winona immediately disappeared down the hall behind her, returning a moment later with a basket in hand.

"Are we going somewhere?" Miri asked. She asked the question a bit perfunctorily, falling into the habits she had mastered over the years—ask coy questions, play along, pretend to care. She had learned all too well how men loved to be indulged even beyond their beds. And Ezra was just another game, after all. Just another disciple to win over. She wondered if he could tell.

"There's something I want to show you," said Ezra. It was only then that she realized his arm was still around her, his hand holding her securely to his side.

As if he had no intention of letting go.

Within moments, Winona handed Ezra a basket filled to the brim with all kinds of warm goods—too many pastries and breads for two people. Ezra handed her a fistful of far too many coins, even for the bounty now in a basket on his arm.

"Keep it," he said when Winona tried to hand him most of the coins back. He turned, guiding Miri gently along with him, and walked back out the door, the morning sun a blistering shock compared to the dimness of the bakery.

"Where are we going?" Miri tried again.

"You'll see," was his only response. Side by side, they made their way to a livery where he retrieved a glossy bay and gestured for Miri to mount.

"I'm not very good with horses. I haven't ridden since I was a child."

Ezra smiled, took hold of her waist, and hoisted her across the back of the stallion with little effort. He lifted himself behind her and wrapped one arm around her waist, saying, "You needn't worry. I'm good enough for the both of us."

"Confident, I see." She snorted, unable to stop the quip.

She did not need to turn around to hear the grin in his words. "I see no reason not to be."

THEY RODE FOREVER. At least, it felt like forever, with his broad chest against her back and his rich voice vibrating against her. It might as well have been an eternity like that. Just the two of them atop the gentle horse, munching on warm breakfast pastries and riding further and further away from the village.

And deeper and deeper into the mountains.

"Where exactly are you taking me?"

"To my favorite spot," he said. The horse dodged a rather large rock in his way, jolting enough that Miri gripped the pommel tightly. Ezra's arm locked around her.

"You're not going to fall."

"Because you're such an excellent horseman?" she teased.

"Because I *am* an excellent horseman. And exceptionally strong," he added with a healthy dose of ego.

"And exceptionally humble." She couldn't help the snorted laugh that escaped her, warmed further by the breathy chuckle that caressed her ear a moment later.

She reminded herself that Ezra's attention was rooted in political gain and nothing more. Last night, Phinehas had surely promised him anything he wanted in exchange for his loyalty. And Ezra had obviously taken the bait. Wherever he was taking her, however amiable he acted—it was all to get what he wanted. To have his fun and then toss her aside as if she had never existed.

After a long while, and a particularly steep climb uphill, at last Ezra brought his mount to a stop and hopped off. He reached for Miri and helped her down as well.

Jutting out from the side of the mountain, the bluff overlooked the lake below, its waters a crushing shade of blue, reflecting the bright skies above. And tucked neatly in a quiet, remote cove of the lake, a castle sat by the water.

No, a castle sat *on* the water.

"How is that possible?" she asked, staring at the formidable building of towers and turrets that looked as if it were floating. Vines fell down the sides of the building, curling around stones and exploding here and there with bright violet and magenta blooms.

"It was built by my ancestors some seven centuries ago," said Ezra.

"This is *your* home?"

"Massahd Castle. Built by my, let's see...great, great, great, great, great—"

"I get the point," she said.

Ezra laughed.

"Is it *floating?*" she asked.

She heard a chuckle as he moved to stand beside her. "No. Its foundation runs deep into the lake, into the world between the mountains."

"How? How did they do that?" The placid lake waters lapped along the foundation, and a thin green line of moss marked a water line that surely ebbed and flowed with the rains. Several verandas and balconies stretched out over the waters, outfitted with cozy seating and inviting tables. Quiet. Remote. Peaceful.

"The legends say that it took years. Decades. That they took their time to build a steady foundation on which the castle would be built. It's said that my forefathers started the project knowing they wouldn't finish it—that it would be a legacy for generations to come. But they moved great boulders into place deep beneath the water, one by one. The stories go that because the lake is so deep, it was only after fifty-seven summers that the foundation was ready to be built upon."

"Who would start a project knowing it would take so much just to make it possible?"

"I suppose some people have a gift of seeing what could be

long before it actually is."

Miri faced Ezra, searching him for a moment.

"It's beautiful. Thank you for bringing me to see it." The gray stones were bright in the morning sun, shimmering here and there. Birds perched on the topmost towers, chirping on the winds.

"Well, this is not what I brought you to see," he said, his voice colored with mirth.

She furrowed her brows, but Ezra only smiled.

"Come," he said, extending his hand. She took it, despite her better judgment. He led her not far from the vista to the edge of the bluff where a deceptively shallow grassy knoll separated them from a rather abrupt drop off.

"You've brought me here to throw me to my death?" she asked, peering skeptically down the horrifying decline looming before them.

Ezra only laughed. She turned to find him lying in the thick grass, folding his hands behind his head. "It's best experienced like this."

She raised a brow, folding her arms across her chest. She knew he was bold, a bit unconventional. But this...? Out here in the open, on the edge of a mountain? This was where he would have his way with her?

Ezra tipped his head back and laughed.

"I'm glad you think this is funny," she groused.

He did not stop chuckling. "I'm not making an untoward proposition, Miri. But you'll need to lie down next to me if you want the best view."

When she was still not convinced, Ezra extended his hand to hers, still grinning like a fool. "Just trust me," he said.

She shouldn't trust him. She should not trust this man for one breath.

But Miri lay down next to him anyway.

"I'm not sure I under—oh!" Miri sat up almost as quickly as she had laid down, propping herself on her elbows as she watched the sight unfold above her. "Winged horses!" she heard herself say.

Yes, winged horses. By the dozens. Flying over them. Vast wings extended from their surprisingly lithe bodies, they glided on the winds in all colors—white, black, gray, dapple, blood bay, and on and on. Some flew close to one another as if family or mates. Others flew alone, separated from the clusters. But they were surprisingly agile in the skies. She had expected winged horses to be clumsy, or even odd on those wings. After all, she had only ever read stories of them. She had never seen them in person.

But there was nothing odd or clumsy about the creatures. They glided over the wind as if they understood it. As if they spoke to it. In a word: majestic.

"How did you know they'd be here?" she asked in awe, unable to take her eyes from the glorious sight.

"They fly down from the mountains every night."

"They do?"

At her side, Ezra kept his eyes on the sight above them, a quiet satisfaction on his face as he spoke. "Unlike their ground counterparts, winged horses bed down high in the mountains at night. I suppose it has something to do with their love for the skies. But in the mornings, they come down from the high elevations to graze and mate in the valleys."

Even as he said it, a mated pair flew over, their wings touching as they glided, as if they couldn't stand to be separated, even in the skies. Ezra watched the pair as he went on. "And unlike their ground counterparts, they only foal every twenty summers or so."

"Twenty summers?" Miri asked, and at this, she turned her attention away from the overhead spectacle to Ezra.

"They're immortal. Or as close to it as possible. If they reproduced the same way horses do, they'd take over the world."

"How long do they live?"

"A thousand years. Maybe more. Most winged horses remain with their human families for generations."

She looked back to the skies, strewn with at least a dozen horses. "They're so beautiful."

"Yes, they are," Ezra agreed.

There was such peace watching the horses fly over them. It was oddly beautiful and soul-filling. Neither of them spoke as they watched.

Ezra did not seem afraid of the silence, for he let long moments stretch between them with nothing to say, no sounds but the halcyon song of the mountain around them—shimmering aspen leaves, chirping birds, the flap of horses' wings. After a while of the peaceful silence, she looked over to him once more. Gone was the tension she hadn't realized he bore anytime she saw him at a formal dinner or gathering of nobility. Here, on this mountain, Ezra was at ease. With himself. With the mountains. With life.

She found she was jealous of that settled calm. Wondered if she had ever known it for herself.

"Are you sure you're all right, Miri?" he asked, shattering the silence. His words were gentle, and his eyes were full of concern. "The way you left last night... I know that I was being abrupt with you, and I wanted to apologize for it."

"I just thought you were in a bad mood," she said, half teasing him, though the observation was honest.

Ezra breathed a sigh. "I suppose the world into which I was born never ceases to amaze me."

"You do not like your title," she said.

"I am not so petty to lament it," he admitted. "But I confess I'm terrible at the games I am supposed to be playing."

"Well, if it helps, so am I."

He searched her face at that, as if he were trying to answer a question. If another man had held her gaze so intensely, she would probably have blushed. Looked away. Feigned coy flirtation. But Ezra's gaze did not intimidate. It did not frighten her. It was not possessive or bold. It was more...curious. Like she was a puzzle he was trying to solve.

So she did something she had never had the courage to do with Phinehas—she bared her soul and gave him the truth.

"I am barren," she said.

"What?" he asked, his demeanor shifting from curiosity to surprise.

"I cannot give Phinehas children," she said, fidgeting with a strand of her hair instead of meeting Ezra's branding gaze.

"How do you know?"

"What do you mean how do I know? I mean it has been seven years and I've not conceived his child."

"Seven?" he asked, though he nearly mouthed the question. She could see him doing the math in his head, wondering if he would think less of her knowing she had been thirteen years old when Phinehas had first taken her to his bed. First whispered his promises to her.

Promises he could never keep now.

But Miri was no anomaly; Phinehas had brought all the acolytes to the temple at such a young age. She had never had the courage to ask him why.

"Is he pressuring you to bear his children?" Ezra asked softly.

Miri snorted. "No. Quite the opposite, actually."

"You want to give him children?"

"I just...thought it would help," she said softly. It took her a moment to gain the courage to meet Ezra's gaze again. But she did not find judgment or even disdain. She found what felt like concern. It gave her the courage to continue. "I hoped that if I could give him a child, he would finally agree to marry me and—"

She realized her mistake the moment it escaped her lips. But she wanted to give Ezra the truth. It mattered, for some reason. So she said, "We are not married. I don't know why I lied to you about it."

Ezra did not seem shocked, or even offended. He simply held her eyes as he spoke. "It's all right."

"It's not all right. I lied to you. You shouldn't trust me." For about a dozen different reasons, she knew that statement to be true. Much more true than perhaps he even realized.

Ezra nodded softly, and something in her heart deflated at the simple gesture.

"You probably shouldn't trust me either," he said. "But I trust you. I know all the reasons I shouldn't. But I find that I do anyway."

"I just admitted that I lied to you about being married," she pointed out.

A soft smile graced his mouth. "Yes, but I figure you had your reasons for it. And I suppose I'm curious enough now to wonder what they are."

Miri huffed a disbelieving laugh. "Well, that would mean having only the truth between us. Are you sure you're prepared for that?"

The question had been intended to humor him. It did nothing of the sort. Something sobering washed over his features. Something she did not understand. But at her flippant question, Ezra's eyes found hers and did not let go.

She found she could not look away either.

"Only the truth between us?" Ezra asked at last.

Miri held his intent stare for longer than she realized, letting the question settle. Letting the implication play itself out in her mind.

Only truth between them.

A glorious, terrifying prospect.

And one she dearly craved.

With someone.

For once in her life.

Even if Ezra was little more than a stranger.

Somehow…for some reason, she wanted nothing more than the sobering proposal set out before her. So she answered without hesitation.

"Yes. Only truth between us."

Ezra seemed at a loss for anything to say for a moment, and she had half a mind to turn her attention back to the skies, but then he finally spoke again. "You present a dangerous proposition, Miri."

"Dangerous?" she asked.

"The truth can be much more damning than lies."

"Don't I know it," she said, deflating.

But Ezra did not let her look away. He took her chin between his thumb and forefinger, holding her gaze for another long moment before he said, "Only truth between us."

Something in her settled. A promise—a whisper of a chance she had never taken before. To have only truth with someone. Only honesty.

So when Ezra reached between them and took her hand in his, when he laced his finger between hers and pulled her hand to his mouth, pressing a kiss to her knuckles, she did not stop him. She did not feign the blush that rose to her cheeks or the breath that was coming up short. She let him see her. She let him look at her.

All of her.

And she did not let herself fear.

Ezra returned to the topic at hand. "You are young, Miri. And you have your whole life ahead of you. I would not let anyone define your worth by the usefulness of your womb."

"Well, you would be in the minority in that opinion," she said. Miri looked away, fixing her eyes on a nearby aspen, its leaves trembling in the breeze. "There is no man in the world who would knowingly give himself to a woman who could not give him heirs."

"There is more than one way to have children, Miri."

She scoffed. "I hardly think most men willingly go into marriage knowing they'll have to sire an heir by a mistress. If the bastard were to be exposed—"

"I'm not talking about a mistress, Miri," Ezra said. "There are many children in the cities who need homes. Loving parents."

"Yes, well, I don't know any man who would give his estate and holdings to a child not of his issue."

"I did," he said.

"What?"

"John Junior. My sister's son. He is the heir to my estate."

Miri turned away. "That's different. He's family. And you'll change it once you have children of your own."

"Possibly, yes. But then again, maybe I won't want to saddle my children with the burden of heirship. It's nice knowing they'll have a choice, anyway. The point is, your story and most certainly your worth are not gone simply because you cannot bear children, Miri."

"I doubt Phinehas would agree."

"How do you know it's you?" The question was soft. Careful.

"What do you mean?"

"I mean, why must you assume barrenness is solely your fault?"

Oh.

"Well, at the risk of impropriety, I can assure you that everything—is in—" She cleared her throat. "Is in working order—for *him.*" Providence help her, she could hardly believe she was having this conversation.

Only truth between us.

She wondered what Phinehas would think of her stark honesty with this man.

Ezra chuckled. "Well, Miri, you can put ingredients in an oven, but there is no guarantee that the end result will be a cake."

"A cake?" she scoffed.

"It's a metaphor."

"I understand the metaphor, Ezra. I'm just not sure why I'm having this conversation with you."

"Miri," he said, laughing softly. He squeezed her hand and set it to rest on his chest. "All I mean is you don't know it's you."

"Even if it's not me, it doesn't matter," she said soberly.

"You speak as if your story is over."

"I wish I knew how to believe that it wasn't," she admitted.

"Well I know for certain that it isn't."

"How?"

"You're alive, aren't you? You're alive and you're young and you're vibrant and your story has only just begun."

He smiled, never letting his eyes leave hers as he pulled her hand to his mouth and pressed another kiss to her knuckles. He laid back again, folding one arm behind his head that he might watch the horses once more. But he kept the fingers of his other hand laced with hers, resting their joined hands on his chest as he watched the spectacle above.

The horses were thinning now. Only a few stragglers flew over them.

Needing a change in subject, she asked, "Have you ever ridden one?"

"Yes."

"You have?" So few ever had a chance to ride winged horses anymore. Most of them were wild. Untamed. That he had ridden one...

"When Queen Adelaide brought the herd to Har-Navah during the Great War, most of them stayed in the plains of Gav and Tsafone Provinces. Over the centuries, they migrated north-ward. Once they found the mountains, they made it their new home. They've been here for half a millennium now, and most are wild. But there are few left that come from the royal line."

"Queen Adelaide's mare, you mean?"

Ezra nodded, squeezing her hand in time with his smile. "Eagle mated not long after the war was over. She and her mate died only a few decades ago. But their foals are still alive today."

"I thought you said they were immortal," she pointed out.

Ezra chuckled softly. "To a human, a thousand years of life is about as immortal as it comes."

She nodded. "Have you ever seen them? The foals of Queen Adelaide's mare?"

"Once or twice," he said.

"Can you show me?"

"I might be able to arrange that," he said, turning his attention back to the skies. Miri, however, turned her gaze to their joined hands resting on his chest. The way his hand covered hers. The way his thumb traced idly along her palm. How lovely and golden his skin looked in the morning sun—as if he spent most of his time outdoors. As if he came alive in these mountains around them.

Only truth between us.

He was a paradox, Ezra. A grand duke—a powerful man in the kingdom. Even with his fine clothes and polished manners, there was something untamed about him. Something wild. Like he kept one foot in these mountains. Like he'd rather be here, lying in the soft grass than anywhere else. Like the winged horses above them —one part rugged and wild, one part refined and ethereal.

The moments passed in peaceful silence before she said, "Ezra?"

"Yes?"

She waited for him to meet her eyes before she said, "Thank you for bringing me here. I needed it."

"You know, so did I, Miri. So did I."

CHAPTER NINE

"Uncle Ezra?"

"Yes, my darling," Ezra said, unable to stifle his smile at the sound of the tiny voice. He turned his attention from the cloudy vista outside the many windows of his sitting room to the boy sitting on his knee. Gentle thunder rumbled in the distance.

"I want to learn to fly," said John Junior.

"You do?" Ezra asked. "Well then, I shall have to teach you."

"Today?"

Ezra laughed. "I'm afraid your mother might protest if I were to teach you to fly in a thunderstorm."

From across the way, Esther raised an eyebrow but said nothing. John Senior stifled a chuckle for his wife's benefit. Ezra's mouth curled into a smile as his nephew went on.

"Is it so very frightening?"

Ezra wrapped his arms around the boy's torso, pulling him closer. Resting his chin on the narrow shoulder beneath him, he whispered, "It's terrifying. In the very best way."

The boy laughed and jumped from Ezra's lap, but not before

Ezra pulled him back and pressed a firm kiss to his temple. Thunder rumbled again.

"We need to talk." This came from Esther, who rested folded hands on her swollen belly, holding Ezra's gaze with unflinching reprimand.

So it was going to be one of *those* conversations.

"Why is it that I cannot have a conversation with a woman these days without it starting off with foreboding?" Ezra lamented.

Just then, Thaddeus, the lanky and well-meaning butler emerged into the sitting room, followed by Helena, the house-keeper. Thaddeus held his shoulders back as he announced in his rich, formal baritone, "Dinner will be in an hour."

"Thank you, Thaddeus," said Esther, as if this were her home. Then again, it had been, not so long ago.

John Junior's bright attention landed on Helena, who stood beside Thaddeus holding out her hand with a warm, grandmoth-erly smile. "I've some goodies in the kitchen for you, my darling," she said.

"You'll spoil his supper again, Hel," Thaddeus scolded under his breath. The look of disdain on his face brought a grin to Ezra's mouth. Thaddeus and Helena had always had a...special relation-ship. After her husband had died when Ezra was only a boy, Thad-deus had become the object of Helena's hovering, feminine attention. And Thaddeus had willingly taken up the post as the curmudgeonly recipient, a fact that had been a great source of entertainment to Ezra for years.

"Oh I will *not* spoil his dinner," Helena spat without bothering to look at Thaddeus. When John Junior reached her side, she took his hand and promptly led him out of the room with a twinkle of mischief in her eyes.

"I'll keep her under control," Thaddeus promised with a stern bow.

Ezra nodded once to show his appreciation for Thaddeus's seriousness, waiting to chuckle until the butler had left the room.

Settled back on the settee, Ezra crossed an ankle over one knee and turned his attention back to his sister. "So what is it that we need to talk about?"

Esther lifted her chin, her black hair pulled in a neat but becoming knot at the back of her head. Providence above, she looked so much like his mother, Lady Leah Kelach, that he was half tempted to smooth his jacket and sit up straight, lest he receive a lecture on manners.

"Am I to understand you have been consorting with a whore?"

"What?" Ezra choked, the question bursting from him with a guttural laugh.

"Do not toy with me, brother. I am in no mood." Esther shifted in her chair, doing her best to hide her discomfort from her pregnancy.

"I have no intention of toying with you," Ezra said. "But you will have to rephrase the question, as I am unsure to which of my *numerous* consorts you are referring."

Perched on a nearby table, John couldn't quite stifle his laugh.

"Enough," said Esther. "Is it true, Ezra?"

Ezra crossed his arms and held his sister's unflinching gaze. "If you are referring to Miri, then I am afraid you have been sorely misinformed as to the nature of our relationship."

"You call her by her first name?" Esther cried.

"How should I refer to her to suit you? Woman Of Whom My Dearest Sister Does Not Approve?"

"Ezra, you realize she is a prostitute, right?"

"I believe the term is acolyte." That was from John.

"Exactly. A temple whore," said Esther. "And don't you dare defend him," she practically spat at John.

John lifted both hands in feigned innocence.

Ezra bit down on the frustration that welled suddenly within him and said sternly, "I am afraid that if you refer to her as a whore again, you'll find that you regret it."

"You rise to her defense?" Esther asked incredulously as thunder rumbled again, a little more loudly.

"She is my friend," Ezra said. "Is it such a crime?"

"Pffft," Esther scoffed, resting her back against her chair for the first time. Her hand found the small of her back, and the motion revealed just how big her belly had gotten. Ezra wasn't sure, but he could have sworn it had grown even since her arrival in the room. "There is no such thing as a man and a woman being friends," she went on.

"Excuse me?" Ezra asked. Gesturing to John first, then Esther, he said, "I seem to recall the two of you were friends for years."

"Exactly," said Esther. "We were friends and now we're married. There is no such thing as a man and a woman spending time with each other without at least one of them growing affections for the other. John was in love with me from the very beginning."

Ezra turned his attention to John, who merely shrugged from his perch. The man never seemed to sit properly on furniture. "She's not wrong."

Ezra shook his head. "You're no help." He looked back to his sister. "And what about you? Did you love John from the beginning?"

Esther turned her attention to her husband, appraising him for a moment, apparently disinclined to answer the question.

"Careful, sister. Your answer is bound to offend one of us," Ezra said, smirking.

"What are your intentions with this woman?" Esther went on, ignoring him. "I've never known you to be the kind of man to take a paramour."

"She is not my paramour," Ezra insisted. He knew she meant well. He thanked Providence he knew her well enough to know that this was nothing more than firstborn concern. Since their parents had died a few years ago, Esther had taken it upon herself to smother him with motherly chastisement.

"If she is not your paramour, then what is she? Your wh—" Esther stopped, apparently rethinking the word at the sight of the stern warning that hardened Ezra's face.

"She is my friend," Ezra said curtly, his tone dangerous.

"Ezra," Esther said, her tone shifting to something piteous. "I know you are in a confusing time. What with the dissolution of your betrothal—"

"Despite what everyone thinks, I am not confused. You will recall that *I* am the one who called off the wedding, not Rachæl."

"Yes, and in times like these," Esther went on, "it can be easy for a man to look for affection—"

"Esther. Stop," he said, gripping the arm of the settee to channel his frustration into the poor, unsuspecting upholstery. "I am not looking to numb myself in the arms of a woman. And your implication is rather insulting."

"Then what exactly are you doing?"

"Like. I. Said," Ezra practically growled. "We. Are. Friends."

"And we have established that it is impossible for men and women to be only friends," Esther insisted.

"Well, you are wrong."

"Does she bear affection for you? Do you feel guilty about it? Is that it?"

"Damn it, Esther," Ezra said, unsure why he was feeling so defensive. Why the thought of Miri as anything but the beautiful, funny, warm friend he had made nearly sent him into a fit of rage... He folded his hands before his mouth and closed his eyes. "Why is this so difficult for you?"

"Your reputation is in shreds as it is," Esther said. "You've paid no attention to your duties as grand duke. If you had attended council once in the past year, you would know that your focus should be on the king and whatever unholy alliances he is forging with Medinah."

"What alliances?" Ezra said, abruptly sitting up, every ounce of frustration falling out of his head. Rachæl had mentioned concern about her father's secret deals the other day. Now Esther was mentioning the same? If two of the sharpest women in the kingdom were concerned about it, he'd better start paying attention.

"I don't know details. But the point is, *you* should," Esther said.

Yes. Yes, he should. He had used the last two years as an excuse to stay away from council. To grieve the loss of his parents and grandparents after their untimely death. But after the grief had settled, he had milked the excuse to stay out of politics.

Providence grant he would not come to regret that.

"What *do* you know?" Ezra insisted.

"Nothing. Are you listening to me?" she asked, frustrated.

"Yes, Esther. I am. But I fail to see how my friendship with Lady Miriam is a problem," he said, and he meant it. He knew what she was. He knew that he was playing with fire too. Wildfire. That she was a game, whether she meant to be or not. But every time he had been around her, he didn't give a damn. Not even a fraction of a damn.

Only truth between us.

The words clamored through him once again. A prayer. An anthem.

Every time he was around Miri, all he could think of was when he would be around her again. And so yesterday, on that mountainside, he had decided he would see her again. And again.

And damn the consequences of spending time with Miri the Wildfire.

"*Lady* Miriam?" Esther scoffed. "Ezra, don't be so naïve. She's an acolyte. And regardless of the honor of your intentions, people are talking. Surely you recognize that."

Yes. Yes, he did. But he had never given a damn about his reputation. He saw no reason to start now.

"She will ruin you," Esther went on, rather adamantly. "You need to think of your future."

"It's a pity you were not born male," Ezra said. "You would have made a fine grand duke." And as firstborn, she would have been. Ezra had never understood the rather archaic system under which they lived and the tradition that only males could inherit titles. King Dægan had even had to issue a special dispensation that he had no intention of siring more children in hopes of a male —a decree that allowed Rachæl to be named heir to the throne of Har-Navah. Providence knew there would be no more formidable monarch than she. And Esther most certainly should have been Grand Duchess of Kinnereth. But there had never been such thing as Grand Duchesses—at least not ones who inherit. Marriage into the title was a very different thing than inheriting it.

"I, for one, am not sorry she was born female," said John, and Ezra couldn't help but chuckle.

Esther, however, ignored the comment completely. "The point is, there are plenty of eligible and agreeable matches for you, Ezra. You needn't bother finding companionship with someone so wrong for you."

"I appreciate the advice, but I will thank you to keep your nose out of my business."

Esther slapped her hands on her thighs, moving to stand up. "This is your life you're talking about! Our lives! All of us—even John Junior! Are you going to throw all of this away simply because you are too stubborn to listen to reason?" Esther stopped, catching her belly and wincing. John was instantly at her side, one hand at the small of her back. Ezra stood too, worried that his sister was working herself into a frenzy.

"You should rest, love," John said. "You don't need to get so upset."

"I wouldn't be upset if my brother would think with the head on his shoulders and not the one in his trousers!"

"And with that rather colorful admonishment, I think we're done with this conversation," John said, attempting to usher Esther back into her chair. But she did not flinch.

"I need to walk," she said, pushing out of her husband's arms and moving across the room without a backward glance. John did not follow her, instead watching her as she waddled like a duck from the room.

"Shouldn't you follow your wife?" Ezra asked, plopping back down on the settee, rubbing between his eyes with his thumb and forefinger.

"Right now? I'd sooner follow a mother bear into a den of cubs."

Ezra couldn't help the chuckle that escaped despite the headache that was blooming.

"She means well," John said, sitting across from Ezra.

"I know. I just wish she could mean a little *less* well. And I'm sorry you had to be in the middle of that. You don't have to choose sides."

"I took on that role when I married my best friend's sister. And just so we're clear, I will always choose her side. Even when she's wrong."

Ezra smiled genuinely. "And that's why I let you marry her."

"You think you could have stopped me?" John asked with a grin.

"I would have burnt the world to Sheol to stop you had you been wrong for her."

John let a beat of silence stretch between them before he spoke again. "She's not wrong, you know," he said. "There was never a moment when it was not her for me. From the time I began to think of such things, I wanted it to be her. The first time I kissed her, I knew she was the only person I ever wanted to kiss."

"Not all of us are quite as sentimental as you are, John."

"Perhaps," John agreed rather reasonably. "But what *are* you doing?"

"I don't understand."

"What is the point of bringing so much Sheol on yourself?"

"I enjoy her. I—" Ezra shrugged, answering the question for himself as much as for John. "I like being with her."

"Are you attracted to her?"

Ezra looked up, considering John before answering the question.

Only truth between us.

That's what Miri wanted. He wondered what she would do if she knew his truth.

"Yes," he simply said.

John sat back against his settee, apparently satisfied with the answer.

"I'm a fool, aren't I?" Ezra asked. If there was one person in his life whose opinion of him he valued, it was John. Low born, John the nobody. John the working-class lawyer who had fallen in love with the granddaughter of a grand duke and had the stones to tell her. To marry her.

"Yes," John said with a conspiratorial smile. "But from one fool to another, just make sure you understand what you're getting into." When Ezra didn't say anything, John went on, his words a little more sober. "There will be Sheol for it. Every day. Likely for the rest of your life, if it comes to that."

Ezra knew John was right. He had seen the way the aristocracy scoffed at John's presence at events and parties meant for the nobility of the kingdom. He had heard the way people talked of Esther—as if she had thrown her life away to marry a low-born lawyer. Six years married, and they still paid for it. When invitations would come for county dinners and balls, Ezra was invited. Esther rarely was.

If it bothered her one way or the other, she had never let it show. She had always held her head high, walking proudly when John was on her arm. And Ezra had respected her deeply for it.

But he had never really considered it—the price she paid for that love. That marriage.

Until today.

But Miri was his friend. Nothing more.

She was just his friend.

"Just make sure she's worth it," John finished. "Make sure she's worth the fight. And if she is...to Sheol with the naysayers."

CHAPTER TEN

Miri worked a comb through Kata's hair, the brown strands muted and dull in the dimness of the common room below the temple. Across the room, Jordie sat at a table, bobbing her foot as she toyed with a pot of rouge. Standing before a small looking glass on the mantel, Galina inspected every detail of the perfection she had concocted for tonight's ball. If one could call it a ball. A county dinner with dancing was more accurate. But Phinehas preferred the more grand definition of the evening, so they had been calling it a ball for weeks.

Kata's dress tonight was simple in comparison to the rest of the girls, as if she had no intention of drawing attention to herself. Not that Miri could blame her. Galina, by contrast, wore a ruby-and-black dress that hugged her figure as if it had been painted on, spilling into a glorious skirt that trailed behind her nearly a foot. As if she were the queen of Har-Navah.

Miri had chosen gold. A simple gown in style, the shimmering fabric was the real draw. And since she had been able to choose her own gown tonight, it was more tasteful. Modest. A gown in which she wouldn't be self conscious with her breasts on display for every man to ogle.

Kata winced when the comb caught in a tangle.

"Sorry," Miri said, continuing to work her friend's rather unremarkable tresses.

Despite the fact that her back was to the room, Miri could see the smirk curling Galina's mouth in the looking glass—and the words dancing on her tongue that she was clearly dying to say.

Kata could see the smirk too, for she whispered for Miri's benefit, "She's gloating because the king has turned his eye to her."

"And you're jealous because he has not turned his eye to you," Galina purred, meeting Kata's eyes through the looking glass for a moment before returning her attention to herself. She fussed with a curl near her cheek, moving it a fraction, as if to find the perfect spot.

"I am not," Kata said.

Galina merely laughed and began applying rouge to her lips.

Miri reached for a tin of pins and began fixing Kata's hair on top of her head.

"What was he like?" Jordie asked, the question almost innocent. Innocent, she most definitely was not. At least not anymore. But she certainly knew how to keep up the appearance.

"Like a bear," said Galina. "All claws and teeth," she added with a wicked grin. Jordie giggled with her.

Kata rolled her eyes and returned her attention to Miri's ministrations at her head.

"Is it all right?" Miri asked, gesturing to Kata's hair.

"It looks fine," Kata said.

"I'm not very good at this," Miri admitted, dropping a pin. She bent to pick it up from the worn carpet and said, "Galina is much better. Perhaps you should—"

"It's fine," Kata interrupted.

"Miriam's right," said Jordie. "Galina is the best with hair."

"I'd be glad to help you," Galina drawled, turning at last from the mirror, a smirk threatening her ruby lips. "I'm sure you'll want to look your best tonight."

"What's that supposed to mean?" Miri asked, furrowing her brow. She tried to work another pin into Kata's hair, but couldn't help but think she was doing a remarkable job at creating a striking resemblance to a crow's nest on top of Kata's head.

"She'll want to look her best for His Holiness," Galina said. And when Kata said nothing, Miri looked at her friend's face in the looking glass—and noticed the heat that had suddenly found her cheeks and neck.

"What is she talking about?" Miri asked.

It was Jordie who answered, bobbing her foot as she spoke nonchalantly. "Now that Galina is occupied, Phinehas has turned his attention to Kata."

Miri froze, a pin in her hand. Kata looked anywhere but at Miri's reflection before her.

Galina practically beamed.

"What do you mean, now that Galina is occupied?" Miri asked.

No one answered.

So she asked again, a little more slowly, *What do you mean, now that Galina is occupied?*

"Well, you cannot exactly expect him to be without companionship," Jordie said. "You're tied up with the grand duke, Galina is with the king, I have my obligations... Poor Phinehas needs someone to warm his bed."

"Phinehas doesn't need anyone to warm his bed," Miri protested. "I am not sleeping with the grand duke!"

"Well, you will be, of course," Jordie said, as if it were common knowledge. "He certainly didn't want me."

"I am with Phinehas!" Miri spat. "We are—together!"

She looked around, hoping for someone to corroborate her claims. Kata's eyes remained steadfastly *not* on Miri.

"Oh, Miri," Galina said, all false pity. "Dear, *dear* Miri."

"Is it true?" Miri asked Kata. "Are you sleeping with him?"

Kata still wouldn't look her friend in the eye.

"Are *you* sleeping with him?" she demanded of Galina.

"Miri, we're all acolytes." Galina tilted her head to one side. "Or did you think you were special?"

Miri looked at her friend in the looking glass once more. This time, Kata finally met her eyes. And when Miri spotted the tears there, she slammed down the tin of pins and marched out of the room.

SHE MADE it up the stairs to the main floor of the temple only to realize that most of the guests had already arrived. The halls bustled with nobles, all glittering and gossiping, all of them headed toward the banquet room that would be the makeshift ballroom for the evening. She pushed against the flow of the crowd, offering her excuses and pardons as she went, her pulse pounding, until at last she broke through on the other side, and found herself alone in the quiet temple sanctuary.

A few candles flickered at the altar, casting ghostly orbs upon the stones and glass. The room was unnervingly quiet compared to the rest of the temple tonight, and it was not lost on Miri just how perfectly this space had been built for peaceful, unhindered reflection.

A table sat at the edge of the dais of the altar, covered in candles, some burned down to uselessness, others new and hardly burned at all. Ivory wax dripped slowly from the few that were lit, and without thinking, Miri reached for a matchstick. Her hands trembled as she lit one end with one of the flickering candles, letting the flame gather its strength before she used it to light another candle.

Kneeling, she blew out the matchstick, set it down once more upon the table, and folded her hands on the rail before her. She released a long breath, letting the words sink in. The implication.

Miri, we're all acolytes.

Had she truly been so blind? So stupid? So naïve?

A lone tear fell down her cheek as she rested her brow on her folded hands. "Oh Ari, I miss you," she breathed, the words as tremulous as her hands. "I wish I could see you just once more."

But her family had all been ripped from her on one fateful night so many years ago. A night she did not let herself think about very often. A lifetime ago. But every once in a while, often when she least expected it, a keen ache for her cousin—her friend—would rob her of her makeshift peace, throwing her face-first into longing for something that would never again exist.

The sound of a soft step tore her from her vigil. Miri quickly wiped an errant tear from her chin, looking up to find Ezra not far away, quiet reverence on his face.

"I did not mean to interrupt you," he said softly. "I could see that you were upset. I hope you don't mind that I followed you."

"It's fine," she said flatly, turning her attention back to the candles.

"Are you all right?" he asked gently. He took a few more steps, standing closer, but made no move to touch her.

"I'm fine," she lied.

"I did not know you were religious," he said after a moment's pause.

"I'm not," she said, following his gaze to the candles flickering before her. "I suppose my prayers are more of desperation than they are devotion. I'm sure Providence is unimpressed."

"I don't know," he said. "I think Providence is just glad to hear from us."

She looked up again, saw the warmth in his eyes, and breathed a dismissive sound.

"May I join you?" Ezra asked, gesturing to the place where she knelt.

She scooted over to make room for him. He took the same matchstick she had used and lit another candle before kneeling beside her and folding his hands before him.

"Are you a religious man?" she asked.

"I've been known to be, I suppose," he said. "Although, like you, most of my religion can be boiled down to pleas with the Almighty and little more." He laughed at that, a small sound that somehow fit the solemn atmosphere.

"Who do you pray for?" she asked, turning her attention to his candle. It flickered lazily in the dim, still room, as if a phantom toyed with it.

"My grandfather," he said. "I know it sounds silly, but I often ask Providence if he will let me speak to him."

"Does he let you?"

Ezra met her gaze. "I like to think so."

"Does he talk back?"

"No," Ezra said. "But I can imagine what he'd say, all the same." There was quiet, peaceful grief in his eyes, a fondness that he could not hide for the grandfather he had lost. She wondered if it had been long ago or more recent.

"You loved your grandfather very much," she said.

"He was more of a father to me than my father ever was. I miss him every day."

"May I ask when he died?"

Ezra gazed upon his candle, and it took Miri a moment to realize that it was emotion that had rendered him unable to answer the question.

"I'm sorry," she said.

"No," Ezra said, resting a hand over hers on the rail. "It's fine. I lost him two years ago. And my grandmother the very next day. My parents both died in the weeks that followed.

"Were they ill?" she asked.

"Yes," he said. "The pox. I was on tour with Rachæl and the royal family. When I returned, my grandparents were gravely ill and my parents were showing symptoms. It took my parents several weeks to die, but my grandparents passed only a day after my return, and within a few hours of each other, as if they couldn't stand to be apart, on this side of eternity or the other."

She could not bring herself to say it—how tragic and beautiful it sounded. A devastating love like that. Something out of a storybook. But not real. Not really. Not for someone like her, anyway.

"Everything I know about love, I learned from my grandparents," Ezra went on. "They were inseparable. Even when they weren't together, they were always united. I remember, even as a young boy, knowing that what they had was different. Special. He looked at her like she was his only purpose. And she looked at him the same way."

"You miss them very much."

"You miss your cousin," he said, nodding to her candle.

"You were eavesdropping," she said with a small smile.

He squeezed her hand, still under his. "I was concerned about you."

She returned her attention to the candles. "Don't be. I'm not worth it."

"I would have to disagree."

She did not look at him again. Did not let his words sink in.

"Anything you need to talk about?" he tried.

"No," she said.

A heartbeat passed between them, and then something

shifted in Ezra. As if a light had come on, Ezra tugged on her hand, urging her to stand with him.

"What is it?" she asked.

"This is a ball, is it not?"

She looked around at the empty sanctuary, flecked with the paltry candlelight. "I believe we're in the wrong place."

"I don't know," he said, pulling her to him. He wrapped an arm around her waist, holding her other hand aloft. He swept her into a gentle waltz before he went on, "It seems perfect to me."

After a moment, unsure what else to do, she finally said, "You're a terrible dancer."

Ezra laughed, and she wasn't sure if it was the gesture or the candlelight that made his eyes sparkle. "I told you I'm not very good with protocol and all of that."

Miri couldn't help the chuckle that escaped.

"Shouldn't we be in there?" she tried, gesturing with her head towards the ball on the other side of the wall.

"Do you want to be in there?"

"Let me rephrase. Shouldn't *you* be in there?"

Ezra smiled. "Yes. But I'd rather be with you."

She looked away, hating the blush that crept up her neck. Her hair spilled across her shoulders, and she looked down to where it fell down her golden gown, cursing herself for forgetting to do something with it before she stormed from the common room.

"You should wear it down more often," Ezra said.

She shot her eyes up to meet his gaze. "It's a mess," she objected.

"It's beautiful. If you didn't look like a wildfire before, you certainly do now. What with your hair and that gown."

She looked down again, suddenly keenly aware of every angle, every curve over her gown. She was thankful that tonight, at least, her breasts were not on full display. But she could feel it—the warmth of his hand through the fabric on her back. And that moment all of her focus, all of her thoughts honed in on that hand. The surety in it. The gentle nudges as he moved her effortlessly in front of the altar.

She had lied to him. He was not a terrible dancer at all. Perhaps he wasn't the most skilled dance partner she had ever known, but he made up for a lack of flair with his easy grace, twirling her around their makeshift ballroom. They were like rivers meeting in a mountain valley, colliding and intertwining into one as they danced, making their way to the ocean. To something bigger than both of them.

Silence yawned between them, making her more nervous than she wanted to admit. So she decided to find a topic to distract her. "I hear there is some treaty in the works."

Ezra's entire countenance shifted at that, his waltz hesitating. "Yes," he said. "So I've heard."

Perhaps she shouldn't have brought it up. Perhaps she had no right to ask. But she did anyway. "Do you know anything about it?"

"Not enough, apparently. But I am looking into it."

"Should I be concerned?" she asked, marveling that she had the gumption to even broach the subject of politics. With the grand duke of Kinnereth, of all people. It was not her place to know. It was certainly not her place to pry. Phinehas had certainly made that clear over the years.

"If I know the king, then yes, Miri. We should all be concerned."

"Why?"

"Because our king is many things, but immune to the lure of lofty promises he is not."

"What does that mean?" she asked before she could stop herself.

Ezra didn't seem to mind her questions, for he answered

without hesitation. "It means that I would not put it past him to do something—how should I put this?—stupid."

Miri couldn't help the laugh that burst from her. "Sorry," she said.

Ezra laughed with her. He pulled her a little closer to him as he turned her about the space, his golden eyes glittered with amusement as his gaze locked with hers.

"You know him well," she said.

"I've had a few more peeks behind the curtain than most," he said. Because he had been betrothed to the king's daughter, up until not so very long ago.

She thought of Ezra dancing with the princess. She painted a picture in her mind of smiles and laughter and quiet secrets. Of a princess who did not bother to hide a blush on her cheeks and a grand duke who loved to find ways to put it there.

It surprised her how much she hated it.

"So what are you going to do?" she asked, mostly to distract herself from the thoughts trying to rob her of sensibility. "I mean, if he's truly up to something awful, what will you do?"

"That's an excellent question, Miri. I am not sure, to be quite honest. I love my kingdom. I will be damned if I stand by and do nothing while it's thrown to the wolves."

"Well, I will help you," she blurted.

"What?"

"I will help you figure out if there is something amiss. And I will help you if there is."

"I cannot let you do that," he said.

"Why? Because I am a woman? An acolyte?" she groused, stopping him from the dance.

"No," he said gently, refusing to drop his hand from her waist or his gaze from her face. "Because I won't let you put yourself in harm's way."

"I won't be in harm's way," she insisted.

"You will, Miri. You do not know this world the way I do."

"I know it better than you think," she said. "And I want to help you."

Ezra stood before her, holding her eyes, searching them. As if he were actually considering it—as if he would actually let her help in some way. Do something that mattered.

"Have breakfast with me," he said.

"What?" she asked, taken aback by the non sequitur.

"Have breakfast with me in the morning," he said again.

In the morning. Tomorrow. She swallowed, understanding his meaning. The implication. His way of asking her to go home with him without having to say it aloud.

Something in her chest tightened.

All of this was still a game, then. That's all it had been. Perhaps a little more drawn out. Perhaps a little different than all the others. But a game all the same.

At last she managed, "All right."

"We'll figure out what the king is up to together," he said.

"What the king is up to," she parroted absently.

He nodded, sweeping her into a waltz once more. There was a lightness in his steps that hadn't been there before. Then again, she had just agreed to go home with him. And disappointment settled in her at the thought. She had spent an afternoon on a mountainside with a man who did not ask anything of her. Who shared stories with her and promised only truth between them. And then he had taken her back to the village without so much as touching her. She had been surprised, shocked, really. That he hadn't asked more of her. Hadn't seemed inclined to. And she had told herself, even without realizing it, that perhaps Ezra was different. That he wouldn't play these games.

Whatever you did to him, keep doing it. He is yours, darling. Yours to command.

But Ezra wasn't different. He was the same. The same as all the rest.

The same as Phinehas, visiting Kata's bed. And Galina's. And Jordie's. And Providence knew who else's...

Bile burned in the back of her throat at the thought.

Ezra turned her once, a smile growing on his mouth before he said, "Tomorrow."

"Tomorrow," she parroted again, and hated herself for it.

CHAPTER ELEVEN

The bell rang over her head, a jarring sound against the quiet mountain morning. Tentatively, Miri stepped inside the small bakery nestled at the mouth of the lake.

"Good morning, Miri!" Joshua chirped merrily. "'Tis a lovely day!"

Miri could only nod, her nerves getting the better of her as she looked around the empty cafe.

"I've got pumpkin challah coming out of the oven in just a moment, if you're interested," Joshua went on.

"I—oh, yes," she said, turning to face him once more. She kept her hand on the knob of the door to stabilize herself. She didn't know why she was here. She didn't know why she was such a naïve fool. But he had asked her to meet him here. And after the events of last night, she wasn't sure why she had believed him.

But before she could stew on the subject any longer, she nearly toppled backward by the pull of the door, the bell ringing again over her head as she collided against a body, solid and sure.

She felt his chuckle against her ear as he said, "Good morning, Miri."

She stumbled, turning to face Ezra before making a complete idiot of herself. "I—sorry," she stammered.

His hands were surprisingly warm on her shoulders, considering the coolness of the morning, and he waited until she met his gaze. "Were you thinking of a quick escape?"

She took a breath before she said, "I was wondering whether or not I was a fool to come here."

He tilted his head to one side, knitting his brows together. "What made you decide to take the risk?"

"The absurdity of your request, I think."

At that, Ezra chuckled, a grin spreading wide across his mouth, accentuating the dimple on his right cheek. "I suppose I should forewarn you then. You see, I plan to ask you to breakfast tomorrow, too. And the day after that. And the day after that as well. But I didn't want to overwhelm you last night. So I only asked you for this morning."

"You want to have breakfast every day? With me?" The absurdity of it, the utter oddness that he hadn't asked her to come to his home last night. Or to some seedy inn. He had simply kissed her knuckles and bade her farewell, promising to meet her here at the bakery just after first light. And now he wanted to ensure that she met him every morning, apparently.

For breakfast.

And nothing more.

Ezra Kelach was perhaps the strangest man she had ever met.

"If it's all right with you, yes," he said, as simple as that.

With that, he offered her his hand and guided her further into the tiny bakery, accepting Joshua's offer of warm, steaming pumpkin challah. Winona followed behind, two mugs and a pot of steaming coffee in hand, bestowing a warm smile on them.

And so Miri joined Ezra for breakfast on the rooftop.

And she joined him for breakfast the next morning, too.

And every morning after that. For weeks.

A breakfast of unfettered, comfortable conversation. Perhaps a casual stroll down the lakeside promenade and then a sweet departure—a kiss to her hand or a soft brush of his fingers on her cheek—before he was off to tend to whatever he had to tend to as grand duke of Kinnereth and she was back to the temple for daily prayers vigils and tedious services celebrating this holiday or that sacred soul.

And never anything more than that.

It went on that way for weeks.

Their little routine became a comfort to Miri—she would meet him in the street and be greeted with a warm smile, Ezra would take her hand and guide her into the bakery and order their breakfast from a bright-faced Winona or a welcoming Joshua before they would make their way to the rooftop together. They would speak of their day—of anything they had discovered about the king or his plans for any unusual alliances with Medinah. On that front, their search had come up mostly short. But neither of them really minded, for every time they came up with nothing, it was an excuse to meet again the next day, hopefully with something new.

Breakfast with Ezra had become the best part of her day for the better part of a month. Scones and challah bread, rugelach and raisin cakes—Joshua and Winona had no shortage of imagination when it came to pastries, and they were eager to keep Ezra and Miri coming back every day. They often found themselves spending half the day on that little private rooftop, just talking. Sharing. Laughing. She found she enjoyed how easily Ezra could make her laugh, how easy their conversations were—as if they'd known each other a lifetime, instead of only a few months.

So it was with disappointment that Miri had woken this

morning, the first hints of autumn whispering on the cooler morning breezes, knowing that she wouldn't be indulging in any of those pastries with Ezra today.

"I had better go to council, Miri," Ezra had said yesterday. "Or I'm afraid they might kick me out."

"Can they do that?" she had asked around a mouthful of chocolate babka.

"No." Ezra had smiled. "But they can certainly give me Sheol about it. Which they do. Besides, I should be there. We've found next to nothing about the king's secret dealings with Medinah. Perhaps I can learn something."

He would only be gone for the day—Chesedelle City was no more than an hour's ride from the village of Shalem. But somehow, that one day seemed to be too much.

"And what am I supposed to do? Suffer the cook's breakfast?" Miri had teased. Though it wasn't much of a joke. The temple cook was less than skilled. Miri was always glad for an excuse to miss breakfast in particular—not only to avoid the girls, but to avoid the food, too.

"I'm sure Joshua and Winona would be more than happy to accommodate you, my lady." He had smiled again. And then he had kissed her hand. And as if that wasn't enough for him, before he walked away, Ezra had pulled her into his arms and held her tightly, resting his chin on the top of her head for a moment longer than she had expected. And then he had walked away without a backward glance.

And that was that.

"What's gotten into you?" Jordie asked, ripping Miri from her thoughts. The girls were gathered around the pathetic excuse for a table in the bottom of the temple, just off the kitchen, already tearing into their breakfast when Miri arrived.

"What?" Miri asked, finding a seat far away from Kata. They hadn't spoken one-on-one since Miri had found out Kata's secret.

That had been nearly a month ago. And their distance had been just fine with Miri. She wasn't sure if she ever *wanted* to speak with her friend again.

"Praise be. The *princess* has decided to join us," said Galina.

"You're in another world," Jordie went on.

"No, I'm not." Miri spooned some fruit onto her plate before taking a pastry from a tray. Chocolate challah. An image of Ezra laughing flashed through her mind—the way his golden eyes glittered, the way his rich voice could sound so free, so uninhibited.

She took a bite of the bread and was instantly disappointed. It wasn't nearly as rich or heady as Joshua's. In fact, it was a bit dry and bland. And the aftertaste was...strange. Earthy, almost.

Miri observed the bread in her hand, wondering why it tasted so pathetic in comparison to the little bakery in the village.

"What's your problem?" This came from Galina.

"Not the best challah I've ever had," Miri mused.

From down the table, Kata eyed Miri over her cup of tea, but said nothing. Miri ignored her.

"I'm used to it," said Jordie. "Cook puts it in our breakfast now. I'm sure it's some old wives' tale that it works best if it's in our belly for most of the day."

"If what's in our belly?" Miri asked.

"I've heard the cooks whisper," said Galina. "They think it's most potent about twelve hours after we take it. Which I say is ridiculous."

"And makes a rather imperious assumption that we're only busy at night," Jordie added with a knowing smirk.

Galina snickered with Jordie. Had Miri not been intent to understand what in Sheol they were on about, she might have marveled at the fact that Galina had shown even the slightest hint of camaraderie with any of them.

"Honestly, it's ridiculous that they think we don't know," Galina went on. "Virgins. That's what they think we are. Never had a man between our legs. And the proof is that we've never conceived."

"Fools that they think we are, I suppose it's still better than ending up stoned in the streets," Jordie added.

"I couldn't agree more," Galina said, lifting her cup of coffee before taking a sip.

"The herb?" Miri asked. She looked again at the bread in her hand and finally noticed it: tiny flecks of green throughout. "They're feeding us the herb?"

The herb.

In her breakfast.

In *all* of their breakfasts.

Phinehas wasn't on the herb. He didn't need to be.

Because *they* all were. The acolytes.

"How long have you known?" Miri asked, dropping the bread as if it were a hot branding iron.

"We're not supposed to know, remember?" Jordie said with a conspiratorial snicker.

"Jordie," Galina scolded. "Watch what you say, you stupid girl." The camaraderie of a moment before was gone now.

"Did you all know?" Miri asked. She looked down the table to Kata, whose face shone with that same apologetic embarrassment she had seen a month ago—when Miri had found out about her sleeping with Phinehas. About them *all* sleeping with Phinehas.

"Don't tell me you really didn't know, Miri," Galina mocked. "Or are you really that stupid?"

Miri pushed away from the table, throwing her napkin down before marching from the room.

She would just stop eating breakfast at the temple, that's all there was to it.

The thought that Phinehas would lie to her.

To her face.

Not only about the herb. But about the girls.

About everything.

It burned in her stomach.

She had hardly spoken to him—hardly even seen him in the last weeks. So wrapped up in her mornings with Ezra, Miri hadn't paid much attention to Phinehas. Or the goings on in the temple. And Phinehas had seemed to be fine with it, anyway. After all, hadn't he been the one pushing her to the grand duke? To learn his secrets?

She wondered what Phinehas would think if he knew she was using all of it as an excuse to see Ezra. To help *him*, not Phinehas. Though on that front, she had been little more than a sounding board for Ezra's wild theories about what the king was up to.

She wondered what Phinehas would do if he knew just how two-faced she really was.

But Phinehas had lied to her. Over and over. Lied to her about the girls. Lied to her about the herb. Lied to her about what she was to him.

Miri was seething with it all when Phinehas walked into her chamber.

"Bastard," she spat at him when he appeared.

Phinehas cocked his head to one side. "Pray, Miri. What seems to be troubling you, my darling?"

"Don't *my darling* me," she spat. "You lied to me!"

"Providence cannot lie. Neither can his holy man," Phinehas said matter-of-factly.

"You're a son of a bitch. Get out of my room," she growled, reaching for a book on her bedside table, lifting it over her head.

"Go ahead. I dare you," he said. "Hit me, Miri."

"I hate you!" she shouted, hurling the book towards him.

He did not flinch. Did not even move a fraction. The book missed him.

"Your aim was as terrible with your father," said the priest.

"At least he had the decency to tell me his treachery to my face!"

"Careful of your accusations, Miriam. You are slandering the king's man of Providence," said Phinehas, slithering towards her like a viper after a grouse.

"Stay away from me!"

Phinehas continued moving towards her with excruciating slowness. "Believe me, love. I would have stopped bothering with you a long time ago, if I could have."

"What is that supposed to mean?" she sneered, her breath heaving.

Still, Phinehas inched his way towards her. As if he would devour her.

"Tell me what you are hiding, Miriam."

"I don't know what you are talking about."

"I think you do," he said. And his words. His voice. They were so different from usual. Gone was his pious superiority. Here was Phinehas, the man she had met as a little girl. Even in her innocence, she had seen him for what he was. Even then.

A snake.

"Get away from me."

"Tell me what you're hiding," said Phinehas.

"Leave me alone, *Tomas.*" She hissed the name—his given name—as a reminder of who he was. And who he was *not*.

Tomas Augustus. A nobody from Nehar Province, born into a family of blacksmiths. He had seen an opportunity to elevate his status and taken it. Changed his name. His entire trajectory.

There were few in the world who knew Phinehas's past, much less his real name.

But Miri knew it. And she relished the look on his face when she reminded him of it.

Phinehas reached her, grabbing her wrists with effortless strength. "Be a good girl now," he said. "And tell me your secrets."

"*You're* the one with the secrets," she snarled, her heart practically pounding in her throat. "I know about the girls. I know about the herb. I know everything," she said, her words a growl in her throat. "Let go of me."

"You're *mine,* my darling," he said, pressing himself against her. Despite his thick robes, she could feel his desire, and disgust roiled in her gut. Phinehas licked the column of her throat, his breath a foul assault when he reached her mouth. She quickly turned away, pressing her lips tight, closing her eyes even tighter.

"Tell me your secrets, Miri," he said, even more demanding, his hands releasing her wrists. He did not let her go, however, pulling her to him with a strength that did not match his lanky form. One hand found her back, the other found her belly and moved downward with sickening slowness. When at last he reached the most intimate part of her, his fingers stopped, hovering. Even through the fabric of her skirt-pants, his hand burned her like a brand.

"Pity," Phinehas said, pressing his lips to her throat. "That you prefer trousers like a man. I rather dislike having to go on the hunt."

"Why do you think I prefer them, you bastard?" With that, Phinehas bit her ear so hard she cried out.

"Yes, my darling. Scream. See if your precious grand duke comes to help you."

Jealousy. It was jealousy she heard buried deep beneath Phinehas's words.

"I hate you," she said, hating even more how the declaration sounded more like a whimper than a fierce declaration of freedom.

"Perhaps," he said. "But you need me, don't you? You're a lost little girl who cannot find her way. You like to pretend like you're obedient. But you like it—the attention. You like the attention of His Grace. You like the attention from every man in the province, knowing they can't have you and wanting you all the more for it."

She hated him for that too. That he had used her. Made her his most prized whore. That he had promised a little girl the world and given a woman a cage of lies. A tear squeezed from her eye.

Phinehas's hand gripped her between her thighs so hard she cried out again, and with the help of his other hand, he ripped the billowy pants from her with little effort. She loathed the whimper that came from her as the bottom half of her clothing fell to the ground.

This time, his grip was against her bare skin. With her eyes shut tightly and her heart nearly pounding out of her chest, she waited, knowing what was coming.

"Tell me your secrets, Miri. I know you're hiding something."

She wondered if he had somehow found out about her promise to help Ezra. If he knew of their daily, candid conversations about the king. About him. Phinehas removed his hand from her back and gripped her chin so hard she wondered if she would bruise. He forced her to face him. "Look at me," he growled.

She refused.

"LOOK AT ME!" he shouted.

At last she opened her eyes. He held her with his menacing gaze, with the grip on her chin that stung, the green in his eyes like a viper's. "You have *nothing* without me. You *are* nothing without me." He gripped her so tightly she whimpered at the pain. "Never forget that, you fucking whore."

With that, he released her so violently, she toppled to the ground like a sack of potatoes, hitting the carpet with such force that her teeth sang and her cheek burned.

She did not hear him leave.

She woke startled, unsure where she was or what time of day it was.

"You've been asleep all afternoon," came a voice from not far away. She sat up abruptly to find Phinehas sitting at the foot of her bed, his shoulders slumped, his hair mussed, and his eyes red and swollen. As if he had been crying. He pushed a shaking hand through his hair, his other holding a glass with only a swallow of whiskey left in the bottom.

"What are you doing here?" she asked, pulling her knees to her chest. She felt hollow. Empty. A phantom pain lanced through her core, and a picture of that morning—Phinehas's hateful grip —flashed back into her mind. She swallowed back a lump in her throat.

"Miri," Phinehas said, his words cracking. "Oh, my sweet Miri."

Phinehas buried his face in his hands and wept.

Wept.

Miri watched him for a minute, wondering what to do. What to say. After a moment, she crawled towards him. The cool air kissed her bare legs, exposed from underneath her blankets. She covered herself when she reached him, placing a tenuous hand on his shoulder.

Phinehas wept harder.

She said nothing.

"Miri, I am sorry," Phinehas finally managed. "I cannot help it. When it comes to you, I cannot help it." He lifted his glass and swallowed the last of the amber liquid before letting it tumble to the carpet. The sound cut through the silence like rumbling thunder.

Miri's hand remained on his shoulder, and absurdly, she

watched it there. As if it were someone else's hand. As if she was not sure what the gesture meant. Comfort? Pity? Hatred?

Maybe all of them.

Phinehas at last looked up from his hands, his face stricken with a kind of grief she had never seen in him. But there were no tears in his eyes. None on his face, either. "I love you. That's why. You make me mad with love for you. I am mad with it. It's different with you. It always has been. And I am mad with it." He buried his face in his hands again, but Miri could not help but notice that there were still no tears, though it seemed as if he were trying to coax them.

"I wish that you loved me as much as I love you," Phinehas went on. "Then you would understand my madness. Then you would understand why I am the way I am. You would understand why I have to go to the other girls. Because I am sickened with need for you. And I try to satiate that need. I try, but I cannot. You've poisoned me Miri. You've poisoned me for other women. With your goodness and your strength and your beauty. You're a better person than I am, Miriam. You are stronger than I am."

"You are a good person, Phinehas," she heard herself say, surprised that she protested his words. He had rescued her, hadn't he? He had gotten her out of her home with a father who beat her and a mother who ignored it. He had gotten her out. He had given her a chance. A life. When she would have had nothing without him. "You are, Phinehas," she repeated. "You're a good person."

"I wish I were good enough for you," he said.

"You are," she said. For she hadn't known it—her effect on him. She hadn't realized how much he loved her. How difficult all of this must be for him, too. She'd had no idea. "You're good enough, Phinehas. I'm the one who's not good enough for you."

And she had betrayed him, hadn't she? She had ignored him. Pushed him away. When he obviously loved her madly. She had thought she was obeying his orders by spending all her time with

Ezra. Befriending him. But she couldn't remember why anymore. She couldn't remember the reason for any of it. And in the process, she had pushed Phinehas away. To madness.

"I'm sorry," she said. And she meant it. "Phinehas, I'm so sorry. It's all my fault."

Phinehas pulled her to him, resting his head on her shoulder, trembling as he wept in her arms and she in his.

It was all her fault. Everything. And she would do better.

CHAPTER TWELVE

For several days, Miri stayed in the temple. She remained mostly in her chamber, reading books or just staring into the empty hearth, offering paltry excuses to miss every prayer vigil or ceremony. For several days, she mulled it all over. What she had done to Phinehas.

What she had done to herself.

She would do better.

She *had* to do better.

She just didn't know what better was. She didn't know what Phinehas wanted. What she was doing wrong. Most of all, she didn't know what he had meant about her hiding something from him.

It was true that she had not lived up to her end of the bargain —she had helped Phinehas become high priest of Har-Navah. She had whored herself at his bidding to curry favor with the right people. And it had worked.

But she had not fulfilled the rest of their plan. Her father's plan. To use the tinge of Adelaidian blood in her veins as an excuse to go after the throne.

A queen on the throne with the high priest as king beside her.

She had het him be her savior...and offered nothing of worth in return.

She had let Phinehas's obsession with his appointment to the priesthood take center stage, hoping in vain that the rest would fall away into forgotten oblivion.

But it hadn't.

And once again, she had proven a woeful disappointment, an utter failure.

Would claiming the throne somehow prove her love? Her loyalty to him?

If so, she feared she would never be enough. For she could not find it within herself to care about that one thing Phinehas so desperately wanted.

She wondered what that said about herself. What that said about her love.

She did not know what to do anymore, her thoughts a mess in her mind—a confusing whirlwind of fear and sadness and disappointment and hatred and worry. She hated herself. She hated Phinehas. But in the same breath, she loved him. Of course she loved him.

And he loved her.

It was love between them.

Love.

The word clamored through her. A picture of quiet smiles and whispered promises and private laughs and hope. Love was hope.

Strange that she should feel so hopeless now.

She wondered if Ezra was back from council yet. She could not remember when he said he would return. Couldn't remember if she had promised to meet him for breakfast again or not. Everything was a blur—a mess of thoughts and worries. And what would she say to Ezra when she saw him again, anyway? Was it right to be his friend? Is that what they were?

Her thoughts remained a blur all day and into the evening. As she dressed for some dinner Galina had gleefully announced at the breakfast table this morning, she found she could hardly focus on her appearance, too distracted to care about pretty dresses and playing the part. She was glad to notice that the bruises on her chin were starting to wane, even if they were still quite sore—a gift from Phinehas's hateful grip. If he'd noticed that he had bruised her, he had said nothing when he had wept in penance before her.

But it didn't matter, did it? The hateful bruises on her face. The lingering ache in the places he had held with his unrelenting hands. She had deserved every bit of it.

"You look like you've seen a ghost."

Miri turned toward the source of the voice to find Kata standing beside her on the edge of the banquet room in the back of the temple. In silence, they watched the handful of nobles fill in around them. She did not know how to answer the friend she had all but ignored for weeks.

Just another person she had hurt. Had disappointed.

"Hey," Kata tried. Miri turned to face her. "Are you okay?"

"I'm fine," Miri lied, turning her attention back to the room. "What is the point of hosting a dinner for the ambassador anyway? Must we have the whole province around every time Phinehas so much as sneezes?"

"You don't know why we're here?" Kata asked the question as if Miri were the only person in the world who did not know the answer.

"Obviously," Miri said, not meaning to sound as harsh as she did.

Kata turned away again, folding her hands in front of her

pretty gown. And Miri noticed she looked beautiful tonight, her pale-pink dress a nice compliment to her soft skin and brown hair. Kata had always been the plainest, simplest of the girls. Then again, compared to Galina, they were all plain. But Kata had never really cared about the typical allure of an acolyte. She had cared more about a roof over her head. And she had been a willing enough acolyte that Phinehas had kept her around, despite her plainness—a fact he had pointed out often enough.

"Kata," Miri asked. Her friend turned her attention away from the crowd and back to Miri. "Why are you here?"

"What?"

"I mean, why did you come here? To the temple? To be an acolyte?" She found she needed to know. Needed to understand. What had brought someone like Kata to this place? To this life?

Kata seemed taken aback by the question. But just as she opened her mouth to give an answer, they were interrupted.

"You look beautiful tonight, Kata."

Jareth.

Miri was nearly flabbergasted that the sage had been so bold in his appraisal of Kata. But there was something in his eyes tonight. Something that seemed concerned. Perhaps he had good reason.

Miri had heard the rumors of the man who would be here tonight. She knew what they said about the Medinian ambassador. His reputation was that of ruthless cunning and unbridled brutality. Anyone who had interacted with the man had come away either terrified or loathing him. Was Jareth concerned that the ambassador was here? That Kata might be asked to accompany him this evening?

Kata, as usual, brushed him off. "Och," she said, and turned away from him.

Jareth nodded to Miri. "You look lovely too, Miriam."

"Thank you, Jareth," she said. And then the sage disappeared into the thickening crowd.

"Why do you ignore him?" Miri asked. "He's obviously smitten with you."

"No, he's not," Kata said.

"Yes, he is! It's obvious to everyone but you, Kata."

"Well, he's wasting his time," Kata said. And Miri wasn't sure why her friend was being so petty. Jareth wasn't bad looking. And he was kind. Why couldn't Kata see that?

"He's here," Kata said, her words haunted, her gaze fixed across the room. Miri turned, half hoping to see raven black hair and a dimpled grin...

But it was not Ezra across the room, and Miri was glad for it. It was wrong to be disappointed that he was not here. It was wrong to wish to see him.

"Who is that?" Miri asked, watching the man enter the room. He was round through the middle, rather like a giant grape. His mustache was perfectly waxed to curl on the ends, and he handed his top hat absently to a passing servant, revealing a thinning crown of brown hair.

"The ambassador," Kata said quietly.

"*That's* the ambassador?" Miri asked.

"Shhh," Kata scolded. "From Medinah. They say he is here on the king's bidding. That he comes to prepare us for a visit from the Empress."

"He looks like an overdressed grape," Miri said, surprised as he strutted his way into the room, all odd angles and ostentatious accessories. He did not look terrifying. He did not look like the horrible man he had been painted to be. If anything, Ambassador Phocas looked like a bloated billy goat, strutting about the room sampling treats and accepting every courteous nod as if he were the emperor of Medinah himself.

Every single swath of fabric on the man was of some fine, obnoxious make—a distasteful cacophony of silk and brocade and pinstripes and lace. Never mind his rotund form meant that there was enough fabric stretched across him to fashion a circus tent. He wore a watch tucked into the pocket of his brocade vest, its gold chain draped along one of his much too short legs. He bore a ring of sweat along his brow, despite the brisk early autumn evening. And he eagerly accepted every nod or bow or handshake offered, as if everyone here were lucky to be in his presence.

Miri resisted the urge to laugh at the caricature of a man. She wondered if Ezra knew he was here tonight—that he was preparing people for the arrival of the Empress. She wondered if Ezra had found out *anything* while sitting on the king's council.

The Medinian ambassador made his way through the room, extending his hand as noble after noble kissed his many rings. He smiled in a way that somehow felt both pleased and greasy—like a tinker might convince a woman of her unfailing beauty for the sole reason of selling her an overpriced bauble. Miri rolled her eyes.

"He's rather...ostentatious, isn't he?" Miri asked.

"I was going to say revolting," Kata said, and Miri chuckled. Kata chuckled with her. And for a moment, it felt like nothing stood between them. Like they were the friends they had always been.

"Are you ready?" Kata asked.

"Ready for what?"

Kata turned to face Miri. "You don't know?"

"What are you talking about?"

"Does anyone know where I can get some decent chocolate challah around here?"

The words were spoken from behind, not far from Miri's ear, and she startled, turning to find Ezra's smiling face. "Hello, Wildfire," he said, pressing a kiss to the top of her hand. "I missed you."

At that show of chivalry, Miri's heart pounded in her chest. She wondered what it said about her. Wondered more what her friend thought of it. Miri glanced at Kata from the corner of her eye. The acolyte watched the interaction with wide eyes, but said nothing.

Ezra did not let go of her hand but instead, laced his fingers through hers. He turned to face Kata, a glitter of amusement in his eyes as he said, "You must be Kata."

Miri's friend nodded in mute wonder. Her eyes slid to where Miri's hand rested in Ezra's, and she kept her gaze there as she said, "It's an honor, Your Grace." She dipped into a curtsey before she finally met Ezra's gaze again.

"It's just Ezra," he said warmly. "Miri has told me much about you."

Kata turned to Miri, eyes wide with question.

Ezra saved Miri from having to say anything. "All good things," he chuckled. "I am glad to meet you."

"The pleasure is mine, Your Gr—er, Ezra," she said, curtseying again.

"Has anything entertaining happened yet?" Ezra asked, gesturing to the ambassador bellowing a laugh on the other side of the room.

"Not yet," said Miri, looking at Ezra. He met her eyes and winked, pulling her a little closer to him with their joined hands until their shoulders touched. And she knew she shouldn't, but she leaned into him all the same.

Kata seemed to take that as some sort of cue. "I, uh, better find Jareth."

She dipped into one more curtsey before disappearing into the crowds without another word.

"Well, that was sufficiently awkward," said Ezra.

"Kata and I are—not exactly on normal terms at the moment," Miri said, before she thought better of it. For to explain would be to convey the horrible secret that was apparently not a secret—that Phinehas slept with all the girls. Likely always had.

And Miri still wasn't sure how to process that information. What to think of any of it.

"I gathered that," said Ezra. He ran his thumb along hers before he let go of her hand and said, "I have news to share."

"You do?" she asked.

He nodded, taking a moment to appraise Miri head to toe. There was nothing possessive in the way he looked at her, nothing greasy or unsettling. A sparkle found his eyes when he met hers again and said, "You are beautiful."

She immediately looked down to survey the dress she had absently chosen. It was a russet color that mimicked her hair in the candlelight. Not her best gown by any means. "I—didn't really pay attention. I just threw on a gown—"

"I wasn't referring to your gown, although it is lovely."

She looked away, disallowing herself to let that comment settle; to allow herself to enjoy it. "What news do you have?" she asked.

"Not here. We'll need to speak somewhere private."

She looked at him, to find a conspiratorial smirk threatening his mouth. And by it, she was transfixed—the way the light hit his lips, ever so softly pink in the candlelight. The smooth column of his neck peeking out from his black cravat. His sun-kissed skin, somehow even more golden in the muted light of the banquet room here in the temple. That one strand of raven hair that refused to be tamed, no matter how perfectly the rest of his hair complied. The way his eyes transformed from burnished gold to sunlight itself whenever he laughed or smiled. Beautiful. Truly, he was beautiful.

"There is something I want to show you." he said, effectively ripping her from her silent vigil.

She castigated herself. *Selfish. Traitor. Whore.* She was defying

Phinehas and obeying him all at the same time, wasn't she? To any casual observer, she was simply paying Ezra the attention Phinehas had bade of her. None knew the betraying thoughts that accompanied that attention. None knew the betraying gallop of her heart, either. She swallowed once, refocusing her thoughts. "What is it?"

"You'll have to come with me."

Ezra held out his hand between them. She looked down to it, hesitant to take it.

"Is it such a risk? My hand?"

"I'm trying to decide that," she admitted. If she went with him...

If she went with him, she'd be obeying Phinehas's orders. She'd be playing his games, just as he asked.

Just as she had promised him.

But Phinehas didn't know—couldn't know—how much she wanted it—to take that hand extended to her. To feel what she so often felt with Ezra—like a person. Like someone who mattered. Someone of worth.

She had promised herself to do better. To be better.

She wondered now who she had made that promise to —Phinehas?

Or herself?

"Have you ever taken a risk, Wildfire?"

"What exactly is it you want to show me?" she asked, looking up to him again. His eyes danced with humor.

And something else.

Something much deeper.

Ezra leaned in a fraction closer. His eyes darted to her lips before he said, "You'll just have to trust me."

"Miri!" Miri startled at the sound of her name, and whirled, keenly aware of Ezra at her back, to see Kata approaching them once more, a look of worry in her eyes. "He is asking for you."

"Who is?" Miri asked.

"Phinehas," Kata said, lowering her voice. "He wants to introduce you."

"Introduce me?"

Kata's eyes widened, as if she couldn't believe Miri was making her say it. "To the ambassador," she practically whispered.

Miri froze, finally understanding Kata's cryptic remarks tonight. Phinehas wanted to introduce *her* to the ambassador. *She* was to be the ambassador's companion. Ezra was not her only conquest, but the godsdamned Medinian ambassador too. She might not have realized she was still standing in the banquet room in the temple if not for the feel of Ezra's hand, which he slipped over hers. He squeezed once, as if to tell her she had a choice. As if to tell her there was another option than the tangled web of deception before her. She was to be the ambassador's companion. Had Phinehas had been planning this all along?

You like the attention from every man in the province, knowing they can't have you and wanting you all the more for it.

Had Phinehas allowed her that bit of distance from the other girls, that sense that she was something more, not because he wanted her for himself, but because he wanted to save her for his biggest challenges? They had moved to the northern province to be closer to the king, but also to be closer to Ezra—the grand duke. The second most powerful man in the kingdom.

Oh and he was close. Too damned close at the moment, his chest nearly pressed against her back, his heat so near that he might as well have been a branding iron. And that hand over hers...

Miri had been planted in Ezra's path from the very first moment. Bait.

And it had worked. Ezra had taken the bait easily.

Too easily. His thumb ran along the top of her hand as if he were confirming her thoughts.

And now Phinehas was moving her to more challenging prey, wasn't he? After all, if Phinehas could get the Medinian ambassador in his clutches, he'd as good as have the empress herself. And with Ezra, with the king, too... He'd have a virtual empire of his own design. All thanks to his most prized whore.

She didn't realize she was squeezing her hand shut quite so hard until Ezra ran his thumb along hers. The warmth of his body against her back consumed her. As if he could protect her from all of this.

As if he *would*.

He slipped his free hand around her waist but remained silent behind her.

"Miri?" Kata asked, sliding her wide eyes to Ezra's hand at Miri's waist. "You should not make him wait."

Absently, Miri leaned into Ezra, who was practically wrapped around her, his warmth a comfort she did not bother to deny. She shut her eyes for a moment to think.

Have you ever taken a risk, Wildfire?

No. She had not. Not once.

But it was no use. There was no way she could get out of this. There was no excuse she could make that would suffice. She was not free. Whether she believed it or not, whether she liked it or not, she was an acolyte.

A priest's whore.

And that's all she would ever be.

"I'll be right there," she finally managed.

At her declaration, Ezra's hand fell from her waist. He moved back a fraction, but even such a small absence was a chilling reminder of who she was. And who she was not.

Kata seemed satisfied and turned to walk away.

When Miri finally faced Ezra, there was a quiet disappointment on his face.

"What do I do?" she asked.

Ezra's disappointment melted into something conspiratorial, and he looked around them for a moment before he looked back at her. "Come with me. Right now."

"Right now?" she asked, looking around the room, half expecting Phinehas to be watching her every move. But he was nowhere to be found. Neither was the ambassador.

"Do you trust me?" he asked, extending his hand to her.

She looked down to that hand, considering the weight of the choice he offered so freely. Unwittingly.

"No," she said, wondering what he made of the lie. When she looked to his face again, she found a grin.

So she took that hand and ignored the pounding of her traitorous heart.

Ezra merely said, "Only truth between us, remember?"

CHAPTER THIRTEEN

Ezra wondered what to make of Miri's hesitation as he took her hand in his and guided her through the room and out a back door that led onto the narrow lawns that separated the back of the temple from the lake. She had been guarded tonight. Lost in herself. So at odds with the bright, vibrant woman he had come to know these weeks.

With his spare hand, Ezra put his thumb and his forefinger in his mouth and blew.

The whistle was so loud Miri startled.

"What do you think you're doing?" she scolded under her breath, though it was rather pointless to whisper, considering no one was out here with them. She soon understood his call, for a creature descended from the sky, landing in front of them with a bow.

"It's a…"

"His name is Ahadah," he said with a smile when she could not finish her sentence.

The dapple gray winged stallion almost looked like starlight in the darkness. Ezra had always loved that about him. His black mane tossed lazily in the lakeside breeze, and he fluttered his wings once, as if shaking off any dust from their ride here. Miri stepped toward him in awe.

"May I pet him?"

"Of course," Ezra said, stroking the horse's soft mane. "But we better leave quickly."

As if she had forgotten they were escaping from an assignment she so clearly did not want, Miri looked over her shoulder, worry shining in her captivating emerald eyes. In that gown, with her fiery curls and those piercing eyes, she looked like autumn itself. Fitting, he thought, considering the season was upon them, the nights turning cooler, the mornings brisker.

He used her worry as an excuse to pull her into his arms. He hoisted her onto the back of the stallion without asking, settling behind her and wrapping his arms securely around her middle.

"We're actually going to—fly?" she asked.

"That's the idea," he said.

"I—I don't know how."

"Well, I do," he said. With a nudge from his heel, the horse extended his wings and took off into a canter across the lawn, straight for the lake.

When the horse did not slow, Ezra could feel Miri's body tense against his. He smiled and pressed a kiss to her cheek. "I thought you said you wanted to fly?"

She reached to grip the horse's mane, but Ezra stopped her. "He doesn't like that."

"What am I supposed to hold on to?" she pleaded.

Ezra laughed. "I've got you, Wildfire. I promise."

He pulled her closer to him, resting his chin on her shoulder. Without hesitation, the old stallion leapt into the air and soared over the lake, the world quickly shrinking beneath them. Soon the great breadth of Lake Yerah was little more than a swath of silver, the mountaintops their companions as they soared dangerously close to the clouds that dotted the night sky. Above them, the stars glittered like a thousand fireflies. Below them, the village glimmered with lantern light, as if they suddenly found themselves deep in the heavens.

Miri could not seem to find words, but he could see the delight in her eyes and feel it in the way her body relaxed into his.

"John Junior had the same reaction," Ezra said, relishing the feel of the night wind on his face.

"What? Horror?"

He laughed and said, "I was going to say trepidation that soon turned to awe, but your description is much more colorful."

"I'm so glad I remind you of your nephew," she said flatly.

Ezra laughed again, loving the feel of her back pressed against his chest. "You most certainly do not remind me of him. Though you are gripping my arms as tightly as he did."

Her hands relaxed a little. "Where are we going?" Her words were difficult to hear over the din of the wind as it raced past them.

"To one of my favorite places."

"I thought the mountainside with the horses was your favorite?"

"It's one of them. This is another place I grew up coming to. You can't reach it, except by winged horse."

"You've had this horse since you were a boy?" she asked, turning her attention from the glorious view to the beast carrying them through the skies.

"Longer than that, I'm afraid," he said.

"How old is he?" she asked.

He was afraid she might ask that. When he did not answer immediately, she asked again, "How old is he, Ezra?"

"We're not sure," he admitted. "But probably somewhere around eight centuries."

"Eight *centuries!*" she exclaimed in shock. The horse startled at her outburst, losing altitude for a moment before composing himself again. Miri's grip was a vice on Ezra's arms. He found he did not mind in the least.

"Shhh," he laughed. "Give or take, yes."

"What do you mean give or take?"

"He is a foal of Eagle, Queen Adelaide's mount. It is believed he was born some two hundred years after the Great War."

"You put me in the air on the back of an...*an old man!*" she grumbled.

Ezra laughed. "He's actually not terribly old for his kind."

"You just told me he's probably eight hundred years old. That's old, Ezra," she said flatly.

"Fair enough. But he's more than capable. Aren't you having fun?"

She looked around again, at the valley below, the little homes that glittered here and there, and at the mountains that towered around them. Most who rode in the skies for the first time were either too sick to remember it or too terrified to look. But Miri just marveled at the view as if she'd flown a thousand times. It made Ezra admire her more.

"It *is* beautiful," she admitted serenely.

Ezra took one of her hands, pulling it to his mouth for a kiss before he extended it along his. With the back of her hand to his palm and her arm outstretched along his, they let the wind beat against them as they flew. And Miri turned her hand this way and that, playing with the wind as if she had wings of her own.

The wind did not cooperate with the knot of hair on top of her head, and soon those curls of hers were loose and wild, as if they too wanted a taste of the skies. Providence help him, he was jealous of the wind as if it ran its fingers through her hair.

"Sorry," she said, attempting to pull her curls away.

"Don't," he said, stopping her. "I like it."

"You're insane," she said, but she did not attempt to pull her hair back up.

Thanks to the impossibly swift speed of his companion, they soon reached their destination—a corner of the mountain forest so remote that it was impossible to reach by foot. Ezra had discovered it one afternoon by accident as a boy, flying over these mountains on this very horse. It had soon become his favorite hideout —a wilderness to rule all on his own. He had wanted to bring Miri here ever since he had taken her to the mountainside to watch the winged horses. Partly because he wanted to show her its beauty, but mostly because he wanted to share with her everything that mattered to him. And the moment he had realized that was the moment he'd realized what she was becoming to him.

And he hadn't been able to return to her fast enough.

Ahadah landed with easy grace deep within a forest clearing, surrounded by a thicket of conifers on the mountainside. Even with the darkness of night all around them, the stars and moon spread pale silver light through the mountain forest, casting shadows hither and thither in shimmering patterns. Ezra slid off the back of the stallion and turned to reach for Miri, who was already dismounting without hesitation. He took hold of her waist anyway, and she did not stop him.

A dark part of him knew that she could be playing Phinehas's games—that maybe she had agreed to come with him not out of a desire to spend time with him, but because she knew she had him in her spell. But he hoped that maybe she had come for a different reason. He hoped that spark in her eyes had been born from somewhere genuine, that she was here with him, in this place of his childhood, because she wanted to be. Because she wanted the risk he spoke of.

Because she was ready to turn the key to the cage she had made for herself.

"Didn't you tell me you have news?" she asked, adjusting her crisp cinnamon skirts before she began finger-combing her hair.

"I do," he said, mesmerized by her fingers as she worked them expertly through her thick curls. Each strand pulled taut, revealing the long length of her hair before bouncing back to a tight, glossy curl. He wondered what she would do if he offered to help, knowing damn well he would be no help at all as he explored those exquisite locks of hers.

"Well?"

Ezra smiled, focusing his attention on the conversation again. "I'm afraid it's not what you might think."

"What does that mean?"

Ezra took her hand and began guiding her along the mountainside, through the dense forest. Pine needles and fallen sticks crunched beneath their feet as they made their way through the trees.

"There is a treaty in the works between Har-Navah and Medinah. I know that for certain. But aside from confirming it, I know nothing more."

"Nothing?" she asked a bit disappointedly. He did not fail to notice how she trusted him when he guided her over roots or stones—how she took his hands and let him lead her without hesitation. A satisfied smile crept onto his mouth.

"Not really," he said. "The king knows how to keep his secrets."

"I thought you said you had *news*," she said, and at her disdain, Ezra chuckled.

"I do. There is a prophet."

"A prophet?" she asked. But at the question, her countenance shifted. As if this was not the first she had heard of a prophet.

"He is coming to Kinnereth. To Shalem, actually."

"Why in the world is that news?" she asked curiously.

"Because," he said, turning to face her. He took hold of both of her hands and guided her over a particularly gnarly root. Her skirt snagged on a knot, and Ezra crouched to release it, revealing a sliver of her smooth leg in the process. He swallowed and willed himself to focus on the conversation at hand. "He's causing an uproar. Apparently, he speaks against the king. And the whole government."

Which included the Sanhedrin. And Phinehas.

Ezra stood again.

"Insurrection?" she asked quizzically.

"No," Ezra said. "Something much worse."

Her brows furrowed, and a small freckle near her nose crinkled with the movement, looking for all the world like her face had been flecked with cinnamon. Ezra wondered if that freckle tasted of the spice.

"What is worse than insurrection?" she asked.

"Reason," said Ezra. Unable to help himself, he ran a finger along her jaw. But with the movement, he noticed a faint discoloring on her chin. Like—like a *bruise.*

Something within him froze as cold as ice.

"What happened to you, Miri?"

Miri turned away, stepping around him now that her skirt had been freed. She walked a few steps before he followed her.

"Miri," he tried again. She was bruised. And he could think of only one person who would do that to her—

"Why does it matter if some no-name prophet is visiting Shalem, speaking against the king?" she asked, tearing him from his thoughts—from the many reasons he was building in his mind to kick the priest's ass. Ezra took a moment to regain his senses before he spoke.

"Well, it wouldn't, except that Phinehas is here," he said. "And as newly appointed high priest, Phinehas has made it quite clear to the Sanhedrin that he will not let anything or anyone threaten him or his position."

"He has?" she asked, facing him again. It was genuine surprise on her face.

He did not know what to tell her. How to convey the truth to her without it looking like he was trying to turn her against the priest. He did not know how to tell her of the threats his own household had received. Promises of ruination from so many of his fellow councilors—not only of Ezra but of Esther as well—should he fail to support the priest's rise to power. His grandparents' deaths had not been the only reason he had steered clear of that brood of vipers this last year.

But even worse, most of Phinehas's supporters had powerful wives in the village—women who had slept with Phinehas in exchange for favors. Money. Promises of power. The list of bribes was extensive. John had uncovered enough to accuse any man of extortion. But Phinehas was not just an ordinary man. He was high priest. Something far more powerful and cunning, indeed. And certainly not someone to be accused without concrete evidence.

And since Ezra had had no wife to seduce, Phinehas had attempted to seduce Ezra in other ways.

With Miri.

The irony, of course, was that it worked. Ezra had taken the bait. He knew that Phinehas's game was simple: with one word of fealty to the priest, Ezra could have all of Miri he wanted.

But Ezra had no interest in making Miri his mistress. He had no interest in using her like a pawn in these games of kings and then moving on when the lure wore off.

He wanted something else. Something far more dangerous. And it both thrilled him and scared the Sheol out of him.

But by wanting her, he was playing right into Phinehas's hands.

"Ezra?" Miri asked, drawing him away from his train of thought.

He looked up, and seeing the concern in her eyes, he stepped towards her on instinct.

"How has he made that clear, Ezra?" she tried again.

Ezra took hold of her waist. "I don't want you to worry. I will keep you safe."

Miri looked down in lieu of a response. He watched her worry those delicate fingers, trying not to think too long about how her hands felt in his. How he had come up with flimsy excuses to hold her hand too many times to count.

"Why?" she asked, the question so quiet he almost missed it.

"Why what?"

"Why keep me safe? Why do you care?"

Ezra wasn't sure how to answer, where to begin. He lifted her chin so that he might meet her eyes. The moonlight glinted off of her skin, and he could see the marks on her again, dark smudges just far enough apart to have been made by a finger and thumb. Most certainly bruises.

Something within him went very cold and very still.

He moved his hand to cup her cheek and willed himself not to let his thoughts carry him off.

"What's wrong?" she asked, and he marveled at how well she could read him.

"Are you all right, Miri?" he asked.

"I'm fine," she said brightly. Too brightly. And with the practiced inflection, he knew for certain she was not all right. Not at all. He could have ripped the world apart for the subtle tremble in her fingers alone.

"Has something happened?"

She did not answer but looked away, towards the thick forest waiting for them just beyond the ridge.

"What is that?" she asked suddenly, pointing towards the forest.

Ezra turned to see what had caught her eye.

"Is that..." she started.

"A stag," Ezra finished, in wonderment as much as shock.

The stag was formidable—twice, maybe thrice the size of a normal buck. Maybe more. White as snow in the moonlight, with antlers that towered over him like the forest canopy. But it was not his size or splendor that held Ezra fast. It was his eyes. Even from this distance, Ezra could see them.

Evergreen.

Richer than the forest around them. And brighter. Like emeralds kissed by the sun. His eyes pinned Ezra to the forest and held him there. Beside him, Miri stood still as a statue.

The stag did not move as he watched them. But he did not seem afraid or even on alert. On the contrary, the stag seemed as if he wanted their attention, *wanted* them to see him.

"The stag is at hand," Miri whispered.

"What?" Ezra asked, turning his attention from the majestic beast not twenty paces ahead.

"The færies—that's what they told me," she said, her eyes fixed on the beast.

"You speak with færies?" Ezra asked, half amused, half in awe.

"They're sort of my friends," Miri said, as if conversing with færies were normal. "I used to build houses for them when I was a little girl. To give them a place to hide from owls and hawks. But my father wasn't too fond of them."

"Why not?" Ezra asked.

Miri only shrugged. "He said it was childish to build them. Though I never understood that, considering I *was* a child when I built them. He always tore them down when I wasn't looking."

"Your father tore down your færy houses?" He was sure he had heard her wrong. Sure that no father could be so callous. Even his own father, as stern as he was, would never have done such a thing.

Miri only shrugged. "Like I said, he thought they were childish. But I always rebuilt them anyway. I didn't care what he thought. They were my friends. I suppose they still are. They visited me. Not long ago."

"You were visited by færies?" he asked. He hadn't heard of færies interacting with humans since the stories of the days of King Ferryl. That they would visit Miri...

"Yes," she said. "They came to me at the temple. And they told me the stag is at hand."

"The stag," Ezra parroted, unsure what to think.

"What do you think it means?" she asked.

"I don't know," he admitted, turning his attention back to the snowy white buck with antlers like trees sprouting from his proud brow.

"I've seen him before."

"You have?" Ezra asked, surprised.

"When I was a child," she said.

The stag turned and walked away from them, but he looked back just once, as if he wanted them to follow.

Miri and Ezra did, without a word. As if it were normal to follow glowing, ethereal stags into thick mountain forests.

"Is this what you brought me here to see?" she whispered.

The stag traversed the steep mountainside effortlessly. Miri and Ezra, on the other hand, had a bit of a time navigating the boulders and trees, not to mention the incline. Over a particularly jagged boulder, Ezra lifted Miri as he said, "No. Just this forest. There is a small pool not far where I used to swim."

"You've never seen the stag before?" she asked.

"Never," he said. "I've seen many deer in these forests over the years. But never that one." He would have remembered such an animal. He was fairly certain he would never forget it.

The stag trekked farther inward, deeper into the forest and closer to where Ezra knew the pool was hidden between the rocks and trees. Something whizzed past Ezra's ear, and he shooed it away on instinct. Miri noticed the movement, but said nothing, her eyes too wide with awe.

The trees were not as Ezra remembered them. Well, they were the same trees. But there was something different about them now. They were bigger, perhaps. Taller. More lush.

But that wasn't all of it. There was something else here. From the corner of his eye, Ezra saw something fly past Miri in a whirl of color and wind.

"Færies," she whispered.

Færies.

Never—not once, had Ezra ever encountered a færy in this forest. Not in all the years he had been coming here as a boy, to hide from his family and his life. And as a man, to do the same. To think. To recharge.

Never once had this forest felt...magical.

He looked around to see there were now many færies filling this forest—bobbing like fireflies among the trees and vegetation. Hundreds of them, in every color he could name and some he could not. They flitted about the leaves and branches, mingling as if in greeting. Yet they all followed the same path, flying inward, the same direction he and Miri now walked.

As if summoned.

Following the white stag, they soon reached the hidden pool. Surrounded on all sides by towering pines and shimmering aspens, the small mountain lake seemed to glow in the starlight, reflecting the stars with crisp perfection, despite the canopy of branches that nearly obscured the skies. Animals of all kinds prowled the edges of the water—squirrels and chipmunks, birds and bear cubs. Beneath the glassy water, and despite the darkness, they watched brightly colored fish swim in merry trails, excited by something. As if their own curiosity had brought them here.

Or perhaps as if they too could not avoid the lure of the stag who now stood on a boulder on the opposite shore, his pure reflection like moonlight spilled over the surface of the waters beneath him. Ezra wondered if his glow was actually moonlight... or magic.

And at the center of the pool, something Ezra could not explain floated above the waters. Something he had never seen before. It was...

"An island?" Miri said in awe. "You brought me to see a floating island?"

No. He hadn't brought her here to see a floating island. Because there had never been one here before. But there it was now, hovering above the waters, a small island, barely big enough for the lone tree that grew on it. A chalam tree, if memory served him. He had read about them in the story books. So few remained here in Har-Navah—the result of over-harvesting and greed. But here it was: a chalam tree standing tall and perfect, growing from the floating, impossible island beneath it. Its roots hung like veins from the bottom of the island, reaching out for the waters below. Its leaves shimmered and glowed, golden and bright despite the night. And even from here he could see the glittering fruits in its boughs. Hundreds of them. Just begging to be plucked and devoured.

"Look," Miri said, tearing Ezra's gaze from the tree island. "A bridge!"

Ezra followed her around the rocky edge of the pool to find that sure enough, just on the other side, a bridge of grass and rocks connected the island to the land, floating above the water in an arc of lush flora.

"Let's go!" she said, collecting her skirts and practically running around the pool's jagged edge. Ezra followed her on instinct, unsure what to think. This forest was nothing like it had always been. As if it had been invaded by the deepest, richest magic possible.

The stag on the opposite boulder watched them in silence. He did not flinch as they moved closer. When Miri reached the arched land bridge, shestepped onto it without trepidation.

"Wait," Ezra said.

Miri slowed, facing him.

"Are you sure it's safe?"

"Of course not!" She beamed. "Why should that stop us?"

Something was different about Miri here. There was a lightness to her that he had not seen on the edge of this forest only moments ago. Lifetimes ago.

She made effortless purchase on the grassy bridge with those lithe limbs of hers. He followed her, a little less fearless as she, but still he made it with ease.

She climbed onto the small island that did not move, did not give to their weight. As if some invisible force held it aloft, suspended midair. She reached toward the chalam and plucked the lowest hanging fruit from its bough. She turned to face him before she took a bite. Her face glowed with the light from the fruit, and her eyes lit like a thousand stars as she bit into its soft flesh. The juices dripped from her chin as she handed Ezra the fruit.

"I think there's a story about this." Ezra smirked. "Isn't this forbidden?" He held the fruit, inspecting it as it glowed in his hand.

"That's another tree and another fruit." Miri laughed. "This is the chalam, Ezra. The *dream tree.* It's a gift to us from Providence."

And then he remembered it—the story of King Ferryl and Queen Adelaide. Before he was a king. Before she inherited her throne. When they were young and innocent. The chalam they shared. And the destiny that awaited them.

Ezra looked to Miri once more, captivated by the smile on her rosy mouth. Taken in by the hope that shone in her emerald eyes.

So he took a bite, marveling as the fruit washed down his throat—the pleasant, sugary warmth it left in its wake.

"You're glowing," she laughed.

"So are you," he said.

She took the fruit from his hand and took another bite. Then another. She handed it back to him, and he did the same. They passed the golden snack back and forth until it was gone. Until nothing but a glowing pit remained.

"Should we keep it?" she asked, eyeing the seed in her fingers.

Ezra took it from her, kissed it once, and folded it in her hands. "Absolutely."

Miri tucked the seed into the bodice of her gown and turned her attention to the shimmering waters beneath them. She sat down on the lush grass of the island, letting her feet dangle off the edge.

"Was it always like this?" she asked.

Ezra looked around, noticing even more about this place around them. The vines that curled up the branches of the trees. The riotous flowers that burst forth. The butterflies that flitted about. And færies—færies on every branch. Every bloom. Glowing almost as brightly as the stag that watched them from not far away. This place was like a dream. And nothing like he remembered.

"No," he finally managed. "It was just a forest."

"What does it mean? Why is it like this?" she asked.

"I don't know," he admitted. When he looked again at the stag on the stone, he couldn't help but wonder if perhaps the creature knew.

Or was the reason. For all of it.

"Did you ever swim in it?" Miri asked, looking down at the pool beneath them.

"All the time," Ezra said with a smile.

Miri offered her own smile—so rich and lush that Ezra

wanted to pull her to him and kiss that smile just to see how it tasted. To see if it was as captivating to touch as it as to witness.

And then without a word, she fell.

Miri flung herself over the edge of the island, falling into the pool beneath, her wild curls following as if she were aflame. She hit the water without a splash.

And did not surface.

CHAPTER FOURTEEN

Galaxies.

Clouds of impossible color—amethyst and amber, cerulean and emerald. Flowing through the blackness like swaths of the finest silk, mingling and entwining in impossible patterns. Ribbons of ethereal, prismatic color that defied definition. And then there were the stars.

Endless, endless stars.

Glittering blankets of stars. Stars that sparkled. Stars that shimmered. Stars that shone as bright as a candle in the darkness, and stars that seemed to flicker like fireflies in a summer twilight. Stars that anchored the churning blackness, and stars that streaked across the sky as if chasing a lover.

Miri had hit the pool without feeling it. And instead of finding herself in black waters, she had found herself in the night sky.

No, not the night sky.

The heavens. Firmament. Another world. A world beyond worlds. Between them. Some distant part of her knew that she could spend the rest of her days here and never take it all in. Or she could spend a century staring at only one star and never uncover all of its secrets.

In the span of a breath, Ezra appeared not far from her, the same look on his face that she imagined was on hers. Awe. Wonder. Unfettered joy. He looked around, the stars reflecting in his eyes and lighting them like flames. His inky hair was nearly obscured by the black night around them, but the starlight flickered off of the glossy strands here and there, bringing it to life like quicksilver.

His gaze finally landed on her, and he held her frozen in the firmament for a moment. Then he moved, floating towards her, like swimming through the sky, moving his arms and legs in graceful tandem. He glided effortlessly through the night that was not a night.

"Where is this?" she asked, knowing a sweet thrill as he came nearer.

His arms came around her, two solid branches of an oak tree that encircled her as he pulled her close. So close that their bodies touched, their legs entwined. He was solid and he was warm and he was beautiful. She smiled, a thrill rushing through her as his arms closed around her. A contented smile found his mouth as he said, "I think the better question is *what* is this?"

She tilted her head to one side in a question. Ezra took it as an invitation and pressed a languid kiss to her neck. His breath was warm on her skin, and gooseflesh spread across her as she sighed at his touch.

"Don't you feel it, Wildfire? This is magic."

"Magic," she breathed.

"Magic," he repeated. Kissing his way up her neck to her chin, he kissed the bruises she had been given only a few days ago. A lifetime ago. A tingling sensation crawled under her skin. "Truth," he said, eyeing her chin. He lifted a hand to her face, running a featherlight finger along the bruises. And she knew what was happening—she knew without having to see it that his touch was healing her.

"Truth," she said softly. Yes. She could feel it. The truth in this place. The truth in Ezra. The absence of fear. Of doubt.

Only magic here.

Only Truth.

So she told him the truth. "I want you to want me, Ezra. I want you to love me."

"Well, you're in luck, my beautiful Wildfire," he said. And then his lips found hers.

His kiss was soft. Gentle. Like lapping waves on the shore of a mountain lake. But then she felt his mouth open, she felt him taste her, and she was consumed. She was claimed. Marked.

Never. Not once had she been kissed like this. A kiss—a promise. Magic in and of itself.

Somewhere—somewhere else she was someone else, the memory of it on the edge of her mind, like a feather tickling her skin. Somewhere else, she was afraid and she was unworthy and she was lost.

But here, she was beautiful. And she was worthy. And she was loved. Loved by this man. Wholly. Completely.

Here, she was home.

He relinquished her lips and found her eyes, searching them for a moment, a hand cradling her head when he said, "I love you, Miriam Sasson."

She grinned widely, at a loss for what to say. Something must have been amusing about her reaction, for Ezra laughed delightedly and kissed her again.

"Why was I afraid? I cannot remember," she said, breaking the sweet kiss. "Why am I no longer afraid?"

"Because there is no fear in love," he said.

She looked around, finding easy comfort in the strong arms around her—as if they had always been around her. Keeping her safe. The stars glittered in the blackness, winking here and there as they passed through clouds of firmament. Colors so vibrant they seemed impossible. A star streaked across the sky, so close she might have been able to touch it had she been fast enough. She reached out her hand anyway. And that's when she spotted it...and Ezra spotted it too. Bringing her hand between them, Ezra traced a thumb along her palm—along the vines and whorls of color and light that had appeared there.

"Magic," he said. "You have magic, Miri."

"It was a gift," she said, the secret she had held so tightly somehow on the edge of her tongue. As if she had been bursting to tell Ezra. To share with him this truth too. "My cousin gave it to me. When I was young."

"Your cousin gave you magic?" Ezra asked as he traced his fingers delicately along her hand, watching as the magic reacted to him—curling around him like a cat at his master's feet. Entwining in his fingers as if the magic knew him. Knew his touch. His tender kindness. His gentle love.

"I don't know why," she admitted.

The magic in her hand grew from her palm like a spring sapling, curling around Ezra's fingers and wrist, lighting his whole hand with the same wonder. Not divided, but multiplied. The magic multiplied between them.

"Shouldn't it diminish?" she said.

"Magic never diminishes, my love," he said. "It only grows. And when there is love, it flourishes."

"Why? Why me? I don't understand why my cousin gave this to me."

"I do," Ezra said, meeting her eyes again. "You have a destiny, Wildfire. You're to set the world ablaze."

"What does that mean?"

"I don't know, but I can feel it. I know it in my bones. As if I've always known it."

She felt it then, the twinge in her heart. The wishing that—

"I will," he said, as if it were perfectly normal to read her thoughts. To know her heart so thoroughly. "I will be with you. I'm a part of it too. We have a destiny. Weaving in and out. Together and apart and then together again."

She felt a tear fall from her eye, its warmth sluicing down her cheek. Ezra leaned in and kissed it away. Kissed another tear as it fell down her cheek.

"I don't want to leave this place," she admitted, basking in the warmth of his breath on her skin, the strength of his arms around her. "I don't want to go back."

"We must go back," Ezra said, and at that, she looked at him again. "This is not our calling. Not here. It is only a taste, my love. But there is a secret. Can you hear it?"

She shook her head, hating that she could not hear whatever it was he could hear.

"We get to keep it," he went on, pressing a soft kiss to her brow and running his strong hands along her back. "We get to take it with us. The magic. It's ours. A gift. If only we will take it."

They floated in the sparkling abyss, entwined in each other's arms. Her skirts floated lazily around them like a blanket of silk. Ezra's body was warm and solid against hers, holding her with gentle surety. She shut her eyes, taking in the smell of him— somehow more vivid here. He was like a mountain breeze. Like a sunrise bursting past a snowy peak. The mountains were a part of him. As if all his years here had shaped him, molded him into who he was. Awe and beauty and splendor, but upon closer inspection —a strength that towered above the rest. A quiet surety of his own formidable power.

Ezra was unlike anyone she had ever known.

And he loved her. Even if he hadn't just told her, she could feel it here. She could see it in the way he looked at her, feel it in the way he held her. He did not hold her with lust in his eyes and greed in his touch like so many before him. Ezra held her with something else. Something she had not known before. Something deep and sweet and gentle and powerful.

And in a quiet place within her—a place untouched, slumbering for so long, she knew the truth of it. A wrecking sort of truth that held and shattered. That thrilled and consoled.

"I love you, too, Ezra," she said. And it was Truth. Shimmering and glittering Truth. Every word of it.

His smile was languid and easy. He brushed his lips against hers. "I know," he said, and then he kissed her savagely. Hungrily. Not with greed or possession. But with a surety that colored every brush of his fingers along her body and every move of his lips with hers.

She did not know how long he held her there, kissing and touching and coaxing something from her that she had never experienced. Maybe it was moments. Maybe hours. Maybe a dozen lifetimes.

She did not care. She had no desire to leave this place—wherever they were. She would stay here in weightless abandon, wrapped in his arms for a thousand centuries and then a thousand more after that.

And then she was consumed with a sudden hunger to give him every part of her. To remove the barriers between them and show him just how much she had meant it, that love she felt.

She moved her arms, sliding them up his solid chest until they were circled around his neck. She played with the dove-soft hair at his nape and brushed featherlight kisses along his jaw, relishing the feel of his stubble on her lips.

Ezra ran his hands down her back and cupped her backside, lifting her to him, fitting her against him like a puzzle. She obliged and wrapped her legs around him, her skirts suddenly heavy and bothersome between them.

He kissed her again, and she smiled at the hunger in it. Up to this moment, Ezra had been nothing but unhurried. Gentle. Now he was a dam breaking under the weight of a mighty river. His hands worked her up and down, exploring and teasing. His lips were a poem, spouting sonnets along her skin as he coaxed every last bit of fear from her until she was supple and willing in his arms.

Still, she could feel it—how careful he was. How mindful of every move he made, every touch. A cherishing sort of reverence. That even here, in this place where the past was forgotten, he was eager to protect her. To guard her. Even here, he would make sure she felt safe.

The irony, of course, was that his gentle reverence only coaxed a wilder hunger within her. His concern only stripped her bare. So she pulled away from his kiss and took in a breath to speak—to grant him every permission—

She startled, sucking in a breath and grabbing Ezra closer.

"What is it?" he asked, sudden worry in his golden eyes.

"The shore," she said, pointing behind him. He turned them, their weightlessness in the abyss like spinning a swath of silk in a pond. Her hair trailed behind her, her curls spilling slowly around her face, as if suspended in honey.

She could see the demarcation line between this world and the other. As black as night, it blended with the sky around them, except for its soft movements, a bit like the ripples of a lake just after a stone hits the surface. But it was getting farther and farther away. They were drifting farther and farther from one world into the next. Ezra looked over her shoulder, to the expanse behind them. An abyss of stars and colorful clouds, galaxies and great, streaking stars.

"Do you suppose it ends?" she asked, following his gaze.

"No," he said without hesitation, his eyes fixed on the infinite sky beyond them. "His magic has no end."

"Are you afraid?" she asked.

He met her eyes again, searching hers in earnest before he spoke. "I was, Miri. Back there," he said, nodding towards the demarcation behind them. "But here, I see it. I see it so clearly."

"What do you see?"

He ran his hands along her back, pressing a kiss to her brow, then to her chin. "I see you, Miri. I see all of you. I see us. And I see what's meant to be."

"What is meant to be?" she asked, wondering why she could not see so clearly what Ezra apparently understood.

"This," he said, kissing her once and softly, enclosing her more securely in his arms. "Us. You are mine, Wildfire. And I am yours."

She could see that. And here, with all that fear gone, all that trepidation, she could see that it had always been so. From the moment she had met him, she had been his. Even before that. She could see her life leading to here—to this place. This time. This person. She had wanted to be his. She had never wanted anything more.

"What do we do from here?" she asked.

Ezra's gaze returned to the border between the firmament and the real world that awaited them. "We take it with us," he said wistfully. "The magic. And we never let it go."

She landed on the lakeshore, a little out of breath. A second later, Ezra landed beside her, equally winded. She looked at him, looked back to the pool, then back to him again.

He was dry.

As dry as a bone.

As if he hadn't just climbed out of the water.

And she...she was dry too! Not a drop anywhere!

"Did you swim?" she asked him.

"I—I don't remember," he said. "Did you?" He looked her over as if he were just now realizing their impossible dryness.

"I think so. I jumped in, didn't I?"

"Yes. And I jumped in after you."

She sat up on the shore, which was mostly rocks and boulders. They had landed on a particularly large boulder that jutted out over the waters. "What happened after that?" she asked.

"I don't remember," he said. "Do you?"

She only shook her head, turning her attention back to the placid water. Then she remembered it—the ethereal stag who had stood in silent vigil over them.

"Where is he?" she asked. "Where is the stag?"

Ezra looked around, too. "He must have left."

She looked back to Ezra. Heart pounding, she admitted her thoughts. "It's him, isn't it? The Promised One."

Ezra nodded, a little wide-eyed. "The time has come."

CHAPTER FIFTEEN

"You are trembling," Ezra said as he lifted her off the back of his ancient winged horse and onto the cobblestone street outside the temple. The night was thick and dark in the village—somehow darker than it had been on the mountain. And their flight home had been one of quiet contemplation, both of them trying to figure out where they had gone, what had happened to them that an entire chunk of their night simply vanished from their minds.

But none of that had given Miri reason to tremble. No, it was something else that plagued her thoughts the closer they got to the village. Something that haunted her like a ghoul in a dark corner, waiting to pounce.

"You did nothing wrong," Ezra said, and it struck her how well he understood her quiet thoughts. How easily he could read her. "I will simply tell Phinehas that I lost track of time and—"

"No," she said. "You won't." The thought of Ezra speaking to Phinehas, of explaining anything of their night to him...she knew no good would come of it. And while she knew the reason behind

Ezra's words was honorable, she also knew it didn't matter. No, she hadn't done anything wrong.

And yet she had done something terribly wrong.

She had chosen Ezra tonight. Over the ambassador. Over Phinehas.

And she knew she would pay for it. When or how, she could not say. But she would pay.

What would be the cost?

"Miri," Ezra said softly, taking her chin. His fingers were gentle. Careful. So different from the way Phinehas touched her. It struck her then—she did not feel a sting of pain along her jaw. As if her bruises were gone. Or healed. Though how they could have healed so quickly, she could not say.

Ezra searched her chin as if he were thinking the same. Even so, his touch remained especially careful. His eyes lingered on the place where those bruises had been for a moment before he said, "I won't let anything happen to you."

She resisted the urge to huff a laugh. To ask him just how exactly he expected to manage that. Second most powerful man in the kingdom or not, what could he really do? Against Phinehas? The high priest of Har-Navah?

She heard the guttural laugh come from her throat anyway, and at it, Ezra's gaze hardened. For a moment, fear lanced down her spine at the look on his face. But it vanished almost as quickly when she realized that darkness in his gaze was not for her…

But for Phinehas.

"Don't," she said. "You don't know what he's capable of."

"And so you're going to be my hero, then?" he asked. "Protecting me from the wicked priest? I know you won't say it, so I will. He hurt you, didn't he?" Ezra's fingers trailed delicately along her jaw, in stark contrast to the roughness of his words or the anger she could tell he was keeping on a short leash.

She did not answer his question, instead looking away.

"Miri," Ezra tried, his voice gentling.

When he did not speak again for a moment, she finally looked at him, taken aback by the war in his eyes. There was something he was not saying. Something he was fighting with himself about saying at all.

A noise from behind her startled them both. She whirled to face the entrance of the temple.

"Someone is coming," she whispered.

"Miri, you did nothing wrong," he said again, attempting to take her hand. She did not let him, turning only slightly, unwilling to fully face him.

"I have to go," she said.

"Wildfire," Ezra pleaded. And at the way he said the name he had given her, she froze in place for a moment to take it in.

But then she released a breath and walked away without another glance.

WHATEVER NOISE she had heard outside the temple did not turn out to be anyone of consequence, and Miri was quietly relieved as she made her way through the dark sanctuary. The few remaining candles guttered softly, holding on to the last vestiges of their wicks as the liquid wax threatened to engulf them once and for all. It made for a haunting stillness in the hallowed room—a quiet that seemed deeper than it should be. Even her breaths seemed to slice the stillness around her with the finesse of a finely-honed blade.

She at last made it to the hall at the back of the room and the stairs that led down to her chambers. She was almost to the door of the common room when she froze in her tracks at the sound of a voice behind her.

"I was beginning to wonder if you would return."

Gian. His voice was liquid night, his words a dark menace.

"I was...out," she said stupidly.

"Mounting the grand duke?" the pirate said, a vulpine lilt to his words.

She turned to face him slowly. Gian was huge—a giant oak of a man, covered head to toe in a variety of weapons that seemed to stand out like lightning against the blackness of his leather pants and loosely-laced ruffled shirt. Beneath the opening of his shirt, she could see a tattoo along his chest, but it was obscured by the fabric and the dimness of the hall and she could not make out what it depicted. His eyes were as icy blue as his stare. Gian was a stark contrast to the quiet reverence of the temple. If this place were a quiet meadow, Gian of Borras was a black-bellied storm cloud looming over it. The king's favorite lapdog, sent here to watch over them.

To spy.

Miri swallowed once.

"He required my presence this evening," she said, hating the words and the implication of blame in them. As if Ezra had had to convince her to come with him.

Gian stepped towards her, and she did not move, did not breathe. She could not have said whether it was out of stupefied fear or quiet wisdom. He was only inches from her, the closeness too intimate for comfort. As close as Ezra had been tonight, with his arm around her waist as they flew on the back of his winged stallion. For a moment, she was back there, in his arms again, Ezra's breaths warm on her neck. Safe. A vision of starlight and his lips on her bruised chin flashed in her mind, gone as fast as it had come.

Gian's breath was hot against her mouth as he spoke. "Everyone's so infatuated with you. I'm not sure I understand what all the fuss is about. I much prefer blondes." His touch was featherlight, but there was nothing gentle about it as he ran a finger down her neck. His callouses scraped along her skin like tiny blades, and she shut her eyes, shutting him out, the pounding of her heart ringing in her ears like a warning drum.

Her skin strained against the cold fury of the hall and the slithering invasion of this man. His finger lingered on her breast, unhurriedly tracing the edge of her gown. She wondered if he could feel her heart pounding beneath his calloused finger.

"Gods, Miriam," he breathed, pressing closer against her. She stifled the urge to run, to cry out, knowing it would only make this worse. "No wonder he follows you like a stag in rut." He bent, stopping just shy of pressing his dry lips to the skin just above her dress. The bittersweet smell of rum on his breath mingled with her own, and she resisted the urge to gag.

"What's this?" he asked, retrieving a golden seed from between her breasts—the pit from the chalam she had shared with Ezra earlier tonight. Something cried out in her heart at the thought of this monster having a piece of her night. She started as he took it from her.

A wicked laugh glittered in his dark eyes, and Gian sniffed the seed, eyeing it greedily for a moment. "Don't want to lose this, little Miriam?"

She reached as quickly as she could, but Gian was faster, clutching the golden pit and grinning. "Tsk tsk, darling. Let this be a lesson to you: what a pirate finds, a pirate keeps." He smiled, but there was nothing amiable about it as he stuffed the seed into a pocket of his leather vest. "Tell me, Miriam. What secrets are you hiding? What is it that has every man here vying for your favors?"

That was as it should be, of course. For even something as simple as a seed could not be hers. Nothing sweet to remind her of anything good in her life. It was only fitting that a monster should steal a worthless token of an invaluable night.

Gian reached for her skirts, and she flinched, waiting for the shock of cold night air as he lifted them. But he did not. Instead, his hands lingered on her, one at her waist, the other just below her breast.

"So innocent," he said, a mocking tone in his voice. "As if you were untouched. No wonder men throw themselves at you."

A tear slipped down her cheek, hot and fast, and she could not stop her lip from trembling.

"You toe a dangerous line, Miriam Sasson," he said, his words nearly impossible to hear. He moved his mouth closer to her ear, pressing himself harder against her. She flinched but said nothing and did not move. "I think you're smarter than this."

The warning sounded sincere. But she could not understand its meaning.

"His patience wears thin, Miriam," he said against the shell of her ear. "This game of yours will backfire. You need to pay attention."

To any passerby, they might have looked like a couple tangled in the darkness. But Gian did not touch her further, his warning rattling around in her mind. She tried to make sense of it—to understand who the warning was about: Phinehas or Ezra.

"Look who decided to join us." A familiar, slithering voice came from just down the dark hall.

Like the snuffing of a candle, Gian stepped away from her. Her eyes flashed open to see him standing a respectable distance, fumbling with one of his blades as if he were nervous. As if he had been caught.

"Apparently His Grace likes to play with his toys all night," Gian said, a wolfish grin spreading across his mouth. "We were beginning to wonder if he'd return you."

"It seems he is not the only one who likes to play," said the dark voice. Miri's heart pounded.

Gian looked genuinely nervous, though Miri was not sure if

his manner was an act. "Can you blame me?" Gian smirked, but the expression shook a little.

Miri turned to see Phinehas emerge from the darkness. "The prodigal returns, praise Providence," he said.

She might have been relieved to see him if it wasn't for the darkness in his eyes.

For Phinehas did not seem relieved she was home. Or concerned in the least.

Phinehas was in a fit of fury.

If Gian was a storm cloud looming over her, Phinehas was thunder and lightning and mighty wind. His eyes bored into her like daggers in the gut of an enemy, and for an absurd moment, she wished Gian had not been caught before he had whisked her away to his chambers.

Because this...

She swallowed back the lump in her throat, suddenly desperately wishing she had taken Ezra up on his offer to explain to Phinehas why she had disappeared tonight.

The thought of Ezra did not help, either, her heart knowing a keen sting at his absence. A palpable worry of what she would do without him to help.

Phinehas took her by her arm and practically ripped her away from the wall, but not before she caught a final glimpse of Gian, whose eyes flashed for a moment before relaxing into impassivity. She wondered what it meant as Phinehas dragged her down the hall with a brutal grip. In stark contrast to his hold, his voice was soft. A mockery of kindness.

"I missed you, my pet," he purred. She strained to keep up with his pace and long stride down the dark hall to his door. She tripped over her skirts twice in the process.

"I...I'm sorry," she stammered.

"You should tell me before you decide to disappear, darling." His words dripped with false sweetness as he dragged her along.

Miri was trying to come up with something to say when she was stopped abruptly by Phinehas, practically tripping over him.

"Oh," said a small voice, and in the darkness of the corridor, it took her a moment to realize that she and Phinehas had almost crashed into Galina.

"Apologies, Your Holiness," Galina went on, her words meek, a stark contrast to her typical swagger. But that was nothing compared to the shock of the way she looked—her usual perfection replaced with hazardous weariness.

"You look like shit, woman. Take a bath. Do you want the ambassador to see you like that?" Phinehas sneered.

At the mention of the ambassador, Galina's eyes widened for a brief moment, and she tried to gather her tangled locks into her hands. In the dimness, it was hard to be sure, but Miri could have sworn she saw the beginnings of a deep bruise blooming on Galina's smooth cheek.

Galina looked terrible. *Too* terrible.

But Miri didn't have a chance to wonder what had happened to the other woman before Phinehas shoved her through his private chamber door and slammed it shut behind him, bolting it before whirling to face her again.

"Explain yourself," he said, his words cold and unforgiving.

She froze, regathering her thoughts, unsure where to begin.

"You better have a good reason why you disappeared tonight," he warned.

"Ezra," she whimpered. "He asked me to come with him." For the second time, she regretted the words. They were true. But they implicated Ezra. Made him the guilty party.

Nothing could be further from the truth.

But she did not know what else to say. Her heart pounded mercilessly, and she felt the urge to collapse. But she held her ground and looked Phinehas in the eye.

She had done nothing wrong, she reminded herself. This was the game he had wanted her to play all along, wasn't it?

"You've let him win, Miriam," Phinehas warned. "Giving him what he wants without anything in return. He has not spoken to me. Not once. Did you know that? He has shown no loyalty. None at all! You're letting him win, Miriam. Do you realize that? You're failing us all!"

"He's not—"

Phinehas started so fast she swallowed her words. The fire in his eyes was enough to stop her short.

"He's not what?" Phinehas asked, his words a quiet fury. The calm before a mighty storm.

She decided the truth was her only option. "He's not sleeping with me," she managed, the words less than a breath.

Phinehas stood motionless in the dark chamber, his eyes unreadable. Miriam wasn't sure which was worse: his anger or his foreboding silence.

Moments passed without a sound. She wanted to explain. To launch into a diatribe of excuses. But she did not. She stood her ground before the high priest of Har-Navah and waited.

Phinehas at last moved. His steps were slow. Deliberate.

"You've not slept with him?" Phinehas clarified, his eyes glittering with something she could not read.

She merely shook her head.

As he crossed the space between them, that silence morphed into a dangerous smile that spread slowly, long and thin across his lanky face. "What a clever little spider you are," he said. "What a cunning little fox."

She swallowed her retort, figuring the rest of the truth wasn't helpful right now. It was far better for Phinehas to be pleased with her than the alternative.

Phinehas at last reached her, slithering his arms around her and pulling her into a wet kiss. His tongue wormed its way into her mouth, and she could not help but feel like she had suddenly forgotten how to kiss a man. Then she realized *why* it was so awkward to be kissing him like this.

Because she had never kissed him like this. He had never kissed her more than a close-lipped peck on the mouth now and then.

But this...this was gluttonous possession. Savage hunger. And something much darker that she could not name.

Phinehas moved her across the room as he devoured her with his lips, ripping her dress from her with terrifying ease until she was as naked as a babe before him, bathed in pale moonlight.

He broke his invading kiss to ogle her head to toe. Her hair spilled wildly down her breasts, and Phinehas sneered with disdain. She quickly moved to pull it up and away, and at her silent submission, Phinehas's snarl turned to a serpent's grin. "My little spider," he purred. "What a pretty little web you weave. What with your coy glances and whispered conversations." He unbuttoned his trousers in a single motion and stood before her, his form long and lean and vicious, almost ghostly in the moonlight of his chambers. "Here I was thinking you had betrayed me. Thinking you had disappeared with the grand duke tonight to escape." He moved his fingers along her skin as he spoke—a touch that was all at once consuming and barely there. She shivered as he continued. "And all along, you were proving how cunning you really are. How clever."

There was nothing gentle in the way he touched her. Nothing sweet as he slithered his long fingers down her body. "He pants for you. Longs for you desperately. And you keep him at bay. Clever, wicked little spider that you are." His fingers trailed lower and lower until they stopped at her most intimate places. A breathy, guttural laugh rose up from his throat. "Perhaps I should thanking Ezra," he said, his words like the purr of a wildcat. "Such a warm welcome from my cunning little fox."

Without warning, he shoved her down on the bed behind her and pounced on top of her—a caracal devouring a gazelle. His body was hard and unforgiving, and she, unprepared for his harsh invasion, cried out against the pain.

"So many secrets, my little spider," he whispered. "So many secrets you keep."

He bit her shoulder so hard that she was certain the entire village of Shalem could hear her cry.

"I was mad with jealousy," he admitted. "Mad with the thought that you had left me. Abandoned me. After all I've done for you. But I understand now. I understand you perfectly. You're as clever and cunning as a witch," he said, nearly grunting the words as he violated her over and over and over again.

Tears fell freely down her cheeks as Phinehas kept up his unrelenting assault. Sharp pain radiated from her but she said nothing. Did nothing but receive the punishment she knew she deserved.

She was a liar.

A traitor.

A whore.

That's all she ever had been.

That's all she ever would be.

"Tell me," he said, the words grinding out through his teeth. "Tell me your secrets, my little spider. Tell me what you hide in the night."

She did not understand. She did not know what he wanted from her. Phinehas's body became an unbearable weight.

"Tell me," he growled in her ear. "TELL ME WHAT YOU HIDE."

"I hide nothing from you!" she whimpered. "I would not hide from you, my lord."

"Yes," he grunted. "Yes, I am your lord. Your master. Your father. Your god. Now tell me. Tell me what you hide."

She cried out at his merciless affection, and in an absurd moment, she found herself transfixed by the straining tendons and veins in his neck as he shut his eyes and bellowed a great cry.

In the span of a heartbeat, Phinehas collapsed beside her, heaving breaths as he sprawled out. Miri lay next to him, looking up at the rafters of his chamber. As if nothing in particular had just transpired, she found herself wondering just how thick the dust was on the heavy wooden beams. Wondering if she could write in it clear enough for someone to read. Perhaps she would write her story in that dust. Leave a tragic tale for someone else to read.

But no one would read her story. Because no one would bother with the story of a traitorous whore.

Phinehas said nothing beside her, which was fine with her, as she had nothing to say. Nothing to give. Nothing left of her.

She was nothing.

Nothing and no one.

CHAPTER SIXTEEN

I t was all a blur.

Well, not all of it. But a strange part of it. As if their night together had been broken into pieces, one of which fell through the rafters into a permanent darkness.

It was strange—to know you did not know something. To remember that you did not remember.

And that strangeness had followed Ezra for four days.

He had only gotten to see Miri for brief moments over the last few days, which was just as well since she had been consumed by quiet contemplation, too. What had happened when they jumped in the pool together? Somehow, it seemed important enough that neither of them could let it go.

It was only in his dreams that he seemed to remember any of it. And even they were a confusing blur of starlight and brightly-colored clouds and the sense that he was home. Home and settled. Whatever that meant.

He would have dismissed the dreams, except that he kept having the same one over and over, every night. In every dream, he caught a glimpse of fiery red curls suspended wildly in the air as if under water. And every time, right when he spotted those curls, he woke with the sensation that he had experienced the dream in real life. Woke and thought of that stag and what it could possibly mean for him. For her. For everyone.

Ezra sat at his polished mahogany desk, sifting through ledgers and papers, pretending to be sorting out the business of Kinnereth Province. But really, he was pondering his night with Miri over and over in his mind.

The day had dawned particularly gray—the kind of gray that signaled the end of any remaining summer warmth and the last of the harvest. It was not bitter cold outside yet, but the mountain air was cool and crisp, a taste of what awaited them in the coming months. The snows wouldn't come for another month or so but in these elevations, the weather acted as if it were preparing all the same, for this morning Ezra had been greeted with a blanket of frost on his gardens. The day had remained mostly dismal, and now, with twilight creeping in, the gray was almost complete, robbing trees and leaves and grass of color.

When Ezra realized he had read the same line of the ledger for the third time, he shut the great leather book and sighed.

"Northern farms still cheating their taxes?"

Ezra looked up to see John standing in the door of his study. He smiled at his brother-in-law.

"John," he said, standing from the buttery leather desk chair. "Where is that precious nephew of mine?"

"I left Esther and John Junior at home. They will arrive later."

And with that little declaration, Ezra knew something was on John's mind—he never left Esther or his son home without him.

"What's going on?" Ezra asked, concerned.

John said nothing as he made his way into the room, lined floor to ceiling with books on shelves of dark mahogany. He fiddled for a moment with a large globe on its stand near one of the bookshelves, spinning the earth as if he were Providence himself.

"John," Ezra tried again, making his way around his desk and perching on the edge of it.

John looked up from the spinning globe. "Are you sure you want to do this?"

Ezra crossed his arms and smiled faintly. "I've never been more sure."

John looked down at the leather satchel in his arm, as if within it, he carried the weight of the world. Ezra supposed that in one way, he did.

"Surely there is another way," John finally said.

"I will make sure John Junior is taken care of," Ezra insisted, hoping to placate his brother-in-law.

"I'm not worried about John Junior," he said. "I'm worried about you. You know this is insanity, right?"

Ezra grinned. "I suppose some would see it that way."

"Not some. All. Everyone will think you've cracked when they learn of this."

"Let them think what they think. They do anyway," Ezra added, but it did not seem to comfort his friend.

John opened the satchel, retrieving one crisp parchment sealed in evergreen wax. With a shaking hand, he handed it to Ezra.

"It seems odd, doesn't it?" Ezra asked, taking the paper and looking it over. "That my whole life—for seventeen centuries before that, everything my family has worked for should be reduced to a few sentences on a fine piece of linen."

John shook his head, apparently without an answer to that. "Can't you just marry her? Wouldn't that be the more sensible way to do this?"

He had thought of that. But it wasn't enough. It wasn't the message he was trying to send. So he looked at his brother-in-law and said, "I don't want her looking up ten years from now thinking that I rescued her. I want her to look up one day and know that she had the courage to rescue herself." He paused, then continued, "It matters a great deal to me, John. That's why it has to be everything and nothing less."

That's what he would offer Miri.

Everything.

John sighed, shaking his head once more. "You love her. I don't doubt that. I just want to make sure you understand what you're getting into."

"I know it's a lot to ask of her, John. But she's stronger than you think. Stronger than most realize. I know she can do this."

"There is so much, Ezra. To learn. To navigate."

"She doesn't see it in herself yet, John. But I do. I see how she handles the pressures she faces at the priest's side, day in and day out. There is a quiet strength to her. I know that with time, and with love, she will see it within herself. And more so, I know that together we will shape a brighter future for Kinnereth than I ever could have alone."

John didn't respond, as if taking in what Ezra had to say. He knew it was absurd. Impossible, even.

But he had spent his formidable years watching his grandfather and grandmother turn the Kinnereth duchy into something noble. Something worth a Sheol of a lot more than a title and wealth and a prestigious family name. They had taught Ezra the value of hard work, the blessing of generosity, and the strength of mercy. Together, they had set a precedent and forged a legacy that Ezra could only hope to live up to.

For the first time in his life, he knew he had found someone with whom he could continue that legacy. Which is exactly what he intended to do, no matter how irrational it looked. For the first time in his life, Ezra had *wanted* to continue that legacy, thanks to Miri. He did not intend to waste it.

So when John met his gaze again, Ezra smiled broadly, offering silent assurance. But when John did not return that smile, he knew this was not the only subject weighing on him. "John, what's going on?"

John looked anywhere but at Ezra, clearly gathering his words. After a long silence he finally said, "It's worse than I thought, Ez."

"What is?"

John sat down on the arm of a chair near the hearth and opened his leather satchel again, pulling out a stack of papers and documents. He thumbed through a few of them. "Here," he finally said, handing Ezra one of the parchments.

Ezra skimmed it over, unsure what he was supposed to be looking at. "What is this?"

"Evidence," John said.

"It looks like a receipt," Ezra mused.

"It is," said John.

"A pearl-and-sapphire ring?" Ezra asked. "I don't understand." He handed the paper back to John, who tucked it back into his stack and handed Ezra another one.

"A locket," Ezra said, reading another receipt. "Albeit a rather expensive one," he added.

"There are fourteen receipts in here," John said. "All of them for exquisite jewels and baubles. And all of them purchased by an anonymous person within the span of the last six months."

"I'm afraid I still don't understand."

"I didn't either," John admitted, his face forlorn. "Until I noticed that all of the wives seemed to be particularly bejeweled at the ball last month."

"They're noblewomen," Ezra chuckled dismissively. "Their husbands buy them baubles to keep them placated as they dally about the countryside. And if their husbands don't buy for them, their lovers do."

"Yes, that's usually the case," said John. "But I found it odd that the jeweler here in Shalem had sold so many items of such value in such a short time. And the jeweler in Har Omer. And in seven cities across Kinnereth Province. I began to suspect they were all purchased by the same person."

"These are anonymous," Ezra pointed out unhelpfully. "How do you know it's the same person purchasing them?"

"Of course I cannot be certain," John admitted. "But all of them—without exception—were purchased with a note from the same bank. In Teman City."

John stood, holding a few of the papers in his hand as he started pacing the room. Ezra couldn't help but notice that his brother-in-law looked like a lot like he should be writing mystery novels at the moment. "I got to thinking. Phinehas came from Teman City, didn't he?"

"Yes," Ezra said. "But we already know Phinehas bribed most of the wives in every village from here to the coast. That's how he got so many votes on the royal council. This is hardly news."

"Just let me finish," John said. "I started digging around, thinking I would find a link to Phinehas. Thinking it was too obvious to be overlooked. Except there was no link to Phinehas. Not a single one. It was not his money that purchased jewels for all the noble wives of Kinnereth Province. All the money came from one account—the lord of Teman City."

"Lord Tamir Sasson," Ezra said, nearly mouthing the words.

"Lord Tamir Sasson," John confirmed, his eyes grim.

Miriam's father.

"But," Ezra said, putting it together in his mind. "Lord Sasson died years ago."

"Exactly," John said. "Seven years ago. And his wealth and title were never transferred to Miriam. When I searched the official records, there was some vague explanation about extortion and bribery and how all of his assets were to go to his debtors. But when I searched the history of his estate, there was no debt. Anywhere. In four centuries, the Sasson family had not accrued so much as a bekah of debt. So either Lord Sasson was very good at hiding a double life..."

"Or someone took his money," Ezra finished.

"Exactly. Someone who needed a great deal of wealth to finance a rather rapid rise in rank. Someone who could use that bottomless wealth to convince an entire council's worth of noblemen to vote him in as the youngest high priest in Har-Navarian history. Someone who convinced those noblemen by bribing their wives. I looked, Ezra. I did some sniffing around Shalem. Rumor has it that several of the noble wives here are on the outs with their husbands, only making public appearances when necessary. One of them is with child. After sixteen years of marriage, she finally conceived. There are similar stories in many of the villages and cities of Old Haravelle.

"It's all conjecture, Ezra. None of it is concrete. But all of it seems too coincidental to be an accident. How did Phinehas fund his rise in rank so rapidly? How did he fund a campaign to convince so many of the king's council to vote for him? And the Sanhedrin? There is rumor after rumor for a thousand miles in every direction—of wives who adamantly supported the rise of the young priest. And noblemen alike who voted for him with no previous knowledge of him. In addition, there is no history of the man himself. No records. I'm not even sure Phinehas is his real name.

"So how did he do it? How could he achieve such a rapid rise in rank with nothing?" John asked, and Ezra did not miss the frustration in his tone.

"He bought them all with Miriam's inheritance," Ezra said, nearly growling the words. Bitter bile stung his throat.

"That's not the worst of it," John said. "Maybe he really did bribe them, but he's done it in such a way that no one could ever point to him. There is no concrete evidence of any of it. Just rumors and hearsay and wild guesses. But it got me thinking. How did he manage to time embezzling an entire estate with the sudden death of its patron?"

Ezra went still, the room suddenly cold as he put it together before John had to say it.

John said it anyway.

"Ezra," his brother-in-law breathed. "I believe it was him. I believe he killed Miri's parents."

Ezra stood. Walking briskly across the room, he retrieved his coat and top hat from a rack by the door.

"What are you doing?" John asked, standing as well.

"I have to find her. Right now."

"Ezra," John said. "Think for a moment. This man is going to any lengths to ensure his power. He is dangerous, Ezra."

"Yes, exactly," Ezra said. He donned his coat in a fluid movement before marching from the room, his hat tucked under his arm. John followed him.

"Ezra, if all of this is true, he is not just a thief and a whoremonger...he is a murderer! You need to tread carefully."

Ezra made his way down the hall to the steps that led to the entrance of Massahd Castle. He took them two at a time, his heart pounding as he descended.

"Ezra," John insisted, catching up and stopping him at the bottom step with a hand on his shoulder. "Think about this for one moment, will you? This is not just a matter of getting tangled with a woman who will ruin your reputation. This could be your life in danger!"

"All the more reason to be worried about *her* life!" Ezra said, and every second John delayed him felt like a lifetime. He had to get to her. He had to help her get out of the temple. Tonight.

The situation was more dire than he thought.

"Ezra, you're not hearing me," John went on. "There's something we're not seeing here. There's got to be a reason he's keeping her."

At this Ezra stopped his harried progress through the castle, turning to face his brother-in-law.

"What do you mean?"

"This is about more than just sex. He has any woman he could want. And then some. There is a reason he keeps her so close to him, Ez. There is a reason he uses her the way he does."

A vision flashed in Ezra's mind—whorls of light like spring vines on a tree growing from a delicate palm. Of that light entwining fingers. Entwining hands. Binding. Growing.

Magic.

Ezra swallowed once and spun around again, even more eager to get to her as quickly as possible.

"Ezra, listen to me," John said. "There is a meeting happening tonight. In the village."

"A meeting?" he asked, heart pounding. "For what purpose?"

"I don't know. I confess, I did not learn much. But Phinehas is meeting with the ambassador. In a secret meeting. For no good reason, of that I am sure."

Ezra whirled around, reaching for the door without explanation.

"What are you going to do? Just barge in there and whisk her away?" John protested.

"I'm going to do whatever it takes," Ezra said, and disappeared into the night.

IT WAS PROBABLY pointless to be here. The likelihood of finding her tonight was slim, and the risk of going to the temple directly was too great. But Ezra had come to the village anyway. Apologizing to John for abandoning the family dinner they had planned, Ezra had mounted his horse and ridden into the village as fast as he could, arriving just before nightfall.

There was no reason to believe Miriam would be in the village attending the secret meeting tonight. At least not any that he could think of. But he could not bear the idea of sitting idly at home and waiting until breakfast tomorrow to see her. If there was a chance of finding her tonight, he would.

Because her plight was worse than he'd thought.

If the evidence that John had uncovered was true, Phinehas was not just a conniving, grasping bastard. He was a murderer.

A murderer conspiring with someone who was rumored to be one of the most vile, horrible humans in existence.

The Medinian ambassador.

Miri needed to get far away from him—and from Phinehas—as quickly as possible. Ezra's heart pounded in his chest as he gave the stable boy a single gold talent and left his horse at the livery.

"Milord," the boy protested. "S'too much!" He waved the talent in the air, but Ezra did not bother arguing with him. It was a hundred times the cost to stable a horse for the night. But Ezra would have paid a thousand times. Ten thousand. And he had no desire to waste time rifling through his purse for the correct coin.

"Keep it," he said over his shoulder as he hurried away.

He could still hear the boy mumbling his excitement as he made his way down the street. Miri was not anywhere that he could see, and it only bothered him more, the knowledge that he had no idea where she went at night when there wasn't some sort of dance or dinner or ass-kissing gathering going on. Phinehas had thrown himself so many parties since he arrived that Ezra had lost count. And in any other circumstance, Ezra would have found an excuse to miss most of them.

But he had been to every one since the day he had met Miri. Not knowing where she was now—if she was safe—it was eating at him.

He thought back on the last few breakfasts they had shared together and her mood of quiet contemplation. He had assumed it was for the same reasons he had been locked in thoughtful silence. But what if it was more? What if Miri wasn't consumed with trying to remember the foggy parts of their night in the mountains?

What if something had happened to her?

Ezra's pace quickened nearly to a run as he made his way from shop to shop in the quiet mountain village.

CHAPTER SEVENTEEN

The temple was quiet.

Too quiet.

Miri had woken from a nap to find herself alone, the rooms dark, the halls silent. She searched Kata's room, and Galina's and Jordie's as well.

Empty.

She left the common room between their chambers and made her way down the near underground halls of the living quarters at the temple.

Silent.

Not even Gian could be found lurking the halls.

She did not know where everyone had gone.

She made her way to Phinehas's private quarters, knocking once. Twice.

No answer.

She knocked again, calling his name.

When no one answered, she reached for the handle and opened his door.

His room was dark.

Empty.

And mostly barren.

As if no one in particular lived here.

Or perhaps he wanted it to appear as if the room boasted nothing of particular importance.

A dark part of her—a deeply cynical part of her—wondered if that was intentional. For she knew, above all else, Phinehas was a man of secrets. And men with secrets knew how to keep them well hidden.

But she had no explanation for his absence. Nor anyone else's, for that matter.

For reasons she could not explain, the need to know where they were weighed on her.

Well, she would just have to find them, that's all.

THE MOUNTAIN AIR was crisp on her face, the smell of peppermint growing from flower beds in front of the shops wafting on the breeze as she made her way down the village road in the waning twilight. Autumn was rapidly changing the quaint little village, and Miri privately wondered how different it would be from the warm, balmy autumns of Teman City. So far, summer in the mountains had been sunny and bright, a bit cooler than the thick, humid heat of the south. But if the crispness of the breeze was any indication, perhaps the coming months would prove to be much colder than what she had experienced growing up on the coast.

She took a deep breath, relishing the cool air filling her lungs, and let it clear her mind. Wherever Phinehas and the acolytes had gone, she did not know. But the more she searched, the more she realized she didn't care, thankful for the momentary quiet free-dom. What had begun as a search had soon evolved into a quiet walk in the village. Perhaps she would sneak into the theatre after the intermission and watch the second half of tonight's play. Perhaps she'd even reward herself with a pastry from Joshua's. With any luck, the few bekahs in her pocket would be enough.

Rounding the corner of the apothecary, whose windows were dark for the night, she noticed a figure walking briskly on the other side of the street. The waning light seemed as if it should be bright enough to tell who it was. But alas, she could only see shadow and silhouette. He bore a top hat and tails and walked with purpose, peeking into every window he passed as if desperately looking for someone. After only a moment of this, he froze on the promenade, looking out across the cobblestones.

"Miri!" she heard the man call, and she recognized his rich baritone immediately.

"Ezra?" she asked, stepping out onto the street without thinking. Ezra cried out, and Miri quickly realized why, flinging herself backward to avoid the carriage careening toward her. She hadn't even heard the clomp of the horses' hooves, too distracted by Ezra and whatever seemed to be so important to him.

When the carriage passed, she brushed her hands down her skirts and took a look down the street before attempting to cross. But she did not even make it halfway before Ezra met her on the cobblestones, taking hold of both of her hands and ushering her to the safety of the empty promenade.

"Miri," he said, sounding half exasperated, half thrilled. "What are you doing here tonight?"

"I just thought I'd go for a walk," she said, with no interest in explaining her curiously free evening.

"I'm so glad you did," he said, and he sounded relieved.

"Why?"

Ezra searched her for a moment before looking around, as if checking to see if anyone might be listening...or watching. When he seemed satisfied, his eyes found hers.

"Miri. I need you to come with me."

"With you? Where?"

"Home. To Massahd Castle."

"What? Why?" she asked, taken aback by his urgency.

With hands still clasping hers, he ushered her off of the promenade into a narrow alleyway between two buildings. The rough road curved upward behind them, following the slope of the mountainside on which the buildings had been constructed. Only the pale yellow light of a window above them shone in the darkness, casting a perfect shape onto the cobblestones.

"Miri," he said, and the way he said her name stole her attention from the shapes on the street.

"Ezra, what's wrong?"

He took a moment to tuck an errant strand of hair behind her ear, the messy knot of curls on her head feeling suddenly heavy and tipsy.

"Why aren't you with them tonight?"

"With who?" she asked.

"Phinehas. And the priests. The acolytes," he said, hesitating on the last word.

"Where are they?" she asked.

He looked over his shoulder once before turning to face her again. "They are meeting. With the Medinian ambassador."

"Why? For what purpose?"

"I don't know. But I need you to come with me. Now."

"Come where?"

"Home, Miri. I want you to come to Massahd with me. Tonight."

"Ezra, I don't understand," she said.

"I will explain. But not here. I need you to trust me," he said.

"You want me to come home with you?" she asked, and upon hearing herself ask the question, she understood what he wanted.

Suddenly and quite unexpectedly, fury boiled in her veins, and she could feel the heat of it climbing her neck and cheeks.

"Oh, I see," she said curtly before he could reply. "Am I to be your mistress then?"

"What? No!" he answered abruptly. "That's not—"

"You needn't pretend," she retorted, hating the hot anger that brought tears to her eyes. "I understand completely."

"No, I don't believe you do," he said.

"Do you deny that you are attracted to me, Ezra? Is that the game you wish to play now?"

Ezra seemed at a loss, searching her for an uncomfortable moment before saying, "No, I do not deny it."

"Good, because I cannot keep playing this game. I cannot," she said, unable to see through the tears that had collected in her eyes. She cleared her throat, scrambling for some semblance of calm. She hated it. Hated what he did to her. Hated that she had let him fool her. Let him make her think he was different. He was no different. He was the same. The same as all of them.

"Miri, what game?" he asked, and she could hear the exasperation he was trying to stifle in his tone.

"It's simple, isn't it?" she retorted. "It merely comes down to what kind of man you are."

"What kind of man I am?"

"Are you a private man? Perhaps you'll take me to an inn and pretend as if no one is the wiser." She ripped her arms from his grip and crossed them in a huff. "Or perhaps you are public man. Perhaps you will take me right here, for anyone in the world to see. I don't care, only be done with it because I cannot keep this up. I cannot keep playing this cat-and-mouse game. I know what you want. There's no reason to pretend. You can put a pretty dress on a whore and call her your mistress, but at the end of the day, she's still a whore. It's all she will ever be."

"Miri," he said, his voice gentling. He took a single step towards her. But she took two steps back.

"What will it be, Ezra? Decide. Because I cannot do this anymore."

"Miri," he said again, crossing the gap between them, taking hold of her arms and disallowing her to move away any further. "I have no interest in making you my mistress."

"I don't care what you want to call it," she spat. "Just—"

"You are not an itch I need to scratch. You are not a plaything for me to fiddle with until I bore of you," he said, his words firm but somehow still gentle. Much like his touch. Even his eyes. "I want you, Miri. I will not deny it. But that is not why I ask you to return to Massahd Castle with me."

"Why then?" she blurted. "What are you going to do? Make me your wife?"

Had he not been holding her steady, she might have fallen straight to the cobblestones when he responded matter-of-factly, "I hope to someday, yes. But not yet."

"Not yet?" she blurted, realizing it sounded as if she were protesting his timing instead of questioning why in the world he would ever marry her.

"I am not proposing to you today," he said, his words quivering with a small laugh. "That will come in time. But—"

"In time? In time when?" she scoffed. "What on earth are you talking about?"

"In time—when you are ready." He smiled.

"And when in Heaven or Sheol am I to be ready?"

"Sooner rather than later, I hope," he said softly. His eyes sparkled with humor, and his grip on her upper arms loosened just a bit. "But I need you to come with me now, rather than wait until then."

When she furrowed her brows, he went on. "I am not making an untoward proposition, Miri." He chuckled again. "There is plenty of room in the castle. You can have an entire wing to your-self, if you wish it."

An entire wing? What in the world was he talking about?

"Only I need you to trust me when I say that you can no longer stay in the temple."

That last sentence brought her back to reality, and she met his eyes, her vision clearing. "Whyever not?" she barked.

"It is too much to explain right now, and certainly not some-thing I am going to explain here," he said, taking a moment to look past them into the streets. Looking back at her, he went on, "Suffice it to say you are not safe, Miri. And I need you to trust me."

"So I am to take you at your word and leave my home for the past seven years, come with you back to your castle for reasons you will not explain, live with you but not as your mistress, and wait until the time you decide I am ready so that you will marry me?"

This was nonsense. Ezra was being absurd. And ridiculous. She wanted to grab him by the shoulders and shake some sense into him. Perhaps he was drunk. She sniffed the air between them for any hint of ale or rum or whiskey, but smelled nothing except crisp mountain air.

"No," he said. "I want you to leave the temple and never look back. I want you to come back to Massahd with me and start your life."

"I have a life, thank you," she said, dismissively.

"You have the life that was handed to you, Miri. You do not have your own life."

"And what exactly would you have me do? Ezra, I have noth-ing. No prospects, not three bekahs to my name. I have no skills besides those on my back. There is not a place in the world that would even rent a room to me. If I were to leave, I would be a street whore within a month. I'd rather be a priest's whore than a street whore."

"What if you were free instead?"

"There is no such thing as freedom for a woman."

"There is for a Grand Duchess," he said.

She darted her eyes to him, completely confused.

"I had John draw up the papers. I renounced my title and made you my heir. It's all yours, Miri," he went on without letting her retort. He pushed a shaking hand through his hair, messing up the perfect coif and coaxing free an uncooperative strand. "The castle, the estate, the title. Every talent in my coffers. It's yours. All of it."

"What is mine? What are you talking about?"

He smiled, and Providence help her if it wasn't dripping with warmth, that smile. "Everything. Your freedom. It's yours, if you will take it."

He wrapped an arm around her waist, resting his free hand on her cheek. "I thought about it—asking you to marry me first. And yes, that would make you Grand Duchess, but only by marriage. Inheritance by law is very different for a woman than it is for a man. I want it all to be yours by your own right.

"I want you to come with me. I want you to find your wings and spread them. I want you to know what freedom is. I want you to hold the keys to your cage. No one else. You can come back with me to Massahd Castle. Become the Grand Duchess. Learn the estate, learn anything you wish. Find out what it is you want out of life, Miri.

"And at the end of it, if you look up and realize it's not me, you're free. All of it is yours. You'll have enough money to start a life of your own." He chuckled, adding, "You'll have enough to start a *kingdom* of your own, should you wish."

"Ezra..." She stopped, trying to take it in. "This is...absurd. What are you to do without your title?"

"I will help you run the estate. I'll be your manager, if you wish. Or if you don't wish, you can kick me out and hire someone else."

"I know nothing about running an estate!" she protested.

"Well, I was hoping we could run it together," he said, pressing a soft kiss to her cheek. "But that will be up to you, Wildfire. For as Grand Duchess, I cannot ask you to marry me. You'll have to do the asking."

"Ezra," she tried, her resolve melting with every soft stroke of his knuckles down her cheek. "Ezra, this is ridiculous."

"I don't care," he said.

"Well, I do!" she retorted. "I cannot possibly steal everything from you!"

"You cannot steal what is freely given," he said warmly, pressing his lips to her brow. "Come back with me, Wildfire. Take the keys to your freedom."

"Ezra," she said, unable to say much more for the emotion welling, welling, welling.

He took her chin, lifting her gaze to meet his. A single tear fell down her cheek. He kissed it away before he said, "Come home, Wildfire."

She wanted to say yes. With every fiber of her being she wanted to shout it out for the entire, sleepy village to hear. She wanted to be brave. Or insane. Or whatever would allow her to say yes. To take the keys to her freedom. To have everything Ezra offered her. Freely. Without restraint. Like a madman.

She wanted to say yes.

But that would be absurd.

And he would regret it. He would regret her. Maybe not today. Maybe not tomorrow. But one day he would regret ever having known her.

"I cannot," she said. "I'm sorry."

"Miri," he said, not letting her go.

She forced herself to push out of his arms. "I cannot, Ezra. I'm sorry."

"Miriam," he said again.

She did not look back at him as she ran from the dark alleyway into the empty cobblestone streets.

CHAPTER EIGHTEEN

Miri hardly slept.

The winds outside the small window at the top of the wall in her room rattled the mottled glass, kissing the air with wisps of icy coolness. She shivered beneath the wealth of blankets, wishing the fire could burn brighter and warmer across the room. She had even reluctantly tried a little contraption Kata had brought her from one of the shops in the village—a gesture of good will, she supposed. Cleverly constructed of what seemed to be a hundred cogs and gears, it was designed to whir with nothing but the aid of magic, a little fan meant to push the heat from the fire farther into the room. But it was to no avail. It seemed nothing was capable of warming her against the coming autumn.

She ran the words over and over in her mind.

Come home, Wildfire. Take the keys to your freedom.

Everything. Ezra had offered her everything.

And she had refused it. Perhaps out of wisdom, most likely out of fear.

But she had refused the beautiful picture he had painted.

And she hadn't been able to relax since.

She wondered how she would explain it to him at breakfast this morning. She wondered what questions he would ask and what answers she would offer. She had no logical explanation, to be honest. Nothing that could offer reason to such a profoundly illogical offer.

So she dressed in silence and sneaked through the quiet temple earlier than usual the next morning, hoping to avoid any explanations or unwanted conversations with the girls, or Phinehas, or Gian. She just wanted to get to the bakery and see Ezra.

The sun was already dawning bright and clear as she made her way down the cobblestone streets. The town tinker was busy hanging his wares from the side of his cart, and he smiled broadly as she passed him.

"Interest you in anything, milady?" he offered, gesturing to the baubles and handmade jewels that clinked against the worn wood of the back of his cart.

"No thank you," she said, uninterested in explaining to him that she hadn't enough coin to purchase anything from him anyway.

You'll have enough to start a kingdom *of your own, should you wish.*

Ezra's words clamored through her mind, and she thought how marvelous it would be to make the tinker's day and purchase every single thing he had to sell. A smile found her face.

"If that smile's for a beau, he'll take one look at it and buy you whatever your heart desires, milady," said the tinker.

She could not stifle the smile, even as it grew on her mouth. "I'll have to remember that," she said, tipping her head as she passed him by. She made her way to the baker, the smell of the pastries wafting and beckoning through the streets.

Pushing through the door, the bell ringing over her head, she caught sight of Joshua and said, "If the smell of whatever you're baking doesn't draw every soul from three provinces in here, nothing will."

"And good mornin' to you too, Miri!" Joshua laughed. "What can I get for you?"

"I'll wait for Ezra," she said, nodding her head towards the narrow steps that led to the roof.

Joshua smiled again. "We'll bring you some coffee while you wait."

"Thank you," she said, and could not stifle the expectancy that welled within her as she practically skipped through the bakery and up the steps.

The sun was blinding as she emerged onto the rooftop and found her way to their favorite table, thankful that the sun had slightly warmed the metal seat despite the crisp air. She had barely begun to sit down when she heard the familiar sound of steps up the stair and turned to see Winona emerge with a tray on her hip. A kettle, two cups, a creamer, and a dish of honey in tow, she set her burden on the table and said, "Morning, darlin'. You're awfully cheery this morning."

"It's a beautiful day, isn't it?" Miri asked.

"'Tis," said Winona. "But I've never known mere sunshine to bring such a look to a woman's eyes," she added knowingly, setting a cup directly in front of Miri. She poured the steaming coffee, lifting an eyebrow before winking once.

Miri merely shrugged, reaching for the creamer. As she poured, she noticed the painting adorning her cup. "I like this one today," she said, lifting the hand-painted porcelain to inspect it more closely. "A windmill."

"That's one of my favorites, too," said Winona proudly. Miri looked across the table to inspect the cup that awaited Ezra.

"What is that?" she asked, squinting to try to decipher the intricately-painted cup.

"Fire," said Winona. "A whole bush of it, to be precise. I thought these were fitting for you two."

Miri looked up at the portly baker, meeting wise, knowing eyes. Then Winona smiled. "I've heard 'im call you Wildfire before. It fits, you know. You're the fire, and he's the wind that fans the flames."

Yes. Yes, he was.

Miri simply smiled and took a sip of her coffee.

Winona grinned. "I'll bring you both some breakfast when he gets here."

"Thank you," said Miri. She watched Winona walk away and then turned her attention to the lake below, waiting for Ezra to arrive.

"Perhaps he got tied up," said Joshua, bringing Miri a third pot of coffee.

Two hours. She had been waiting on the rooftop for two hours. In the first half hour, she'd waited with expectation. But every minute after that, her heart sank a little further. Now she sat alone in the brisk autumn sun on the rooftop out of sheer embarrassment.

Ezra was not coming. That much was clear.

"Yes. Tied up," she said absently, pushing away from the table at last, her muscles stiff and sore from sitting so long in one place.

"It's not like him," Joshua offered. "He wouldn't miss a day with you if he could help it."

Miri found she could not come up with a reasonable response. Anything but the truth would sting. And the truth would sting too much to say aloud.

I refused him, Joshua. That's why he's not here. He offered me the world, and I refused it.

She swallowed against the lump she did not know was in her throat.

"Why don't you eat something, darling?" Joshua tried. "Winona just took some raisin cakes from the oven."

"I'm not hungry," she said, pushing past him, unable to look at the pity in his eyes.

"He used to visit us, you know. Before you came along." Miri froze, her back to the baker as he went on.

"He would come visit the shops of the village faithfully at least once a month. Sometimes more. Felt it was his duty as grand duke," Joshua said. "But not every day. Never every day. Even if he wanted to, he has so much on his plate. It was tragic, what happened to him and his poor sister. Whole family gone. In an instant. One moment he's a carefree young lad with the world ahead of him, next minute he's got the weight of the world on his shoulders.

"But he loves it. This place. These people. This life. And he's good to us. Takes care of us. He's the patron of the theatre, for goodness' sake! He always makes sure this place can make ends meet. Stay afloat. All of us.

"But he rarely came into the village so often, Miri. Not until he met you."

Miri turned to face Joshua at last, looking blankly into the baker's kind eyes, as warm and sweet as the breads and cakes that came from his ovens.

"If he's not here, there's a damn good reason, if you'll pardon my language. He would not miss a chance to see you. Not for nothin' in this world."

Miri hated the lone tear that escaped down her cheek. Hated it so much that she refused to wipe it away or even acknowledge it.

For she had brought this upon herself. And she knew the *damn good reason* he wasn't here today.

The reason he would not come back.

"Thank you for your kindness, Joshua," she said.

And then she turned and left.

CHAPTER NINETEEN

The soup was cold, but Miri stirred it absently, resting her jaw on her free hand, practically draping herself across the small table in the kitchen underneath the temple.

Across from her, Kata sat at the table, silently eating her soup as Jordie prattled on and on about this lord and that, all of whom were apparently eager to earn her affections. It made Miri nauseous to hear the young acolyte speak of sex so freely, as if it were nothing to give herself over and over again. As if all that attention were real, all that affection from one man after another anything but a farce. Miri hated it, the way Jordie spoke.

Like looking into a glass from the past. A mirror of the girl she had once been.

She had once relished it—the life Phinehas had made for her.

When she was as young as Jordie—when Phinehas had first brought her to his temple—she had relished all the attention, all the baubles, all the flimsy gowns and dances with strange men. She had once reveled in the affections they practically begged from her. All the while, Phinehas's promises ringing in her ears.

He can help us, my darling, Phinehas would promise her as he brought aristocrat after aristocrat to her. *His influence is what we need. We'll make our dreams come true.*

She wondered what her dreams were anymore.

Certainly not this. Cold soup at an empty table in a dank kitchen beneath a temple that felt more like a prison with each passing day. Certainly not this emptiness that welled every time she thought of all that had happened since she had come to Kinnereth Province. And certainly not the barren chill of her bed each night and the knowing that nothing would change. Ever. No matter how hard she tried.

Like a fool she had gone to the bakery this morning again for the third morning in a row.

And like a fool, she had waited in vain for a friend who would not join her.

She spooned up some of the gray, lumpy soup again, watching it plop into her bowl. The next moment, she realized Jordie was gone.

"Where did she go?" she heard herself ask.

Kata looked up from her empty bowl. "To bed."

"Where is everyone else?" Miri asked to keep the conversation going. She hadn't seen or heard from anyone in a few days. Too busy with their meetings with the ambassador, she supposed.

She didn't really care.

Miri looked up from her soup after a pause that had gone on too long.

Seeing the look, Kata finally answered. "The ambassador has kept Phinehas busy. And Galina has *selflessly* offered her companionship in your absence."

Miri rolled her eyes. Good. Let Galina play Phinehas's whore for a while. Miri was tired of every bit of it. "Where is Jareth?" Miri decided to prod. But when her friend did not answer, something sharp rose within her.

Kata eventually shrugged. "I'm sure he's lingering not too far from here."

Miri looked out the dark door of the kitchens, then back to her friend across the table, indignation welling. "Why do you insist on ignoring him?" Miri challenged.

Kata did not match Miri's sudden temper, but remained a bit forlorn at the opposite end of the table. She said nothing.

Miri slapped her hands on the table. "He's obviously in love with you!" she spat. "Why do you ignore that? Do you think you're too good for him?"

Still Kata said nothing, which managed to infuriate Miri more.

"What's going on with you lately?" Kata said instead. But Miri could tell she was deflecting.

"Nothing," she groused, and returned her attention to the lumpy soup.

"It's not nothing. I know you, Miri. Something is bothering you."

Miri looked up, but schooled her face into blank neutrality. She had no desire to talk about Ezra. About the offer she had turned down and the friend she had thrown away in the process.

"Did something happen with the grand duke?"

Miri froze, uncomfortable with the idea that Kata knew her business so clearly. Even now. After Miri had basically ignored her friend for weeks. Could she even call them friends at this point?

"What have you heard?" Miri spat under her breath.

"Nothing," Kata quickly answered. "I just know you. And you've been so occupied with him for months. Now all of a sudden, you're not. Did something happen between you? Did he hurt you?"

"Never," Miri said quickly. "He would never—" She was saying too much.

"Then what's going on? Your temper is on a short leash, Miri. Worse than normal."

Miri knew her friend well enough to know that the comment was supposed to be a joke to lighten the mood. But it did nothing of the sort.

But she needed to talk. She *wanted* to talk about it. She needed someone else to reassure her that she hadn't been a fool. It was Ezra who had been the fool. To offer something like that to a whore. It was ridiculous. Of course it was!

"He offered me his estate," Miri blurted out, immediately regretting it at the look that came over Kata's face.

"What?" she asked, slowly setting down her spoon. "What do you mean *his estate?*"

"I mean he offered me his estate. Everything," Miri said, and hearing it out loud only underlined how foolish the whole thing had been. How asinine.

"As in... 'Here, Miri. Have all my wealth. It's yours.' As in that?"

"Something like that," Miri said, dejected.

When Kata did not say anything for a long moment, Miri finally demanded, "What?"

"What did you tell him?"

"I told him no, of course! I'm not an idiot!"

"Are you sure about that?" Kata asked, and the question only fueled Miri's ire.

"I'm not talking about this," Miri said, standing.

"Why in the world did you turn something like that down, Miri?"

"Because it's insane!" Miri said. She rubbed between her eyes with her thumb and forefinger, releasing a tight breath.

"Every girl here dreams of something like that happening. Some foolish lord with too much money on his hands offering her everything if only she'll come with him. Be his mistress. It's the perfect way out, Miri. It's the perfect game."

Except Ezra hadn't asked Miri to be his mistress. In fact,

considering he hadn't so much as laid a hand on her, it was fairly clear that Ezra wanted nothing of the sort from Miri.

So what *did* he want?

Slowly, Miri sat back down as Kata went on.

"Take him up on it, Miri! If he's stupid enough to do such a thing, that's not your fault. Do whatever he wants for a while—be his whore. Or his mistress. Sheol, be his *wife* if he wants. Let him spoil you. Buy you fine gowns and take you to royal balls. All of it. And then when he tires of you, take what you want and leave. He'll be glad to be rid of you, and you'll have a pretty nest egg to start over. Do do whatever you want. Go wherever you want. Don't you see it, Miri? It's your ticket out of this Sheol hole!"

She knew somewhere in the back of her mind that Kata wasn't wrong. It was an easy way to start over. To be free.

But Ezra had offered her that. Without the caveat of sex. He had offered her everything. Every bekah in his coffers.

Surely—surely there was some sort of catch. Some game he was playing. Something he was much too clever, too sinister for Miri to pick up on.

So she was glad. Glad she had avoided that spiderweb. Glad she had been wise enough to see through it. To know there was always a string attached. It was always a game when it came to men. There was always an angle and it was always in their favor.

"Why in the world are you still sitting here?" Kata asked, shattering Miri's thoughts.

"Why in the world aren't you with Jareth, then?" Miri blurted, regretting it the moment she saw the look on Kata's face shift from incredulity to something much, much darker.

"I know he's in love with me, Miri," Kata said softly.

Miri paused, surprised by the admission. "You *know*?"

"I...I think I love him, too," Kata admitted, her words small, her shoulders slumped.

"Then why aren't you with him?"

Kata looked down, slowly stirring the remains of her soup with her spoon. "Because," she finally said.

"Because why?" Miri asked, exasperated.

"Because," Kata retorted, at last showing some passion when it came to the sage who followed her like a pup. "Because I don't want to!"

"Do you know how ridiculous that sounds?" Miri shot back. "You have a chance at something more. Something...real. Why would you throw that away?"

"Because I have to," Kata said.

"Because why?" Miri demanded.

"Because he deserves better!" Kata burst out before leaping to her feet and disappearing into the darkness beyond.

BECAUSE HE DESERVES BETTER.

Miri hated how much she understood Kata's refusal to embrace what was right in front of her. She hated how reasonable it sounded. And as she walked through the village the next morning—not to sit miserably on the rooftop and wait for Ezra who would not come, but to distract herself—she hated how much of herself she had seen in Kata last night.

Miri stared into a shop window, lined with all manner of whirring, magical gadgets and inventions. She wondered why *anyone* would have need of a perfume bottle that sprayed itself for you anytime you walked by. In one corner of the display rested a strange-looking contraption with spider-like arms that held your book and turned your pages for you. Miri was instantly reminded of her cousin—he'd had something similar when they were children. In another corner, draped across a handwoven basket, she noticed a blanket with a sign that read: *guaranteed to stay warm no matter how cold the weather.* That, she decided, seemed a delightful use of magic.

"I have a much better blanket than that," came a voice from behind, startling her. "One my grandmother made herself."

Miri whirled to find Ezra standing not three feet from her on the promenade, his smile a bit crooked, emphasizing the dimple on his right cheek.

"Hello, Wildfire," he said. "I missed you."

He stepped forward and reached out, taking both of her hands and lifting them to his mouth, kissing one, then the other, before lowering them again. He did not let them go, however. "How is it possible that you are even more lovely than the last time I saw you?"

She did not know what to say, jutting her chin backward at his declaration.

"May I say that?" he asked, tilting his head to one side.

"Yes," she said, hesitantly.

"Good," he replied. "It would be a pity not to." He turned, and tucking her hand into the crook of his arm, he began walking down the promenade in the direction of the bakery. "I have so much to tell you. So much I could not put in my letters. Sufficient to say—"

"Your letters?" she asked, abruptly stopping.

"Yes," he said, also stopping and facing her. "I did not want you to worry. I know that I frightened you, and I know that I put a lot of pressure on you the other night. I am sorry that I dropped it on you so abruptly. I should have given you time to think it over. Then, of course, with everything going on, I—"

"Everything going on?" she asked, confused.

"Oh Miri," he said. "It has been one nobleman after another. For three days, they haven't stopped darkening my door. I told Thaddeus this morning that if he allowed one more soul through my doors he would be sacked," Ezra added with a chuckle.

"Thaddeus?" Miri asked stupidly, unsure where to begin unfolding what he was saying.

"My butler. You shall meet him. He's not nearly as much of a curmudgeon as he likes to let on," he said amiably. "Anyway, like I said in my letters, there is all manner of hubbub over this prophet. He is coming to Shalem, Miri. Can you believe it?"

"I did not get any letters," she said, and at her declaration, Ezra paused again.

"What?"

She said nothing, merely shaking her head. Trembling. She was trembling because of his nonchalance. The way he spoke to her as if nothing was wrong. As if nothing had transpired. As if she hadn't refused him three days ago and then he'd disappeared as if he'd never speak to her again.

"Oh Miri," he said. "I did not know. I did not realize you weren't getting the letters." He placed warm hands at the top of her arms. "You are trembling. Oh my Wildfire, I'm sorry. You must have wondered..."

She couldn't help the tears that began to fall freely down her cheeks. Ezra pulled her into his arms without hesitation, kissing the top of her head before he said, "Don't cry, Wildfire."

But she did cry. Like a little girl. She cried and pressed her tears into the warmth of Ezra's chest. He wrapped his arms tightly around her, running gentle hands along her back.

"I thought..." she tried to say, but she hiccoughed a small sound before continuing. "I thought you were so angry. I thought..."

"Angry?" he asked, pulling back just enough to lift her chin with one hand. "Why in the world would I be angry?"

"Because I refused you!" she said, sniffling.

She could see it—the laugh he tried to hide behind pursed lips. "Oh Miri," he said, pulling her back into his tight embrace. "I am not mad at you."

"Shouldn't you be?"

"You're allowed your own opinion, you know. Even if it is different from mine."

"I hardly think a refusal is a mere difference of opinion," she added, wondering why she was countering her own argument.

At that, Ezra finally chuckled, pulling back from their embrace again to meet her eyes. "If you're trying to get rid of me, you're going to have to do a lot better than that."

Relief. It was relief that flooded her eyes with a new wave of tears. Ezra moved both hands to her face, using his thumbs to wipe away her tears. "I was going out of my mind, you know," he said. "I can hardly stand to go a day without seeing you. Three days, and I was practically coming out of my skin!"

"So was I," she said, her voice small.

"Oh good!" he declared.

"Good?" she protested, furrowing her brows.

Ezra's chuckle sent a puff of air across her brow as he kissed it. "I'd hate to be the only one, Wildfire. Now come with me. Let's get some breakfast. We're going to need it."

"Why?" she asked, allowing him to lead her along the promenade.

"Because we are spending the day together."

"Aren't you a terribly important and very busy aristocratic man?"

"Yes," he chuckled. "But nothing is more important than you."

"DOESN'T it seem like a bit of a waste of magic to you?" she asked, climbing rather gingerly into the gondola that had magically rowed to them the moment they stepped onto the promenade at the edge of the lake. The intricate glass wobbled beneath her feet, and she gripped the arm Ezra offered a little more tightly as she stepped inside. The glass beneath her feet sent a wave of nausea straight through her, and she quickly averted her eyes from the uninhibited view of what lurked beneath the waters.

"Whoa there, you all right?" Ezra asked with a chuckle, coming to her aid as he too, climbed into the glass boat. He wrapped a steady arm around her waist, and she let herself lean into his solid sureness.

"I'm fine," she said.

"You're green," Ezra countered.

She did not doubt him. She had never been in a glass gondola. She had never even heard of one before moving to Shalem. But according to Ezra, they were a risk worth taking—and an attraction that the locals loved to enjoy. And after breakfast, he had insisted on taking her to one.

No oars, no one to row it, the boat was powered by magic alone, and would take them as far out onto the lake as they wanted, with nothing more than a few pats on the side to inform it where to go and how far. Ezra settled onto the narrow glass bench in the middle of the boat and gestured for her to sit beside him. She welcomed the security of his arm around her as he pulled her close to him.

"Autumn is settling in, isn't it?" she said, trying to distract herself from the dizzying effect of floating on top of a crystal clear lake in nothing but glass so pure, it felt like there was nothing beneath them at all. She squinted her eyes shut to keep from catching a glimpse of the busy lake waters beneath her feet.

Ezra puffed a chuckle. "You don't know the half of it," he said, and then he pressed a kiss to her temple as he used his spare hand to tap the side of the gondola three times. The magic of the boat set the intricate gears and cogs embedded in the sides to a gentle whir and they set off away from the shore with unearthly smoothness.

"You going to be all right?" he asked.

She decided to risk a slight peek through her squinted eyes, only to realize that the gondola was not moving nearly as quickly as she had imagined. It glided along the water at a rather calming pace—enough to truly enjoy the breathtaking scenery around and beneath. From this perspective, the lake was nothing more than a mirror of the towering mountains. Great pines and aspens turning a violent shade of gold reflected off the glassy waters, and the white, fluffy clouds above them seemed to dance on the surface. The mountains themselves were somehow taller from this angle, their snowcapped peaks like mighty giants guarding the valley. Beneath them, the waters were so deep it seemed as if they might never find the bottom of the lake. Brightly colored fish darted through the depths, their scales reflecting the morning sunlight. Great plants waved lazily in the placid waters like old friends offering salutations.

Ezra rubbed a soothing hand along her arm. "It's not so bad once you get used to it," he said.

She looked up at him, suddenly realizing just how close he was, his breath warm on her cheek. For all the scenery, for everything around her that could attract her attention, truly nothing compared to him. Beautiful. That was the only word to describe him. Ezra was a beautiful man. It wasn't just his piercing eyes, his inky hair, or even that dimple on his cheek. It was something else about him—something deep, profound—he was beautiful inside and out.

A soft breeze played with the curls that had spilled out of the pile of hair on top of her head, and Ezra took the opportunity to tuck a strand behind her ear, letting his fingers linger along her jaw.

"My grandparents took me on a gondola for the first time when I was only a boy of five or so. I was terrified then too," he offered with a warm smile.

"You were a child. I think you had an excuse."

Ezra laughed. "Well, Grandfather told me that he was a teenager the first time he got on one of these, and he spent most of the ride vomiting off the side. My grandmother was less than impressed."

"She was with him?" Miri asked.

"He was trying to woo her." Ezra laughed and Miri joined him, covering her mouth with her palm.

"That's terrible!" Miri lamented, a laugh catching in her throat. "Then again, I believe someone once told me that no woman can resist falling into a man's arms when she's in one of these things."

"I should certainly hope not," Ezra said. She looked up, catching a hint of a grin on his full mouth.

She bit her lip, something dancing in her gut when she said, "I see. Is this your attempt to woo me, then?"

"Yes," he answered without hesitation. "Is it working?"

She searched him, too stunned to come up with an answer. She narrowed her eyes before she finally dared to say, "No."

His lips turned into a humorous pout. "Too bad."

The fact that Miri could not think of a response unsettled her, to say the least. She looked down, opting to fiddle with her fingers instead. Ezra seemed undaunted.

"The lake is a lot deeper than it looks," he offered, and the idea didn't help the nausea one little bit. "They say there are ancient creatures in its depths."

"Mmm," she said, closing her eyes once more, willing her senses to calm. "So if you cannot woo me with the romance of a glass gondola, is it your plan to force me into your arms with the constant reminder of my own nausea?"

Ezra grinned like a fiend. "It was worth a shot, wasn't it?" When she leveled a flat look at him, he laughed. "Do you want me to take you back?"

"No," she said quickly, shutting her eyes once more. "Just—give me a minute."

He moved his arm away from her back, and the absence had her taking the risk to open her eyes.

"Give me your hands," he said, and she looked down to see his palms open between them. She rested her hands in his, and he immediately began massaging her palms. The pressure sent a surge of relief through her.

"What sort of magic is this?" she asked, practically moaning the words.

Ezra chuckled. "No magic. It just helps. Don't ask me why."

She shut her eyes at his ministrations, marveling at how thoroughly it worked.

"The boat is not running on magic, either," he added. "Not real magic, anyway."

She opened her eyes again, tilting her head to one side in question.

"None of these silly little conveniences are real magic," he went on. "Stirring spoons and teapots that never cool. Even winged ships and steam carriages... They're just manmade versions of magic. But they're nothing like the real thing."

"The real thing?" she asked.

"The lake. The forest. The stag. That was real magic, Miri."

"Real magic?" she asked. "Wouldn't you say railcars and flying ships are real?"

Ezra chuckled. "Of course they're real. That's not what I mean. But that sort of magic is...well I don't think it's really magic. I think that's just what we call it, instead of what it actually is. Innovation. Industry. Infrastructure. Powerful stuff, to be sure. But I don't think it's really magic."

She furrowed her brows for a moment, contemplating his meaning. "Then what is magic?"

He didn't answer for a moment, kneading her wrists. "I

haven't been able to stop thinking about it since we went there," he eventually said. "It was magic, Miri. That's all I know. All these things—all these conveniences. That's all they are—convenience. That lake. That stag. Those stars. That was something else. Something more." His hands continued kneading down her wrists, the nausea steadily subsiding with every move of his strong fingers.

"Does it really matter? The difference?" she asked.

"I don't know," he admitted. "I suppose we'll find out."

She watched him. Watched his powerful fingers working along her skin before she asked, "What do you suppose happened to us?" She didn't clarify, knowing he would know exactly what she was asking.

Where had they gone when they jumped into that starlit lake? And what had happened to them while they were there?

Ezra searched her face for a moment, his hands going still. Then, with his eyes still locked on hers, he moved his thumbs to her palms, tracing delicate patterns there, as if remembering something. An image danced in her mind—silver wisps of light, dancing on her palms.

Ari, kissing her brow.

There is only one true magic, Miriam. Never forget that.

Ari had given her the gift of magic when she was only a girl. She had never questioned it until now. Never thought how strange it was that he should gift such a thing. That he should even be *able* to gift such a thing.

It was a part of her she had kept curled tightly within—a story she had never told another soul. Not even Phinehas. It was something she did not fully understand.

"I have magic," she said, so softly she wondered if Ezra had even heard her.

But when she met his eyes, there was no surprise in them, no question. Only quiet peace. He nodded once, bending to kiss her palms.

"I think I knew that," he finally said. "Somehow, I think I already knew."

She took hold of both of his hands, pressing her palms tightly to his. She shut her eyes, unsure what she was doing. Unsure what she wanted to do. But as if of its own will, a warmth rushed to her hands and a light flared brightly enough that she opened her eyes, looking down to their joined hands resting on her lap. Ezra's hands glowed, and his own eyes flared for a moment. He took his hands from hers, raising them to inspect more closely. Whorls and curls of rich silver and blue covered his golden skin, giving off a pale glow.

"Did you give this to me?" he asked quizzically, mesmerized by his own hands.

"No," she said, knowing it was the truth in her gut. Finally understanding what had happened between her and her cousin all those years ago. "I just woke what was already in you."

CHAPTER TWENTY

Magic. Deep and pure and...shared. Ezra and Miri *shared* magic.

Ezra gazed stupefied at his glowing hands. Miri lifted hers to meet his, and palm to palm, they laced their fingers together, the magic between them glowing white-hot before disappearing altogether. He stared at their joined hands a bit longer, waiting for something else to happen. The light was gone, but the heat lingered. When he met her eyes again, silver tears lined them.

"You all right?" he asked softly. Miri nodded. He released her so he could take her face in his hands. Soft. She was so soft. And so warm. Like a blanket of summer grass on a mountainside. He loved how he felt when he was with her. Like home. Settled. Like the thing he had always known was missing was finally found. Only a few months ago, he had questioned everything about his life and the impulsivity of throwing away his marriage and his future with the royal family. Only a few months ago, he had jumped off of a cliff without knowing where he would land.

All that risk seemed so small now, looking at her. Seeing her. Feeling her.

For the first time since losing his family, everything made sense when he looked at Miriam Sasson. A smile found his mouth before he realized what was happening. He found himself transfixed by her lips—supple and rosy and glistening. So very inviting. So very...familiar.

"Miri, have I—?" But that was silly. Of course he hadn't. Ezra knew he had never kissed Miriam before. He would remember it.

He realized Miri was nodding softly when he felt her face move in his hands. He cleared his thoughts and focused again. Blushing, Miri looked down, and Ezra took the opportunity to pull her closer to him.

"The lake," she said, and he nodded.

"Yes. The lake." He had kissed her in that lake. He could almost remember it now. Almost feel it. See it. A picture of starlight and whorls of colorful clouds and soft lips flooding his mind...

"Ezra, the lake," she said again.

"It's technically a pond, Wildfire," he said, leaning closer to her, a smile finding his mouth. "I kissed you in that pond, didn't I?"

Miri did not answer his question. "What's in the lake?" There was a hint of horror in her words.

Ezra stiffened, pulling away from her, following her gaze to the glass beneath them.

To the scales that slithered beneath the boat, practically glowing beneath the dark waters, much too large to be fish scales. Ineffable shades of amethyst and emerald, opaline and silver, the scales were curled around a rather long tail, covered in deadly black spikes all the way to the end. They appeared just beneath the glass bottom of the gondola, curling up high enough to see before disappearing again into the black depths.

He had heard the stories—the tales of a leviathan, cursed to live in these waters. Even as a boy, one of Esther's favorite ways to scare the living shit out of him was to tell him those stories. But he never really thought they were true. Just stories. Folk tales. Dragon lore.

But now, seeing those scales... Something stirred in Ezra. "Mother of kings, it's true," he heard himself breathe.

"What's true?" Miri asked, looking up to him.

He met her stricken gaze. "The legends. Legends of dragons."

Miri's eyes danced, her brows furrowed as if searching the depths of her memory for something.

"Bound by the sea for all eternity, Leviathan awaits her destiny," she whispered.

Ezra nodded, finishing the verse. *"By fire and flame she sets the world ablaze for the coming of the new age."*

"But what does that mean?" she asked.

"There are dozens of stories about it. Most say the dragons are cursed to lurk beneath the waters until..."

He looked up, wide-eyed and wondering.

"Until what?" Miri asked, squeezing his forearm.

He focused on her again as he finally managed to say, "Until the wildfire."

"Is that why you call me Wildfire?" she asked, accepting his help stepping off the gondola and back on to solid ground.

"No," he said truthfully. "I just started calling you that because of your hair. I had never put that together until now."

Miri brushed her skirts and fussed with the knot of curls on top of her head for a minute before she said anything. "It doesn't mean anything, then. It's just coincidence."

"Yes, of course," he agreed, though privately, he couldn't help feeling as if it was anything but coincidence. But he could see the worry gnawing at her as they walked along the lakeside. It remained in her as they shared a quiet lunch in a village bistro and all the rest of the afternoon, while exploring some of the abandoned villas on the mountainside.

He decided a distraction was in order. "I have an idea," he said, loving the way the waning sun bathed her skin in gold.

"What's that?" she asked absently, balancing along a low rock ledge at the edge of one of the ancient homes.

"Let's go to the theatre."

She looked up, her arms extended on either side for balance, making her look like a bird about to take flight. Delight flashed in her eyes for a brief moment before disappearing completely.

"I'm not properly dressed," she said, deflating.

"Well, that's rather easy to remedy," he said, stepping towards her and offering his hand to help her off the wall.

"I don't think going to the temple right now—"

"There's a wonderful clothier right here in the village," he said.

She blushed, turning away from him just a bit as she said, "I haven't any money."

He grinned, taking her hand and lacing his fingers between hers. "You have more than you could fathom."

"ANTONIUS!" Ezra said amiably as the dressmaker greeted them eagerly from behind the counter of the clothier shop.

"Ezra, old friend!" said the slender man, bustling around the counter and taking Ezra's hand in his.

"And who is this lovely thing?" the dressmaker asked, turning his attention to Miri. He was immaculately dressed in a perfectly tailored pinstripe suit of a rich blue and pale gray. His cravat was the same shade of silvery gray as the pinstripes. His wingtips were polished so perfectly they might have passed for a looking glass.

"This is Lady Miriam Sasson of Teman," Ezra said. It had been so long since Miriam had heard her full title that she hardly recognized it. She shot a wide-eyed gaze to Ezra, who winked, squeezing the hand he kept wrapped tightly in his.

"Lady Miriam," said the dressmaker with a small bow. "What an honor to meet you. Please tell me I get to dress you."

"We're headed to the theatre tonight, and we need something suitable," said Ezra. "Do you have anything ready-made?"

"You're in luck. The tails you sent for tailoring last week are ready," Antonius said, clapping his hands sharply to summon a portly assistant. She wore dress of simple make but fine fabric. A measuring tape fell from her shoulders, and a cushion of pins was strapped to her wrist.

"Hadriana!" he called rather abruptly, in stark contrast to the glowing approval he had shown Ezra. "See to it that His Grace's tails are a proper fit."

Then Antonius whirled to face Miri. "As for you..." he said, a measure of delight in his cunning eyes. He took her by the hand and practically yanked her along. "Come with me."

"I do not keep many ready-made gowns around," Antonius said. "There is not much occasion for them around here, you see. Most of the noblewomen want something custom-made." The dressmaker circled Miri once before stopping in front of her. He stepped back, crossing his arms and appraising Miri head to toe. After a moment, the dressmaker gave a *hmph* before reaching up and pulling the tie from Miri's hair, letting the mess of curls spill down her shoulders. Appraising once more, he at last nodded as if satisfied and turned to march across the room.

As Antonius gathered dresses, Miri eyed several in the small room before pausing on a black gown on a nearby dress form. In a word, it was sumptuous. A fitted gown encrusted with the perfect amount of glittering onyx on the bodice that hugged the form all the way down to a small skirt that spilled out just below the knees. Of fine make and fabric, the dress likely cost more than Miri's entire wardrobe—over the course of her entire life.

"I'm sure anything you have will be fine," Miri said.

"Nonsense. With that figure? You need something that shows you off, my little cocoon. I shall give you wings yet. I have a few things that might work just perfectly."

Behind the door, Miri had left a chuckling Ezra to the ministrations of the portly tailor. She was both glad and terrified of Ezra's absence from this room, for while she had no desire to parade a wardrobe of gowns for him, or anyone else for that matter, she also had no idea what gowns like these must cost. She had no desire to pick something overly expensive and take advantage of Ezra's kindness.

"Do you like this?" Before Miri could answer, Antonius shook his head and tossed the gown aside with a *tsk*. "Too plain. Perhaps something in red?" He held up a crimson, feathered contraption that looked more like a puzzle than a gown. Galina would have probably loved it.

Antonius tossed it aside without waiting for her reaction as he pulled the next gown forward. "Emerald, I think. It will bring out the colors in your hair."

"That's fine," Miri said, and obediently took the gown, stepping into the curtained-off dressing room beside her. She emerged a moment later, covered head to toe in velvet and jewels and gold accents and...

"She doesn't need all of that, Antonius," said Ezra. Miri whirled to find him stepping into the room, dressed in black brocade tails that fit his broad, chiseled frame perfectly. The crisp white shirt beneath his jacket was perfectly accented with a pale gold silk cravat and a single, diamond pin. The assistant followed behind, frantically removing pins from Ezra's shoulders before crouching beside him, marking something on the side of the coat with a worn piece of chalk. At her aid, several measuring tapes went to work, slithering along his back and shoulders without her help, measuring and moving along. Miri spotted a quick scrawl appearing on a small slip of paper in the assistant's hand; the magical measuring tapes were registering Ezra's every measurement. Ezra all but ignored the entire thing.

"Yes, it's a bit much for me," said Miri, looking down.

"The gown is not too much for you," said Ezra. "You wear it exceptionally well. But you're too beautiful to be covered in all of that fuss."

Antonius seemed a bit miffed by Ezra's assessment, but quietly acquiesced, picking another gown—this one a sky blue. He held it aloft for approval. Ezra nodded, shrugging, so Miri took it and tried it on. More complicated than the emerald number, she could not fasten the back on her own, mildly horrified when the assistant unceremoniously flung open the curtain to her dressing room with a huff and rather viciously drew the laces of the gown. Miri could see in the looking glass before her that Ezra had politely averted his eyes, busying himself with a swath of fabric as if he hadn't just caught a glimpse of Miri's bare back.

"What sort of corset is this, girl?" Hadriana grunted through clenched teeth as she pulled each ribbon tight.

"I—it was a gift," Miri admitted quietly. A gift from Phinehas. A corset made to display her assets. Nothing a fine lady would wear. A corset for a whore.

The lacing ceased for a moment, and Miri looked up into the mirror before her to see Hadriana's eyes widen with understanding.

"Wouldn't't've thought His Grace would be seen in public with the likes of you," she muttered, returning to drawing the laces a bit more roughly.

Miri wanted to point out that she felt the exact same way, but chose to say nothing.

When at last the gown was laced, Miri stepped out, turning once for Ezra's benefit. He gave her a once-over, his face showing nothing of his thoughts.

"Do you like it?" he asked.

Miri shrugged. The gown was lovely. It would do just fine. She wanted to leave this place.

Ezra eyed her for a moment, running a thumb and forefinger along his jaw before he said, "Let's do that one," pointing to the black gown Miri had first spotted.

"No, not that one," Miri said.

"You don't like it?" Ezra asked.

"No, I love it. I just—"

"Then try it on," he interrupted.

"His Grace has excellent taste. One of my finest gowns," Antonius said, unlacing the gown from the form with a proud smirk.

"Ezra," Miri whispered through her teeth.

"Humor me," he said, a sparkle of mirth in his eyes. The dressmaker's assistant had returned to fussing with Ezra's new clothes, stitching here or there, huffing little puffs of frustration then and again when Ezra moved unexpectedly.

Before she knew it, Miri was in the dressing room again, and once again, Hadriana entered just in time to lace the gown for her. It was as soft as silk and as warm as velvet. And it fit like it had been custom-made for her. She took a moment to stare at herself in the looking glass. Hadriana supplied a pair of pale-gold silk gloves to complement the ensemble perfectly, helping Miri slip them on her arms.

Of all the fine dresses she had worn for Phinehas—all the revealing, flimsy outfits he had chosen for her—never once had she felt so elegant, so beautiful. And when at last she turned and opened the curtain that separated her from Ezra, she did not feel like a plaything on display for a man's tawdry imagination.

She felt... She felt...

Ezra stood before her in silent appreciation, and she could not help the blush that crept up her cheeks as his face melted into a radiant smile. He stepped towards her, running a single knuckle down her cheek.

"You make a handsome pair," said Antonius, breaking the silence between them, crossing satisfied arms across his chest.

Not knowing what to say, Miri pushed a hand through her hair. "I'll need to do something with this."

"No," said Ezra, gently taking hold of her wrist. "It's perfect. You're perfect." Ezra tilted her chin up to get a better view, so close to her that she thought he might kiss her right in front of the dressmaker and his huffy assistant.

"You are an artist, Antonius," Ezra said, never breaking his gaze with Miri.

"I know. I'll mark it on your ledger," he said with smug enjoyment, and then he left the room, wordlessly taking his assistant with him.

Miri watched them leave, unsure she wouldn't just come apart at the way Ezra continued to stare into her. Through her. His knuckle lingered under her chin, and she could taste the sweetness of his breath against her lips.

"I don't deserve you," Ezra said at last.

Miri finally met his eyes again. Ezra wrapped his free arm around her waist and leaned to press a gentle, lingering kiss to her cheek. But she wanted more—she wanted to wrap her arms around his neck and pull him as close as possible and kiss him until she could scarcely breathe. But a gentleman would never kiss a lady in public. Never mind she was no lady. And before she could move, he was moving again, offering her his arm.

She took it, resting a glove-covered hand in the crook of his elbow and letting him lead the way.

"WHAT IS THE SHOW TONIGHT?" Miri asked, gingerly lifting the skirt of her gown with trembling, nervous fingers as she and Ezra ascended the grand staircase in the lobby of the theatre. People stared. *Everyone* stared. Whispered to their companions. And when she caught words here and there, she understood why.

"I never took him for a whoremonger."

"I suppose any man would be desperate after losing the princess for a wife."

"He doesn't look desperate to me. He looks rather...satisfied." That was followed by a fit of quiet snickering behind silk gloves.

"Ignore them, Wildfire," said Ezra, leaning close to her when they at last made it to the top of the stairs.

"I cannot blame them. I suppose it's not every day a grand duke shows up with his whore on his arm—"

Ezra stopped abruptly, moving in front of her and forcing her to meet his eyes. They were serious. Hard. A wave of fear washed over her, and she used every bit of restraint not to cower.

"Never use that word again."

She swallowed once, holding his gaze, relaxing only a fraction when his face softened. He tucked a strand of hair behind her ear before he leaned closer and added with a raised eyebrow, "People will always talk, Wildfire. Why not give them something to talk about?"

"I don't think I'm very good for your reputation," she said.

Ezra chuckled. "I never had one to begin with."

"Yes, you did," she said.

"Let me rephrase that: I never had one that was accurate. I see no reason to start now."

"So I'm a game for you?" she asked, hoping the humor would calm her own nerves.

But Ezra's face turned serious again, and he made sure he had her full attention before he said, "Never."

Keeping his eyes on her, he lifted her hand to his mouth and pressed a soft kiss to the top.

Then he offered her his arm again and continued walking.

"My lord," said the usher, standing straight-backed beside a finely carved door. His double-breasted tails were perfectly pressed, the gold buttons polished to glimmer in the candlelight. His hands were covered in white gloves that seemed to glow as he extended his hand, ushering Ezra and Miri inside. "It is good to see you, my lord."

Ezra bowed his head to the usher. "And you, Felix."

"You're going to enjoy this one. It's one of my favorites so far," said the usher warmly.

"I've no doubt," Ezra said. With a gentle hand at her back, he ushered Miri into the small room before them.

"A private box? I should have known," Miri said with a laugh. Two velvet seats were positioned at a small angle just before a balcony rail. Heavy, red velvet curtains framed the opening, and gaslights flickered on the back wall, illuminating the gold filigree that ornamented the space.

"Isn't this where you first saw me?" Ezra asked, pulling out the chair closest to the stage for her to sit. She obliged, fixing her skirts before she answered.

"I suppose it is. It just never occurred to me that I'd join you here one day."

"You'll join me here many days, if I have anything to say about it."

Miri pursed a laugh and turned her attention to the stage, mesmerized as the orchestra settled into their many seats below, plucking and tweaking their instruments, finding notes and playing them out.

"What are they playing?" Miri asked, fascinated.

"They are tuning," Ezra said. "Listening for the overtones and matching them. Making sure the notes are perfect before they begin."

Miri faced Ezra, who was now occupying the chair beside her. He had moved it to be closer to her, resting his arm on the back of her chair. "You know about music?"

A chuckle. "Like most boys, I was expected to learn the pianoforte. I was never any good at it. But I found the mechanics of music fascinating. Studying how it works was much more exciting than actually learning to play."

"So you know everything about music and have nothing to show for it?"

A grin. "A love for the arts is nothing to show?"

Miri shrugged and turned her attention back to the stage. "It's hardly impressive," she quipped.

Ezra's chuckle was a surprise puff of warmth on her neck. With his hand resting on her waist, Ezra whispered onto the shell of her ear, "Tell me how I shall endeavor to impress you, my lady, and I shall do my best to oblige. I've offered you a glass boat ride, which you saw right through. A romantic lunch and afternoon of exploration. A new gown. I was hoping perhaps the theatre might convince you, but I can see that you are much too clever for all of that. So tell me how I may win your affections, and it shall be yours."

Gooseflesh spread across her neck and exposed shoulders, but she dared not turn to face him as she said, "I'll try to think of something."

Another chuckle, this one skirting along her skin. She thought

Ezra might kiss her cheek or neck, as close as he was. But he did nothing of the sort, instead leaning back into his chair again. She tried not to let her disappointment show.

All of this today—a game of some sort. She did not understand it, what Ezra was up to. What he wanted. Most men would have long-since taken her to their beds and have finished with her by now. Instead, Ezra had spent the last few months laughing with her over morning coffee. Taking her to his favorite places. Offering her endless distractions from her life in the temple, with nothing more than a kiss on the cheek at most. Then four days ago he had offered her everything, and when she had refused it, he had just continued on as if nothing in particular had transpired between them.

No, she did not understand whatever it was that Ezra Kelach was up to.

She did not understand it at all.

CHAPTER TWENTY-ONE

The show was gorgeous. An opera, which she had never seen in her life. Sung in the old language, she did not understand a single word of it. But it moved her. In deep, passionate ways. Every haunting note told a story. Every lilting aria forged a masterpiece. Every lively jaunt painted a portrait to explore. And by halfway through the second act, she was riveted, clutching her skirt in harrowed frustration as the story unfolded.

"Careful," Ezra whispered with a chuckle, and his words jolted her back to reality long enough to realize how close he was sitting to her. His body warm against her back, he placed a hand over hers, running a thumb along the top of her hand, coaxing it to relax. "You're going to rip your dress if you're not careful," he went on.

"Sorry," she said, relaxing a bit when she realized he was right.

"There is no need for apology. This is tragic," Ezra said.

"How can he leave her?" she practically begged, an unexpected tear falling down her cheek. The man sang with a haunting tenor, and though she did not understand his words, she understood the look of abject horror on the woman's face. He was leaving her. He did not love her.

"He feels he has no choice," whispered Ezra, his words warm on her ear.

"Why? Why doesn't he have a choice?"

"Because he loves her. And he must save her. She is trapped, and he knows it. The only way to set her free is to let her go."

Miri hated it. She could not see why it should be so. The song rose and fell in a harrowing melody that ripped anew with every lilting turn. Miri vaguely felt Ezra move behind her and realized why a moment later, as he extended his handkerchief to her.

"Thank you," she breathed through sobs.

Ezra pressed a soft kiss to her shoulder but said nothing else.

When the song ended, the audience made no sound. For a moment that felt like an eternity, the theatre was silent. Then the lights dimmed completely, the curtains closed, and at last, the orchestra played a single note for several measures. A note that wrapped itself around Miri as if to console. To understand. To agree.

She thought it was over and was about to decry her protest when the curtains suddenly opened again to a shocking scene.

The man lay sprawled on the ground, stretched over the motionless body of his lover, her master standing above them both, holding a dripping dagger.

The audience gave a collective gasp, and the notes of the symphony decayed, leaving them in silence once more. Then, in a most shocking turn, the woman sat up straight, inadvertently rolling the man she loved off of her. When she realized what she had done, she sang a piercing note and turned, deftly retrieving the dagger from her master and turning it on him.

She was free. Her wicked master was gone.

And the love of her life was dead.

Miri covered her mouth with Ezra's handkerchief, unable to stop the tears that fell as the final notes rang out and the gaslights below brightened once more.

"It's *over?*" She wasn't sure if she had mouthed the words or spoken them aloud.

"I did not realize quite how harrowing this one was," Ezra said, his eyes fixed on the stage as the heavy, crimson velvet curtains drew to a haunting close.

"How could he do that? How could he just die?" she demanded, finally turning to face Ezra.

"He had to die. To save her."

"Surely there was another way! Surely he could have lived!" she protested.

"Yes, he could have lived. But then she would have died."

"Well, that's ridiculous! He should not have died!"

"He would do anything to save her. Even give his own life."

"That's lunacy!"

Ezra chuckled. "I think that's called sacrificial love. It was more important to him that she have her freedom than she have him."

"She should have both!" Miri croaked, dabbing more and more tears from her cheeks. Why she was so upset... Why it was getting to her... "I don't understand why I'm even bothered by this! I didn't understand a damn word of it!"

Ezra cupped her cheek with one hand, turning her to face him. "I didn't mean for this to upset you, Miri," he said gently.

"Well, how can this be right? Shouldn't love win? Shouldn't they be together?"

"Love did win," he said. "She will always have him in her heart."

"That's not the same," she huffed, crossing her arms.

"Perhaps not. But I think the truest love is the kind that does what is best for the other person."

Miri looked at Ezra, calming at the surety in his words, the gentle way he spoke them to her.

"How could I be moved so much by something I didn't even understand?"

"Perhaps language is not the only way to understanding."

"What does that mean?"

"Oh, I think the most precious things in this world transcend spoken word," said Ezra.

"Like what?" asked Miri curiously.

Ezra looked down, brushing a knuckle along Miri's arm before he spoke. "Music, I think. It speaks to us in ways language never could. Hope is another one. Faith." He looked up again, meeting her eyes before he added, "Love."

"Love," Miri echoed, the word setting her heart at a gallop.

"Can you define it? Can you put it into words, really? Men have tried. Through the centuries we've tried to put it into songs and sonnets and poems and plays. We've built temples and carved sculptures in the name of love. We've waged wars and drawn swords for it. But if you ask us to tell you what it is, to explain it, we cannot. Because at the end of the day, we know love in our hearts, but we cannot really put it into words."

"Do you know love in your heart?" Miri asked.

"I do now," Ezra said without hesitation. "I had observed it before. Knew that it was real. But I did not know its full measure until now."

"Until this opera?" Miri asked, her heart pounding so hard she wondered if Ezra could hear it.

A smile ghosted across his mouth, but his eyes were locked with hers. "Right. Yes. Until this opera."

The gaslights in their private box brightened, bathing them in sudden, unexpected light. Miri turned her attention behind them as the usher opened the door and even more light from the hall spilled onto them.

When she looked back at Ezra, his eyes were still fixed on her. She wondered if he had ever taken them off of her.

"I don't want this day to end," she said.

"Good. Neither do I. Let's go for a walk," he said, standing and extending a hand to help her up. She took it and let him lead her out of the room.

"G'night, my lord," said the usher as they passed him.

"Goodnight, Felix."

"Do you know everyone in the village by name?" Miri asked as they walked down the hall towards the grand staircase.

"Shouldn't I? My family has served these people for centuries." Ezra led Miri gracefully down the steps that led to the front hall and doors. Throngs of theatregoers were now leaving their suites and the seats below, the din of conversation rising with every step they took.

"Your Grace," said a nobleman who tipped his hat to Ezra as he passed. Ezra nodded his head toward the man and his wife with a smile.

"And do they all adore you?" Miri asked as another aristocrat greeted Ezra.

Ezra puffed a laugh. "No. They don't adore me at all. Few of them truly know me. And even fewer care."

"Then why do they all say hello?"

"Because I'm richer than they are," said Ezra matter-of-factly.

She had never really heard him talk of his wealth before, though she had always assumed he had plenty of money. Most dukes did, in her experience. And considering he was the grand duke...

You'll have enough to start a kingdom of your own, should you wish.

She looked at the splendor around them—noblemen and noblewomen alike clothed in the finest gowns and tails, dripping in jewels and pearls. Proof of their wealth.

And yet, the way they ogled Ezra...the way they made a point of currying favor with him. She could only imagine the kind of staggering wealth and power he must possess that would give them reason to behave in such a way.

And he had offered every bit of it to her.

And she had turned it down.

She wondered what all of those groveling aristocrats would think if they knew he had offered all that wealth to her, no strings attached.

"I've only been grand duke for a few years. Hardly enough time to prove myself," Ezra went on, oblivious to her musings. "And considering that I ended my betrothal to the crown princess, I can only imagine what they think of me now. Reckless, to be sure. Naïve, perhaps. They're likely salivating at their notions of how easily they could manipulate such a fool as I."

Indeed. That much was evident in their shameless whispers and stares.

But Ezra was anything but reckless and naïve, despite how it looked. Ezra was calm and collected. Idealistic, yes. But he was thoughtful, deliberate, not impulsive.

And yet he had offered her the world. His world, anyway.

Maybe it really hadn't been some wild notion on his part but something he had been planning. Something he actually had *wanted* to do. For her.

Why had she been stupid enough to say no?

"Shall we walk on the promenade?" he asked, shattering her train of thought.

"Oh. Yes," she agreed, and followed his lead into the cool night.

THE PROMENADE WAS EMPTY. The night was dark and cool, and what little light the moon provided was hardly enough to keep the streets full. So they had the walk to themselves, the lapping lake at their side their only company. Which was perfectly fine with Miri, as she much preferred not to be distracted by the whispers of passersby.

Ezra was surprisingly quiet as they walked arm in arm along the lakeside. She wondered if perhaps she had done something to offend him and was about to ask him so when he stopped and turned towards her.

"I made a mistake, Miri," he said abruptly.

"What?"

"I see it now, the error in my thinking."

"What are you talking about?" Miri asked, confused.

Ezra took hold of her hands, looking down at them for a moment before he lifted his gaze to hers again. It was only then that she realized he was nervous.

"I thought I was doing the right thing. I thought I was doing you a favor by giving you my estate, by offering you my home, my life, with no strings attached. But I see now that I was wrong.

"I've spent the last four days trying to figure out how to convince you. How to prove to you that I meant what I said, but I see it now. They're just words, Miri. Just pretty promises. And you've been given pretty promises your whole life that meant nothing. And there I was, standing before you, promising you that you'd be free, with nothing to back it up. No proof of my love and my promise."

"Ezra..." Miri tried to stop him, but he dropped to one knee before she could even collect her thoughts.

Reaching into his jacket, Ezra pulled out something, placing it in the palm of her hand. "This belongs to you, Miri."

It was a ring.

Not just any ring.

A cluster of diamonds around a crest carved into heavy gold. It was heavy in her hand.

"What is this?" she asked breathlessly.

"The signet of the Kinnereth duchy. My grandfather had it made for my grandmother. He did not name her Grand Duchess by law, but they ran the estate as equals. Together. He gave her this ring to symbolize that. I suppose I just wanted to take it a step further."

Miri looked to him, speechless. But he was undaunted.

"I want to spend my life you. Not someday. Today. Now. I want to spend the rest of my life with you, because I am in love with you. And I didn't tell you that because I thought you might fear it. I thought you might think it a trap.

"But love isn't a trap. Not the real kind. It's... I'm rambling. Mother of kings, Miri. I just want to marry you. I want you to be my wife."

Miri froze, unsure what to say. She was trembling so violently she thought she might drop the ring and watch it shatter into a million tiny pieces at her feet.

Seconds passed. Maybe minutes. Ezra rose to both feet again, taking hold of her arms before he finally said, "Say something."

"I just thought you were going to ask me to come back with you again."

"Well, I am," he said with a small laugh. "But I want you there as my wife, not my ward. I didn't offer you the estate to be your savior, Miri. I offered it to you because I love you. And because I want it all. With you. Everything. I do not want to hold anything back."

Miri couldn't bring herself to find words—to form cohesive thoughts.

"If you're not ready that's all right. I can wait. Of course I can, I just—what I mean to say is—I want all of this. With you. I want to share it all with you. Every bit. And—"

"Yes," she finally said, although the word was smaller and meeker than she had intended.

Ezra stopped, meeting her eyes. "What?"

"I'll marry you, Ezra. I... I *want* to marry you."

"You do?" he asked.

She could only nod before his mouth found hers—crashed into hers, really. Ezra kissed her fiercely, holding nothing back. He pulled her tightly against his chest and kissed her breathless, and she could not help but think that was how kisses should always go—consuming and bright and heady and beautiful. So she snaked her arms around him and lost herself to him completely.

When Ezra relinquished her mouth, he reached up, taking her hand from his neck, removing the ring from her palm before slipping it onto her finger.

"What are you doing?" she asked, alarmed. "We're not married yet!"

Ezra grinned. "You're already the Grand Duchess, Miri. Technically, I can't propose to you. You'll forgive me for the breach of protocol. This isn't a wedding ring. It's the signet of the Kinnereth duchy. And yours as Grand Duchess."

"Ezra," she said flatly.

"What?" he asked, his tone innocent, pulling her back against his chest. He kissed her once, a soft, swift kiss.

"I am not Grand Duchess," she said.

"Oh yes you are. Will you please let me be your duke?"

"Stop playing like that. I don't like it."

Ezra's face turned serious. "I'm not playing, Miri. It's all yours. Every bit of it. Technically, I'm a freeloader currently trespassing in your castle."

She shook her head, unable to stop the little laugh that bubbled up. "You're ridiculous."

"Well, you agreed to marry me. I heard it. You can't take it back now."

"I don't want to," she said, and she meant every word of it. Even if it was preposterous—Grand Duchess. Even if it wouldn't matter once they were married, anyway. He was offering her the world on a gilded platter. Freedom. But more than that, he was offering her his whole heart. The only sufficient answer was to give him all of her in return. A smile crept slowly onto her mouth, and she did not bother to hide it.

Ezra took the opportunity to kiss that smile. She did not protest.

"Miri, I love you. I am so madly in love with you I can hardly think straight."

"I know. You asked me to marry you. Clearly, you're delusional."

"Allow me to spend the rest of my life showing you why it's the best idea I've ever had."

CHAPTER TWENTY-TWO

She kept eyeing the ring on her gloved finger every time she got the chance, and the sight made Ezra grin. He had not seen that ring on a hand since his grandmother wore it. He had not given it to Princess Rachæl either, for she would not have become Grand Duchess of Kinnereth upon their marriage. She was already Crown Princess of Har-Navah. No need for a lesser title. He'd had half a mind to give the ring to Esther long ago, but never did, for reasons he did not understand until recently.

The ring belonged to Miri. It belonged on her finger. He was glad he had kept it for her.

Ezra stifled a laugh as he watched her surreptitiously steal another look. The carriage he had hired jostled as it rolled along the cobblestones through the village, and Miri sat close to him in the darkness, nestled under his arm.

Home. They were going home. Together.

He couldn't help but kiss her again. She did not protest, which only gave Ezra reason to deepen that kiss, pulling her so close to him that nothing but fabric separated them.

He had been a bumbling fool for most of the day, so desperate to find a way to convince her of his love for her that it was robbing him of sense. By the time he had found the nerve to propose, he had fumbled it so much he thought she would laugh him off as an imbecile.

Instead, she had accepted. He had hardly believed it when he heard her answer. And when she had vowed forever to him only moments ago at the rooftop at Joshua and Winona's bakery, he could hardly contain his joy.

Wife.

She was his wife now. Jareth—a sage from the temple that Ezra had observed to be something of a friend to Miri—had agreed to meet them on the rooftop tonight, the final piece of Ezra's plan for their day. He had sent Jareth a letter a few days ago, asking for his help. The sage had happily agreed, promising to keep it quiet. So Jareth had married them in the peace of the village of Shalem. Under the stars, under the pale moonlight, Miri had given him her forever. And he had given her the same. There was something profoundly beautiful in the simplicity of those promises. That those vows had not been made as a matter of show as so many aristocratic weddings were. As his wedding to the princess surely would have been.

No, with just him and Miri there on that rooftop under the stars, there was something magical about it. Serene. Holy. Somehow, Ezra knew that they weren't really alone. That his grandfather had been watching—had seen the whole thing. Had smiled upon them.

Only truth between us.

Here was his truth. Pure and simple and beautiful.

Wife. This woman, this treasure was his wife.

And now, they were going home. Together. Ezra ran a finger down her delicate cheek, marveling at the way she practically purred at his touch. So many things—he had so many things he wanted to say to her. Share with her. Show her. He was brimming with the anticipation of taking her home. Starting their life, running the duchy together. Just as he'd observed his grandparents growing up. Partners. Equals.

He let his finger trail down her chin and neck, marveling when she did not stop him from exploring the soft swell of skin above her gown. He bent to press a kiss just above her dress and nearly came undone right there when she sighed, wrapping herself around him. An invitation.

He would not decline.

Gently, reverently, he laid her back against the carriage seat. He slipped those glorious silk gloves from her hands, taking a moment to put her ring back on her finger before he trailed kisses from her fingers down one arm, then the next. He pressed his lips to her neck and tasted the chalam-sweet skin he found there. She was a living flame and he was a willing victim, consumed by her every touch, every sigh, every sensuous move.

He was contemplating how he might undo the laces of her gown in such a cramped space when he heard his name in a hushed tone.

"What is it, my Wildfire?"

Miri met his eyes, and even in the darkness of the carriage, he could see the worry in them. He sat up, pulling her up with him. "What's wrong?"

Had he gone too far? Had he pushed her past what she was ready for? Never, *never* would he want to hurt her. To be just another one of the men who took and took and never gave anything in return.

"Ezra, I need to go back to the temple."

"What? Why?"

"I forgot something. Something I must get."

Ezra smiled in relief, pressing his lips to her neck. "Whatever it is, I'll buy you ten of them."

"It cannot be bought," she said. "Please, Ezra."

Ezra pulled away again, meeting her eyes. They were serious. Almost begging.

He put his hands on either side of her face. "Of course, my love. We'll go back right now."

He knocked twice on the roof of the carriage, and immediately, the driver slowed, turning the carriage around and heading back into the village.

"What is it you forgot?" he asked.

"A gift. From my cousin," she said.

Ah. Something to remember him by. Ezra understood that. How many little tokens and mementos did he have of his grandparents? Things to remember them by. Things he could not part with.

The carriage wound back through the village streets and up to the temple.

"I'll come with you," said Ezra.

"No," she said quickly. "You cannot."

"Of course I can," he said, smiling.

By now the carriage had come to a halt and the driver had come down from his seat. He was in the process of opening the door for them when Miri said, "Don't you see? If you come with me, they'll know. You've never come to my chambers before. They'll know something is different this time."

"Well, it *is* different. You've married me," Ezra pointed out.

Miri kissed him softly, a smile lingering on her mouth. "Yes, I have. Just let me run inside. I won't be ten minutes."

"I don't like you going back there," he said, unable to shake the worry dancing through his thoughts. He knew he had no concrete reason for that unease—only his gut and the flimsy pile of evidence John had uncovered about the high priest of Har-Navah. Maybe it proved nothing, maybe it proved every misgiving he had entertained since meeting the man. In the end, it didn't matter; he did not want her facing that man alone even once more.

"It will be fine," she said. "I will be back shortly. No one will think twice of it."

"Miri," he tried to keep her back, taking hold of her hands.

Miri kissed him so thoroughly that he forgot the rest of his argument.

"Ten minutes. Wait for me here," she said.

And then she disappeared out the carriage door.

"You've been a busy little bee, haven't you?"

Miri whirled in the darkened corridor. Not ten steps from her bedchamber, she thought she had made it through the temple unnoticed. Of course not. Of course *he* would find her.

"What do you want, Gian?"

Gian strolled casually towards her, as if an old friend come for small talk. He slipped his hands in the pockets of his black leather pants before he said, "Such interesting letters we receive around here. To you. To the sage. Jareth, I believe is his name?"

"You were the one who kept my letters," she said, her voice as low as a growl.

Gian only smiled, though it did not meet his eyes. "Your precious duke is the world's biggest fool, writing you like that. Be glad I did not let Phinehas get ahold of them."

"Give them to me," she spat.

"Where did you go today, little Miriam? Did your illustrious savior whisk you off into the night?"

"I don't know what you're talking about," she lied, squaring her shoulders.

Gian stepped closer, a sweet, spiced warmth on his breath—a

drink she did not recognize. "I thought you had finally used your brain. Instead, I see you never had one to begin with."

"What are you talking about?"

Gian looked her up and down. "My, my. Such a sumptuous gown, Miriam. Did His Grace buy that for your special day?"

She lifted her chin, refusing to answer. Gian's lips curled into a grin. But she had no interest in trying to figure out whatever game this monster was playing. She just needed to get her things and leave. She started to turn away from him, when a heavy hand on her shoulder stopped her in her tracks.

"You should not have come back here." Gian's words were merely a breath, but his bright cerulean eyes were two living flames.

"You needn't worry. I won't stay."

"You won't be able to leave now," he said darkly.

She furrowed her brow, dread pooling in her gut at the way he looked at her. At the implication of his words.

"If you're so concerned, you could make sure I leave without harm." She did not know where the gumption came from. Did not know her own courage in that moment. But Gian's eyes shifted to something dark.

He shook his head as he spoke. "It doesn't work that way. I cannot be your savior now. No one can. Not even your *husband.*"

She met his gaze with as much fury as she could muster. "I don't know what you want, I don't know what you're up to, Gian. But stay the Sheol away from me."

He laughed through his nose, running a featherlight finger along her arm. "You should have stayed away while you had the chance."

"Get your hands off me," she growled.

"By the time this is over, you will wish it was only my hands on you," said Gian.

"What is that supposed to mean?" she asked, but Gian did not answer, only sneered, baring his teeth to her.

Miri furrowed her brow, about to ask Gian what the Sheol he meant by any of it, but she heard steps from behind. She whirled to find Phinehas standing close—too close. How had she not noticed him before?

"Phinehas!" she breathed, slightly relieved. He did not seem angered or even perturbed. He just stood there, watching her.

"I didn't see you there!" she said inanely, placing a hand on her chest.

"Did you enjoy your day with His Grace?" Phinehas asked, his words as sweet as syrup.

Too sweet.

"Yes," Miri said, deciding that lying probably wasn't in her best interests at the moment.

"I do hope he hasn't *tired* you too much," said Phinehas.

Miri shook her head, scrambling for something to say. An excuse to end this conversation. She just wanted to get to her chambers and then get out of here. For good.

"Excellent," said Phinehas sweetly, reaching to take hold of her hand. He brought it to his mouth to kiss when he paused. "What's this?" he asked, pulling the ring Ezra had given her from her finger.

"A—a gift," she stammered, heart pounding.

"A rather generous gift," Phinehas agreed.

"What can I say? I have him eating of my hand," she said, hating the lie. Though it wasn't a lie, not really.

Phinehas met her eyes at that, a serpentine grin curling his narrow mouth. "Indeed, my pet, you do. Though I do wonder about his lack of loyalty to me." He curled his hand around the ring, tucking it into a pocket of his embroidered tunic. "Perhaps it's time to see if you're better served elsewhere. Galina, after all, has proven a woeful disappointment. But you, my dove. I know you will prove worthwhile."

Phinehas turned, tucking her hand into the crook of his arm.

"I—" she started, unsure what to say. Unsure what lie she could use to get away from Phinehas tonight.

"I've been worried about you, my little dove. You've been so preoccupied I feared I might have lost you." Phinehas walked slowly with her by his side—like two lovers strolling down a moonlit path.

"You could never lose me, Phinehas." Liar. She was such a liar. Liar and whore.

He paused, facing her. "I confess I am glad to hear it. You should hear the rumors, my darling. The things they are saying about you. And the grand duke. My heart is gladdened to know that you are not conspiring against me, as so many terrible people are saying."

Who? Who would say such a thing? And for what purpose? Miri's heart pounded as she raced to think of a way out. Some way to get back to Ezra and just get out of here. She looked over her shoulder, to perhaps plead with Gian—though why, she could not say. It's not as if the bastard would help her. He'd already proven that by delaying her.

But she looked back anyway.

Gian was nowhere to be found.

She did not recognize the room. It was farther down the hall than she had ever ventured. And dark. The room was eerily dark without even the small windows that lined the ceiling of most of the rooms below the temple.

The fire had burned down to cinders in the hearth, and the room was shockingly cold as a result.

"Where are we?" Miri asked, looking around. Phinehas stood by the door, tilting his head to one side as he looked her up and down, but he did not say anything. She wondered if he realized the gown she wore was not one of his choosing—not one she had ever worn in his presence. She wondered if the words were branded on her brow for him to read plain as day:

I betrayed you. I married another.

And there's nothing you can do about it now.

"Phinehas?" she asked, but before she could say anything else, a figure darkened the door beside him. A portly man, as round as a grape and about a head shorter than Phinehas.

"All those promises, and she's here at last?" said the man, his words heavy with an unfamiliar accent.

Phinehas did not move. "She was worth the wait, I can assure you."

The round man moved enough that pale light shone across his face and Miri recognized him immediately. Dread pooled in her gut.

"The ambassador has been dying to meet you, my little dove," said Phinehas.

Miri did not move, did not breathe.

"Leave us," said the ambassador without bothering to turn to Phinehas.

Phinehas seemed to hesitate, and for a brief moment, Miri could have sworn that fear shone in his eyes, as if surprised. As if this were not part of the plan. "I—"

"I said leave us," the man said again. This time, Phinehas did not argue. He shut the door quietly, and Miri watched as the ambassador turned, locking Phinehas out.

And locking Miri in.

The man stalked towards her, surprisingly agile for such a rotund form. "I've heard so much about you, girl," he said. "Your master won't quit going on and on." He stalked towards her, a wolf hunting his prey. He stopped shy, looking her up and down but saying nothing more.

Words failed Miri as she watched the ambassador remove his jacket. He laid it carefully across the back of a chair and then turned to a small table, reaching for a snifter and downing a healthy gulp of amber liquid. The room was quiet, still, the only sound the crystal connecting with the table when he set his empty glass back down.

"I was beginning to think you were a figment of his imagination. You are one scarce little whore."

Miri forced herself to breathe. To think. To find an excuse to get away from this man.

He stepped closer to her, and as he did, she was assaulted with a foul stench that forced a gag from her throat. He watched her for a moment, his eyes unreadable. Sweat beaded his shiny brow and stained a dark line along the shirt under his suspenders.

"Why do you tremble?" he asked. A simple question, though there was no concern in it.

She did not answer, could only focus on breathing. One breath. Another.

The ambassador reached for her, tracing a finger along her collarbone, down the fabric across her breasts, and to her navel.

"You are a tempting little thing, aren't you?" he mused. Casual, light. As if speaking about the changing weather. "The priest wasn't wrong about that. But you seem frightened, darling. Are you frightened?"

Something danced in his eyes at that question—delight. Hunger. Anticipation. As if her fear were as fine as wine.

She did not lie to him. She did not see a reason to. So she nodded her head once before shutting her eyes.

The ambassador breathed a laugh. "A whore playing the part of a scared little girl. Why, men must blaspheme their very souls for a chance at you."

Miri felt a tear fall down her cheek.

The ambassador stepped closer, his breath, his malodor assaulting her as he leaned close and licked that tear from her skin.

"I think I shall rather enjoy this," he said, and at his words, she squeezed her eyes as tightly as she could.

He ran featherlight fingers along the skin on her arms. "Do you scream, Miri? When you are afraid?" His questions were light, almost a whisper. "Or do you whimper like a babe?"

Tears fell freely, hot and fast, dripping from her chin. She did not bother to wipe them away, her eyes still closed, her breath ragged.

"I think," he went on, "that you like to hide your fear as long as possible. That you like to square your shoulders and lift your chin and pretend that you are strong. That you are someone worth something."

He reached around her then, taking to the laces at the back of her gown, encompassing her in his thick arms, his belly grazing hers. "And I think," he said, "That I shall enjoy very much as I uncover the fear inside you." He pulled at the laces, loosening her gown bit, by bit, by bit. "And I think I shall rather enjoy learning the sound of your screams."

CHAPTER TWENTY-THREE

It had been more than eight minutes. Maybe nine. Certainly not yet ten. Ezra was tired of counting. And tired of waiting. He jumped out of the carriage, unable to stand it any longer.

How he was going to just waltz into her chambers and get her, he did not yet know. Perhaps he would find Jareth first, let the sage help him for the second time tonight. He didn't care. Something wasn't right. Something was…off.

And he'd have bet good money it had something to do with Phinehas.

He marched more quickly across the cobblestones to the temple entrance. He hadn't even managed to take hold of the latch when the front door swung open.

"Your timing is shit, Ezra."

"Get out of my way, Gian." Ezra moved to push past him, but the giant man did not move.

"I'm afraid I can't let that happen."

"Where is she?" Ezra ground through his teeth.

Gian merely crossed his arms.

"Where. Is. She." Ezra could feel panic welling with every passing second. Something had gone terribly, terribly wrong.

"You cannot help her now. No one can," said Gian.

"Bullshit," said Ezra, and used his shoulder to shove Gian out of his way. But Gian was fast. Too fast. He grabbed Ezra and spun him around, landing his fist right in Ezra's teeth.

Ezra spit blood, seeing red as his vision focused again. "You're going to regret that."

"A shame. I rather enjoyed it."

Ezra lunged, rage and fury in his veins. But before his fist could meet Gian's chin, a sharp pain lanced through his gut. He froze, the world suddenly going silent. He looked down to find a dagger in Gian's hand, the blade having disappeared into Ezra's gut—all the way to the hilt.

A killing blow.

When he looked up again, Gian's eyes were unreadable, but he shoved Ezra off his blade with brute force, and Ezra collapsed in a heap of useless bones.

And then there was black.

End of Part One

PART TWO

CHAPTER TWENTY-FOUR

"What do you want?" the ambassador groused as if disturbed from a good book when came a knock at his door. He shoved Miri away from where he perched on the edge of his bed. She collapsed to the ground in a heap of bones, the carpet burning her cheek, her bare shoulder, her thigh and calf with the force of her body. Every muscle ached, barking in pain. A wave of nausea swept over her and she wretched onto the ground, not bothering to wipe her mouth or to even move away from the puddle of sick before her.

The voice on the other side of the door spoke again. "May I enter, my lord?"

Somewhere in the recesses of her mind, she knew that voice. Knew its familiar cadence. The ambassador—Phocas, that was his name—merely grunted his consent, not bothering to cover Miri before accepting the visitor.

Hesitantly, the door on the other side of the room opened. Miri watched through swollen eyes as Phinehas entered, freezing at the sight before him: Ambassador Phocas, standing with his back to the door, fastening his trousers and tossing aside a handkerchief he had used to clean himself; Miri naked and prone on the floor, a puddle of her own vomit beside her, tinged with blood. Her own blood.

No one bothered to offer her a blanket to cover herself. As if she did not exist.

Perhaps she didn't. Perhaps she never had.

Too weak and sore to move, Miri didn't bother to try to find a blanket—not because she was ashamed, but because she was cold. So very cold. She trembled, the air biting along her bare skin.

"Well?" the ambassador demanded.

Phinehas at last took his eyes from Miri.

"I do apologize, Your Excellence. I did not mean—"

Uncomfortable. Phinehas was markedly uncomfortable by the sight before him. Then again, he hadn't been in here to see her. Not once since he had delivered her into the brutal hands of Ambassador Phocas. Days ago. Weeks ago. Years ago. She did not know anymore.

With no windows in the room, and no discernible pattern to the ambassador's visits, she had lost track of time almost immediately. Everything was a blur of screams and darkness and pain. Endless, unyielding pain. It echoed along every place in her body. Her body was a canvas on which Phocas painted his masterpiece —in blood and bruise and shame. In screams and nightmares and untold horrors.

Phinehas cleared his throat. "I thought you would like to know..." He paused, the uncomfortable distraction clear in his tone. "I thought you would like to know that the prophet is here. In the village. He has been proselytizing for most of the day."

Phocas at last turned to face Phinehas, his trousers hanging at odd angles from his awkward form, perspiration staining along the straps of his suspenders. "And just what does he proselytize about, *Your Holiness?*"

"He speaks of the same nonsense they all do," said Phinehas.

"Is that so," said Phocas, making his way across the room. He poured two fingers of whiskey into a snifter before downing the whole thing in one swallow. "Tell me, Phinehas. Why are you so threatened by him?"

Phinehas did not deign to answer. From the corner of her blurred vision, Miri could see the priest eyeing her on the ground again. There was something dark in his countenance. Dangerous.

"There is no threat, my lord," said Phinehas, finally taking his eyes from Miri. "But I did think you would want to know."

"I don't," said Phocas. "But your king will. So will Her Imperial Majesty."

With that, the ambassador disappeared from the room.

A long silence passed, and Phinehas did not move toward her. He only stood near the door, watching her. Breathing. A silent, unmoving vigil. She watched him from the carpet. She held his gaze with her own, the only sound in the room her shallow breaths. Even breathing hurt thanks to Phocas, whose preferred method of castigation involved his perfectly polished boot in her ribs. Repeatedly.

"What have you done to yourself, Miri?"

She ground her teeth, tears threatening to fall. But she did not answer him. She did not answer this man before her. She did not know him anymore.

"My innocent little dove," he continued. "What have you done?"

Miri closed her eyes, shutting him out. Phinehas did not offer her a blanket. He did not offer to help her. He offered no explanation.

He simply left her there alone.

CHAPTER TWENTY-FIVE

Everything felt heavy. Like trudging through quicksand and honey. Slow and heavy and murky. He tried to open his eyes, but found the light too bright to bear. Sitting up was no easier, a sharp, keen burning sensation punching him in the gut when he so much as wiggled a toe.

"You need to keep still," came a familiar voice.

Ezra wanted to point out that he couldn't move if he wanted to, but even his voice seemed lost.

Focusing was difficult but not impossible, and after a minute of blinking away the fog, Ezra realized he was looking at a mirror image of himself—except a much lovelier version. Raven black hair, a dimple on her right cheek, piercing golden eyes.

"Esther," he groaned.

"Stop trying to move, you ass. You're going to make it worse."

He didn't see how that was possible, but he obeyed his obstinate sister nonetheless.

He felt a cool rag at his brow and welcomed the soothing sensation.

"Drink," she said, tipping a glass to his mouth.

He sipped, surprised at first by the taste. But then he continued, enjoying the soft burning liquid as it poured down his throat.

"Whiskey," he managed to say.

"I figured you wouldn't mind the relaxation," said Esther.

Ezra did not disagree. The whiskey did wonders to ease the edge off his sore stomach rather quickly, but losing that edge meant clearing his mind of the fog that seemed to engulf him. And that's when it hit him.

Bolting upright and crying out against the sharp sting, Ezra blurted, "Where is she?"

"Lie back down, Ezra," said Esther harshly.

"Where is Miriam?" he demanded, ignoring her. Ignoring the pain that was now throbbing down his legs and up into his arms. He looked down, moving the blanket from his bare chest to expose a rather large bandage on his abdomen. He lifted it enough to see the angry red skin and dried blood beneath.

Stabbed.

He remembered it now. Gian had stabbed him. While trying to get to Miri...

"Where is Miriam?" he demanded again.

"I take it he's awake," came a man's voice. John appeared in the room with Helena behind him.

"Thank Providence," said the housekeeper.

"John, I have to get to her," said Ezra, panic rising in his pained gut.

John looked at Esther, who looked back seriously. But neither of them said a word.

"Damn it, where is she?" Ezra demanded.

"If you don't lie back down, I'm not telling you anything," said Esther. Her very round, very pregnant belly rested on her lap in the chair beside the bed, and even with it, she was no less intimidating. But Ezra would not be daunted.

Helena appeared on the other side of the bed, a bowl of something steaming in her hand. "Try this, darling. You need to eat something."

"Ezra, you must relax, do you understand me?" Esther said.

"Not until I know she's safe," he said.

"If you don't relax, you are going to bleed out," said his sister. "And if you die after all of this, I am going to come down to Sheol myself and torture you just for spite. Now lie. Back. Down."

"John. Please," Ezra pleaded with his best friend.

"She's right, Ez. You need to heal. You lost a lot of blood."

And was still losing it, by the looks of the bandages.

He didn't give a fraction of a damn.

Shoving the blankets aside, Ezra tried to sit up, only to collapse a moment later from the excruciating pain.

"Damn it, Ezra. You are such a stubborn ass!" snapped Esther, fixing his blankets over him, tending to his bandages.

"Please," Ezra panted around the pain. "Please tell me she's all right."

John hesitated for a moment, but then, placing a hand on Esther's shoulder, he finally said, "We don't know what is happening to her, Ez."

Ezra sucked in a breath, trying to sit up again but thinking better of it. Tears stung his eyes. Maybe from the pain. Maybe from the frustration. Maybe both. "John," he heard himself whimper.

"You almost died," said Esther. "Do you understand that? We almost lost you. I am not—" Esther could not continue, placing a hand over her mouth to quell a rare show of emotion.

"How long have I been in this bed?" Ezra asked, reality dawning on him.

Once again, his brother-in-law, his sister, and his housekeeper all hesitated to answer.

"How long?" he barked.

"Three weeks," John finally admitted.

Three weeks.

Three *weeks*.

She could be... She could be...

"Please," Ezra pleaded, desperation taking over any sound thought. "Please, you have to help me find her. Bring her home."

Ezra grabbed John's hands, squeezing them tight. "Please John. Help her."

John looked at Ezra for a moment, and he could see the understanding in his friend's eyes. If he had been in this situation...

"I'll see what I can do," John said quietly.

"John," said Esther, wide-eyed. "He is a monster. You see what he did to my brother!"

"What do you want me to say, Es? Do you think I wouldn't beg the same if I were in his shoes and that was you out there?"

Esther looked to Ezra for a moment, contemplating. Something small shifted in her countenance. A resignation of sorts. "Why'd you have to go and fall in love with her?"

"She is the love of my life, Es," said Ezra, taking his sister's trembling hands.

"Yes, and you're the world's biggest fool," she said, a tear slipping down her golden cheek.

"I know," he said. "I know."

Helena made a small sound, fluffing his pillows and pouring him tea. When at last she presented a tray and set it across his lap, he could not ignore how good the food smelled.

"Eat," Helena said. "You've hardly had a bite for weeks. Eat."

Ezra obliged as Esther stood from her vigil and walked from the room. Helena followed her.

When the girls were gone, Ezra finally said to John, "Tell me what happened. How did I get back here?"

John walked to the large set of windows across the room, clasping his hands behind his back as he took in the gorgeous view of the mountains and the lake.

"John," Ezra tried again. He needed to know.

John sighed. "When you didn't come home that night, Helena knew something was wrong. She sent for me, and I went into the village to find you." John turned, facing Ezra once more. "I figured you had just been with her all day. You had said you were going to spend the day with her. But Helena wasn't wrong—it was late. And something was off. I went to the temple, but it was dark and no one would answer. I wasn't stupid enough to try to get into the private quarters. Not without a plan.

"So I decided to regroup. I was going to come back here, get some of your soldiers, and come back to find you with some rein-forcements in tow.

"I was walking back towards the livery in the village when I heard a sound. I followed it behind the temple to the lakeshore. It was dark enough that all I could make out was a figure lying on the ground. And then you moaned. And I realized you were bleeding out. You were dying. You probably *would* have died if I had found you even ten minutes later. Someone had left you for dead. I figure I know who that someone is," John added.

"So I brought you home. Esther has been nursing you back to health every second since you arrived. She hardly sleeps. She's worrying me, Ez. But she won't rest. Not as long as you're not well."

John walked across the room, placing his hands on the back of the chair Esther had occupied a short while ago. "I will help you, Ezra. I will help you find Miriam. Because you are my brother and because I know you love her. But I need you to promise me that you will not do anything stupid. That you will listen to your sister and you will heal.

"You almost died, do you understand that? She almost lost you. We all almost lost you. I can't see that pain in my wife's eyes again. I can't. So you will stay in this godsdamned bed and you will heal and you will let me help you. Do you understand?"

Ezra nodded but couldn't bring himself to say anything else.

John nodded curtly before marching out of the room.

A week.

It had been a week since Ezra had woken in this bed. A week since he had found out that he'd nearly died.

Which meant it had been nearly a month since he had seen Miri.

A godsdamned month.

If he didn't die of this stupid wound, he would surely die of panic wondering if Miri was all right.

If she was even alive.

"You ready, darling?" came a familiar voice. Ezra turned his attention from the ledgers spread across the clean, white linens of his bed, the business of Kinnereth all chronicled on sheets of parchment. Helena bustled into his chambers with a pair of boots in hand—Ezra's most comfortable pair. It was time for another walk.

Helena had never had children of her own, and Ezra had never had the heart to ask her why. But she had always treated him and Esther like her own. She had doted on them and looked after their every need with the affection of a mother. And Ezra had loved her dearly for it.

Ezra sat up, stifling the urge to wince at the pain that was still sharp in his belly. He was so damned tired of being in this bed that he had insisted on getting up days ago. But that had proven a much more taxing endeavor than he imagined, and like an elderly man, his days had been reduced to the bed for most of the daylight hours, with a walk here and there as he could stand it.

"You lasted an extra ten minutes yesterday," Helena said helpfully as she knelt before him and worked a boot on his foot.

"I'm useless," Ezra grumbled.

"Nonsense," the portly housekeeper said. The gray in her curls caught in the afternoon light, shining like strands of living silver against the darker strands of her more youthful brown. It did not help Ezra's mood that an aging woman had more vitality than he these days. It did not help to know that he had been so throughly wounded that he was recovering at a snail's pace.

You're lucky to be alive. That's what Esther had said when last he had lamented how pathetic he was. Maybe he *was* lucky to be alive.

He could only wonder if Miri could say the same.

"She'll be all right, darling," said Helena, looking up from where she had finished working on the second boot. She stood, albeit a bit more slowly than he might have, had he been whole and well. But she stood much more rapidly than he could now, and her extended hand to help him was equally as welcome as it was offensive.

But he took it nonetheless and stifled another groan as his muscles ached in protest.

Too damned weak to help the woman he loved.

She deserved much better than him.

"Come on, darling," said Helena, offering her his arm for support. "The sun will do you some good."

IT DID. Along with the mountain breeze and familiar smells of conifer and aspen. Ezra felt better. A bit.

Nothing could soothe the worry for Miri. But the fresh air had brightened his mood at the very least. He supposed that was good, considering the look on his brother-in-law's face at the moment.

"Nice walk today?" John asked as Ezra made his way into his

sitting room on Helena's arm. He sat—or collapsed really—onto the settee and gladly took the steaming cup of coffee a servant offered him.

"It was fine," he said, opting not to sip before he went on. "What is it, John?"

John sat perched on the arm of the opposite settee—his usual seat of choice. No papers in his hand. Nothing of the curious, thorough lawyer Ezra called his friend. No, John carried nothing with him but guilt in his eyes. It did not sit well with Ezra.

"What do you know?" Ezra prodded.

"Not much, I confess," John said.

"Tell me anyway."

"She's alive, Ez. I know that for certain."

The fact that he said it with such apology scared the living shit out of Ezra. "What are you not telling me?"

"I don't know, Ezra. I really don't. I swear. All I have is hearsay. Conjecture."

"Don't give me your lawyer bullshit, John. Tell me what you've heard."

John looked down for a moment before he spoke. "The Medinian ambassador. He is rumored to be...quite pleased with his...ah, *accommodations*," John said, looking up at Ezra before he added, "at the temple."

Ezra could feel his heart beating in his chest and found himself absurdly focused on it as John went on. "The rumor is that he's so pleased he has decided to write his mistress—the Empress of Medinah—and convince her to come to Har-Navah in person."

"For what reason," Ezra ground the words through his teeth.

"To sign a peace treaty."

The way he said it... "Occupation," Ezra breathed.

"Occupation," John confirmed.

The king would sign away the autonomy of their kingdom,

just as they had all suspected. In the name of peace. Medinah was going to take over this country, one promise at a time. One treaty at a time. And the king was going to allow it willingly. All because the ambassador was pleased. Pleased with his visit here. Pleased with how his ass was kissed. Pleased with his *accommodations*.

Ezra did not need to think long on the other implication there.

The ambassador was pleased by whatever Sheols he had been subjecting Miri to. For the last month.

Bile burned hot in the back of Ezra's throat. No, not bile.

Vomit.

Ezra dropped the steaming cup of coffee into his lap, unable to cry out before he vomited right onto the plush carpets of his sitting room.

"Thaddeus!" John called, jumping to his feet. Undaunted by the sick now splattered around his friend, John came to Ezra's side, wrapping a steady arm around Ezra's shoulders. "You okay, my friend?"

Within a breath, Thaddeus appeared in the chamber, coming to Ezra's other side. A few servants followed him, turning to fetch some towels and a bucket of water, no doubt.

"I'm sorry," Ezra said. "I'm so sorry."

He wasn't sure if he was speaking to Thaddeus or Miri.

CHAPTER TWENTY-SIX

"Miri," she begged, shaking her friend for the third time. "Miri, please. Can you hear me?"

Miri did not move, did not stir from the filthy carpet where she lay sprawled, naked and clammy. If it weren't for her breast rising and falling in a shallow cadence, Kata might have thought her friend dead. She shook Miri again, the skin under her friend's eyes sallow.

Fever.

She should have come sooner.

That's all she could think when she saw her friend like this. She should have stopped this sooner. But she hadn't. Too scared to do anything—what with the rumors of what the ambassador did to anyone who defied him—Kata had hidden away for weeks, keeping her head low.

Survive. She just wanted to survive all of this.

She just wanted to leave here and never look back.

Now, seeing Miri, she wondered if her friend ever would.

Riddled with bruises and dark places on her body that defied explanation, Miri was little more than a heap of skin and bone.

Her lush locks were a tangled mess of knots, matted with dried blood and Providence knew what else. What had the ambassador had done to her? What sort of evils had he inflicted to render her so incapacitated?

She hadn't quite believed Galina's account. When the acolyte had returned to their shared space one night weeks ago, cold and disoriented, Kata had thought her lying. Or at least exaggerating. But then Galina hadn't really recovered. A week went by, and then another, and the snooty, holier-than-thou acolyte had remained quiet and distant, her eyes haunted with stories she might never tell.

That had been the first time Kata realized she should be worried for Miri.

They thought she had left forever. Disappearing first thing in the morning, Miri hadn't returned to the temple all day and well into the night. All the acolytes had assumed she'd run off with that handsome duke. And Kata, remembering the conversation she'd had with Miri only days prior, knew it was probably true. The way the duke looked at her, the way he was consumed by Miri as if she were his entire world... It hadn't surprised Kata at all that Miri had changed her mind, taken the duke up on his offer of the world, and run off into the sunset with him. Given half the chance, Kata would have done the same.

It wasn't until a week later that she heard the rumors that Miri had returned and had been deposited directly into the arms of the ambassador.

No one had seen her. Not once. No one knew what was happening to her. Where she was, if she was even in the temple.

And certainly none of them had any idea what the ambassador could be doing with her.

But Kata couldn't do nothing, especially not when she remembered the haunted terror in Galina's eyes a few weeks ago.

So she decided to investigate for herself. When she heard

whimpers and cries from the end of the hall in the dead of night, she realized her friend was in real danger.

And she was powerless to do anything about it.

She was risking her life to be here now. But seeing Miri—knowing her life was on the brink—she didn't give a damn anymore. Let them draw and quarter her like some barbarian.

She had to help her friend.

Now she just had to figure out how.

Twenty minutes later, and after many heart-pounding close calls with the temple guards, Kata had sneaked her way back into the ambassador's chambers. He was gone for the night, Providence only knew where. And it gave her a chance to help Miri. Getting some broth from the kitchens was only the first step.

"Miri," she whispered, kneeling beside her friend. "Can you hear me? Please wake up! You need to eat."

Miri did not stir. Kata tucked a matted strand of those fiery curls she had always envied behind her friend's ear. "Miri," she said again, the name cracking in her throat.

Miri groaned softly, attempting to move her arms. Tiny beads of sweat peppered her brow despite the fact that the dark room was ice cold. Kata hadn't dared light a fire in the hearth lest someone figure out she was here. She hadn't really had a plan. She had just wanted to know Miri was all right—that Miri was alive at all. She hadn't thought past that when she dared to sneak into these godsforsaken chambers. The foul smell of the ambassador still clung to the stale air in here, as if he were hiding around a corner like a spider waiting to pounce.

Kata moved to kneel behind Miri, using every ounce of strength she had to lift Miri under her arms and prop her up to a sitting position. She fetched a blanket from the nearby rumpled bed and wrapped it around Miri's bare shoulders. Miri made another small sound, her head lolling sickeningly to one side.

Kata grabbed the steaming bowl of broth and, sitting behind her friend, spooned small helpings of the liquid into her friend's mouth. Miri rallied at the shock of heat on her lips, but soon grew limp again. Kata held Miri's brow with her free hand, tilting it back enough that she could drip the broth down Miri's throat.

"Miri, you've got to eat. *You've got to,*" she whispered. Miri barely moved, barely reacted to the sustenance her friend attempted to give her.

At this rate, would Miri survive the night?

From this angle she saw more bruises and wounds on her friend. Knees raw and scabbed from the burn of the carpet, thighs littered with what looked like the remnants of many firm grips, a long, slender bruise that striped her abdomen. And the bruises were only the beginning. A month of wasting away in this darkened pit had left Miri's skin sallow and pale, her hair reeking of vomit, her body growing thinner with every day that she didn't eat. What sort of monster would do this to a woman? What sort of monster would want a woman in such a condition?

Bile burned Kata's throat as she spooned drop after drop of the broth into Miri's mouth. It was hard to tell if she swallowed any at all. But Kata would try. She had to try. She couldn't leave Miri like this.

She had barely gotten in her third knock before the door swung open before her. Jareth stood long and lean in nothing but a pair of trousers, a look of utter disbelief on his face.

"Kata!" he exclaimed. He whirled to grab a shirt from a nearby chair in his private chambers, hastily slinging it over his head as he ushered Kata inside. "What's wrong?" he asked as he shut the door behind her.

Gone was the shy sage whose dearest companion was his own brevity. Gone was the pretense of decorum. Kata couldn't help but feel as if she was speaking to a friend she'd known her whole life.

"I'm afraid, Jareth," she said, a tremble taking over her whole body. "She won't eat. She's barely awake. I'm afraid she's going to die. I don't know what he's doing to her in there, and I don't know how to get her out."

"Slow down," Jareth said, placing his hands on her shoulders. She looked up, meeting his eyes for a moment. When she saw the concern there, she could not stop the tears that poured freely.

"What's going to happen to her, Jareth?"

She sobbed, heaving great gulps of air as she dropped any sense of dignity. Jareth pulled her to his chest and ran his hand over her hair, breathing soothing sounds as he let her weep in his arms.

She wrapped her arms around him and held on to him as tightly as she could, feeling the tears soaking into his shirt.

"We'll get her out," he said softly. "I promise you."

She could not be sure, but she thought he might be trembling, too. She let herself weep in his arms—let herself be soothed by his touch, by his concern. It was the first time in such a long time that anyone had seemed to care at all.

"I should have helped her sooner. I should have known that monster—"

"What happened, Kata?" Jareth interrupted, pulling her away from his chest just enough that he could see her face. He kept his arms around her.

"The ambassador," she said around sobbing breaths. "He—I don't know what he's doing to her—so many bruises—he's a monster, Jareth. We have to get her out of here."

"We'll find a way to get her out. But Kata, you have to listen to me. You have to get out, too. She is not the only one in danger. The priest will not stop with her. I can't keep him at bay much longer."

"Keep him at bay? What you mean? What are you doing, Jareth?"

Jareth's face heated, and he did not answer immediately. "You have to get out of here, Kata. Please trust me on this."

"I won't leave without her," she said.

"We'll come back for her. We'll figure out a plan and—"

"No," she said sharply, cutting him off. "I won't leave without Miri."

"Kata, you don't understand—"

"No, *you* don't understand," she protested, pushing free from his arms. He did not stop her. "She is my friend, and I won't leave her here to die by that monster. If you won't help me, then I'll get her out myself."

And with that, Kata whirled and stormed from Jareth's chambers.

CHAPTER TWENTY-SEVEN

Jareth's heart pounded as he stood before the closed door, wondering whether he should go after Kata. He had never been good at talking to her, never been good at much of anything except watching her from afar like a psychopath. So when she had knocked on his door tonight, he'd thought he might shit his pants.

He had known the ambassador was a madman. His reputation had preceded him, so his arrival at the temple had been as unwelcome as it had been obscene. But Jareth hadn't seen Galina to confirm Kata's claims—to know for certain if she really was as bad off as Kata seemed to think. All he had known was that the snooty acolyte had been quiet and distant for weeks. He hadn't asked why.

The look on Kata's face alone had made him realize time was running out. He had to get her out of here. Tonight. He could not risk it any longer. The games he had played with Phinehas regarding Kata would not work with the ambassador.

Phinehas had been easily convinced that Kata was best kept serving the lesser nobles. It was a foolish idea Jareth had come up with months ago—convince Phinehas to use Kata as bait for the easier prey and keep Galina and Jordie busy with the higher-ranking officials. Jareth had nearly exhausted himself night after night to keep those lesser nobles distracted, telling one lie after another to keep their stories crossed, their facts wrong, and their greedy hands far, far away from Kata. With a few exceptions, it had worked surprisingly well. And despite the fact that he knew he was lying to her—to so many—it at least kept a roof over Kata's head and the pretense that she was consistently busy with her duties as an acolyte.

Never mind he knew she shouldn't be here. That she had only come here out of gross naïveté. Like so many before her, Kata had come to the temple at a far too young age out of true devotion to Providence. Instead of religious piety, she had found herself ensnared in a web of lies, deception, and sexual games. And she could not get out. Not on her own.

There was no acolyte in the world who could ever leave and return to a normal life. The world didn't work that way.

So Jareth had stayed too. Drawn to the allure of the temple by his love for history and art and culture, once he had met Kata, Jareth had stayed long after his own disillusion with the Sanhedrin. Protecting her had become his religion—she the goddess he worshipped.

But the ambassador was a different game entirely. And when the bastard had arrived, Jareth knew he was on borrowed time when it came to protecting Kata. It would only be a matter of time before the ambassador turned his unholy attention to her. And Jareth would slit the man's throat before he let him anywhere near her.

THE HOURS STRETCHED thin into the night, but Jareth took the risk and sneaked into the ambassador's chambers anyway, hoping that the Medinian representative was still gone for the night. He was—the portly bastard was nowhere to be found. That fact alone came with an equal dose of hope and horror.

Because Miri was exactly as Kata had described her—cold, limp, and lifeless on the floor. The blanket around her shoulders did little to hide her nakedness, so Jareth found another to cover her. An empty bowl sat nearby, a few drops of broth left in the bottom. A flicker of hope came to life for a brief moment before he noticed the pool of vomit near her mouth. She was eating, but she could not keep anything down. He had to get her out now or not at all. There would be no hiding her, no nursing her back to health here. There would be no tomorrow for Miri—not as long as the ambassador was still here.

But how would he do it? He had been pondering that the entire time he crept down the empty corridor, praying to Providence above that he wouldn't be seen. Now, seeing Miri like this, he prayed again—that somehow he could get both her and Kata and the rest of the girls out. Alive.

Tonight.

JARETH KNOCKED SOFTLY but no one answered. He decided to risk knocking louder and waking the rest of the sleeping priests and servants in the temple. But when there was still no answer, Jareth took it upon himself to enter the common room of the acolytes' chambers.

It was empty, the only sign of life the dying fire in the hearth. He had no idea which chamber was Kata's—he had never visited her before, despite the fact that he had thought about it at least a thousand times. He hated how often he had entertained the notion of taking Phinehas up on his offer: to have Kata whenever he wanted as a reward for his loyalty to the priest. He hated how many times he had thought of giving in—of using that offer as an excuse to get past his own damned nerves.

But he never had. Now, in the dead of night with time not on his side, he wished he at least knew which of the doors to knock on.

"Jareth?"

He whirled to see Kata standing in the door of one of the rooms on the left. She was still in her dress, her long chocolate hair down and unkempt—a sight he so rarely saw from Phinehas's gaggle of perfect acolytes. In her hands, she held a hastily-folded dress. As if she were packing.

"What are you doing here?" she went on.

He crossed the room in three steps. "I'm going to get you out," he said, reaching to take her by the hand. She quickly moved away.

"I told you, I'm not going without—"

"All of you," he said. "I'm going to get you all out. Tonight. But I need your help. We don't have much time, and I will need help with Miri, but I think if we—"

Before he could finish his sentence, Kata had dropped the garment and thrown her arms around him, practically devouring him with a devastating kiss. After a brief moment of shock, he let himself pull her so close he could feel the whole length of her body against his. He let himself get lost in that kiss—let his hands and his lips tell her when words had failed him for years.

"I love you, Jareth," she said, a bit breathless when she finally broke the fierce kiss.

"Oh Providence, Kata. I'm so in love with you." He kissed her again, forcing himself to break it after only a moment this time. "We have to get out of here, though. We cannot wait."

"I know," she said, but she kissed him again anyway. He did not stop her.

"Finally find the balls to mount her, Jareth?"

Jareth tore his lips from Kata's, whirling to face Jordie entering the common room from the hall outside. At the same time, Galina emerged from another bedchamber door. From the high windows above them, the morning light was slowly growing. Panic welled in his chest; time was running out.

"Girls," he said. "We don't have much time."

"Come now, Jareth," Jordie snickered, plopping down onto a thick chair. "Surely you can last a *little* while."

Galina stood near her doorframe, wordlessly eyeing the exchange.

"We're getting out of here. All of us. Tonight," he said, wrapping an arm around Kata's waist and pulling her close to his side. "But we don't have much time. Miri needs our help and—"

"You seem *desperate* to help Miri." This from Galina—but it was not sarcasm in her tone, it was disdain.

"He didn't know," Kata said. "Not until tonight. He didn't know how bad it was. Neither did I."

"You didn't know? Is that your excuse?" sneered Galina. "You didn't *know* what sort of fucking monster he is?"

From the chair nearby, Jordie giggled. "He's not so bad," she said lightly.

"You haven't been near him, girl," Galina hissed.

"I made him bathe first, of course. But he rides like any other man," Jordie said nonchalantly, playing with the ends of her hair.

Galina's eyes went wide with horror.

But it was Kata who asked, "You've been with him?"

Jordie shrugged. "Where do you think I've been tonight? He got tired of all the complaining. I thought I'd show him that some of us are more devoted to the cause than others."

Galina's eyes seethed with rage. "You know nothing of which you speak, you stupid whore."

"Seems to me like you're the stupid whore here," Jordie returned, twirling a strand of her blonde locks around a finger. "You're in good company with Miri."

"What is that supposed to mean?" Kata asked, and Jareth could feel a tremble settle along her. He pulled her closer for good measure.

Jordie laughed, and something in Jareth seethed with rage. How could such a young girl be so blind? So ignorant?

"She was the only one of us stupid enough to get herself pregnant."

"What?" Kata burst out.

"Jordie, what are you talking about?" Jareth asked, his voice urgent. They were running out of time before the temple awoke again and the ambassador returned.

The young acolyte twirled another strand of hair around her finger, reveling in the way everyone in the room waited with bated breath for her response. "It's all the servants are talking about. Her linens have been clean for weeks now. And she can hardly keep food down."

"That's because he's beating the Sheol out of her!" Kata protested.

Jordie shrugged. "Maybe. But my guess is she's pregnant. She's stupid enough to do something like that just to get back at Phinehas. And you all heard her at breakfast weeks ago—complaining about the herb. She hasn't taken breakfast here in months. She practically planned this!"

"She planned nothing of the sort, you imbecile," Galina sneered.

Jordie simply laughed again. "I wonder who the father is? The ambassador? Or Phinehas? Oh! Or perhaps that gorgeous duke she's always riding!"

Kata erupted, launching herself across the room towards Jordie. It was all Jareth could do to stop her from clawing the girl's eyes out. Galina shouted too, though what she was saying, Jareth couldn't tell, too busy trying to hold Kata back. Galina, on the opposite side of the settee that separated them, restrained Jordie with surprising strength. But Jordie was stronger, and agile thanks to her youth and small frame. She wrangled free from Galina and launched herself off of the back of the settee. Jareth pulled Kata just far enough away that Jordie landed with an unbecoming plop on the carpets beneath them.

At that moment, both Phinehas and Ambassador Phocas burst through the doors of the common room. And in the span of a single breath, Jareth knew he'd never get Kata or anyone out alive. Not tonight.

Maybe not ever.

"What the Sheol is going on?" Phinehas snapped. Kata froze, and Galina cowered in such a way that Jareth had never seen. But Jordie lay nonchalantly on the floor where she had sprawled. She bent a leg, her skirts falling to reveal a slender calf and knee. In that one movement, she transformed from disheveled child to alluring acolyte.

"We were just discussing the happy news," Jordie said with a feline grin. She let her hair fall down her breast, twirling it around a finger once more.

Jareth, seeing how she trembled and damning what Phinehas would think, pulled Kata back against him, wrapping his arms around her middle and letting her lean against his chest.

"What news?" the ambassador asked, eyeing Jordie as if she were a feast he planned to devour. For the second time tonight, apparently.

Jordie toyed with the hem of her skirt as it slowly drifted higher up her thigh, and disgust roiled in Jareth's gut. He had not seen any of the acolytes so brazen before. Most of them at least tried to keep up the pretense of devoted virgin. In this moment, Jordie looked more like a street whore luring a potential customer.

"About our darling Miri," Jordie answered. "We were wondering who the father might be!"

All the color in Phinehas's face drained, and his eyes narrowed to slits as he asked Jordie to repeat herself.

The acolyte smiled coyly. "Sweet Miriam is with child."

And at this, Phinehas exploded.

The priest tore through the corridor like a hurricane devouring the seashore. Wild-eyed and practically salivating, the ambassador followed eagerly behind. Jareth, heart pounding, took hold of Kata's hand and turned her to face him, stopping her from following.

"Stay here," he said firmly.

"I will do no such thing!" she protested.

"Kata," he said, and she did not miss the warning in his tone this time. "Stay here. Do not leave the common room until I come back for you."

He could see the hesitation in her, but he took her by the shoulders and pulled her to him, pressing a single, fierce kiss to her soft lips before marching out of the room.

By some mercy, Kata did not follow.

"What the Sheol is wrong with you," Galina growled as the three acolytes watched the priest, the ambassador, and the sage disappear into the corridor.

Jordie merely stood, straightened her skirts, and took her place on the plush chair once more.

"Who are you?" Kata begged. "You're not who I thought you were."

Jordie shrugged, playing with her blonde strands again. "Maybe you weren't paying attention," she said simply.

"You'll be the reason she dies," Galina said. "You do realize that. You'll be the reason she's beaten to death in the public square. That's the punishment, according to the sacred law. She'll be ripped apart, limb by limb for everyone to watch. All because of you."

"I'm not the one who got pregnant," Jordie said. "I'm not the one who was stupid enough to stop taking the herb."

"She didn't stop taking it!" Kata protested, panic welling from deep within.

Jordie sniffed contemptuously. "She's been having breakfast away from the temple every morning for months. She knew we took the herb at breakfast. You heard her. She knew it. And she still chose to take breakfast with that duke every morning. She did this to herself. And now she'll pay for it."

"Like Sheol she will," Kata growled, and despite Jareth's impassioned plea, she marched out of the common room and into the corridor beyond.

She followed the sounds of shouting and screaming. Her stomach turned as she heard the words, the accusations against her friend.

"Tell me it isn't true!" Phinehas shouted.

Kata ran down the corridors towards the ambassador's chambers. She arrived to find Phinehas flailing his arms as he raged against Miri, who had been propped up against the edge of the bed. No one had bothered to cover her with a blanket, and her once beautiful, glowing skin shone sickly and bruised as she lay bare before them all. At Phinehas's side, the ambassador stood silently, crossing his thick arms across his fat belly. Jareth stood just behind them, and she could see plainly that he was thinking —calculating a way to get Miri out of this.

Miri was conscious, though only just. She looked at the high priest through hazy eyes but said nothing as he flung his accusations.

"Do you know what the punishment is? For fornication and debauchery? Do you know what will be done to you, whore? Do you?" A vein pounded in Phinehas's temple as he raged and shouted. "I will not have it, do you hear me? I will not have such brazen debauchery in my holy place! I will not have such wretched sin against Providence smear my good and holy name! Do you understand me, you stupid, fucking whore! You have brought shame upon me!"

Deny it, Kata wanted to scream—to shout at the top of her lungs. *Deny it or you will die!*

Phinehas knelt before Miri, grabbing her hair and yanking so violently Kata thought he would pull it all out. But Miri kept her face impassive, her expression calm as she looked him right in the eye.

Defend yourself, Miri, she pleaded silently. *Don't let him win!*

"What have you to say for yourself?" Phinehas raged. "Do you deny it?"

Miri said nothing.

"Are you with child, Miriam Sasson of Teman?" Phinehas demanded.

Miri held his gaze, and with unflinching calm, said, "Yes."

"NO!" Jareth screamed, forcing his way into the room as Phinehas yanked Miri by the hair, lugging her across the room and to the hall outside.

Kata's heart pounded as she watched her friend being dragged like a corpse through the temple. She had not denied it. She could not possibly know if it was true or not. She could not possibly have confirmed a pregnancy in such a state.

But she had not denied it.

And Kata finally understood why.

Miri wanted to die.

PHINEHAS DRAGGED Miri through the rough stone corridor and down the steps that led to the kitchens and other rooms beneath the temple. Kata followed quietly behind the ambassador, who seemed to be practically giddy. Jareth followed too, unsuccessfully trying to pull Miri from Phinehas's arms over and over. Too consumed by his rage, Phinehas did nothing to stop Jareth. And Jareth, too consumed by his own fury, did not notice Kata following the spectacle.

Phinehas deposited Miri into a room Kata had never seen before. Windowless and dark, only torches lit the space, which was made of stone and little else. In the center, a single long table stood empty, save for a white linen that covered it. The high priest of Har-Navah heaved the limp, bloodied acolyte onto the table with the help of the ambassador.

It took Kata much too long to understand what she was seeing. The slender, sharp knives Phinehas retrieved from a nearby shelf, a long, thick strand of dirty, rusted wire, a heavy chunk of wood that the ambassador picked up to examine for a moment, a smile curling his mouth to mimic the curl of his mustache.

Miri made no sound as Phinehas strapped her to the table with leather belts across her arms and chest.

"You will not do this, you bastard!" Jareth screamed as Phinehas began sharpening one of the slender blades. "YOU WILL NOT DO THIS!"

The ambassador did not say a word, simply lifting the heavy

wood level with his shoulders as if waiting…waiting for permission to strike.

Kata could not help the scream that burst from her, causing Jareth to spin around. When his eyes landed on her, they grew wide with horror.

"Run, Kata!" he yelled. "RUN!"

She stood frozen to the ground as she watched the ambassador deliver the damning blow.

She did not move as she watched the blood spray from Jareth's mouth and nose.

She could not scream as she watched him hit the hard stone floor, his body slamming against it with a sickening, splintering crack.

She could not make herself leave as the ambassador delivered a second blow.

Heart pounding and ears ringing, Kata watched the pool of blood grow beneath Jareth's absent eyes as he lay sprawled on the ground. She did not notice what happened next until she heard the screams and looked up to see her friend's knees bent, her body flailing against her restraints, the ambassador watching with bright-eyed delight as Phinehas used those wicked blades.

Blood poured freely from the edge of the table where Miri lay.

Only then did Kata manage to scream, a single word running through her mind.

Run.

Kata ran.

CHAPTER TWENTY-EIGHT

"I don't particularly care," Ezra said as he slipped on the second boot.

Esther stood with arms akimbo across the room. Her belly protruded so far that he wondered how his sister could stay upright.

"You will care when you bleed out and die," she said matter-of-factly.

Ezra stood, thankful for the feel of the blood rushing through his limbs as he stretched once. His stomach ached in protest, but at least he didn't feel the wound stretch open again. He rolled his shoulders once, twice, then marched across his bedchamber, retrieving a coat he had flung over an armchair.

"I won't bleed out, sister," he said casually. "The wound is healing nicely."

"Right. *Healing*. Not healed. You're not ready yet."

"I'm fine," he said.

"It's going to rain," Esther pointed out.

"I'm going into the village," he said as he straightened the brocade lapels of his favorite jacket.

"Why now? Why today? I don't understand why you just woke up and decided you needed to risk your life."

Ezra breathed a laugh through his nose, reaching his sister's side and pressing a swift kiss to her cheek. "Because I'm fine," he said, grabbing his top hat and disappearing into the hall.

He had kept his manner light on purpose, for he knew Esther well enough to know that if he had let on the real reason for his going to the village today, she would have protested vehemently.

But he had awoken this morning with a profound sense of urgency. To the point that he could not ignore it as he gulped down his breakfast. Nor could he ignore how the urgency seemed to increase as he watched the autumn storm rolling in from the north. Esther and John had come over for the evening last night and decided to stay. She was far enough along in her pregnancy that even the short carriage ride across the valley to their home was proving uncomfortable. So whenever she showed the least bit of discomfort, John would insist they stay.

Ezra didn't mind. He loved the company. He certainly loved having John Junior around.

But this morning, he had known that he needed to leave the house. He had known without knowing why that he needed to get to the village.

Now.

Esther didn't need to know why. Sheol, *Ezra* didn't really know why.

But he could guess.

And he knew his guess would not be a sufficient answer for his well-meaning, overprotective sister.

But Miri needed him. She was still there in that temple somewhere. That's all he knew.

He'd break down the doors and burn the whole damned building down, ancient landmark or not. He'd do whatever it took to find his wife and get her home. Today.

He'd almost decided to take his winged horse, Ahadah, before he thought it through. What if Miri was ill? Or weak? She'd need to ride home in a carriage, not sprawled on the back of his horse flying through the air. So he had suffered the extra time it took to prepare the carriage. Now, riding quietly on the hour-long trip down the mountain, he was second-guessing his wisdom. Ahadah could have had him to the village in less than half an hour.

But he was almost there now. It would be fine.

He would find her.

He would bring his wife home.

Today.

It would all be fine.

The village was surprisingly quiet. No one roamed the streets, bustling in and out of shops, as was usual on an autumn morning in Shalem. No passersby waved salutations. No tinkers lauded their wares. Ezra could not understand the reason for the ghostly emptiness of his beloved little village until his carriage traveled further into town. At first, the sounds were indecipherable, but the closer he got to the village square, the more he realized that everyone was here. And everyone was shouting.

Crowds gathered shoulder to shoulder in the open square. Unintelligible words hovered over the throng: some were chanting, some were yelling. The dark clouds of the oncoming rain hung fat and heavy over the village.

Ezra had never seen such a sight in his life. He knocked twice on the carriage for the driver to stop, and without explaining, he hopped down onto the cobblestones, practically running towards the gathering of villagers.

He ignored the sting in his stomach as he shouldered his way father inward, muttering apologies and excuses as he shoved people out of his way. Some noticed who he was and made room. Others wouldn't have cared if he was the king himself—they wanted to see the action as much as he did, and they were not budging. But driven by that urgency, he managed to keep going. And the further inside the crowd he got, the more one chant was clear.

Whore!

Whore!

Whore!

Ezra's heart fell right through his gut.

He pushed harder through the crowd, which was now so tight he could hardly move them. The sheer volume of the revelers made it impossible to speak any excuses or apologies, so he simply lifted and bodily moved anyone who stood in his way until at last he reached the final layer of people lining the edge of the inner circle, his head pounding and his stomach clenching with pain. He pressed a hand to the tender scar on his belly, looking past heads and shoulders to scan the open space before him, trying to understand what he saw.

A woman lay sprawled on the cobblestone, her naked body limp and bruised. She had been beaten. Severely. It wasn't until he saw the fiery curls tangled in bloody knots that he understood who the woman was, and Ezra gulped down a scream, his heart pounding in his throat.

Miriam.

The world seemed to stop turning as the scene unfolded before him.

"What say you, good people of faith!" shouted a man. Ezra looked up to see Phinehas dressed in pristine white robes and a brightly embroidered bib. He wore a tall hat adorned with an eight-pointed star and carried a scepter in his right hand.

The high priest of Har-Navah, his might on full display for all here to see.

"What is the punishment for her crimes?" Phinehas continued, walking slowly and purposefully around the circle, his voice loud and clear.

The crowed erupted with a sort of glee. *Kill her!*

Kill her!

Kill her!

"You son of a bitch!" Ezra screamed, tearing like a caged wildcat against the crowds holding him back. But his words hardly registered above the din of frenzied onlookers. The ancient laws, written by high priests many centuries ago, were as uncompromising as they were archaic. Few practiced them anymore, meting out justice in the civilized barbarism of the courtroom, not the vulgar barbarism of corporal punishment. But every once in a while, stories would manifest of priests who had resorted to the old law out of necessity. A crime too gruesome to be ignored. A grievous injustice that deserved the highest punishment. If memory served him, the ancient punishment for harlotry was swift and brutal: public dismemberment, limb by limb.

Ezra's whole body raged in protest.

The crowd's frenzy grew to dizzying levels, so loud that no single person could be heard over the shouting. Phinehas's eyes danced and burned, drunk with the power he wielded here. The ambassador stood near Miri, watching her with a revoltingly pleased leer. In his hand, he held a massive bludgeon, stained with dark blood on the end. Ezra knew—just knew—the sick bastard would eagerly use it on his wife if she dared to make a single move.

But Miri did not seem capable of moving, and Ezra soon realized why. Blood, thick and dark, pooled freely around her middle.

What had the monster done to her?

His ears rang with the blood pounding through his veins as he cried out and tried to shove his way past the final layer of onlookers. One of them seemed to figure out what he was doing and grabbed him by the upper arm. "He'll kill you," the man said.

Ezra didn't care. He had to get to her. Now. He had to get her out of here.

But the stranger persisted. "Don't be a fool. He'll kill you, Your Grace."

Ezra struggled against the man—two men, one on either side—who were holding him back. But they kept him at bay.

Then the crowd suddenly stilled. From raging melee to eerie silence in one fell swoop.

Ezra stopped struggling and looked around to see what had calmed the frenzy.

A man crouched at the edge of the circle. He was simply dressed in brown trousers, unpolished and scarred leather boots, and a dusty white shirt peeking underneath a dusty brown jacket. His build was as unremarkable as his clothing. In fact, there was nothing particularly distinguishing about the man except his hair and eyes. Strands as white as bones baking in the sun framed eyes clear and keen, greener than a Haravellian emerald.

He said nothing. Not a single word. But with his finger, he drew upon the gray cobblestones, words appearing in a trail of faint blue light.

From this distance, Ezra could not make out what they said. But Phinehas apparently could, for with one look at the magicked words, the high priest froze as still as death.

So did the crowd. Even the ambassador.

Ezra dared to glance at the high priest. Abject horror colored his narrow, pointed features. He seemed to be barely breathing.

The silence stretched thin, the only sound the caw of a crow. Above them, even the thick gray clouds seemed to still.

Thunder rumbled once, and it seemed to give Phinehas the stones to say something, though he was unable to hide the quaver to his voice. "What say you, prophet? Are you not learned in the holy laws? She has committed carnal sins against Providence himself. She took the vows of chastity, honor, and virtue. She took them before Providence. And now she has spit in his face by lying with a man and finding herself with child. She has brought shame upon this holy temple and upon my blameless name!"

Phinehas squared his shoulders, preparing to deliver the damning blow. The crowd was at his mercy again, and he knew it.

"What is the punishment for this woman's fornication? *This debauchery?*" He hissed the last words, and an answering hiss ran through the crowd.

The prophet did not move, as still as a statue. He looked once at Miri before lifting his eyes to Phinehas again. Beneath him, whatever he had written seemed to glow more brightly on the cobblestones. When he spoke, the already silent crowd seemed to quiet more, holding their breath in anticipation.

"May the blameless among you be the first to exact judgment."

Ezra knew those words. Knew where they originated.

The ancient texts.

He had quoted the ancient texts.

The same texts Phinehas had cited for Miri's punishment. The high priest knew it, too, for he did not move, did not dare speak. He simply stood before the melee he had created and gaped. Like a fish out of water. Like a fool.

The crowd became a frenzy of whispers. Fat rain drops began falling slowly from the sky, and thunder rumbled lazily again.

The prophet stood at last, taking the few steps that separated him from Miri. Phinehas did not try to stop him; neither did the ambassador, too stunned to do a thing as the prophet knelt beside her bruised, matted form.

Ezra sucked in a breath to protest before he realized that the prophet only meant to tend to her. The man tucked a strand of her disheveled hair behind her ear, bending to whisper something to her. Had Ezra not been watching so closely, he might not have seen her eyes flutter as the prophet spoke, nor would he have seen the brief flash of blue light that passed from the prophet's hand to Miri's temple. In an instant, the dried blood covering her gaunt body disappeared. Then the prophet removed his jacket and covered her with gentle reverence.

From the corner of his eye, Ezra saw the ambassador drop the bludgeon like a stone. Even Phinehas's shoulders sank, knowing he had lost the crowd—lost the momentum, the frenzy he had drummed up in the name of his crooked justice.

With one sentence, the prophet had silenced every one of them.

The prophet stood again, ignoring Phinehas and the ambassador and completely undaunted by the rage now sizzling in their eyes. He turned and faced Ezra fully.

Heart frozen for a moment, Ezra was not sure what was happening. Not until he heard the prophet say, "Take her home."

Ezra didn't hesitate.

Pushing past the people around him, he strode to Miri in all of three steps. He knelt before her, ignoring his screaming abdomen as he scooped her into his arms. She was as limp as a straw doll and just as light. And covered all over in wicked marks and bruises. Ezra choked back a sob and pressed a tremulous kiss to her brow.

"Oh my Wildfire," he said before he looked around again, just waiting for the priest or the ambassador to dare to try and stop him.

But Phinehas and the ambassador had disappeared, nowhere in sight of the dissipating crowd. Ezra didn't care. He would deal with them later. Standing with Miri in his arms, Ezra turned to thank the prophet.

He was nowhere to be found.

On the ground at his feet, Ezra read the words the man had written, the glow dimming rapidly in the falling rain.

Phocas Antonius — Extortion, Treason

Tomas Augustus — Fornication, Murder

CHAPTER TWENTY-NINE

Fire spread across her lower back, throbbing and aching. She grimaced, sucking in a breath and reaching behind. Her arms ached, too. So did her head. Her whole body, really. Everything hurt and seemed to curse in protest. She let out a particularly colorful word of agreement.

When Miri opened her eyes, it took her mind much too long to catch up with what she saw. Plush curtains draped down large, picture-frame windows. Rich carpets spread across the polished marble floors of a vast bedchamber. A large fire burned brightly in a hearth large enough to be a bedroom in and of itself.

Miri had no idea where she was.

Panic set in, as quick as lightning. Her heart pounded mercilessly in tandem with the pounding in her head. She sat up, crying out against the pains shooting from her middle down her legs and up her torso and arms. It felt as if no part of her had been spared a thorough and violent beating. Judging by the bruises marring her skin, that assessment was probably not too far from the truth.

Wherever she was...they would surely beat her again.

She looked around again. Cathedral ceilings adorned with

heavy, intricately-carved wooden beams reached down to thick stone walls covered with all manner of detailed paintings: a mountain-scape of a glorious sunset bathing a pool of water in golden light; a white wolf howling at the moon; an evergreen forest rich with færies. Another painting of a couple—a tall man with hair as black as ink standing next to a woman with thick, long, chocolate tresses. The man looked familiar, but Miri could not place his features: either that deep dimple on his right cheek or that cowlick at his temple. Dressed in old-fashioned clothes, the couple was clearly not modern.

A beautiful, plushly furnished prison.

Her captor had a particular fondness for finery, that much was clear. And brutality, if her aching body was any indication.

She needed to get out of here.

Miri heard a sound, reaching on instinct to cover herself with the luxurious blankets of her bed, only to realize she was wearing a soft silk shift—one she had never seen before. Her blankets were richly made of fine damask and thick down. And at her feet draped a white fur blanket that gleamed in the moonlight spilling across her bed from those vast windows.

She looked outside to see the full moon glinting off of the placid lake below. Such a vast, uninhibited view in comparison to her chambers in the temple. And high up, as if suspended over the lake. Second story, then. Maybe third. Mountains towered all around, casting mighty shadows across the waters.

Magnificent.

A glorious, decadent prison.

She needed to get out of here quickly.

Heart pounding, Miri turned her attention to the door now opening across the room. A small, thin servant entered, carrying a silver basin.

"Oh!" said the servant. "I didn't realize you'd be awake!" She hurried across the room, setting down the obviously heavy bowl onto a nearby table before retrieving a bright white towel and dipping it into the contents of the basin. Her ash-blonde hair was pulled tight into a bun atop her head, a few thin strands spilling from the sides. On the side of her head, just above her ear, she wore a comb embellished with what looked like butterfly wings. She wrung the white towel a few times before making her way to Miri, offering it to her.

"I thought you might want this," she said. "Poor thing. Your fever has been up and down. I figured it was about time for it to break again."

"My fever?" Miri said, absently taking the towel from the servant. When she did nothing with it, the servant giggled, taking it back. She pressed it to Miri's brow, simultaneously fluffing the pillows behind her.

"You should lie back down, Your Grace. You need the rest. But oh, how happy everyone will be when I tell them you're awake!"

"Don't do that," Miri blurted.

The servant's eyes grew wide.

"I mean," Miri corrected, "let's not wake them of course."

The servant giggled again. "Of course. We'll let them sleep. Though I'm fairly certain Helena will have my head for that."

Helena. The name rang vaguely familiar. But Miri brushed it aside, trying to figure out how she was going to get out of here. All this plush lavishness. All this decadence. It did not take her long to figure out where she was.

The ambassador.

This had to be his manor. Some ostentatious castle the king had provided for him upon his stay in Har-Navah. The ambassador had obviously tired of dealing with Phinehas's interruptions and taken her to his own home instead.

Miri resisted the urge to vomit as dark images danced in her mind. Phantom pains shot through her gut, and she felt the world spinning around her.

"My lady," said the servant, patting the towel on Miri's head again. "You need to lie down. You're getting stronger every day, but you're not well yet."

The girl was surprisingly strong as she tried to force Miri to lay back down. Or maybe it was just that Miri was weak. So weak.

"Perhaps some broth would do you good?" the servant asked. Miri only nodded, taking hold of the towel when the servant placed her hand on it.

"Good!" she said brightly. "I'm Kit, by the way. Kitty, that is. I'm so glad you're awake, my lady! I'll bring you something to eat right away!"

The bright young servant practically danced from the room, apparently giddy to bring Miri some sustenance. A small part of Miri was sorry that she would not be around to oblige the eager young girl by partaking of it.

Quickly, Miri jumped from the bed, intending to make her way out of the room. But a glimpse of something dark caught her eye, and Miri whirled to face the bed, only to see a broad and glistening stain.

Blood.

There was blood on neatly-folded linens, tucked under where she had been laying.

More blood than she had ever known from her courses. She checked the back of her shift to find that it, too, was soaked in crimson.

A pang of worry rang through her at the same moment pains shot through her belly like lightning.

Hands covering her stomach, Miri looked around, trying to understand. Trying to catch her breath.

She spotted a wardrobe just across the way and ran towards it. Rifling through the contents, she found a robe and quickly covered herself in the fur-lined velvet, hoping it would be enough against the brisk night air. Next she pulled on a pair of soft, warm slippers.

Without considering that she had no idea where to find an exterior door in this castle, not to mention the fact that she was bleeding, Miri escaped into the corridors and into the unknown.

THE HALLS WERE WARM—SURPRISINGLY warm for such a vast manor. With the chill outside, it seemed a bit surprising how warm and inviting the whole place was. Gaslights burned softly along the corridors, lighting the plush carpets in a rich, golden hue. Though she knew she would need it once she got outside, Miri quickly found that the warm clothing she had procured from her chambers was a bit much for this cozy place.

It bothered her—how perfect everything was. How inviting.

Just the same way a spider made her web inviting to any unsuspecting moths. Miri's pace quickened as she made her way through the winding halls.

THE PLACE WAS HUGE. Too big to possibly comprehend, with labyrinthine corridors and winding staircases. She'd never find her way out. It did not help that she was bone tired and weary. Her body seemed to scream in protest of her harried escape. Every part of her wanted to collapse in that plush, warm bed where she had woken and sleep for a thousand winters.

And hungry. By Providence she was starving, fairly certain she could eat an army's worth of food right now.

But she had to get out. She had to leave.

She had no choice.

The ambassador would surely find her soon.

She sped through the maze of halls and stairs, hysteria growing with every new turn, every new corner.

SHE WASN'T sure how long she had been running through this place. Maybe ten minutes. Maybe an hour. It was all a blur of massive paintings and colorful tapestries and intricate sculptures. One hall blurred into the next with no sign of any formal entryway or exit.

The panic had settled into her bones, but Miri kept running.

Running until she collided into...

"Miri!" came a voice, as rich as it was familiar.

Dazed, it took her a moment to realize who she had run into.

"Ezra?" she asked, her mind foggy.

"Where are you going?" he asked, taking hold of her upper arms in order to keep her from toppling like stalk of wheat at the scythe.

"Ezra," she heard herself say again. "Oh Ezra, thank Providence! You have to help me! I cannot find the door! I cannot find how to get out!"

"To get out? Miri, what are you talking about?"

Ezra's thick arms pulled her close to himself, wrapping around her. She let herself collapse against him for only a moment before she regained her thoughts. "I have to get out. Please, Ezra. You must help me!"

"Miri," he said, his words soft and placating. "Shhhh." He ran a hand down her hair and held her close against him. "It's all right," he said. "You're safe now."

"Please. He will wake any moment! Please, Ezra. Help me!"

"Miri," he said, his words irritatingly calm. "It's all right, Wildfire. You're home. You're safe."

She was no such thing. But Ezra did not seem to care. Then again, why was he here?

"How did you get here?" she asked.

Ezra pulled her away enough to search her face. He tilted his head to one side. "Do you remember anything?"

She closed her eyes, those dark images coming back much too eagerly. Pain. So much pain. And blood, dark and dripping freely from a tall, cold table on which she lay. Words, coming to her in bits and pieces.

You will pay, you whore.

You will not do this!

And pains—the pains lancing her stomach, her most intimate places… The blood that stained her linens when she had gotten out of bed…

She shuddered, nearly collapsing. Ezra pulled her against his chest once more. "Never mind," he said soothingly. "I brought you home, Miri. You're home. And you're safe."

"The ambassador—"

"He's gone, Miri. He will not find you here. I have doubled the guards. And stationed my men in the mountains. No one will come here unless they're invited. You're safe, Miri. I promise."

"Your men?" she asked, beginning to understand. "This is… your home?"

Ezra pressed a soft kiss to her brow. "*Our* home, Wildfire. Welcome to Massahd Castle."

Miri pushed out of his arms, looking around her. Everything spoke of Ezra, somehow. She could see it now. A colorful history of family and legacy on every wall and every tapestry. This castle was a testament to the rich legacy of the Kelach family.

"Oh," she said stupidly. "Oh. I'm sorry."

"Why in the world are you sorry?" Ezra asked with a soft laugh. "I'm so glad you're awake, Miri," he went on without waiting for her reply. "You look better. Do you feel any better?"

She met his eyes again. "I'm..." But what was she? Fine? Tired? Better? Terrified? She could not make sense of her thoughts at the moment.

Ezra smiled, pressing a kiss to her brow. "Overwhelmed, I think," he said. He wrapped an arm around her waist, and the movement made her jump back.

"I'm sorry," he said carefully, his eyes flashing with quiet horror. "I didn't mean to—"

"It's fine," she blurted. "I'm fine."

Ezra searched her for a moment, his countenance shifting to something else. Something profoundly sorrowful. "Are you hungry?"

"No," she lied. Looking around, realizing the darkness around her, she asked, "What is the hour?"

"It's the middle of the night," Ezra said.

"Why are you awake?"

"I couldn't sleep," he admitted with a shrug. "I take it neither could you."

"I'm not tired," she lied again. "I feel like I've slept for days."

"You have," he said.

"What?"

"Miri, you've been unconscious for four days," he said, pain in his eyes at the words.

"Four days?" she blurted. "I've been here for four days?"

She did not remember it. Not a single moment.

"It's all right, Miri. You need the rest. Perhaps you should go and lie down again. You seem—"

"I'm not tired. And I will not bother you anymore. If I could have a horse, I could—"

"A horse?" Ezra asked with another soft chuckle. "Miri, what do you need a horse for?"

"I don't want to be a burden. I—"

He took her face in his hands, warm and gentle. "You are never a burden, Wildfire."

Miri met Ezra's eyes, saw the concern in them, and looked away once more.

Ezra moved those warm hands to her shoulders. "Perhaps a hot bath—"

She shrugged away from him. "I'm fine. I'll just go back to sleep." She whirled to go back in the direction from which she had come. Never mind she had no idea where her chambers were now.

"Miri," Ezra tried.

Miri ignored him and disappeared into the labyrinthine halls of Massahd Castle.

CHAPTER THIRTY

Snow fell softly outside the windows. Autumn had made her glorious, colorful appearance, but the snows had only just begun to really stick. The smell of pumpkin, apples, and warm spices wafted through the dining room of Massahd Castle. Lords and dukes and even the king himself would host parties and gatherings to celebrate the changing of seasons. His favorite season.

Ezra sighed and took a sip of his coffee. Miri had been here for days and had yet to emerge from her chambers except for the other night. She had been so confused, so scared. And it had broken Ezra's heart to see her in such a state, silent worry gnawing at him day and night.

"Your morning post, my lord," said Thaddeus. The butler presented Ezra with a silver tray littered with parchment. Ezra took them unceremoniously.

"Thank you, Thaddeus." He thumbed through the letters. Appeals. Inquiries. Invitations. The usual.

"Autumn is upon us," Thaddeus said, looking wistfully out the vast windows of the dining room.

"Indeed it is," Ezra concurred. "The lake will be freezing over soon."

Thaddeus nodded. "John Junior will have many plans for that frozen lake, I have no doubt."

Ezra chuckled his agreement. "Have one of these scones with me, Thaddeus. They're delicious." Ezra gestured towards the array of pastries before him. Someone might as well enjoy them. Miri hadn't joined him for breakfast once since arriving. Not that he blamed her.

Quite predictably, the butler refused with a wry smile before disappearing from the dining hall once more.

Ezra had had the breakfast brought in from Joshua's bakery this morning, hoping the familiar pastries might brighten Miri's day. Because after yesterday...

The doctor had visited yesterday. After sleeping well into the day, Miri had finally woken and the doctor had called. She had hardly spoken since.

Ezra knew she was recovering—sorting thorough the myriad of evils she had faced in her month with the ambassador. Ezra, too, had been sorting through it all, swallowing back tears when the doctor shook his head gravely. Miri had been so violently abused, so wickedly violated that her recovery would be long and slow...and most likely her ordeal would leave lasting effects.

Miri had not reacted, not shown any sign that she understood the doctor at all. She had simply gone back to bed. Ezra could hardly stand it. He could hardly think past the hatred simmering in his soul. The next time he saw the priest or the ambassador... well, he could only imagine how he would react. What he might do. It didn't help that he had no idea where to begin with Miri— what to even say or how to apologize for failing her so thoroughly. If it hadn't been for that prophet, he shuddered to think what would have been her fate.

Ezra took another sip of his coffee and opened the first letter.

"Council. Wonderful," he muttered. The timing was—

"You're going to council?"

Ezra looked up, standing abruptly when he saw Miri emerge into the dining room at the opposite end of the long table.

"Wildfire," he said, surprised she was here. Surprised she had finally left her room. A smile grew from deep within at the sight of her. She had regained some of her color since arriving a few days ago. But her body was still painfully thin and frail. Despite the fact that he knew Kit had spent the better part of a morning combing through it, Miri's hair hung limp, her curls heavy and lacking their usual bounce. Her face was still gaunt—much too gaunt. But somehow, she was still the most gloriously beautiful creature he had ever laid eyes on.

He wondered if she would allow him to tell her so.

He pushed away from the table and made his way to her, reaching to take her hands. She snatched them away before he could touch her.

Something within his heart cracked.

He smiled anyway.

"Good morning, my love," he said gently. "Are you hungry?"

Miri eyed the table, her gaze landing on the pastries and stopping. Something in her features shifted, and a wild fear washed over her expression.

"Scones," Ezra tried. "I thought you might enjoy—"

"I'm not hungry," she interrupted.

Ezra wasn't sure what to say, wasn't sure what was happening. "Perhaps...perhaps some eggs then?"

"Are you leaving?" she asked, ignoring his suggestion.

Ezra searched her. "There is a mandatory council meeting tomorrow. I will have to attend. But you are well protected, I promise."

Miri said nothing, her gaze growing distant and unfocused.

He wanted to reach out to her. He wanted to take her into his arms and hold her until all of her pain disappeared. Until she knew that she was loved and safe and that the darkness was over.

Instead, he asked, "Are you feeling better?" She was out of her chambers, which was something. The bleeding hadn't stopped yet. The doctor had said yesterday that if it didn't stop within the next few weeks, it might never. Not to mention the implications of that kind of injury...

Whatever Phinehas had done to her had been thorough. Creatively brutal. Sickeningly violent.

Ezra's fist clenched at his side just thinking about it.

"I'm fine," she said flatly. And then she turned, walking back towards the door.

"Would you like to go for a walk with me, Miri?" Searching. He was searching for something—anything to convince her to stay. Anything that could help her. Sheol, something that would just let him be with her. Even in strange, contemplative silence.

"You must prepare for council," she said without turning. Then she disappeared into the hall again.

Ezra followed.

"I've written some letters," he said. Miri did not bother turning as she walked like a ghost through the broad foyer. "I'm trying to find the prophet. I've invited him here. To Massahd. I'd like to thank him in person."

Miri paused, turning slightly, her brows furrowed.

"You would not be here without him," Ezra said gently. He reached to touch her arm, but she pulled it away.

A lump formed in his throat. "I owe him a debt of gratitude. Do you remember anything about that day?"

She looked off, her eyes growing distant again. "No," she finally said.

It was probably better that way, but Ezra was not sure what to make of her lack of memory. Not to mention her distance. From him. From reality. From herself.

"I want you to meet him. He's different, Miri. Different than most of the charlatans who call themselves prophets. And I think you will like him."

Miri nodded faintly before walking away again.

"I will not be leaving until midday tomorrow," Ezra said, deciding not to follow her any further. Clearly, she wanted nothing to do with him.

Miri did not respond.

CHAPTER THIRTY-ONE

The snow made for slower travel than he had anticipated. Had the king's letter not been abundantly clear—this was a council meeting he could not miss—Ezra never would have left her. But the possibility of the priest and the ambassador being at Chesedelle today was much too high to take her with him.

So Ezra had reluctantly left a quiet, distant Miri alone in one of the libraries at Massahd. She hadn't even looked up when he said goodbye.

The entire ordeal was tearing away his soul, chunk by chunk.

Ezra hadn't really allowed himself to consider what he would do if he saw Phinehas or Ambassador Phocas today. Not until the carriage ride through the mountains. He hadn't let himself go down that road, to consider what might happen were he to see either one of those monsters. He had just remained focused on keeping it together for Miri. Being strong in her weakness. Steady for her storm-tossed soul.

But now, away from her and drawing closer to Chesedelle

with every clomp of the horses' hooves, one thing was clear: he wasn't ready. Not by a mile. Not by a thousand miles.

Ezra was not equipped to face Miri's monsters.

He couldn't save her from them. He couldn't even get out of the damned bed when she needed him most.

He was not enough for her.

It was rage and something else—something much darker—that burned in his heart as he felt for what was probably the fiftieth time beneath his jacket, reaching for the dagger tucked away beneath his clothes. One word, one wrong look from either the priest or the ambassador, and Ezra would end them. Even if it meant imprisonment.

Ezra would gladly gut both of the bastards. And relish it.

"Your Grace?" came a voice. Ezra cleared his mind and focused his vision again only to realize the carriage had stopped and the driver had opened his door. He wondered how long the man had been standing there in the cold, waiting for Ezra to emerge.

He wondered if the driver knew the thoughts swirling in Ezra's mind or understood the weight of the dagger at his hip.

There were many things he wondered the entire walk to the castle doors.

THE KING'S council would not convene in the usual place: the royal council chambers. For this meeting, King Dægan had moved the council to the throne room at Chesedelle—a massive, ancient chamber of towering pillars and seats that lined the perimeter. The space was more suited for a ceremony than a meeting to discuss the goings on of Har-Navah.

Ezra really hadn't had time to think about politics, to consider the weight of the treaty the king had recently signed—handing over the autonomy of the great kingdom of Har-Navah. In the name of peace. The king had signed *everything* away in the name of peace. Ezra wondered what sort of madness had led the king to do such a thing. He hoped that today he would understand at last.

And when a woman walked in behind the king, adorned head to toe in gold, Ezra thought he might have his answer.

The woman was...there was not a sufficient word to describe her.

Impossible.

Perfect.

Perfect in a terrifying sort of way. Her rich golden gown matched her heavy golden diadem, adorned with black-diamond moths whose wings fluttered of their own accord. Her eyes were heavily lined with gold kohl, and her skin was as milky white as freshly-fallen snow. Her crimson hair, pulled into intricate braids and curls and swirls, was fashioned around her diadem in such a way that it was hard to tell where it ended and the crown began. A sheer, gauzy black veil fell from the back of the diadem, down her slender back, exposed by a deep vee opening in her gown. Her fingers were empty, no jewels adorning them. But her fingernails were long and thin—sharp as dagger blades and painted black like the night sky.

She emerged into the throne room on a cloud of purple smoke. Ezra watched the king as he walked before her, holding a heavy iron censer aloft, spreading the cloying smoke around the throne, basking in its intoxicating shimmer. With a flicker of his hand, that smoke disappeared, leaving behind nothing but glittering speckles in the air. The king had apparently learned a few new tricks from the high priest. He had always loved dark magical displays of power. He had taken to learning those tricks years ago, using them when necessary as a show of power. Of might. Of fear. Today would be no exception, the king displaying the fanfare for all the court here today as if the empress were a high priestess herself.

No, as if she were a goddess.

Behind the empress, four maidens followed, carrying the long train of her heavy golden gown. They were also adorned in finery, and had they not been standing near the woman, might have been splendid of their own accord.

But compared to her... Gods, *anyone* compared to this woman...

She was sin and vice and wicked beauty. She was Heaven and Sheol and night and day.

She was extraordinary.

She made her way one ghostly step at a time to the dais, taking her seat not on the smaller throne designed for the king's esteemed guests, but on the king's throne itself.

The strange woman sat down on the ancient throne of Har-Navah.

That move alone should have had her beheaded. Instead, the king welcomed it with a gesture that was practically gleeful. Ezra did not fail to notice that the queen of Har-Navah was nowhere to be found.

The king lifted the woman's hand to his mouth and pressed a kiss to her skin. A kiss so lingering, so possessive, Ezra couldn't help but feel as if he were intruding on an intimate moment between lovers.

Perhaps he was.

"Esteemed Council," the king finally said, his voice echoing like a hundred voices in the massive chamber. "I thank you for your attendance today."

Ezra looked around the throne room, eager to see the faces of his fellow councilors. The noblemen in the room were as wide-mouthed and stupefied as he knew himself to be. But of those in attendance, two faces in particular were conspicuously missing: High Priest Phinehas and Ambassador Phocas.

Ezra searched the room again, just to be sure. But he wasn't wrong; neither were in attendance today. He wondered what it meant.

But then he spotted two familiar faces who *were* in attendance: Princess Rachæl, standing just off of the dais, looking for all the world like she wanted to rip the woman limb from limb. And just to Rachæl's right...

Gian of Borras.

Rage welled white-hot and quite unexpectedly at the sight of the man who had nearly taken his life. The man who had denied Ezra the ability to save Miriam from the darkness she had known in the temple.

Perhaps Ezra would not face Phinehas or Phocas today. But perhaps Gian would taste Ezra's blade instead.

It would serve him right, the bastard.

"It is my humble honor to introduce to you today someone who is an asset to our kingdom. Someone who will lead us into the future with cunning grace and ruthless cleverness. I have had the privilege of getting to know her over these past months, and I can attest that there is no greater ally to our good kingdom. Councilors, I give you Empress Lilith of Medinah!"

No one said a word. Not a single word. In fact, in that vast chamber with nearly every councilor in attendance, Ezra was fairly certain he could hear his own heart beating.

Empress Lilith stood, her ethereal gown perfectly positioned by her attendants to flow like a river of sunlight down the steps of the dais. She said nothing, looking out over the crowd with a muted expression.

Suddenly and quite unexpectedly, voices rang out. Ezra looked above them to the mezzanine that circled the chamber to find a choir of boys adorned in robes of similar gold to the empress. They sang out in a droning chant of the Medinian language, their high voices rich and clear, echoing off of the marble pillars and walls of the chamber. He did not know all the words, his knowledge of the language broken and minimal. But the sound consumed Ezra, body and soul. A haunting, repetitive rhythm. But from what little of the language he knew, he did not recognize the familiar cadence of any ancient credos.

This was not some ancient hymn, some tribute to Providence or his creation. This was not some familiar verse set to melody. This was something else entirely.

And then the empress sang.

Her sublime voice rang out clear and high above the boys, harmonizing in and through the melodies like a sprite might dance through a meadow. All around him, mouths hung agape at the spectacle of sound immersing them all.

She, too, sang in her native language, and the lyrics were again not any song Ezra recognized. But he picked up some of the words:

> *Alea iacta est.*
> *Ad meliora.*
> *Peace.*
> *In newness of time.*
> *The splendor of the earth and the heavens.*
> *The power of magic. The magic of men.*

Not a word to Providence, as in the temple chants. Not a mention of Eloah, the name given to the Creator in the old language. Nor Deus, his Medinian name. No, this sonnet was an ode to the splendor of something else.

Something new.

Something...*other*.

A sensation dark and otherworldly slithered along Ezra's bones.

THE SONG RANG on for at least a half an hour. No one moved a muscle as the empress sang with an impressive range of rich soprano and guttural baritone, the boys in the mezzanine above accompanying her with haunting perfection. When she was done, the empress stood silent before the adoring crowd for a moment that turned the hairs on Ezra's arm on end. She looked out across the crowd, her eyes bright, her fiery curls spilling in wild familiarity around her face.

Ezra watched those curls, transfixed by them—by the way they swayed ever so slightly, as if alive. He watched them, longed for them, loving them and hating them all at once.

"Great people of Har-Navah," the empress spoke, her voice many and one, ancient and young, seductive and terrifying. "On the wings of this newly-formed alliance, we usher in a new era. We usher in the promise of tomorrow.

"No longer do we wait in vain for the promises of yore—of heroes who never rise or prophets who never speak truth. No longer do we wait for folk tales and legends to come to life.

"You've all heard the stories—by your bedside as your mothers whispered tales, by your fireside as your fathers spoke of one who would to save us all. You've spoken those fables for a thousand years and for a thousand before that. You've waited in vain for færy stories to come to life. Stories of one who was promised to save us all. Promised to make the world anew.

"I come to you now to proclaim that your wait is over; your vanity is no more. I come to you to proclaim the new world is in order, and the new era has begun. I come to you to tell you that there is a new promise.

"By the alliance between our great nations, we shall make the world anew, and set forth the age of industry, the age of enlightenment, a better world for all of us.

"We are the people of tomorrow, and this is the future before us. And the future is magic. In all its glory. In all its innovation. In all its advancement. In all its power. No longer will it be reserved for the few. No longer will magic be an enigma, only given to those deigned worthy enough by some distant, unknown god.

"In this new world we will make, in this future we forge together, magic will be for all. Magic will be for everyone, young and old, rich and poor.

"Magic is the future. Magic is the power—the promise you've been waiting for."

A deafening silence filled the throne room as her words sank in. No one dared breathe, no one dared move. They only stood before her, watching her, their eyes wide and their mouths slack.

And then someone shouted, "*All hail Empress Lilith! All hail Empress Lilith!*"

The crowd erupted. Cheers and shouts, great cries of joy. The people of Har-Navah welcomed this woman and her promises with open arms and shouts of fealty.

Ezra stood in shocked silence as he watched the scene unfold before him.

Without another word, the empress turned, allowing her maidens to gather the hem of her gown, and walked out of the chamber. The king followed her like a salivating pup following a leg of lamb. He hadn't bothered to say a word.

And that was it.

Ezra did not know what to make of it.

"That was a farce if ever I saw one."

Ezra whirled to find Rachæl standing beside him. Gian, he noticed, was a pace behind her, watching her with keen eyes. Whatever he was doing, whatever reason he had for being so near the princess, Ezra knew it was not good. He made sure Gian took note of his glare before he turned his attention back to the princess.

"What in the world was the purpose of that?" Ezra asked his former betrothed.

She watched the door through which the king and the empress had just disappeared as if waiting for it to sprout wings and fly. "I don't know. But I'm going to find out."

"Is it really true?" Ezra asked. "Did your father really sign the treaty without the council's involvement?"

"He's been rather busy with a lot of things he didn't bother to involve you in. Or me," Rachæl said.

Ezra turned his attention to the door Rachæl stared at. "Something is very, very wrong with that woman."

"Tell me something I don't know," said Rachæl. She looked over her shoulder, nodding once to Gian, who leveled a smirk at Ezra before moving to follow the princess from the room. But Ezra grabbed the pirate's arm as he passed.

"Going so soon?" Ezra asked.

Gian cocked his head to one side. "How are you feeling, Ezra? You seem a bit under the weather."

Ezra let a growl escape through his teeth. "What are you doing with her?"

Gian let a smirk curl his lips. "Something bothering you, Your Grace?"

"I don't know what it is you're up to, but you will stay away from her."

Gian sucked in a breath between his teeth. "You see, that will be difficult considering I'm watching over her at her father's behest."

"Bullshit."

"Is that jealousy I detect, Ezra? How very predictable."

"You know nothing of what you speak. Stay away from her," Ezra spat. As if of its own accord, his hand slowly inched toward the dagger at his hip. One move, one wrong word, and he would gut the bastard. Right here, right now. And deal with the consequences later.

"What a tired story," Gian said. "Poor, bored nobleman leaves his intended for a whore, only to bore of her as well and realize what a mistake he's made."

"Never call her that again," Ezra growled. His hand reached the dagger, and he wrapped it around the hilt.

Gian noticed, glancing down at Ezra's waist before meeting his gaze again. He snickered. "What are you going to do with that? Take your revenge?"

"I have about a dozen reasons to gut you right now."

Gian stepped closer, eye to eye, nose to nose. "Do it then."

Ezra did not move. He did not breathe. He contemplated it—how good it would feel to slice Gian open right here, right now, this instant. How right. Take out some of his revenge for what happened to Miri by killing this arrogant ass.

Gian smirked again. "I didn't think you had it in you." He moved, brushing past Ezra a little too firmly as he continued speaking. "You should thank me, you know. I saved your life that night."

"You gutted me and left me for dead," Ezra snapped.

Gian turned to face him, all arrogance in his stance, his grin. "Come, Ezra. Do you really think me so inept with a blade that I couldn't manage to kill you? If I had wanted you dead, you'd be rotting in your mausoleum right now. And if it weren't for my blade, you'd most certainly be rotting at this very moment."

"Am I supposed to believe you did me a favor, then?" Ezra asked. The hilt in his hand turned heavy, but he kept his grip firm.

Gian closed the gap between them, nose to nose once more. "You have no idea what that bastard is capable of. That you think you could have marched in there as her white knight and saved her shows how stupid you really are."

Ezra froze, unsure what to say. Gian watched him for a moment before sneering and turning to walk away once more.

"What are you doing with her?" Ezra asked, staying the pirate with his words.

Gian turned to face Ezra once more. "What you didn't have the balls to do."

What the Sheol was that supposed to mean? Ezra's hand lingered on the dagger at his side, but he did not move to withdraw it. "Stay away from her," he warned.

"I'm quivering in my boots," Gian mocked, a hand to his chest.

Ezra's fist crashed across Gian's mouth before he could think better of it. His knuckles barked with the pain as they collided with Gian's teeth. Blood sprayed, and the pirate lord eyed Ezra with a mixture of shock and delight as he wiped his mouth.

"Good to know you have a pair. I was beginning to wonder."

"I mean it, Gian. Stay away from the princess."

"How about you mind your business and I'll mind mine." With that, Gian turned and followed where the princess and the rest of the councilors had disappeared from the chamber.

Ezra had half a mind to hurl his dagger straight into Gian's back. For reasons he could not understand, he did not.

He stood in silence for a moment, watching Gian saunter away—a wolf walking away from a carcass. The room was silent again, but the strains of the empress's song still lingered high above like a storm cloud. A heavy hand on his shoulder had him turning to see one of the remaining councilors wearing a broad, fascinated smile on his face.

"She was remarkable, wasn't she?" asked the councilor. His eyes...they were distant, almost haunted. As if he had been stupefied.

"She was definitely something," said Ezra.

"That chocolate hair, that rich, caramel skin. Gods above." The councilor spoke as if in a dream.

"Chocolate hair?" Ezra asked, wondering if the man had taken to the bottle early today. "Her hair was red. Fiery red curls, like—"

Like Miri's hair. Eerily similar, now that he thought about it.

The councilor squeezed his shoulder, those distant eyes widening to an eager smile. "What a joyous time for our kingdom."

Ezra had no response to the remark, taking a moment to try to understand. Had the empress appeared differently to him than to the others?

He scanned the room as the rest of the councilors slowly exited. They, like the councilor before him, bore wide eyes and dazed, absent smiles.

As if...as if they were under a spell.

The councilor smiled again before following the rest from the throne room, leaving Ezra alone in the vast chamber.

It was expectation alone that had Ezra staying for dinner with the king, the empress, the princess, and a few councilors. The queen, yet again, was nowhere to be found—almost as if she was waging her own silent protest to the empress's presence.

If Ezra knew anything of Queen Gelleia, that was likely exactly why she had been conspicuously absent today. She was as formidable as she was stubborn—a character trait Rachæl had certainly inherited.

But in truth, Ezra was glad the queen had not been present to witness the king's blatant ogling and ass-kissing of the enigmatic empress. He was glad she had not been present for his unapologetic disrespect.

But it was not the presence of the empress, but another guest at the dinner table that had occupied Ezra's thoughts.

Gian of Borras.

In the years Ezra had spent at Chesedelle, betrothed to the princess, Gian had made himself indispensable to the Ramagi family. As the king's lap dog, Gian had reduced himself to whatever Sheols King Dægan asked of him. Happily. And in between those assignments, he had spent most of his time lurking around the royal family—namely the princess, bawdy quips his conversation of choice.

But never once in all those years had Ezra witnessed Gian sit at the king's table or dine with the king's family. Not once.

Now, the man who had come between him and Miri had somehow wormed his way into the inner circle of the royal family. Ezra needed to understand why.

So after dinner had concluded, he did not hesitate to pull Rachæl aside.

The princess leveled a flat look at him. "You want to speak alone?" she asked, repeating his question back to him.

Ezra merely nodded, glancing about the room once before looking back to her. He nodded towards a small antechamber just off the king's dining hall. It would be quiet and private, even if a bit conspicuous to anyone watching them—which was likely everyone in the room.

He didn't give a damn at the moment.

Rachæl nodded and followed Ezra into the small room. A servant had lit a fire in the small hearth of the room, bathing it in a warm glow. He waited until he had closed the door behind himself before he spoke. "I need to understand something."

"What is that?" the princess asked skeptically, crossing her arms as she faced him. She did not bother to take a seat in one of the two chairs in the room.

"What are you doing with him?" He knew she knew to whom he referred by the way her countenance melted into annoyance.

"You forfeited the right to care when you ended things between us, Ezra."

"I heartily disagree," he offered, stepping towards her. It was strange to be alone with her again. He hadn't been alone with Rachæl in this castle in many months. In the last months before he had ended their betrothal, their moments alone had waned to near nonexistence. It had taken ending everything for him to understand why.

"I trust him," Rachæl said with matter-of-fact confidence.

"You should not," Ezra said. "He is not who you think he is."

"He is exactly who I think he is," she countered.

"He mentioned that the king has made him your personal guard. Is that true?"

She snorted a laugh and turned away from him, facing out the set of windows at the edge of the room. The night was gilded in silver moonlight. "Is that what he said? He is my father's eyes and ears, Ezra. You know that as well as I. He's been commissioned to keep an eye on me since you no longer will."

"I never did that," Ezra protested, taking a single step towards her. He halted when she did not face him. Is that what she thought? That their betrothal was as much a future marriage as it was a chance for Ezra to keep an eye on Rachæl for the king?

"I cannot be trusted. I'm too much like my mother," Rachæl went on. "Father needed to ensure that my loyalties remain in their proper place. Thus, I inherited a watchdog."

"He seemed like more than that to me," Ezra said. He could not put a finger on it—what it was between them. But it seemed a great deal more than a guard and his charge. He did not want to linger too long on what a man like Gian would want with a woman like Rachæl.

"You are misinformed," she said.

"He is a dangerous man, Rachæl. You need to stay far away from him."

"I am trying not to be insulted that you have come here to pull me aside and let me know that I am too weak, too pathetic to know when I am in danger."

"That's not—"

"Gian is not a threat. No more than you are. My father trusts him. So will I. You needn't feign concern, Ezra. It's pathetic."

Ezra knew her—perhaps better than she realized. And he knew it was officially time to drop the subject. So he did. He sighed and walked toward her, waiting until he reached her side before he spoke again. He faced the silver night out the windows as he continued, "There is something I need to tell you."

Rachæl turned to face him, but said nothing.

Ezra swallowed once, wishing there was an easier way to break the news. Wishing it would not hurt her as much as he knew it would. But it had to be said. And it had to come from him. "I have taken a wife."

Rachæl did not say a word, the only indication she had heard him the knitting of her pale brows. "Her name is Miriam. She moved here from Teman City last spring. With the high priest." He added the last sentence with a modicum of hesitation.

"I didn't want to believe it," Rachæl said, "when I heard the rumors you had taken a lover. But never in my wildest dreams would I have guessed you'd be stupid enough to *marry* a whore."

He leashed the frustration that welled at the vile word and instead said, "I wanted you to hear it from me, not from rumor."

She turned back to face the windows, her shoulders back, her chin high.

She was a force to be reckoned with, this princess before him. He had always admired that about her. She was a queen, even though she did not yet hold the title. Any other woman would have raged or melted into a puddle of tears at such a declaration. Especially so soon after their betrothal had ended. Rachæl had achieved making Ezra feel like a complete and total ass simply by squaring her shoulders.

"I don't want to hurt you," he tried. "And one day, when you are ready, I want to tell you the story."

She ignored him. "You told me there was no one else. You told me you would never take a lover behind my back."

"I didn't," he said, touching her at last. He took hold of her arm, his grip firm. A plea. "I swear it, Rachæl. I did not meet her until a few weeks after we..."

"I see," she said. "So in fifteen years of betrothal, you could not find a quality in me redeeming enough to make you take me as your wife. But within a matter of months, you found those qualities in an acolyte."

"It was nothing like that, Rachæl. She is..." He wanted to say it, to share it all. To tell Rachæl what Miri was to him—his best friend, his heart, his very soul. But he knew none of that would help. He knew to share what Miri had so quickly become to him would only wound her. And that was the last thing he wanted.

Angry or not, no matter what had come between then, he admired Rachæl. Respected her. He loved her, truly, though he knew she would not understand that right now. She would not see any sort of confession of his love for her as anything but an insult.

But Ezra loved Rachæl as deeply, as fiercely as he loved John and Esther. She was family to him. And she always would be. He was grateful for the years he had had with her. Grateful that stepping away from her had afforded him the luxury of learning just how much he cherished her.

But in that moment, he prayed that one day it would be different. He prayed that one day Rachæl would understand what she was to him. What she would always be.

"I am thrilled for you," she said, but there was no sincerity in the declaration. "I hope you are truly happy."

She turned then, marching her way back towards the door.

"I do not trust the empress," he called, staying her with his declaration. "I think she might have put a spell on the court today. And I am worried for what is to happen."

Rachæl did not turn to face him before she spoke. "After months of not bothering to attend to your duties as council, do not dare to come into my castle and tell me what I should be concerned about." She turned then, meeting him with hard, hazel eyes. "You can leave the concerns of this kingdom up to me. You can stop pretending like you care about what happens to this kingdom or to me. Go back to your whore, Ezra."

He knew it would only upset her more—only make thing worse. But he said it anyway. "Despite what you think, I am on your side, Rachæl. And I care about you. I am still your friend."

She paused, holding his eyes for an uncomfortable moment. She did not say anything, and Ezra would have given his soul in that moment to know what she was thinking. But Rachæl was a fortress, silent and unyielding. She remained silent before him, simply lifting her chin, turning, and pushing through the door, leaving him alone, the sound of the crackling fire his only companion.

AFTER DINNER, most of the councilors retired to their personal quarters in Chesedelle, resorting to drinking and cards and Providence knew what else, as was usual after a council meeting. They'd return home to their wives tomorrow on the pretense that the meeting had run far too long to return home in any reasonable amount of time. Most wives didn't question, too busy dabbling in their own affairs to care.

But Ezra had not stayed. He didn't want to be in that castle a minute longer than necessary, unsure what he would do knowing Gian was there somewhere. The punch had felt good. Too good. He worried that if he lingered any longer, he'd find out how good the dagger felt, too, especially in light of his conversation with Rachæl.

And then there was Miri... It would be the middle of the night when he got home, but it was better than waiting until morning.

So Ezra had ridden home. The familiar cadence of the carriage through the winding mountain roads was a balm of sorts. He let the gentle vibrations numb his mind, his heart. He let himself relax for the first time in a long time.

The moon was so bright it cast a silvery glow across the snow-kissed forest, painting shadows through the trees. He knew this forest like he knew the back of his hand. Thanks to his grandfather, his love for the wilderness had been a part of him since boyhood.

A jolt brought the carriage to an abrupt stop on the dense forest road. Boots crunched on the snow, and Ezra heard muffled, aggressive voices berating the driver. He pushed open the carriage door and stepped into the still night.

"Halt, sir, or find my blade in your back." The gruff voice came from behind, and even through his thick coat, he could feel the blade at his spine. Ezra heeded the warning, lifting his hands.

"You put that blade in my back and I'll flay your sorry carcass and roast your liver on a spit," Ezra responded, his words low, guttural.

Their faces obscured by the dim night, the two men at the front of the carriage who had been badgering the driver froze. So did the man behind Ezra.

"You couldn't flay a *squirrel*, you pampered ass," said the man behind Ezra. A muffled laugh came from his throat.

Ezra turned and faced his aggressor. Large—like a giant oak by a river basin—the man was at least a head taller and twice as thick as Ezra. "You're doing your job a little too well, Cosmas."

"You're the one who stationed us out here in this godsforsaken wilderness. In the dead of winter, no less." Cosmas sheathed his sword.

Ezra laughed and reached to embrace the well-armed and heavily armored soldier.

"It's not the dead of winter yet," Ezra pointed out. "Unless you're such a cumberworld you can't handle a little snow."

"His Grace always knows how to fling a well-mannered insult." This from one of the men up front.

"I don't remember asking your opinion, Vitus," Ezra quipped, turning to face the other soldier. As large as Cosmas but years younger, his face was fresh and bright, in stark contrast to his towering size. Vitus donned a lopsided smile before embracing Ezra as well.

"Nothing new to report, Your Grace," Vitus said. "So far these woods have been a bore."

"Let's hope it stays that way," Ezra said.

"What's got your underthings in a twist anyway?" This came from the third man: General Albus Hirtius. Thirty-one and well past worrying what anyone thought, the sun-weathered general was always the first to say what everyone else was thinking.

When Ezra did not immediately respond, Albus tilted his head to one side, raising his brow. "Don't tell me this really is all for a skirt. I didn't want to believe all those fireside stories these boys have been concocting."

"I heard she's a real looker," Vitus said. Young and wild-eyed, his face lit up with what Ezra could only imagine to be all manner of indecencies.

Cosmas slapped a heavy hand on Ezra's shoulder, half incredulous, half amused. "You called half your army out here to keep the competition away?"

Ezra decided the truth was a bit too complicated to get into tonight. After all, he was their commander—it wasn't their place to ask questions. It was entirely his prerogative if he wanted to appoint all of the king's army to protect Miri. He would, if it ever came to that. A few dozen soldiers was a drop in the bucket. "Something like that."

"Something tells me there's more to this story," Albus said.

"There always is," Ezra pointed out. When he did not expound, Albus searched his face.

"This is not just about a woman."

Ezra still did not answer.

"What's that supposed to mean?" Cosmas asked, crossing his arms.

Albus continued his appraisal of the grand duke of Kinnereth before he, too, crossed his thick, armored arms. His words curled like mist in the air before him. "It's about that godsdamned priest, isn't it?"

Ezra looked up. "What do you know about him?"

"Enough to know that every lord for seven provinces would like his balls in a vice. He's a whoremongering piece of shit, that's what."

Ezra looked down, wondering what he should explain here in the cold darkness.

"Did he do something to your woman?" This from Vitus.

"I need you to keep him far away from Massahd. Do you understand?" Ezra asked. "Do not let him or anyone on these lands. Not the high priest. Not the Medinian ambassador, not even the king or his lapdog, Gian of Borras. Is that clear?"

The three soldiers stood stoic and resolute before Ezra when Albus finally said, "Understood, Your Grace." There was no sarcasm in his tone this time. Only sober resolution from the general.

"Good," Ezra said. "Now I'll appreciate it if you would stop badgering my driver and let me get home."

"I'll bet she keeps that bed nice and warm for you, eh?" Cosmas elbowed Ezra with the question.

"You're doing your job well, boys," Ezra said, turning towards the carriage. "But try not to attack my personal carriage again, if you don't mind."

"Your wish is our command, Your Grace," Vitus said with a bow.

"Kiss ass," Cosmas mumbled.

Ezra chuckled under his breath as he climbed into the cab.

SOLDIERS. Ezra's army. He'd wondered if his men would think him petty when they learned the reason for his bringing them here. The moment he brought Miri home, he had commissioned his best men to patrol these mountains. For miles in every direction, men camped in these snowy woods, prepared to strike anyone who tried to come to Massahd Castle uninvited.

Meeting them tonight had been good—a reminder that his men were loyal. That they would serve him, even without question. It was a brand of loyalty he knew he had not earned, but one he benefitted from thanks to his grandfather's legacy with this army.

The *king's* army. That Ezra's family commanded.

Ezra swallowed once, trying to clear his mind.

Those men were the only reason he had been able to leave Miri at Massahd this morning. Of course he trusted his staff with his life. But the household staff alone would not be enough against whatever Sheols Phinehas was capable of.

Providence only knew what sorts of magic that man resorted to. Dark magic. Ezra was not ignorant of its effects. He had seen King Dægan dabble in it enough to know that he would not take the risk where Miri was concerned. And today, whatever the Empress had subjected them to...it had reminded him too much of the dark magic the king had tampered with so many times. He could only imagine what it meant—what nightmares she had unleashed in her song today.

So he would keep Miri safe—without apology. And he would use every tool in his arsenal to do so.

He did not know when Phinehas would strike again. When the high priest of Har-Navah would come looking for his prized possession.

He only knew that he would. For reasons he had yet to understand, the priest considered Miri something of a trophy. He imagined it had to do with the magic Miri had once showed him—the pure, raw magic that ran through her veins. But he did not know what it meant. Why Phinehas would want that. He did not understand it. Not yet. So Ezra's only objective was to remain vigilant. Prepared for anything.

The soldiers prowling these woods were only a start.

CHAPTER THIRTY-TWO

The night was still. Quiet. Ezra tried to keep it that way as he made his way through the dark castle to his chambers after arriving home. Miri slept across the hall from his private quarters—the mirror suite to his own and the only two on this floor of this wing of the castle. Hopefully, she was sleeping soundly, recovering the strength that had been robbed from her.

He wanted to check on her. He *had* to check on her. But he did not want to frighten her. So he had turned away from her door and faced his, wishing he knew how to help her. Wishing he knew what she needed.

He had only pushed open his door when he heard a sound. Soft and small at first, it was coming from Miri's room. He turned, crossing the hall and pressing an ear to her door. The sound grew louder. A whimper—like a cry for help.

"Miri," he said softly.

She did not answer.

"Miri, are you all right?"

She whimpered again, this time more loudly.

"Miri, may I come in?"

Miri cried out—a great gasp that tore through the quiet night like thunder before a storm. Damning the consequences, Ezra barged into her chamber without waiting for her approval.

She was sprawled across her bed, her shift tangled around her flailing arms and kicking legs. She screamed as if she were being mortally wounded.

Ezra clambered onto her bed, taking hold of her wrists. "Miri, it's me. It's Ezra! Wake up, Miri. Wake up!"

She did not. She screamed, flailing like a fish out of water, sweat beading her brow. Her curls were a knotted, sweat-dampened mess all around her head, and Ezra used all of his might to try and restrain her, to no avail.

He climbed on top of her, straddling her torso and pulling her wrists above her head. "Miri, listen to me. Listen. It's Ezra, Miri. It's me. You're home. You're safe. They cannot hurt you anymore."

Miri cried out, gasping for air as if she were being suffocated. Ezra loosened his grip on her wrists but kept her pinned beneath him.

"Wildfire!" he cried.

At the name, she stilled.

"Wildfire," he said again, more gently this time. "Wildfire, it's me. Open your eyes and look at me." Miri whimpered, a sound so sad, so broken Ezra thought his heart might have shattered just hearing it.

"Wildfire," he said gently. "Look at me, my love."

Miri opened her eyes. Though her gaze was upon Ezra, her eyes were distant, unfocused. A phantasm given flesh. Seeing and unseeing all at once. She stilled slowly, her body releasing its tension breath by breath. When her muscles had at last released their strain, her gaze focused, her face morphing into recognition.

There was nothing but ice in her pale face.

"Get off of me," she said. Her words were low and sharp. Ezra immediately complied, moving to sit beside her on the bed.

"You were crying out," he said. "You were having a dream."

She fixed her gaze on the ceiling, her only movements the breath in her chest. "He's always there. When I close my eyes. He's always waiting for me," she said, her words so soft, so tremulous Ezra hardly heard them.

But he knew who she meant. White-hot anger boiled within him. He reached for, but she gave no indication that she felt his touch, her hand remaining limp beneath his.

"He cannot hurt you anymore," Ezra said.

At his declaration, she slowly slid her eyes to him. A darkness crept over her countenance as she said, "He never stopped."

She sank back into her blankets, pulling them up tightly to her neck. Her eyes were wide and distant as she lay back against her pillow, staring at the rafters once more.

He wanted to comfort her. He wanted to take her into his arms and hold her, soothe her until she found a measure of peace. "Miri," he said, reaching to brush a hand down her arm.

She turned to her side, away from him.

"I'm right here, if you need me," he said, croaking the words. He swallowed hard against the lump forming in his throat. When she did not respond, Ezra stood from her bed and left her alone in the quiet of her chambers.

Miri had not slept yet again.

Another night of fits and rage.

Another night of nightmares.

Weeks. It had been weeks of fitful, sleepless nights.

And every night, the same dream. For weeks, the same nightmare.

Phinehas, coming to her, beckoning her. Holding out his arms like a father might reach for his child. His face colored with concern, his arms wide and welcoming. Miri would go to him like a lamb to the slaughter.

That's a good girl, he would say. *That's a good, good girl.* And every time, only upon reaching Phinehas would she realize what he reached for.

A child—*her* child. Nestled safely in her arms. Suckling at her breast, the child was warm and content and safe. Phinehas would reach for it. And the moment he touched it, the moment his hands touched her child, Miri would scream.

Except no sound came from her throat. The harder she tried to scream, the more her throat closed. And the more Phinehas laughed.

He laughed delightedly as he took her child from her arms. As he kissed the child's feather-soft brow and then stripped it of its blankets, holding the fat, naked little body up as if it was a sacrifice to the gods. And Miri would try to scream again.

And still no sound would come.

It had been the same dream every night since she first awoke here after being taken from the temple.

Bleary-eyed from sleep deprivation and weary from the dream, Miri crawled out of bed in a blur. She did not want to face another day of avoiding Ezra and trying not to think about her nightmares and trying to ignore the lingering pains in her stomach. But she was equally as tired of her room and her bed and the endless silence of her solitude.

So she got up and decided to dress for the day, at the very least.

But something snagged her attention across the vast bedchamber she had been given. She walked with bare feet across the thick carpets, making her way to an ornate fern stand positioned near a spread of tall windows overlooking the lake.

There, perched on the marble, was a small house, fashioned with a tiny door made of a playing card. Its roof was made from a match box, and its walls were a balm tin stood on its end. It was decorated in all manner of brightly-colored stones and carefully-whittled sticks. Someone had taken a great deal of time and care to outfit the tiny house with stepping stones leading to its door. There was even a wreath fashioned of grass sprigs and tiny wild-flowers hung over the doorway.

A færy house.

Miri's heart leapt. How many had she made as a little girl before her father tore them down, ripping them to shreds and scolding her for her childish nonsense? A part of her wanted to hide it away on instinct, for fear her father would come and take it away.

The young servant, Kit, emerged on the other side of the room, a dress draped over her arm.

"Good to see you awake, my lady!" said Kit brightly. She laid the dress lovingly along the back of a nearby chair and made her way to Miri's side.

"Isn't it lovely? His Grace asked for my help to find all the stones. But he wouldn't let me help him make it, no matter how I begged." She added that last bit with a hint of a laugh in her young voice.

"His Grace made this?" Miri asked.

At the question, Kit's eyes went wide, as if remembering something of great import. "I—I wasn't supposed to say anything," she admitted. "Oh mistress, I am sorry! He didn't want me to tell you that he made this for you. He said it might make you happy—something about your father always taking yours away, though I could not understand why any father would do something so mean."

"Ezra made this. For me," Miri parroted, turning her attention back to the little house. It was perfect. Every detail so carefully crafted. It was better than any færy house she had ever made all those years ago.

"Took him weeks," Kit said. "I've been a bonafide stone hunter for the better part of a month," she added with a laugh before turning away, back to the dress she had laid aside.

Miri eyed the house, unsure what to say. What to think. Then she spotted a small parchment, rolled and tied with a soft blue ribbon. She unrolled the paper to find a handwritten note inside.

To my færy whisperer. We get to take it with us. The magic. It's ours. A gift. If only we will take it.

Those words... spoken in another place, another life. Words he had given her in that lake of stars where they had found a magic so deep, so pure it had wiped away every modicum of fear.

She remembered it now—that night, that magic. She remembered how it felt in her heart. The way it had felt in Ezra's arms. The hope it had birthed in her.

A hope she had carried, savored, even without realizing it.

Until it had been ripped from her by the ambassador. By the horrors he had inflicted upon her over and over again.

We get to take it with us. The magic.

She wasn't sure how she could do that anymore.

Miri set the note down, her hands trembling, and gladly turned away from that little house when Kit arrived back at her side. Oblivious to the emotions swirling within her, the young servant began removing Miri's shift without waiting for her permission.

"You're getting better every day, Your Grace. I only had to change your linens once last night. That's much better!"

Fresh shift in hand a moment later, Kit slipped it over Miri's head, next reaching for a corset.

The maid worked in silence, but Miri could not bear it. She did not want to think about Ezra's kindness. She did not want to think about why he had bothered. When a pain lanced her stomach, she flinched, holding her belly. Kit watched her with mute worry.

"Why am I bleeding?" She blurted the question a bit more harshly than she intended, but it was done. Out there.

The maid seemed hesitant to answer. "No one told you?" The servant's words were small. Worried.

"No one tells me anything. I'm a porcelain doll everyone is afraid to break," Miri sneered.

Kitty did not speak for a moment. "You've been through so much, my lady," she said. "We all just want to see you well."

"What happened to me?" Miri insisted. The servant could scarcely meet her eyes.

"Kit," Miri demanded.

Kitty fidgeted with her fingers. "I don't rightly know all of it, Your Grace."

"Stop calling me *Your Grace* and tell me what you know."

At this Kitty finally met Miri's glare. There were tears lining her young eyes. "They shouldn't have done it to you, Your—er, my lady," she said around the emotion welling in her voice. "He's an evil man; I don't care what they say."

Miri wondered if the girl was talking about Phinehas or the ambassador.

"But the doctor says you're healing well," she said, her words brightening.

"Healing from what?" Miri demanded.

Kitty looked down again, mumbling some words Miri could not decipher.

"What?"

"They took your baby."

Miri froze, letting the words settle.

Her baby.

A baby.

She had been with child.

Phinehas's child. Or the ambassador's. Providence only knew.

But they took it from her.

A vision of Phinehas from her dream stole over her once again —holding her child aloft, a look of wicked victory in his eyes.

"The doctor says you're healing nicely," Kitty went on, but Miri hardly paid attention. "And I know in time all will be well, I don't care what the doctor says. Miracles happen all the time, that's what my momma always told me. And I don't see why Providence should keep a miracle like that—especially from you. I mean, you're so nice and His Grace loves you so much and you've been through so much and I just think—"

"A miracle? What miracle?"

Kitty took a moment before she spoke. "To have a baby again, my lady. I just know the doctor is wrong."

MIRI MADE her way down to the dining hall that beckoned her with smells too delicious to ignore, her mind reeling with Kitty's declaration. Whatever Phinehas had done to her... It had been nearly a month and yet she still bled. She still woke with pains that lanced her belly like fire. The tears in Kitty's eyes had been enough to spell it out clearly.

Miri would never bear a child again. Phinehas had made sure of that.

Her stomach rumbled, not with pain, but hunger; she was perhaps hungrier than she had ever been in her life. But food could not seem to satiate these days. And what seemed like the most appetizing meal would only turn to ash in her mouth. Though she made her way to the dining hall, she knew this morning would be no different.

Sitting at the end of the long table, reading through his many morning letters, Ezra was dressed in his usual black brocade, this time with a pale steel-blue cravat. Beside his hand, a pen danced across a paper of its own accord, scrawling feverishly as he spoke aloud a list of tasks and reminders for himself. Miri watched it absently for a moment, appreciating that small magic, the way it served Ezra well. He was a busy man, that much was certain.

When he saw her come in, his whole face lit up with delight.

She did not want his delight. She certainly did not want his pity.

When she looked at Ezra, all she could hear was one word: *shameful.*

"Good morning, my Wildfire," he said, standing from his ornate chair. The pen fell onto the table with a thud, waiting for him to give it commands again. But he ignored it, his eyes fixed on her. He looked so very much like a king in a throne here in this plush castle he called home. The servants doted on him, to be sure. In some ways, the grand duke of Kinnereth was as important and well served as the king himself.

Ezra reached her, and seeing him lift his hands even slightly, knowing that he wanted to touch her, Miri shut her eyes, breathing in once and holding that breath.

Ezra did not touch her.

"Coffee?" he asked instead. She did not miss the hurt in his voice. It was subtle. Perhaps if she hadn't gotten to know him so well, she might not have picked up on it. But she could hear it. And she knew she was the reason for it.

Shameful.

Worthless.

Filthy.

Miri said nothing. Instead, she pulled a chair from the table and sat down. Ezra stood behind her, quiet as a temple mouse. Then he reached around her, pulling a cup and saucer towards her before pouring some coffee from the kettle on the table. Wordlessly, he fixed the warm drink precisely to her liking—a benefit of having shared breakfast together for months.

It was because of those breakfasts they shared that she had

not partaken in the temple breakfasts, laced with the herb that kept her from bearing Phinehas's child—from revealing to the world that the acolytes were indeed the priest's own whores.

Because of breakfast with Ezra, Miri had conceived Phinehas's child. Or maybe the ambassador's. It didn't really matter—the pregnancy alone would have destroyed everything Phinehas worked for.

So he had made sure it wouldn't.

Because of *breakfast,* Miri would never bear a child again.

Bile burned in her throat, and she shut her eyes. When she opened them, Ezra was seated at the opposite end of the table again—a thousand miles away.

She quickly looked away when his gaze met hers and instead focused on the morning fare spread across the table. Challah, rugelach, raisin cakes... The familiar pastries could only be from one place.

"Brought them fresh this morning," Ezra said.

Ezra had brought her breakfast from Joshua's. Trying. He was trying. A lump welled in her throat. She used the piping hot coffee to wash it away, the cup rattling against the saucer as she set it back down.

"Good?" Ezra asked, trying to make conversation. She could hear the concern in his voice.

Miri might have shrugged; she could not be sure.

Nausea roiled in her belly, and Miri looked down, hating herself. Hating her filth. Hating that she should even have the nerve to sit here at this table with this man who would ride two hours to and from the village just to bring her the pastries they had once both enjoyed. Hating that she could not find the words to thank him for the færy house. Hating that she could not even find the courtesy to eat.

Hating his pity most of all.

"I have good news," Ezra said, his words bright. "John has

located him—the prophet. I wrote him, inviting him to our estate. He will be here in a few days. I thought—"

"The prophet?"

Ezra tilted his head. "The one who saved you. He—"

"The *prophet* saved me?" she interrupted.

Not Ezra. The prophet. A stranger had saved her.

Her mind stilled, her thoughts too many to decipher.

Ezra had not come for her. In fleeting moments of consciousness, in the quiet between the darkness of the ambassador, she had wondered why he had not come to the temple. Why he had not tried to find her. To get her out.

She had wondered why had left her there.

Why he had left her to the Sheol of the ambassador's hand.

He had not even tried to get her out.

Not once.

The no-name prophet had saved her.

She swallowed hard against the lump in her throat, blinking back the sting in her eyes.

He had not even tried to save her.

He had offered her his whole world. Everything.

But he had not bothered to help her out of her own.

"He's an incredible man, Miri," Ezra went on, oblivious to the emotions welling, welling, welling. Anger. Hatred. Rage. Terrible sadness. Emptiness.

Alone.

Miri was alone.

Ezra had not come for her.

Though she did not blame him, she hated him for it all the same. Perhaps that færy house was nothing more than a pathetic attempt to apologize for the fact that he hadn't cared enough to help her.

"I've never seen anyone like him," Ezra said, as if he were excited to tell her. Excited to share all about the man who had bothered to help her when he would not. "I am looking forward to getting to know him. And to thank him."

"I don't want to meet him," she said. She would not meet his eyes.

"I—" Ezra stumbled, obviously looking for words. "He will be here day after tomorrow. John and Esther too. I thought we could perhaps—"

"Fine," she said. "I don't care. It's your house."

"Miri," Ezra started. She would not meet his eyes, fussing with a stirring spoon instead. Solid gold. The spoon was solid gold. Heavy.

Because he had everything. Needed nothing.

Her certainly did not need her.

Ezra's tone shifted to something else. Something that sounded a lot like resolve. "I thought I might show you the estate today, if you'd like. You haven't had a chance to see it all yet." His words were light. Conversational.

She hated them.

But she considered it. A walk. A distraction. The fresh air would probably be nice. And if this castle was anything like what she had seen so far, it was a gorgeous tour awaiting her. But she could not stomach it. She could not keep up the charade, knowing what she knew. That she was a fraud. That Ezra was a liar. That all of this was a farce and she the court jester.

Only truth between us.

Indeed.

The truth was glaring between them.

Ezra had not come for her.

He was as ashamed of her as she was of herself.

She pushed her chair from the table and, without bothering to look at Ezra, simply said, "No thank you," before walking from the room.

Ezra watched her leave. She was more a ghost than a person as she floated from the dining room and into the foyer beyond. He watched her until she disappeared completely. He watched long after that.

And then he felt it, the tears that would not be stopped. He was a child, weak and pathetic. But he cried, wept for Miriam. For the empty soul that once held a bright and burning fire. He wept for the woman that was lost and nowhere to be found.

He wept for himself, for his selfishness where she was concerned. Silent tears fell down his face as he mourned for the woman he loved. And for himself—for the hurts he did not know how to fix. For the pain he did not know how to take away. For the wounds he did not have the skill to heal.

It had been weeks since she had left that temple.

She had barely spoken to Ezra in that time.

A week ago, when John Junior had visited with his parents, taking to Miri as if he had known her all if his young life, Miri had not said much. The boy had been undaunted, telling Miri all about the fat toad he had caught and intended to keep as a pet and the excellent shooting skills he had acquired practicing with his father's bow, but Miri hardly said two words to the boy. Ezra could see it, the delight Miri wanted to take in the boy, the longing deep within her to enjoy his simple pleasures. No one who encountered John Junior walked away without smiling; he was the sort of lad that brought joy wherever he went.

But even John Junior could not bring a smile to Miri's face.

"She will get better," came a voice from behind, a warm hand on his shoulder.

Helena. Ezra did not bother to face her.

"Just give her time," the housekeeper continued.

Ezra swallowed hard against the lump in his throat.

"I believe that," he admitted. "I truly do. I know that one day she will find peace. One day she will heal from all of this. But I am terrified, Helena. And I know now what a liar I am."

"What in the world are you talking about?" Helena asked, sitting down in the chair beside him. She moved her hand from his shoulder to cover his hand resting on the table.

"I promised her," he said. "I told her long before she ever came here that all of this was hers. That she could have it, with no strings attached. I told her that she could find her own life, her own way, and that I would not stop her. I promised her that when she found what she was looking for, if she realized it was not me, I would not get in her way. She would be free. Free to leave. Free to live her own life. Free to do what she pleased. She's never been free, Helena. She's never had a choice. I wanted to give her one."

Ezra turned his attention away from that empty doorway to Helena at last. The portly, aging housekeeper held nothing but concern in her wizened eyes. "I know now that I am the worst kind of liar. That I meant nothing of what I said. I know it because I fear that is exactly what is happening. I fear that she is choosing anything but me. And it is tearing me apart."

Helena rubbed the top of his hand, running a thumb across his wrist as she let him blubber like a fool. "Weep, my boy," she said with her rolling lilt. "Soothe your heart with your tears and then listen to me."

Ezra looked up, meeting Helena's intent gaze before she continued. "That girl is lost right now. Searching. She is lost in the darkness of another man's making, and she cannot find her way. She needs you now more than ever."

"I wish that were true," Ezra protested. "But she pushes me away. She—"

"Because she is ashamed, my boy," Helena interrupted. "She is frightened by what has happened and ashamed of who she thinks she has become. She is deep in a well of darkness, and she does not know how to find her way out. So you climb down there with her. You climb into that darkness and you take her by the hand and you climb—claw your way out if you must. But you do it together. The only way either of you will heal from this is together. I should know."

Ezra merely tilted his head, letting Helena continue. "I wanted to hate him, my late husband. I wanted to let him pay for his own sins. When we could never conceive, when we could never have children, he took to that bottle and he did not put it down for years. And I wanted to hate him for it.

"But I loved him. And I could not stop loving him. I tried everything—pleading and begging, shame and silence. I tried reason and logic, and all of it to no avail. Nothing would convince him to put down that bottle. Nothing I said, nothing I did. I could not give him a child, and he could not face it.

"It was only once I realized that I had to fight *with* him, not for him, that I saw any change. It was only once I realized that it wasn't the bottle that was his problem, but the shame he had learned to believe that I knew what I had to do. And it's the same thing you have to do. If you love her, then you climb into that darkness with her. You help her find the light again. And then you climb your way back into it together.

"When Salvatore died, he died a sober man. And we were happy, Ezra. For the first time in decades, we were finally happy. We found our peace. I know that only happened because we fought together. Not apart. Not alone. Together.

"She needs you, Ezra. She needs you to fight this with her. She needs your strength because right now, she hasn't any of her own. So don't you dare give up. If you love her, you better not ever give up. Not ever. You climb into that darkness, and you claw and fight and kick and scream your way out. But you do it together."

Ezra looked back to the empty doorway, at that empty space

where Miri had stood moments ago. He felt a warm hand wipe a tear from his chin. He looked back at Helena, lifted her hand and kissed it.

"I love you, you opinionated, nosy old woman."

Helena grinned, slapping the top of his hand. "I know."

CHAPTER THIRTY-THREE

"Aunt Miri! Aunt Miri!"

A bright, small voice came echoing through the foyer and up the grand staircase. Miri could not miss it.

John Junior. She had almost forgotten that Ezra had mentioned they would be visiting.

Miri made her way down the hall towards the top of the stairs, but made it no further before a tiny body collided with her legs, wrapping his slender arms around her. Something hit her from behind—some new delight he wanted to show her, no doubt. Every time had visited since she'd arrived, it had been with some contraption he could not wait to show her: a new toy, a favored book, a helpless creature he had procured from the woods. From the first time she had met the boy, he had been keen to share with her his latest obsession—as if he had known her his whole life and not only a mere month.

Miri placed a loving hand on the boy's raven black hair and John Junior looked up, a smile broad and uninhibited across his cherub face. So Miri knelt, putting her hands on the boy's waist. "Hello, sweetheart," she said.

John's smile grew conspiratorial as he pulled something from behind her.

"Look, Aunt Miri! Look what Father brought me!"

"Aunt Miri?" Miri asked, puzzled. A chuckle from the bottom of the stairs drew her attention to Ezra, John Senior, and Esther, congregated at the foot.

"He asked me why you live here now," Ezra said, color staining his cheeks.

John added, "I told him that Uncle Ezra loves you very much, and he decided he much prefers you as an aunt over that, and I quote, *boring old princess.*"

Ezra puffed an embarrassed laugh, but Miri said nothing, swallowing back a protest when she took another look at the boy before her, now dangling a pair of ice skates between them. A soft whir buzzed from their polished blades, and John Junior's eyes were as bright as two summer moons.

"They're magicked!" the boy announced. "The blades won't collect ice at all!"

"That's wonderful," she said, forcing a smile for the boy's benefit.

"Will you skate with me, Aunt Miri?" he begged.

Dread pooled in her gut.

"I haven't any skates," she said, thankful for the excuse. The boy turned and ran back down the stairs towards his very pregnant mother waiting at the foot. Miri stood, descending the steps much more slowly than the boy. The aching had subsided a great deal today. She felt better than she had in a while, but she still moved gingerly, afraid any sudden movement might ignite the lingering pains.

"Father," John Junior called. "Can you purchase some skates for Aunt Miri, too?"

John turned a conspiratorial grin towards Ezra, who held a crisp, white box in his hands. "I don't think that will be necessary."

Miri made it to the bottom of the steps before Ezra handed the box to her. She did not have to guess what was inside.

"I don't think so," she said, handing the box back to him.

"Oh please, Aunt Miri! Take them!" said the boy.

"You know what's in this box?" she asked him. The boy nodded eagerly. "A conspiracy then. I see."

"You should give it a try." This from John Senior, who stood with a hand on his wife's back. "Skating is quite fun."

Esther grimaced quietly, but not quietly enough for John to miss. "Sweetheart," he said. "You should sit down."

"I'm fine," Esther snapped. "Stop coddling me. I'm not the first woman in the world to give birth, you know. Not to mention I've done this before."

John turned a wry look to Ezra, who only shrugged.

"Surely you are close now, my darling," John tried.

"Of course I'm close!" Esther barked. "That doesn't mean I'm an invalid! Now are we going to skate or what?"

"*You* are not going to skate. *You* are going to rest," said John.

"*You* are getting on my nerves," said Esther, marching through the foyer and to the hall beyond.

John followed, a pair of skates slung over his shoulder. Miri realized Ezra had a pair slung over the shoulder of his black wool jacket, too. He wore a scarf and gloves and a top hat lined with a red sash. His smile was anything but apologetic.

"Come, Aunt Miri," said John Junior. "Let's go skating!"

MIRI WASN'T sure why she was following the boy, except that she found she could hardly refuse him. She would watch from the lakeside, just to appease him. But she would not skate. She had never skated a day in her life. She was not about to start. Not in front of Ezra, that was for certain.

Outside, the day was bright thanks to the snow that had fallen fresh the night before. The sun glinted off the white expanse with dizzying brightness. Miri trudged through the soft snow behind the skating party, wearing the crimson fur-lined redingote and thick woolen gloves Kitty had *miraculously* procured for her the moment Miri nodded her agreement to skate.

Conspiracy, indeed. The whole house had apparently been in on it, for Miri was fully prepared for an excursion onto the ice within minutes of agreeing to join.

They made it to the edge of the lake not far from the castle fairly quickly. From this vantage point, it was clear just how little of Massahd Castle actually touched land—almost the entire estate, huge as it was, seemed to float over the frozen waters of the lake. She remembered the first day Ezra had brought her here to see the castle. From the mountainside, it hadn't looked nearly this big.

And while it was the same lake that was home to the village of Shalem, this was a remote corner, hidden behind a bend in the mountains, unseen by the village and far removed from anything else. A world unto itself. Right now, with autumn giving way to winter, it was a breathtaking sight. Snow covered the grounds in a thick, downy white carpet, every limb and branch heavy with a blanket of white. And the lake stretched out before them, smooth as glass.

"Are you sure it's frozen enough?" This from Esther. Miri had wanted to ask the same question.

"This end always freezes first, Es. You know that," said Ezra. "We've skated this lake since we were kids."

Esther didn't seem quite convinced, motherly concern written all over her face. She grimaced again.

"Another pain?" John asked, coming to her aide. She took a seat on a bench by the lakeshore.

"Yes," she said, exasperated. "I'm fine. Now go skate before I make *you* go for a rest!"

John reluctantly acquiesced, puffing a quiet laugh and pressing a soft kiss to his wife's lips. Esther donned a becoming blush at her husband's gentle affection and Miri looked away as if she had intruded on a particularly intimate exchange. A moment later, John knelt to help his son don his new skates.

Before Miri knew it, Ezra, John Senior, and John Junior had all laced up their skates. She, however, merely eyed the white box sitting near her feet.

"Need some help?"

She looked up to see Ezra walking towards her rather gingerly on his skates through the snow.

"No, I don't think so," she said. "I'll just stay here with Esther. She may need—"

"I don't need a thing," Esther interrupted.

Miri swallowed and Ezra crouched on the ground before her. He opened the white box, pulling a pair of bright-white, fur-lined skates from inside. Embroidered on the heels with a delicate pattern of whorls and crimson flowers; they were lovely and obviously unworn.

"Did you have these made for me?" she asked.

Ezra only smiled, loosening the laces. "You'll need to sit down. They're easier to put on that way."

"I—"

"Aunt Miri! Look at me!" shouted John Junior. She looked toward the lake, where the small boy was gliding across the ice with the help of his father.

Ezra watched him too, chuckling. "It's his first time, though he likes to speak as if he were an expert. He insisted on coming out here today. I checked the ice last night just to be sure it was ready."

John Junior's face was lit with uninhibited delight. Then again, so was John Senior's as he towed the boy around.

"It's fun," Ezra said, facing Miri again. "I promise."

"I don't know," she said.

"Just give it a try," Ezra said, his words warm and filled with promise. She nodded once.

Ezra pushed her skirt just above her boots and began unlacing them. Another woman might have balked when he slipped the boots from her feet—when his fingers brushed her stockings while he worked on the skates. Another woman might have found such things too personal, too intimate.

It only seemed paltry when compared to all she had faced. To feel his hands on her ankles, to watch him work at her feet—it felt like nothing at all in comparison to what the ambassador had subjected her to. The indecencies he had treated as if they were as simple as lacing ice skates on a stockinged foot.

And she hated herself. She hated that she did not blush at his touch. She hated that it did not embarrass her as it should. That she did not blush as Esther had blushed at her husband's affection. That she would never be that innocent. That whole.

So when Ezra finished, when he stood and extended a hand to help her stand as well, she refused it. Looking down, she played with her fingers in her lap to hide the frustration she knew was on her face and said instead, "Can't John help me?"

From the edge of her vision, Ezra's fingers curled inward, but he kept his hand extended for a moment. Then he walked away towards the lake without a word. A moment later, John was at her side.

"IT'S NOT SO BAD, SEE?" said John with a grin. He held both of her hands, practically pulling her around the frozen lake while he skated backwards with little effort. Her knees remained locked, and her ankles felt like they carried the weight of the world.

"Relax, Miri," John continued. "You're doing well."

"No, I'm not," she countered, unable to take her eyes from her feet.

John chuckled. "Well, you haven't fallen. The first time I skated, I fell on my ass about a dozen times. I was sore for a week."

Miri looked up at John, who smiled amiably at the memory.

"You were a child, weren't you?" she pointed out.

He shrugged, and Miri looked down to her feet again, terrified that if she didn't keep an eye on them, she'd fall.

John glided over the ice with expert skill, and from the corner of her eye, she could see Ezra doing the same not far away. He pulled John Junior in a similar manner, and the boy squealed with delight every time Ezra twirled him around or sped up at all. Ezra's smile was broad and unrestrained as he watched his nephew.

John Senior looked across the lake, eyeing his friend and his son with a hint of envy in his eyes. He had wanted to teach his son to skate today, that much was clear. And Miri had robbed him of that simple joy.

Because she was selfish and she was shameful.

Heat colored Miri's cheeks. She could feel it creeping up. But John seemed oblivious.

"I know you feel like you don't belong here," he said, turning her carefully around a bend in the lake. "I feel the same way, you know."

"You do?" she asked before she could stop herself.

John smiled softly. "I never belonged here. But they accepted me with open arms anyway. I'm a nobody born into a nothing family. My father was the family lawyer. I grew up playing with Ezra and Esther simply because my father worked for the grand duke. And they always accepted me with open arms. Treated me as part of them from the beginning. I fell in love with Esther long before I had the stones to do anything about it. But when the time came to tell her, neither she nor Ezra scoffed. To my shock, she told me that she returned the feelings. And Ezra was happy for us.

"He was happy for me, Miri. For loving a woman beyond my birth. He was happy to have me in his family. All my life, I will be a part of this family knowing I didn't deserve it. But they loved me anyway."

John looked over, pulling Miri along as he skated backwards with effortless ease. He watched Ezra pick up John Junior, skating quickly with the boy perched on his back. John Junior squealed with delight as his uncle practically flew with him across the ice.

"He's in love with you, Miri. I can tell you that for certain. I know him. He's my best friend. He's had plenty of opportunities to fall in love over the years."

Miri looked at John, her brows furrowed. John chuckled. "A betrothal never stopped a young man from looking at his options. And Ezra did, believe me. Women from all twelve provinces threw themselves at him, hoping for a chance to turn his eye. Even if he didn't call off the betrothal, a bastard child of the grandson of the grand duke of Kinnereth could set a woman up for life.

"But he never took them up on their offers, Miri. He never fell in love with any of them. He never fell in love with the princess, either, though I think he was fond of her. He never once looked at her the way he looks at you. Or spoke of her the way he speaks of you. And that's when I knew he loved you, Miri. When he spoke of you the way I speak of Esther. When he looked at you the way I look at her—like you are his whole world.

"Because you are, Miri. You are his world now. And he won't give up until you let him back in. No, that's not true. He won't give up. Period. He's the most stubborn bastard I've ever met, and now that he's made up his mind, he won't give up on you."

"He should," Miri said under her breath.

"But he won't," John countered easily. "He—" John froze, his eyes darting to the other side of the lake where Esther sat on the bench. Miri followed his gaze to see Ezra's sister bent over her belly, holding it as if it were on fire. John dropped Miri's hands without a word and sped across the ice toward his wife.

Abandoned and unable to maneuver herself on the ice alone, Miri watched John stumble off the ice and onto the snow-coated bank, running awkwardly on his skates to his wife. She nodded when he reached her, and even from the distance, Miri could see what had happened.

A dark spot stained Esther's dress below her belly.

A moment later, John Junior skated effortlessly past her, and she was envious of the boy for picking up the skill so quickly. Knees locking, Miri nervously began to try to maneuver the ice, but soon found herself unable to move so much as an inch for fear of falling flat on her face. The next moment, an arm wrapped around her waist, and a familiar warmth enveloped her. She momentarily forgot about all the reasons she should not allow herself to bask in Ezra's touch.

Ezra noticed, for he took hold of her hand between them and smiled. "I think it's time," he said, guiding her back towards the shore.

"Her waters have broken," Miri pointed out.

Ezra nodded. "Do you know much about childbirth?" he asked, his body close. Too close. She fit against him much too easily. And his smell was familiar and musky and heady; Ezra's whole being threatened to consume her. Miri tried to move away, to put some space between them. But her lack of skill on the stupid skates made it impossible.

"No, not really," she said. "But I know that when it's time, a woman's womb will break, and the waters—" She stopped herself, realizing the conversation was inappropriate.

"Yes, it means the baby is ready. Her pains will increase now," he said. Ezra seemed undaunted by the topic, as if childbirth were not some gruesome topic, best suited for women to endure and men to pretend as if it didn't happen at all.

"Do you know much about childbirth?" she asked.

Ezra smiled, revealing the dimple on his right cheek. "Enough to know that Esther won't want a man anywhere within fifty miles of her while she's giving birth. Not John anyway." Ezra chuckled softly. "In case you haven't picked up on it, he can be a bit...smothering when it comes to my sister. I think she secretly loves it, but she keeps up the pretense of annoyance."

Miri watched John and Esther as Ezra glided closer to the lakeshore, sweeping her with him. Esther nodded, and John moved to help her stand. Contented and oblivious, John Junior sat nearby, unlacing his magicked skates and tugging on his boots. When Esther was finally on her feet, she stooped, wincing again and grabbing her belly.

"We need to get her inside," Ezra said.

Ezra and Miri reached the shore, and Ezra stepped onto the snow as if he had done this a thousand times. Miri, however, eyed the transition with trepidation. Ezra chuckled, holding out both hands. "Just hang on to me. I won't let you fall."

Miri pursed her lips but wordlessly obeyed, letting him hold her up while she clumsily shifted her weight from ice to snow. Her back heel almost slipped when it remained on the ice, but Ezra held her firmly, preventing her from falling. The motion pushed her farther into his arms.

"Have your balance?" he asked, holding her against him with a smile.

"I'm glad you think this is funny," she countered flatly.

"I'm always looking for activities that will afford me the opportunity to hold beautiful women in my arms. Ice skating is brilliant on that front, wouldn't you say?"

Miri rolled her eyes and stooped to scoop up her boots.

CHAPTER THIRTY-FOUR

"She is doing well," Ezra said, closing the door behind him. From the occasional chair where she sat with John Junior in her lap, Miri looked up.

"Keep reading, Aunt Miri," the boy protested.

"Just a moment, darling," she said. "And John?" Miri asked Ezra.

The grand duke of Kinnereth smiled, stifling a laugh. "He'll make it."

"Should we send for the doctor?" Miri asked as Ezra made his way to the chair across from them. Esther had decided she wanted to give birth in her old bedroom at Massahd. It was a suite of chambers that boasted a cozy sitting room adjacent to the bedchamber where she now lay, crying out every few minutes with the pains of childbirth.

"Whyever would we do that dear?" asked Helena, bustling about the room folding towels and prepping a basin with water warmed by a magicked kettle.

"Well, she's giving birth!" Miri pointed out. "Shouldn't someone who knows what he's doing be here?"

Ezra and Helena both chuckled. "I think we can manage, dear," said Helena. She hung a stack of folded towels across her arm and walked into the adjoining bedchamber with a laugh still on her mouth.

"Aunt Miri," John Junior demanded. "Don't stop the story now!"

Distracted, it took a moment to realize that the boy had spoken to her.

Ezra laughed and held out his arms for John Junior, who hopped down from Miri's lap and onto his uncle's, handing him his book. Ezra began to read quietly.

Miri stood and began pacing the room to calm her nerves.

What if something went wrong? Why was everyone so calm? A phantom pain darted through her stomach, and she wondered if it was some sort of sympathy for the pain Esther was surely experiencing or a true echo of the pains she had been recovering from for the past month.

"Are you sure, my darling?"

Miri looked up to see John stepping backward out of the bedchamber where his wife was giving birth.

Esther's reply was inarticulate, but it made the point quite clear. John reluctantly nodded, shutting the door behind him.

"Kick you out, then?" Ezra said without looking up from the book he was reading his nephew.

"She just likes her...space," John replied, sweat beading his brow. Ezra laughed and kept reading.

"She asked for you, actually," John said.

After a beat of silence, Miri looked up, realizing John was addressing her.

"What?"

"She wants you, Miri," John repeated. Miri shot an incredulous glance to Ezra, whose face shone with a soft smile.

"You better get in there," he said, nodding towards the

bedchamber door. Miri hesitated before finally taking the few steps across the room. Her hand trembled on the knob, but she didn't even have to knock before she heard Helena invite her in.

ESTHER WAS A WARRIOR GODDESS QUEEN. That's all there was to it. She endured through each pain with a quiet strength that privately amazed Miri.

She had never once witnessed childbirth, but she could never have imagined it to be such a show of grit and grace. Somehow, even sweat-dampened and red-faced, Esther looked absolutely gorgeous.

Helena bustled about the room, prepping Providence knew what, muttering words of affirmation as Esther endured one wave of pain after another. When one of the pains subsided, Esther opened her eyes and held out her hand for Miri. Reluctantly, Miri crossed the space between them and took it.

"I promise it's not as bad as it seems," said Esther with a weak smile.

Another pain rolled over her like a wave. She shut her eyes, holding her breath through the worst of it and squeezing Miri's hand so hard Miri thought it might come off.

"I highly doubt that," Miri finally said when the pain subsided again.

Esther snorted a sardonic laugh. "I had to kick John out. He's absolutely useless, huffing and puffing around the room as if he's the one doing this. It's unbearable. Let's all pray to Providence that Ezra is not as ridiculous when it's your time."

The words took a moment to register.

Her time.

In Esther's perfect world, Miri would bear Ezra's children, fill this house with them just as Esther filled John's home. In Esther's world of wholeness, of innocence, Miri would be wife and mother —innocent and worthy and wanted.

Tears stung at her eyes. She blinked them back, swallowed hard, and squeezed Esther's hand.

Esther shut her eyes again, straining against the pain. "It's coming, Helena," she said through clenched teeth. "It's time."

Helena, as calm as a sky after a storm, gathered a few of the towels she had been preparing and walked to the foot of the bed. Lifting Esther's shift, she exposed clammy legs. Miri could see the blood-stained sheets beneath Esther and privately understood John's worries. It seemed a gruesome task, this business of childbirth. But within only a few more of those waves of pain, Esther had given birth to a fat, healthy baby with hair as black as a raven.

"A girl," Helena said proudly. "And as beautiful as her momma." Laying the newborn in a loose blanket, she handed her lovingly to Miriam. "Hold her for a moment."

Miri froze, vaguely registering Helena with a small blade. But Miri could not take her eyes from the child.

She looked exactly like Ezra. The resemblance was uncanny. Hair as black and glossy as a raven's. Lips plump and full. The tiniest dimple on her right cheek. Her features crumpled into a grimace, and she attempted her first sounds, which came out more like the screech of an owl than a baby's cry. But even her facial expressions looked so much like her uncle.

A wave of sorrow washed over Miri as Helena tied a small band of twine at the baby's belly. Without a word, Miri handed the baby to Esther, who took her with welcome, eager arms.

"She's perfect, isn't she?" Esther asked, proudly beholding her newborn daughter.

Miri found she could not answer.

"Why don't you go and tell the boys while I get her cleaned up?" said Helena.

Miri, holding back a wave of emotion, nodded without speaking and disappeared from the birthing room.

She burst through the door to see the two men stand abruptly, Ezra practically dropping John Junior to the floor as he did. The boy was unscathed and unruffled, simply reopening his book and reading it from his place on the carpet.

"Well?" John Senior asked.

Miri swallowed hard to quell her emotion. "It's a girl," she said, and then she looked at Ezra. While John practically kicked the furniture aside to get across the room to his wife, Ezra stood in place, his gaze fixed on Miri.

And she could not stop them, the tears that overflowed. The sobbing hit her so hard she felt she might collapse, but strong arms came around her and within a breath, she was sobbing against Ezra's chest.

He held her, brushing a soothing hand down her hair. He held her close and did not say anything, simply resting his cheek on her head and rocking her gently, standing there in the sitting room of his sister's childhood chambers.

On the other side of the door, she could hear the delicate sounds of a baby's first cry and wept harder.

She felt a gentle kiss on the top of her head before Ezra said, "I know, Miri. I know."

But did he? Had he allowed himself to consider the implications of everything? Did he know that he loved a broken, useless remnant of a woman? Did he know that he soothed and comforted a whore who would never be whole again?

She could not bear it any longer. Pushing out of his arms, she did not look at him again before tearing across the room and out the door.

"You should eat something, my lady," said Kit. Miri rubbed her eyes and sat up, pulling the thick white fur blanket from the foot of her bed up over her shoulders. It seemed the only thing that could stave off the chill of winter anymore.

"I'm not hungry," Miri lied.

Kit did not seem convinced. "You're still regaining your strength. Every little bit helps. At least have some coffee." She did not wait for Miri's response; bustling over to a silver tray near the bed, Kit set about fixing a cup of the hot, steaming beverage. "You've been cooped up in here enough. I thought we were past that," she went on.

"I just—" How could she explain it to a young, innocent girl? How could she help her understand? Seeing Esther—watching her give birth, knowing she would never know the feeling...would never know that kind of joy...

She had not been able to take herself out of her chambers for several days.

"Did I ever tell you what His Grace told me the day he met you?" Kit said, surprising Miri with the non sequitur.

"Well, let me correct—it wasn't the day he *met* you," she went on without waiting for Miri's response. She handed Miri the cup of coffee and sat on the edge of the bed. "It was the first time he saw you. In the theatre. He came home that night, and there was something about him—something different. And I knew it wasn't my place to pry, but I had to ask. I had to know what had altered him so indisputably. Do you know what he said?"

Miri only shook her head, sipping from her cup as Kit prattled on. "He said that for the first time in his life, he had heard the voice of Providence."

Miri furrowed her brows but did not know what to say. Kit seemed undaunted. "Yes, he said he heard the voice of Providence. I didn't know what in Sheol he was on about, of course. But I could tell something had gotten to him, so I asked him to explain. Do you know what he said? He said, 'Only truth between us.'"

Miri went very still, the cup of coffee trembling softly in her hands.

"Now I don't know what that means, but I suspect you do," Kit went on. "And it wasn't until later on that I found out he had seen you that night. Seen you and heard Providence say, 'Only truth between us.'

"Miri, I'm not a smart person, but I know my master. I've served in this house from the day I was born, practically. And I knew that night that something had changed in him. For the first time in years—since his family had died—I saw light in him. I saw something that looked like hope. Life.

"And he didn't even know you yet, Miri. He hadn't even learned your name. But he heard the voice of the Almighty say something to him that apparently meant something—and judging by the look on your face, it means something to you too." Kit stopped, reaching across the bed and resting a hand on top of Miri's.

"All I know is, His Grace found life again when he found you. And I know you're scared, my lady. I know you've been through Sheol. But I know he'll go through Sheol with you, if you'll let him. He'll willingly walk into darkness if he has to. Just to be with you. Just to be near you.

"Don't you let that darkness stop you from seeing that light. The light in him. The light in you both. Don't miss it, my lady."

CHAPTER THIRTY-FIVE

Miri had not come out of her room. Ezra had tried to visit her chambers, to no avail. She had not answered the door, and he had not been sure if she would welcome his uninvited intrusion.

So he had just worried. Several sleepless nights had left him groggy and bleary. And not knowing what to do, not knowing what Miri needed was taking its toll. He kneaded the space between his brows with his thumb and forefinger, a cup of coffee in his other hand going cold as he sat alone in the sitting room of Massahd Castle.

A sound had Ezra looking up to see his sister emerge into the room, dressed simply in a soft blue gown, her hair down and loose, brushed into soft curls—a rare sight for her. Though Esther had been born knowing she would not inherit Kinnereth, she had never once presented herself as anything but the granddaughter of the grand duke—fine gowns, immaculate tresses, glittering jewels. Even after marrying John, she had kept her fine things, despite the fact that she had technically forsaken her title upon her marriage to the lowly lawyer. But over the years, Ezra had watched his sister evolve a softness to her hard edges, a loveliness to her propriety and decorum. It made her more beautiful with each passing year.

Now, here in the home in which they grew up, watching his sister walk through the formal living room in a simple gown with her hair down brought a smile to his face. That she was finally learning to be comfortable in her own skin, learning to embrace who she was without apology, only made her more lovely.

"Perhaps we should postpone," said Esther.

"Postpone what?" John asked, walking in behind her. He carried the baby in his arms as if she were a treasure of Hasamayim Province.

"Dinner," said Esther, sitting down gingerly. She winced softly, but made no sound of distress.

John eyed her carefully nonetheless, sitting beside her on the settee. When the baby made a soft coo, all of John's attention fell on her, his eyes lighting with delight. He pressed a soft kiss to his daughter's brow and asked, "What dinner?" Though it was clear he was not particularly interested in the conversation, too fixated on his daughter.

Dinner. Ezra had almost forgotten. He had written the prophet who had saved Miri's life, not knowing where to send the letter, where it should go. But somehow, though the man was nearly impossible to locate, his messenger had found him and delivered the letter. The prophet had responded that he would be delighted to join them.

"Are you too tired?" Ezra asked his sister as he set his cold cup aside. "I admit the timing is terrible."

"I'm fine," she said. "But *you* seem exhausted."

Ezra met his sister's appraising gaze. "I'm trying to decide if that is a veiled insult," he said jovially, attempting to lighten his own mood.

Esther did not miss a beat as she said, "No veil intended." A moment later, her lips curled into a lopsided smile and Ezra breathed a laugh.

"Where is she?" Esther went on.

Ezra knew who she meant. Turning his gaze to John and the baby, Ezra said, "I haven't spoken to her since you gave birth."

That had been two days ago. He hadn't even seen her. Not at mealtime, not any time throughout the day. She had kept herself holed up in her chambers without a word. The only reason he knew she was all right was because Kitty brought him brief reports on her health.

"I think I upset her," Esther said, her words almost regretful.

He did not have the heart to explain it to her, to bring any shame on his effortlessly fertile sister. He did not want to explain it.

Not right now.

At Esther's side, John's attention remained solely on his daughter. Ezra watched the way John looked at her with loving eyes. The way he played with her delicate fingers while she slept peacefully in his arms. It seemed like only yesterday John Junior was that little.

Jealousy, heavy and hot, washed over Ezra.

"Dinner will be ready in an hour, sir." This from the lanky butler who walked into the room from the dining hall just beyond.

"Thank you, Thaddeus," Ezra said, still looking wistfully at his newborn niece.

"Do you want to hold her?" John said. Ezra looked up to his friend, who was smiling softly. Ezra wasn't sure what his answer would be. But he did not have time to figure it out before John was placing the tiny, warm bundle in his arms.

Providence above, she was beautiful. As beautiful as his sister. As beautiful as any of the women in his family.

"Have you settled on a name?" Ezra asked.

Esther looked to John, who smiled lovingly at his wife.

"Leah," John said proudly. "Leah Esther Rennius."

Leah. Ezra and Esther's mother. They would name their daughter for her. Somehow, it made the jealousy a little worse.

"Mother would be proud," Ezra managed to say, swallowing against a lump in his throat.

The little one cooed softly, and Ezra smiled, nestling her a little more deeply into his arms and pressing a tender kiss to her feather-soft cheek.

When he looked up again, both his sister and his brother-in-law were watching him with gentle sorrow in their eyes. He did not want to think about that pity, did not want to dwell on it.

Just then, a knock came at the door. Ezra looked over his shoulder, hearing the telltale sounds of Helena bustling her way to the foyer so she could receive their guest, John Junior trailing behind her, probably with some sort of forbidden treat. Ezra stood along with Esther and John and handed the little one into Esther's outstretched arms. He turned, making his way to the foyer just in time to see Helena open the front door.

The prophet stood at the entrance, a little worse for wear in what Ezra could only assume were the same dust-brown jacket and trousers he had been wearing the day he rescued Miri from certain death. He was not dirty, nor unkempt by any means. But neither was there any indication that the prophet cared very much for petty things like fashion. His smile was warm and genuine as he met Ezra's gaze.

"Your Grace," he said kindly.

"It's just Ezra," said Ezra stepping up to greet the man with a handshake. The prophet gripped Ezra's hand with surprising strength. "I am so glad you are here," Ezra went on. "Please do come in."

The prophet accepted and stepped inside Massahd. It seemed as if the gas lamps and candelabra only accentuated the starkness of his white hair. Not from age—no, the prophet was young. Perhaps near the same age as Ezra. But his hair was as white as moonlight across Lake Yerah.

And his eyes...this close, Ezra could see that the man had eyes as green and vivid as Miri's.

Realizing he was on the brink of gaping, Ezra turned rather ungracefully and said, "This is my brother-in-law John Rennius. And my sister Esther."

The prophet smiled brightly. "And who is this?" he asked, eyeing the baby.

John's smile spread wide and proud across his face. "This is my daughter Leah. Born only two days ago."

"And my name is John too!" This from John Junior, who appeared from behind Helena's skirt, holding a half-licked, twisted confection in his tiny hand. The prophet turned his attention to the boy and bent at the waist.

"Barley sugar?" the prophet asked.

"Mrs. Helena gave it to me," the boy admitted proudly, obviously fearless of his mother's disapproval.

From the corner of his eye, Ezra saw Esther's brows furrow. He kept his chuckle behind closed lips.

"Those are my favorite," said the prophet.

"Want one?" John Junior asked, reaching into the pocket of his knickers and retrieving a rather dusty, broken bit of amber-colored candy.

"I do not think he would like that very much." This from Esther.

The prophet took it with a chortle, inspecting it closely. "When I was a boy," he said, "my cousin and I would sneak these from her father's confection dish every time we could find them. And seeing as I kept them in my pockets most of the time, I'm rather used to a little lint. Adds character."

"Your cousin?" Ezra asked. "Do you have family near?"

The prophet met his eyes. "I believe I do," he said. And the way he said it...

A beat of silence passed before Ezra said, "I feel terrible that I do not know your name."

"*Ari?*"

The party congregated at the door made a collective turn towards the landing of the stairwell that spilled into the foyer.

Miri stood there, wide-eyed and as still a statue.

It took a moment for the name to settle—for Ezra to understand what she had said. But when he finally looked back at the prophet, the man was smiling, and Ezra could have sworn a thin line of silver shone in his emerald eyes.

"Hello, cousin."

MIRI TOOK EACH STEP GINGERLY, afraid she would fall face-first on the plush carpets if she did not. Her hand trembled as she used the rail to steady herself.

Ari.

Ari was *here.*

In Kinnereth.

At Massahd Castle.

"What are you doing here?" she asked.

Ari's smile was as warm as it was familiar. "Well I *was* invited, you know."

Miri choked on what was either a laugh or a sob—she could not be sure. But when she at last made it to the foot of the stairs, she did not care anything for dignity or decorum as she ran across the grand lobby and flung herself into Ari's waiting arms.

He held her close, running a hand down her hair and pressing his cheek against her brow.

"I missed you. I missed you so much," she said between breaths.

"I missed you too, Mir."

"Where were you? Where did my father send you?" she asked, pushing herself out of her cousin's arms. From the corner of her eye, she could see the Kelach family staring at the exchange in disbelief. But she did not care. Ari was here.

Ari was alive!

"You and I both know I could not have stayed," he said.

"But...you left?" she asked. "Father said he made you leave."

Ari smiled softly. "I knew it was coming, Mir. It was only a matter of time."

"Why? Why didn't you tell me? I was so worried. I—"

Ari took her face in his hands, waiting for her to calm, to look him in the eye before he continued, "I have always told you—I am at my father's command. You needn't worry."

"Ari, you have no father!" she protested.

Bastard born. That's what he was. The son of a no-name. That's why her father hated him. Why her mother never showed him any love. Because he was a thorn in the perfect Sasson name.

Ari breathed a laugh and kissed her brow. "Of course I have a father," he said. "Now come, Mir. Introduce me to your friends."

SITTING around Ezra's table with Ari next to her was...strange. An odd picture of the only piece of her family she had ever loved mixed in with the family she had been handed. She could plainly see on Ezra's face that he was trying to understand it too. To put it together and make sense of what had transpired, that he had unknowingly invited Miri's beloved cousin to his castle. She wondered if it was jealously that colored his features—that worried smile, those perfunctory laughs.

A part of her wanted to console him, to ensure him everything would be fine. But another part—a dark, broken part, hidden in the shadows—*that* part of her wanted him to wonder. Wanted him to worry. Wanted him to be jealous of Ari.

After all, it was *Ari* who had rescued her. Ezra had said so himself.

Ari had saved her.

Not Ezra.

A part of her understood it. Ari had always been there. Always come through. It did not surprise her that he had again. Somehow, Ari would always be the miracle in her life.

Ezra had given her promises. He had painted a beautiful picture for her. But when push came to shove, it was Ari who had saved her. Ari who had freed her from the Sheol where she burned.

Burned and burned like a wildfire.

Ari had saved her.

Not Ezra.

She hated herself for it—the darkness that spoke to her. That relished Ezra's jealousy.

But she hated everything about herself these days. It was nothing new.

"You've caused quite a stir, it seems," said John, shattering Miri's thoughts. They had spent the better part of dinner discussing Ari's travels. Apparently, he had spent the last few years in the many towns and villages across Har-Navah. Getting to know the people, the cultures, the land itself. Miri was jealous of him. Of that freedom. To go. To be. To do whatever he wanted.

But she was glad for him too. Glad that he had escaped.

Even though she had not.

And might never.

Ari chuckled in his throat. "I'm afraid I have not made many friends."

"Well, that's not true," said Esther. With expert skill she cut her meat on her plate as she spoke. "They say there are crowds who gather wherever you go, just to hear what you have to say."

"That's more out of morbid curiosity, I would hazard," Ari said.

"In all fairness," John said, "you do have some rather bold things to say."

"What? Pointing out that the throne is a man-made concept? That there is only one true magic? Surely it cannot be *that* controversial?" Ari laughed.

John laughed too. Even Ezra cracked a grin at Ari's sarcasm.

"The truth is, most people love to *hear* the truth, so long as they do not have to live it or be held accountable to it," Ari went on.

"And what is the truth, then?" John asked before sipping his wine.

Ari eyed him for a moment, his expression unreadable. Miri wanted her cousin to flay him. To say something that would expose him—all of them—for the pampered princes they were. All this lavishness John had married into. It was all unnecessary, wasn't it? A man-made farce, just as Ari had said.

She hadn't thought about it, not until she had seen Ari tonight. Until the memory of him flooded back into her like a tidal wave. Everything else in the world seemed a farce in comparison to Ari. Fake. Unnecessary.

"I think you more than most know Truth, John Rennius," Ari said.

John did not say anything. Neither did anyone else.

Ezra was the only one brave enough to end the silence. "What do you mean?" he asked after a moment.

Miri looked up at him, so far away at the other end of the table. But the moment he met her stare, she looked away.

Ari turned to Ezra. "Most people do not like what I have to say for the simple reason that they fear it. But here, in this home, there is no fear. There is no need for it."

"What does that mean?" Esther asked.

"If you were to ask the king this very moment what magic is, what do you suppose he would tell you?" Ari asked.

John was the one who answered. "Magic is power."

Ari nodded. "Power. Yes. Most would say that's what it is. Maybe some would call it convenience. Or some would call it innovation. Or industry. But when you boil it down, most everyone would agree that magic is a kind of power—whether that power is as simple as making your life better or as grand as ruling the world, magic has been redefined in this modern era to become something it was never intended to be. Something it can never be."

"Then what do you say is magic?" Ezra asked.

Ari held his gaze. "Love," he said simply. "Love is magic."

"You speak brazen words, sir," John said, amused. "For to say such a thing would be to imply that magic is within all of us. Not just the powerful."

"That's right, John," Ari said. "My father's magic is not meant to be wielded by those who would call themselves powerful. It was not meant to be used by those who make thrones for themselves. It is meant to be yielded to. Magic is meant to be given and received. True magic is love. And true love is sacrifice.

"And that's why, John Rennius, you would know more than most what Truth is. Because in this home, there is love. You have known it firsthand—in your wife. In this family who accepted you, took you in. In Ezra, who is as much a brother as he is a friend to you. You know in the purest way that love is the only true magic."

The table fell silent again, along with Miri, who found that she could not meet anyone's eyes. Especially Ezra's. How he knew that—how Ari knew any of that... About John. About Ezra. Their family.

Miri was not sure what to make of it.

It was only once a maid unknowingly assaulted that silence, pouring more wine as she made her way around the table, that anyone spoke again.

"Well, we owe you a debt of gratitude." This from Esther, who seemed a bit flustered. "We are all grateful Miri is alive. None more than my brother."

"Had I not been there, I have no doubt Ezra would have gone to whatever lengths to get Miriam home," Ari said.

To that, Miri privately scoffed.

Right.

Except that Ezra had done nothing. Had not come back for her that night. Had not come back for her at all.

The truth of it hit Miri so hard, she clenched her fist in her napkin beneath the table.

Ezra had wanted to be her hero. But he had not wanted to save her.

That was the truth between them.

"Believe me, he tried," said Esther. "I doubt he would be alive if I had let him go." She let out a little laugh that sounded more nervous than humorous. Miri did not understand its meaning. But Esther went on, "I thought for certain he would tear down the walls while he was cooped in that bed. The moment he woke, all he could think about was getting to her."

"The moment he woke?" Miri asked, failing to understand.

Ari looked around the table as if he knew what was coming. But none of the rest seemed to want to speak. Especially not Ezra.

"What do you mean, the moment he woke?" Miri pressed.

"He was unconscious," Esther said. "For days. We nearly lost him." With the last sentence, Esther could not hide the emotion that lurked behind her eyes.

"Lost him? Lost him how? What do you mean?"

"Miri," John said. "Ezra nearly died trying to get to you."

MIRI PACED a small library that sat just beyond the grand foyer. At John's declaration, she'd left the table, almost tripping over her own feet in her haste. She had to get away. She had to think. To understand.

As she marched across the thick, brightly colored carpets in the dim room, she let the silence fill her head. Fill her thoughts. She looked through the windows before her and let the view of the autumn mountain evening fill her, body and soul.

"You were never very good at hiding your emotions."

Miri whirled to find Ari standing in the door of the library, a sad smile on his face.

"I missed you so much," she said. The weight of it all came crashing down on her as Ari walked into the room, crossing the small space and pulling her into his arms.

Ari.

Ari was alive.

"I missed you too, Mir."

"I've been so scared," she said. "So afraid."

"I know," he said, his touch familiar. Soothing. Even his smell —wild berry bushes and heady mountain herbs. Something in her heart settled at the feel of him, the scent of him.

He pulled her away to meet her eyes.

"I didn't even know if you were alive," she said. "I thought Father had..."

Ari's hands settled on her shoulders. "He made it clear that it was time for me to leave. I didn't want to leave you yet, but I knew there would come a day when I had to."

"He's dead, did you know that? He owed tremendous debts,

apparently. Someone came to cash in on them. They killed Mother, too."

Ari sighed, his shoulders falling softly. "The priest told you that."

Miri knitted her brows. "Yes," she said. "What are you implying?"

Ari cupped her cheek and said, "He fears you most of all, Miri."

"Phinehas? He does not fear me. Not at all. He—"

"He does, Mir. He fears that you will one day see what is within you. The strength you possess. The wildfire in your heart. He fears that you will use it against him. He has kept you close to his side all these years for that very reason."

Miri turned away from Ari, facing the fire dancing in the hearth. "How disappointed he will be when he learns that there's nothing inside me but cowardice and shame."

"You're wrong about that, Mir. So very wrong."

She hugged herself tightly, swallowing against the lump forming in her throat. "Look what I did to Ezra. Because of me, he nearly died. And I didn't even know it! He nearly gave his life. For a whore!"

She heard rather than watched Ari take a seat on the settee behind her. "He does not see it that way. No one who has the privilege of knowing you sees you that way, Mir."

She turned, facing her cousin, the light from the hearth casting him in a warm, golden hue.

"He never told me," she said. "He never told me he was stabbed. Left for dead. Nothing. I did not know. Ari, I didn't know."

She had thought...she had thought Ezra hadn't come for her. Hadn't tried.

Instead he had nearly died.

Ezra had nearly given his life for her.

"Maybe he did not tell you for a reason," Ari offered.

"And what reason is that?"

"Maybe he did not want you to feel guilty. To think it was your fault."

"It *was* my fault!" she shouted. "He told me not to go, Ari. He told me not to go back to the temple. And I did not listen to him. I did not listen. And then—"

Ari stood, coming to Miri in three quick steps. He took both of her hands in his, waiting for her to meet his gaze before he spoke. "Miriam, it's not your fault. None of this is. None of it."

Before she could sob, before she would let herself disappear into the rage of emotions swirling around her, she said, "Where did you go, Ari? Why did you leave all those years ago?"

Ari did not flinch, nor did his eyes hold apology. "To prepare."

"Prepare? Prepare for what."

"Magic, Mir. My father's magic. I left to prepare."

"Ari, I don't understand."

"The stag, Miriam. The stag is at hand."

CHAPTER THIRTY-SIX

Miri had left dinner so quickly that neither Ezra nor his family dared follow. Only Ari had left the table with an apologetic smile and followed her into the downstairs library.

And it was jealousy that washed over Ezra again. Jealousy that her cousin would console her, not him. That Miri would not turn to Ezra, would not even look at him the way she had looked at her cousin. Not for the first time tonight, Ezra reminded himself that she had once scoffed—laughed it off when Ezra had asked her if she were in love with her cousin.

Tonight, he hung onto those words as a last thread of hope.

He did not know what to make of that delicate balance of being both immeasurably grateful to someone and irrationally jealous. He certainly did not know what to make of the fact that he liked Ari. That his amiable nature and easygoing demeanor made him someone Ezra knew he could get along with easily. Maybe even call a friend.

He did not know what to do with any of it. So Ezra had merely kissed his sister on the cheek and bade his family goodnight before making his way up the stairs to his bedchamber, leaving Ari to tend to Miri in the library.

Dismissing his manservants for the evening, he dressed for bed in a bit of a blur, donning his drawers and nightshirt before tending to the fire in his bedchamber. In the quiet of the cold evening, Ezra found a robe and wrapped it around himself, lost in his own thoughts.

Something caught the corner of his vision, and he turned to look out the massive windows that lined one side of his bedchamber. The night was far enough along now that the mountains and lake were obscured in darkness. But it was not the view that had snagged his attention but the figure now standing on his balcony. The balcony he shared with Miri's chambers.

It was not the reason he had chosen those rooms for her. No, he had simply chosen the closest ones to him. So that he could be there should she need him. So that she would be close.

Though their doors were across the hall from one another, their chambers were both on one end of a section of the castle that jutted out over the lake. And from this vantage point, the mountains were particularly vast. Both her bedchamber and his boasted a wall of glass and doors that opened out onto a large balcony. A balcony they shared.

A fact he had almost forgotten until seeing her there tonight. And he wondered what she would do if she knew how close they really were. How close they had been all along.

She leaned on the balustrade overlooking the lake, and it was clear that she was cold, shivering softly in the brisk night air. She wore no robe, only a long, woolen shift. Her curls hung long and loose down her back. He looked around, wondering if Ari was somewhere on that balcony with her. Maybe he had followed her to her chambers. Maybe she had turned to him for comfort. And maybe, just as he had opened his arms to her in the foyer earlier this evening, he had offered her a comfort Ezra never could.

Something tightened in his chest, and Ezra scoured the shadows of the balcony. But Miri's cousin was nowhere to be found.

After a moment, and mostly out of a desire to make his presence known, Ezra quietly pushed to open the massive glass doors and slipped out onto the balcony.

Miri did not turn, did not even acknowledge that she had heard the soft squeak of the cold metal hinges.

"Wildfire?" Ezra tried.

The breeze caught a strand of Miri's hair, tossing it softly across her back. But still she did not turn.

"Aren't you cold?" he asked.

He might have second-guessed himself when he thought he heard her say yes had it not been for the faint nodding of her head. Without hesitation, Ezra looked around, spotting the thick, white blanket his grandmother had made many years ago. He'd had the blanket placed in Miri's chambers the moment she arrived, hoping she would use it. Hoping she would find comfort in it the way he had from the time he was a boy. A magic blanket —that's what his grandmother had always said. No, not the paltry excuse for magic that most gadgets and trinkets boasted these days. Something else.

Maybe it was nothing more than nostalgia. Nothing more than the precious memories attached to the wolf fur and wool, the intricate white hand embroidery along the edge. But Ezra had always believed it.

He fetched it, moving to wrap it around Miri's shoulders when he reached her side. To his relief, she did not stop him. He hadn't ever told her how much Miri reminded him of his grandmother Lady Judith Kelach, Grand Duchess of Kinnereth. He did not imagine any woman would appreciate the comparison. But it would be the highest compliment he could give. What with her quiet strength, her gentle kindness, her quick wit. But at the sight of her standing here on this balcony, wrapped in this blanket, something pulled tight in his heart again.

So he moved to stand beside her, leaning on the rails that jutted over Lake Yerah. This corner of the lake was frozen solid now, the nights too cold for any of the waters to remain free. Snow banked the edges, thick and fluffy. Tonight, the skies were clear and the stars shone brightly overhead.

"It's a beautiful night," he said gently.

Miri did not answer, looking peacefully out at the view surrounding them. Ezra took a risk and moved a little closer to her, hoping to offer his warmth. To his surprise, she did not move away.

"My grandmother always told me that the fur on that blanket belonged to Queen Adelaide. That it was once a cloak given to her by King Ferryl."

Miri remained silent and unmoving, but Ezra went on. "I was never sure whether or not to believe her. That would make the fur at least a thousand years old, if not more. But that's what she always swore. Of course, if it had been a full pelt, there would be much more of it than the little bit lining the edge of the blanket. But then again, if it really is a thousand years old, I suppose that's all that would be left."

He was rambling, looking for something to say, something to spark a response.

It wasn't working.

"My grandmother wasn't one for tall tales. Perhaps she was telling the truth. But it always seemed too fantastic to me. After all, the legends say that Queen Adelaide's wolf hide was magic. A protection, or something or other. I can't remember. Anyway, all I know is that I always felt safe when I had that blanket over me. I was hoping you'd feel the same way."

Miri's head moved ever so slightly, as if she might look at him. But she must have changed her mind, looking out over the black waters once more.

Silence pulled taut between them, and Ezra twisted his fingers.

"I like him," Ezra said, deciding a change in subject might help. "Your cousin. He's wonderful, Miri. I can see why you're so close."

Still, Miri said nothing. But Ezra kept trying. "I am glad he came here. I am glad I got to meet him. I know what he means to you. And—"

"You heard the voice of Providence?" Miri asked, turning to face him.

"What?"

"That night—the night in the theatre, when you first saw me —you heard the voice of Providence?"

"How...how did you know that?"

"Never mind that. What did he tell you? What did you hear?"

"I heard..." Ezra swallowed once, clearing his mind. "I heard him say, 'Only truth between us.'"

"I don't understand," she said, flustered. "How could you have known what that meant? How could you have understood it?"

"I—Miri, you must understand," he said. "I had spent my formative years betrothed to the princess. She was my friend— she *is* my friend. But there was no love between us. Not...like that. And I lied to her. I lied to her over and over again, lying to myself too. Telling myself we were good together. That we would be fine. That we would be happy. And she lied too. She lied to herself, she lied to me. Not vindictively, you see. That was the trouble of it. She was not vindictive or malicious. I had no reason to end it with her. We were friends. It was fine. It was all just fine on paper.

"But I knew I was lying. And it was only when I admitted that to myself that I understood what was missing all along between us.

"Truth, Miri. There was no truth between me and the princess. Only lies. Only a farce.

"So I ended it. I took the risk of ruining what was already a precarious reputation as the apathetic duke—the boy who would never live up to his grandfather. But I took the risk and called off the marriage anyway. Because I wanted truth. With someone. With anyone. I wanted to find myself. And be myself. Fully and wholly and truly. I wanted to be the man that my grandfather thought I was.

"That night—that night in the theatre—it was your hair, your glorious curls that caught my eye. And I looked over, and I saw you, a beautiful living flame seated across the way. And it hit me —hard and sudden, like lightning. Four words. So clear I knew from where they had come. Four words that changed everything.

"*'Only truth between us.'*

"I knew that I had to meet you. I knew I had to know you. To find out if I was insane. Perhaps I am. But I had to know. So I showed up to that ridiculous dinner. And the next. And the next one after that. I would never have gone. Never have bothered except for you. For you and for those four words that danced in my mind every time I saw you.

"And when you said them on the mountain that day—when you said you only wanted truth between us—that's when I knew, Miri. That's when I knew what you were. I already knew it in my heart. I was watching it unfurl before my eyes. But when you said it, when you confirmed it... Miri, I knew I had certainly heard Providence that day in the theatre. He had shown me you. He had paved the path that led me straight to you."

"I want to see it," Miri said abruptly, her bottom lip quivering.

Ezra froze at the intensity in her eyes.

"I want to see the wound. The scar. Whatever it is. I want you to show it to me." Her words were as soft as they were intense.

So Ezra complied.

Untying his thick robe, he pulled it open and slowly lifted his shirt, revealing the thick, angry scar just above his drawers. Miri stood silent before him, her eyes fixed on his stomach. She did not move, did not speak. Only stared.

Then her hand was there, running a cold, delicate finger along the sensitive skin. He clenched his stomach on instinct.

"Does it hurt?" she asked, her words dripping with worry.

"It is sore," he admitted. "But it gets better every day."

She did not take her eyes from his stomach, but her hands trembled harder the longer they lingered on his skin.

"I didn't know, Ezra. I didn't know," she said softly. So softly.

"I know, Miri."

She finally met his eyes before she continued, "Why didn't you tell me? Why didn't you tell me that you almost *died*?"

"I didn't want you to worry. I didn't want you to think—"

"That it's my fault?" she interjected, a tear falling down her cheek. "Well, it is. It's all my fault!"

"No, it's not," he said. "It's not, Miri. It's *my* fault. I'm the one that failed you. I'm the one that left you there. The one who could not get you out. It's my fault, Miri. All of it."

There it was. The truth. The truth between them. Bald and ugly. Out of the shadows of his mind. Plain between them.

"No," Miri said, shaking her head. "You tried, Ezra. And I did not know. You tried to save me. And all I've done is push you away. All I've done is hurt you. You nearly died. For me. And all the thanks I've given you is hurt."

"No, Miri," he said. Damning the consequences, he put his hands on her waist and pulled her a fraction closer. "No, it's not your fault. You did nothing wrong. Nothing." He could not help them, the tears that fell down his face too. He did not try to stop them.

"I'm the one that failed you," he said. "I'm the one that's sorry. So sorry. Miri, I am so sorry."

To his shock—to his utter surprise—Miri wrapped her arms around his waist and wept onto his chest, great, gulping sobs and fat tears that soon dampened his shirt. He pulled her closer against him and wept into her hair, letting his own tears fall, fast and hot.

"I'm sorry, Ezra," she said onto his chest. "I'm so sorry."

"You do not apologize, Miri," he said. "Not for this. Never for this. Never."

She wept harder, the tears shaking her shoulders. He held her close against him, rubbing her back as he let his emotions run free too. "You're so strong, Miri. Do you know it? You're the strongest person I know."

"I'm not strong. I'm a mess," she argued, pushing away enough to meet his eyes.

"No, Wildfire. You're strong. Stronger than anyone I've ever known. To face what you have faced and to come back from it. Miri, you are brave and strong and beautiful, and I'm proud of you. So proud of you. I know it's not over, Miri. I know there is so much left to sort through. So much left to face. But you're doing so well. And you're so brave and I'm so proud of you."

He tucked a strand of hair behind her ear, struck by the way she looked at him now. Not with regret. Not with fear or worry or sorrow. But with something else. Something profound and rich and brave.

Something that looked a lot like love.

He could have sworn she moved a fraction closer to him. When she moved her arms and clasped her hands behind his back, he knew he hadn't been wrong.

So he took a risk and moved his lips just a little closer to hers.

Just a fraction. And she did not move away, his brave, beautiful Wildfire. She did not fear.

Ezra pressed his brow to hers. He let his breath mingle with hers, closing his eyes and taking in her nearness. That nearness he had craved for so long. So very long.

"Ezra," she whispered. He moved just enough to meet her eyes again. A tear fell down her cheek, and he watched it sparkle in the moonlight.

"I want you to want me, Ezra. I want you to love me."

Something in his heart leapt at her words. The sincerity in them.

He had heard them once before, the words they had shared that night in the starlit pool. In the magic that had stripped them of fear.

Love—it was love. Love was the magic that had given them a glimpse of hope that night. He had remembered it all. And he had understood that the stag had led them there. Providence himself. The Promised One. To give them a taste of hope. To show them that love could overcome all fear if they let it.

And perhaps to show them that no matter what would come, they could always—*always*—cling to hope.

So he smiled softly and leaned close enough to speak onto her lips words he had spoken to her before. "Well, you're in luck, my beautiful Wildfire."

And he kissed her.

So soft, so unhurried were her lips against his. A gentle, languid kiss that soon deepened into something consuming, something rich and heady. To his surprise, she broke that kiss rather abruptly and said without hesitation, without a modicum of fear or hesitation, "I love you. I love you so much, Ezra."

He could not help the smile that spread across his mouth. "I love you, Wildfire. And I know that I'll love you forever."

For the first time since they had met, for the first time since the Sheols she had faced at the hand of the priest and at the hand of the ambassador, Ezra knew she believed him. So he clung to her —he clung to that hope, fledgling and delicate and beautiful between them. And he did not let go.

End of Book VI

ACKNOWLEDGMENTS

My sisters always told me I was weird. Considering this is my sixth fantasy novel, replete with flying horses, magic ships, and glowing deer, I suppose they weren't wrong. What I once loathed as a thing to be hidden away, I have come to appreciate: namely that kernel of Strange that guides the creative bones in my body and urges me to put pen to paper, so to speak.

But even so, I could never have imagined that there would be people in the universe who want to listen to, read, and participate in my little weird world. I never thought there would be an army of weirdos who would DM and comment and email, asking when my next book is coming. To all of you I say: I have no words for your kindness, your support, and your rabid need for more of my respites into the great unknown. I have no way to express my gratitude. The English language is simply lacking in that regard. So please know as you read these acknowledgments that I am overwhelmed, grateful, and truly honored by each one of you.

Thank you.

To my StoneWater family, you guys blow my mind. Always supporting, always encouraging, leaving notes, asking questions, and generally making me feel like I'm doing something worthwhile. What a gift it is to live life and sing and worship with each one of you.

To my sisters, thank you for making me feel weird. It paid off. *grins*

To mom and dad, thank you for all the piano lessons and head shots and new keyboards and demo tapes and late night toleration of my piano playing. As you can see, all of that really created a novelist... But hey, I lead worship on Sundays, so I guess it was worth it.

To my sweet Lance, you are the wind to my flames. You give me life and you give me joy and you are dead sexy and I HAVE NO REGRETS FOR TYPING THAT FOR ALL THE WORLD TO READ. Thank you for choosing me and thank you for being my biggest cheerleader year after year, creative endeavor after creative endeavor. You are the reason I wake up each morning. Now let's go watch a stupid movie while mom and dad watch the kids. I have a good one in mind...

To my sweet Adeline, you fill my heart so full I fear on a near daily basis that it might burst. I hope one day (when you are old enough to read these) that you see your thumbprint all over them. You bring magic into my world with your wonder. You'll stop the entire family to gawk at a rock. You'll make us late just so we look at the moon together. I want to be more like you when I grow up and I love you more than my own life. Big squish hugs, baby girl.

To my Virgil Bear, I wish I could express what it means to me that you tell everyone you know that I'm an author, that you ask to bring my books to school just to show off to your friends, and that you tell the cashier at Chick-fil-A that I'm YouTube famous. I'm not, but you make me feel like I am. Like your dad, you're my greatest supporter and cheerleader. I love you, Buddy Bear.

To Arielle, once again I cannot even begin to thank you for late night Messenger conversations, your checking-in texts, and your ruthless pursuit of perfection in these pages. You challenge me to be better, you encourage me to keep going, and you make every sentence sing. I absolutely adore you in every way.

And finally, to the One who inspired this whole series, I hope I

can do you justice. I hope I can tell the world in my own weird
little way what you've been for me. I hope that white stag hiding
in the forest gives people just a glimpse of your magic. And thank
you for letting us take it with us.

ABOUT THE AUTHOR

So let's just be real here... My name is Morgan and I'm a chronic over-achiever and avid binger of *The Office.* When I watch *Lord of the Rings,* I watch the extended versions, and they're still not long enough. I won arguments in elementary school by out-quoting everyone with my vast knowledge of *The Princess Bride.* So yeah, I'm kind of a big deal.* I used to have a mohawk‡. And once I had purple bangs‡. But I try not to let that dictate my current fashion choices, which are just as confused, I confess. Bless.

In my spare time, I write. A lot. Songs, stories, articles, novels... It's just this thing in me that I have to get out. The book you're reading, part of *The Chalam Færytales,* is sort of a magnum opus of all the things that have been stirring in me from the time I was a kid—musing about the existence of humanity, pondering the wonder of God and the ongoing work of redemption...you know, kid stuff. I'm real proud of it. (That's my Texan coming out. Fight me.) I'd be honored if you left a review of it somewhere on the interwebs. (Consequently, I'm convinced that novel writing is just an acceptable form of psychosis, but it's definitely a beast within me that roars to be freed. So I pet it and feed it and let it dictate my fingers on the keyboard without regrets.)

But even if you don't ever read another one of my novels or listen to one of my songs, I can't thank you enough for reading this one. I hope I can bring a little magic to your world in some way.

The art in me manifests in various forms—from my books, to my music, to my digital art and even the occasional article. I get confused about what I should call myself: author or musician or songwriter or graphic designer or armchair theologian. I think it's probably safe to say I'm just an artist at heart exploring the magic around us. Thanks for exploring with me!

*This is sarcasm.

‡This is not sarcasm.

instagram.com/morgangfarris

youtube.com/morgangfarris

pinterest.com/morgangfarris

ALSO BY MORGAN G FARRIS

The Promised One (Book I)

The Purloined Prophecy (Book II)

The Parallax (Book III)

The Perdurables (Book IV)

The War and the Petrichor (Book V)

SIGN UP FOR THE NEWSLETTER

I don't send out newsletters a lot. Honestly, it's a pain. But I do use them from time to time to update you when things are releasing, or when something new is happening, or when I set out on another out-of-the-blue artistic endeavor. So that being said, I don't do the whole spammy, weekly, buy my stuff email thing. It's obnoxious.

You're probably wondering why I'd bother asking you to sign up to begin with. Well, it's because all the experts tell me I need a newsletter. And I suppose it's also a sort of doomsday when-all-the-social-media-fails-us mindset on my part.

So yeah, sign up for my newsletter in the event of Armageddon, or if you're so inclined to support a lowly author like myself.

When you visit my site, this annoying pop-up shows up asking you to sign up. Just add your email there.

Man, I should go into sales.

Morgan G Farris.com